In Bed
with the Boss

She would do his bidding…from 9 to 5!

Three passionate novels!

In December 2007 Mills & Boon bring
back two of their classic collections,
each featuring three favourite
romances by our bestselling authors…

IN BED WITH THE BOSS
Bedded by the Boss by Miranda Lee
The Boss's Proposal
by Cathy Williams
In Her Boss's Bed by Maggie Cox

BRIDES FOR CHRISTMAS
Claiming His Christmas Bride
by Carole Mortimer
Christmas Eve Marriage by Jessica Hart
A Surprise Christmas Proposal
by Liz Fielding

In Bed
with the Boss

BEDDED BY THE BOSS
by
Miranda Lee

THE BOSS'S PROPOSAL
by
Cathy Williams

IN HER BOSS'S BED
by
Maggie Cox

⊚™ MILLS & BOON®
Pure reading pleasure

*Harlequin Mills & Boon Limited,
Eton House, 18-24 Paradise Road, Richmond, Surrey TW9 1SR*

IN BED WITH THE BOSS
© by Harlequin Enterprises II B.V./S.à.r.l 2007

Bedded by the Boss, The Boss's Proposal and *In Her Boss's Bed*
were first published in Great Britain by Harlequin Mills & Boon
Limited in separate, single volumes.

Bedded by the Boss © Miranda Lee 2004
The Boss's Proposal © Cathy Williams 2001
In Her Boss's Bed © Maggie Cox 2004

ISBN: 978 0 263 85530 2

05-1207

*Printed and bound in Spain
by Litografía Rosés S.A., Barcelona*

BEDDED BY
THE BOSS

by

Miranda Lee

Miranda Lee is Australian, living near Sydney. Born and raised in the bush, she was boarding-school educated and briefly pursued a career in classical music, before moving to Sydney and embracing the world of computers. Happily married, with three daughters, she began writing when family commitments kept her at home. She likes to create stories that are believable, modern, fast-paced and sexy. Her interests include meaty sagas, doing word puzzles, gambling and going to the movies.

CHAPTER ONE

'So what would *you* like in your Christmas stocking, Jessie? I'm going present shopping tomorrow. There's only just over two weeks till Christmas and I hate leaving things to the last moment.'

Jessie stopped applying her mascara for a second to smile wryly across the kitchen table at her elderly friend—and landlady.

'Do you know a shop which sells men?' she asked with a mischievous sparkle in her dark brown eyes.

Dora's own eyes widened. '*Men?* You told me just ten minutes ago that you thought most men were sleazebags and you were better off without one in your life.'

Jessie shrugged. 'That was ten minutes ago. Getting myself dolled up like this tonight reminded me of when I was young and carefree and didn't know the truth about the opposite sex. What I wouldn't give to be that girl again, just for one night, going out with some gorgeous guy on a hot date.'

'And if that fantasy came true,' Dora asked, still with a sceptical expression on her face, 'where would this gorgeous guy be taking you?'

'Oh, somewhere really swish for drinks and dinner, then on to a nightclub for some dirty dancing.' *After which he'd whip me back to his bachelor pad and...*

5

This last thought startled Jessie. In all honesty, ever since she'd had Emily, she hadn't missed men one bit. Hadn't felt like being with one at all.

Now, suddenly, the thought of having some gorgeous guy's arms around her again was quite pleasurable. *More* than pleasurable, actually. Almost a necessity.

Her female hormones, it seemed, had finally been jump-started again.

Her sigh carried a measure of frustration. And irritation. It was something she could do without. Men complicated things. They always did.

Useless creatures, all of them.

Except in that one department!

Now that her hormones were hopping again, she had to admit there was nothing to compare with the pleasure of being with a man who was a good lover.

Emily's father had been pretty good in bed. But he'd also been a feckless, reckless fool whose wildly adventurous spirit had finally been the death of him, snowboarding his stupid way off a mountain and into a crevasse even before Jessie had discovered she was having his baby.

Jessie had finally come to realise at the wise old age of twenty-eight that the members of the opposite sex who were good in bed were rarely good at commitment. Usually, they were charming scoundrels. She suspected that even if Lyall had lived, he would not have stuck by her and his baby.

No, she was better off without men in her life, in any capacity. For now, anyway. Emily was still only four and very impressionable. The last thing she needed was for her mummy to start dating guys who were only interested in one thing. There was no future in that. And no happiness.

Men could indulge in no-strings sex without suffering any lasting emotional damage. Women, not so easily.

Jessie had taken a long time to get over Lyall, both his death and the discovery she'd made afterwards that she hadn't been the only girl in his life.

'What I really want for Christmas more than anything,' she said firmly as she packed her make-up essentials into her black evening bag, 'is a decent job in an advertising agency.'

Jessie had worked as a graphic artist before she'd fallen pregnant, with an eye to eventually being promoted to the position of creative designer. She hadn't wanted to spend the rest of her life bringing other people's ideas to life; or having them take the credit when she improved on their designs. Jessie knew she had considerable creative talent and dreamt of heading her own advertising team one day; being up close and personal when the presentations were made; getting the accolades herself—plus the bonuses—when she secured a prestigious account for Jackson & Phelps.

That was the advertising agency she'd worked for back then. One of Sydney's biggest and best.

Having Emily, however, had rearranged her priorities in life. She *had* planned on going back to Jackson & Phelps after her maternity leave was up. But when the time came, she'd found she didn't want to put her baby daughter into day-care. She wanted to stay home and take care of Emily herself.

She'd thought she could work from home, freelance. She had her own computer and all the right software. But a downturn in the economy had meant that advertising budgets were cut and lots of graphic artists were out of work. Freelance work became a pipedream.

Jessie had been forced to temporarily receive state benefits, and to move from the trendy little flat she'd been renting. Luckily, she found accommodation with Dora, a very nice lady with a very nice home in Roseville, a leafy northern Sydney suburb on the train line.

Dora had had a granny flat built on the back when her mother—now deceased—had come to live with her. It was only one-bedroomed, but it had its own bathroom and a spacious kitchen-cum-living room which opened out into the large and secure back yard. Just the thing for a single mum with an active toddler. Emily had turned one by then and was already walking.

The rent Dora charged Jessie was also very reasonable, in exchange for which Jessie helped Dora with the heavy housework and the garden.

But money was still tight. There was never much left over each fortnight. Treats were a rarity. Presents were always cheap little things, both on birthdays and at Christmas. Last Christmas hadn't been a big problem. Emily hadn't been old enough at three to understand that all her gifts had come from a bargain-basement store.

But Jessie had realised at the time that by this coming Christmas, Emily would be far more knowing.

As much as Jessie had enjoyed being a full-time mother at home, the necessities of life demanded that she get off welfare and go back to work. So last January, Jessie had enrolled Emily in a nearby day-care centre and started looking for a job.

Unfortunately, not with great success in her chosen field.

Despite her having her name down at several employment agencies and going for countless interviews, no one in advertising, it seemed, wanted to hire a graphic artist who was a single mum and who had been out of the workforce for over three years.

For a while, earlier this year, she'd done a simply awful—though lucrative—job, working for a private investigator. The ad in the paper had said it was for the position of receptionist. No experience required, just good presentation and a nice phone voice. When she'd got there, she was told the receptionist job had been taken, and she was offered investigative work instead.

Basically, she was sent out as a decoy to entrap men who were suspected by their partners of being unfaithful. She'd be given the time and place—always a pub or a bar—plus a short biography and photo of the target. Her job had required her to dress sexily, make contact, then flirt enough for the target to show his true colours. Once she'd gathered sufficient evidence via the sleek, hi-tech mobile phone which the PI supplied—its video recording was excellent—Jessie would use the excuse of going to the powder room, then disappear.

It had only taken Jessie half a dozen such encounters before she quit. Maybe if, just once, one target had resisted her charms and shown himself to be an honourable man, she might have continued. But no! Each time, the sleazebag—and brother, they were all sleazebags!—wasted no time in not only chatting her up but also propositioning her in no uncertain terms. Each time she'd dashed for the ladies', feeling decidedly dirty.

After that low-life experience, she'd happily taken a waitressing job at a local restaurant. Because of Emily, however, Jessie refused to work at night or at the weekends, when the tips might have been better, so her take-home pay wasn't great. On top of that, her expenses had gone up. Even with her government subsidy for being a single parent, having Emily in day-care five days a week was not cheap.

The only bonus was that Emily adored going to her pre-school. Jessie sometimes felt jealous over how much her daughter loved the teachers there, and the other kids. She'd grown up so much during this past year.

Too much.

She was now four, going on fourteen.

Last weekend, she'd begun asking questions about her father. And had not been impressed when her mother tried to skirt around the subject. A flustered Jessie had been pinned down and forced to tell Emily the truth. That her daddy had died in a tragic accident before she was born. And no, her mummy and her daddy had not been married at the time.

'So you and Daddy aren't divorced,' she'd stunned Jessie by saying. 'He's not ever coming back, like Joel's daddy came back.'

Joel was Emily's best friend at pre-school.

'No, Emily,' Jessie had told her daughter in what she'd hoped was the right sombre and sympathetic tone. 'Your daddy is never coming back. He's in heaven.'

'Oh,' Emily had said, and promptly went off, frowning.

Jessie had found her in a corner of the back yard, having a serious conversation with her life-sized baby doll—the one Dora had given her for her fourth birthday in August. Emily had fallen ominously silent when her mother approached. Jessie had been very relieved when her daughter had finally looked up, smiled brightly and asked her if they could go and see Santa at K-Mart that afternoon, because she had to tell him what she wanted for Christmas before it was too late.

Clearly, Emily was too young at four to be devastated by the discovery that the father she had never known was in heaven.

But Emily's reminder that Christmas was coming up fast—along with the fact that Jessie already knew the main present Emily wanted for Christmas—was what had brought Jessie to make the decision to do one more wretched job for Jack Keegan. The PI had said to give him a call if she ever needed some extra cash. Which she surely did, because a Felicity Fairy

doll was the most expensive doll to hit the toy market
in ages. Jessie would need all of the four-hundred-
dollar fee she would earn tonight to buy the darned
doll, along with all its accompaniments. There was a
fairy palace, a magic horse and a sparkling wardrobe
full of clothes.

Speaking of clothes…

Jessie stood up and smoothed down the short skirt
of the black crêpe halter-necked dress she'd dragged
out of her depleted wardrobe for tonight's job. It was
the classiest, sexiest dress she owned, but it was six
years old and Jessie feared it was beginning to look
it.

'Are you sure this dress is OK?' she asked Dora
in a fretful tone. 'It's getting awfully old.'

'It's fine,' Dora reassured. 'And not out of fashion
at all. That style is timeless. You look gorgeous,
Jessie. Very sexy. Like a model.'

'Who, me? Don't be ridiculous, Dora. I know I've
got a good figure, but the rest of me is pretty ordinary. Without my make-up on, no man would give
me a second glance. And my hair is an uncontrollable
disaster if I don't drag it back or put it up.'

'You underestimate your attractiveness, Jessie.'

In every way, Dora thought to herself.

Jessie's figure wasn't just good, it was spectacular,
the kind of body you often saw in underwear adver-
tisements these days. Full breasts. Tiny waist.
Slender hips and long legs. They looked even longer
in the high, strappy shoes Jessie was wearing tonight.

It was true that her face wasn't traditionally pretty.
Her mouth was too wide, her jaw too square and her

nose slightly too long. But anchored on either side of that nose were widely set, exotically shaped dark brown eyes which flashed and smouldered with sensual promise, the kind of eyes that drew men like magnets.

As for her hair...Dora would have killed for hair like Jessie's when she'd been younger.

Blue-black, thick and naturally curly, when left down it cascaded around her face and shoulders in glorious disarray. Up, it defied restraint, with bits and pieces escaping, making her look even sexier, if that was possible.

Dora hadn't been surprised when that private detective had snapped Jessie up to do decoy work for him. She was the perfect weapon to entrap cheating husbands. And possibly non-cheating ones as well.

'Is this the guy?' Dora asked, picking up the photo that was resting in the middle of the table.

'Yep. That's him.'

'He's handsome.'

Jessie had thought so too. Far better looking than the other creeps she'd had to flirt with. And younger. In his thirties instead of forties or fifties. But she had no doubts about the type of man he was.

'Handsome is as handsome does, Dora. He's married with two little kids, yet he spends every Friday night at a bar in town, drinking till all hours of the night.'

'But lots of men drink on a Friday night.'

'I doubt he's just drinking. The particular city bar he frequents is a well-known pick-up joint,' Jessie pointed out drily.

'You could say that about any bar.'

'Look, the wife says this behaviour is out of character with her husband. She says he's changed towards her. She's convinced he's being unfaithful to her and wants to know the truth.'

'Doesn't sound like compelling evidence of adultery to me. She might wish she hadn't started this.'

'What do you mean?'

'You know, Jessie, I've never thought it was very fair on the men in question, sending a girl like you to flirt with them. This man might not have been unfaithful at all. Maybe he's just working very hard and having an extra drink or two at the end of the week to relax. Then you come along tonight and give him the eye, and he might do something he wouldn't normally do, something he might regret.'

Jessie had to laugh. Dora made her sound like some kind of siren. Irresistible she was not! Just ask all the male bosses who hadn't given her a job this past year.

No, poor Dora didn't know what she was talking about, especially regarding tonight's target. Still, Dora *was* sixty-six years old. In her day, maybe more men had more honour.

'Trust me, Dora. By the time wives go to see Jack Keegan and spend the kind of money he asks for, then there really isn't any doubt over their husbands' philandering. All they're looking for is proof to show the lawyers. Our Mr Curtis Marshall here,' she said, taking his photo out of Dora's hand and looking down into his baby-blue eyes, 'is not some poor, hard-working, misunderstood hubby. He's been playing out of his patch and he's about to get caught! Now I really must get going,' she said as she slid the photo in a zippered side-section of her bag. 'I'll just go check on Emily before I leave.'

Jessie tiptoed into the bedroom, where a sound-asleep Emily had kicked off her bedclothes. The evening was quite warm, so Jessie switched the overhead ceiling fan on to the slow setting, then pulled the top sheet up around Emily and tucked her in. Emily had not long given up her cot for a single bed and looked such a dot in the larger bed.

Pressing a kiss to her temple, Jessie straightened before just standing there and staring down at her daughter.

Her heart filled with love as it always did when she looked down upon her child.

That was what had surprised Jessie the most when she'd become a mother. The instant and totally unconditional love which had consumed her from the moment she'd held her baby in her arms.

Had her own mother felt like that when she'd had her?

Jessie didn't think so. She suspected that any love her mother had had for her had been overshadowed by shame.

Jessie pushed this distressing thought aside and bent to stroke Emily's dark curls back from her forehead before planting another gentle kiss on her daughter's cheek.

'Sleep tight, sweetie,' she whispered. 'Mummy won't be long.

'Thank you so much for staying here and minding

her, Dora,' Jessie said on returning to the combined kitchen and living room.

'My pleasure,' Dora said, already settled on the sofa in front of the television.

'You know where the tea and biscuits are.'

'I'll be fine. There's a good movie on tonight at eight-thirty. That's only ten minutes off. You'd better get going. And for Pete's sake, take a taxi home after you're finished. It's too dangerous on the train late at night, especially on a Friday night.'

'Hopefully, I won't be too late.'

Jessie didn't want to waste any of the travel expenses Jack had given her. She wanted to make as much profit out of this rotten evening as she could. Why waste thirty dollars on a cab?

'Jessie Denton,' Dora said sternly. 'You promise me you'll take a taxi home.'

Jessie gave her a narrow-eyed look from under her long lashes. 'I will if I need to, Dora.'

'You can be very stubborn, do you know that?'

Jessie grinned. 'Yep. But you love me just the same. Take care.' And, giving Dora a peck on the cheek, she swept up her bag and headed for the door.

CHAPTER TWO

KANE sat at the bar, nursing a double Scotch, and pondering the perversities of life.

He still could not believe what his brother had just told him: that he was miserable in his marriage and that he spent every Friday night drinking here at this bar instead of going home to his wife and children. Curtis even confessed to going into the office on the weekend sometimes to escape the tension and arguments at home.

Kane could not have been more shocked. There he'd been these past few years, envying Curtis for his choice of wife, his two gorgeous children and his seemingly perfect family!

The truth, it seemed, was a far cry from the fantasy world Kane had woven around his twin brother's home life. Apparently, Lisa was far from content with being a stay-at-home mum. She was bored and lonely for adult company during the day. On top of that, two-year-old Joshua had turned into a right terror this past year. Four-year-old Cathy threw tantrums all the time and wouldn't go to bed at night. Lisa could not cope and their sex life had been reduced to zero.

Curtis, who was never at his best at the art of communication, had started staying away from home more and more, and Lisa was now giving him the silent treatment.

He was terrified she was thinking of leaving him and taking the kids with her. Which had prompted his call of desperation to his brother tonight.

Kane, who'd been working late at the office, solving the problem of a defecting designer, had come running to the rescue—as he always did when his twin brother was hurt or threatened in any way. He'd been coming to Curtis's rescue since they were toddlers.

'I love my family and don't want to lose them,' Curtis had cried into his beer ten minutes earlier. 'Tell me what to do, Kane. You're the man with all the solutions. Tell me what to do!'

Kane had rolled his eyes at this. OK, he could understand why Curtis thought he could wave a magic wand and fix his problems with a few, well-chosen words. He *had* made a fortune teaching people how to be successful in getting what they wanted out of their working life. His motivational seminars drew huge crowds. His fee as an after-dinner speaker was outrageous. His best-selling book, *Winning At Work*, had been picked up in most countries overseas.

Earlier this year he'd gone on a whirlwind tour in the US to promote the book's release, and sales there had been stupendous.

His hectic schedule in America had drained him, however, both physically and emotionally, and since his return he'd cut back considerably on his speaking engagements. He'd been thinking of taking a long holiday when his friend Harry Wilde had asked him to look after his small but very successful advertising agency during December whilst he went on a cruise with his wife and kids.

Kane had jumped at the chance. A change was as good as a holiday. And he was really enjoying the challenge. It had been interesting to see if his theories could be applied to any management job. So far, so good.

Unfortunately, his strategies for success in the professional world didn't necessarily translate into success in one's personal life. His own, especially. With one failed marriage behind him and no new relationship in sight, he was possibly not the best man to give his brother marital advice.

But he knew one thing. You never solved any problem by sitting at a bar, downing one beer after another. You certainly never solved anything, running away from life.

Of course, that had always been Curtis's nature, to take the easiest course, to run away from trouble. He'd always been the shy twin. The less assertive twin. The one who needed protecting. Although just as intelligent, Curtis had never had Kane's confidence, or drive, or ambition. His choice to become an accountant had not surprised Kane.

Still, Kane understood that it could not have been easy being *his* twin brother. He knew he could be a hard act to follow, with his I-can-do-anything personality.

But it was high time Curtis stood up and faced life head-on, along with his responsibilities. He had a lovely wife and two great kids who were having a hard time for whatever reason and really needed him. Regardless of what a lot of those new relationship gurus touted, Kane believed a husband was supposed to be the head of his family. The rock. The person they could always count on.

Curtis was acting like a coward.

Not that Kane said that. Rule one in his advice to management executives was never to criticise or put down their staff or their colleagues. Praise and encouragement worked much better than pointing out an individual's shortcomings.

In light of that theory, Kane had delivered Curtis one of his best motivational lectures ever, telling his brother what a great bloke he was. A great brother, a great son, a great husband and a great father. He even threw in that Curtis was a great accountant. Didn't he do his brother's highly complicated tax return each year?

Kane reassured Curtis that his wife loved him and no way would she ever leave him.

Unless she thought he didn't love her back. Which Lisa *had* to be thinking, Kane reckoned.

At this point he sent his brother off home to tell his wife that he loved her to death and that he was sorry that he hadn't been there for her when she needed him. He was to vow passionately that he would be in future, and what could he do to help?

'And when Lisa falls, weeping, into your arms,' Kane had added, 'whip her into bed and make love to her as you obviously haven't made love to her in a long time!'

When Curtis still hesitated, Kane also promised to

drop over the next day to give his brother some moral support, and to provide some more proactive suggestions which would make his wife and kids a lot happier.

Hopefully, by then, he could think of some.

One divorce in their family was more than enough! Their parents would have a fit if Curtis and Lisa broke up as well.

Kane shook his head and swirled his drink, staring down into the pale amber depths and wondering just why he'd married Natalie in the first place. For a guy who was supposed to be smart, he'd been very dumb that time. Their marriage had been doomed from the start.

'Hi, honey.'

Kane's head whipped around to find a very good-looking blonde sliding seductively onto the bar stool next to him. Everything she had—and there was plenty of it—was on display. For a split-second, Kane felt his male hormones rumble a bit. Till he looked into her eyes.

They were pretty enough, but empty. Kane could never stay interested in women with empty eyes.

Natalie had had intelligent eyes.

Pity she hadn't wanted children.

'You look as if you could do with some company,' the blonde added before curling her finger at the barman and ordering herself a glass of champagne.

'Bad week?' she directed back at Kane.

'Nope. Good week. Not so great an evening,' he replied, still thinking of his brother's problems.

'Loneliness is lousy,' she said.

'I'm not lonely,' he refuted. 'Just alone.'

'Not any more.'

'Maybe I want to be alone.'

'No one *wants* to be alone, lover.'

The blonde's words struck home. She was right. No one did. Him included. But divorce—even an amicable one—made a man wary. It had been fifteen months since he'd separated from Natalie, three months since their divorce had become final. And he still hadn't found anyone new. He hadn't even succumbed to the many offers he'd had for one-night stands.

Women were always letting him know they were available for the night, or a weekend, or whatever. But he just wasn't interested in that kind of encounter any more. He'd been hoping to find what he thought Curtis had. A woman who wasn't wrapped up in her career. A woman who was happy to put her job aside for a few years at least to become a career wife, and mother.

Now he wasn't so sure if that creature existed. The sort of women he found attractive were invariably involved with their jobs. They were smart, sassy, sexy girls who worked hard and played hard. They didn't want to become housewives and mothers.

'Come on, lighten up a bit,' the blonde said. 'Get yourself another drink, for pity's sake. That one's history.'

Kane knew he probably shouldn't. He hadn't had anything to eat tonight and the whisky was going straight to his head. He wasn't interested in the blonde, but neither did he want to go home to an empty house. He'd have one more drink with her, then make his excuses and go find a place in town to eat.

CHAPTER THREE

THE bar Curtis Marshall frequented every Friday
night was called the Cellar, so Jessie shouldn't have
been surprised to find that it was downstairs from
street level. Narrow, steep stairs. Stairs which made
her walk oh, so carefully in her four-inch-high heels.
The last thing she wanted was to fall flat on her face.

The music reached her ears only seconds before
the smoke.

Jazz.

Not Jessie's favourite form of music. But what did
it matter? She wasn't there to enjoy herself. She was
there to do a job.

The bouncer standing by the open door gave her
the once-over as she slowly negotiated the last few
steps.

'Very nice,' he muttered as she walked past him.

She didn't answer. She straightened her shoulders
and moved further into the smoke haze, her eyes
slowly becoming accustomed to the dimmer lighting
as they scanned the not-so-crowded room. Nine
o'clock, she reasoned, was between times. Most of
the Friday after-work drinkers had departed, and the
serious weekend party animals had not yet arrived.

She'd never been to this particular bar before.
She'd never heard of it. It was Jack who'd informed
her that it had a reputation as a pick-up joint.

The décor was nineteen-twenties speak-easy style, with lots of wood and leather and brass. Booths lined the walls, with tables and chairs filling every other available space. The band occupied one corner, with a very small dance floor in front of it.

The bar itself was against the far wall, semicircular in shape, graced by a dozen or so wooden-based, leather-topped stools. A long mirror ran along the back behind the bottle shelves, which gave Jessie reflected glimpses of the faces of people sitting at the bar.

There were only half a dozen.

She recognised her target straight away. He was sitting in the middle, with a blonde sitting next to him on his left. There were several vacant stools to his right. As Jessie stood there, watching them, she saw the blonde lean over and say something to him. He motioned to the barman, who came over, temporarily blocking Jessie's view of the target's face in the mirror.

Had the blonde asked him to buy her a drink? Was he right at this moment doing exactly what his wife suspected him of?

Jessie realised with a rush of relief that maybe she wouldn't have to flirt with the creep after all. If she got over there right now, she could collect evidence of his chatting up some other woman without having to belittle herself.

Jessie's heart pounded as she headed for the bar, nerves cramping her stomach. She still hated doing this, even second-hand.

Think of the money, she told herself as she slid up

on the vacant stool two to the right of the target. *Think of Emily's beautiful, beaming face on Christmas morning when she finds that Santa has brought her exactly what she asked for.*

The self-lecture helped a little. Some composure returned by the time Jessie placed her bag down on the polished wooden bar-top. Very casually she extracted the mobile phone, pretended to check her text messages, turned on the video then put it down in a position which would catch what was going on to her left, both visually and verbally.

'Thanks,' the blonde purred when the barman put a glass of champagne in front of her. 'So what will we drink to, handsome?'

When the barman moved away, Jessie was able to watch the target's face again in the mirror behind the bar.

There was no doubt he *was* handsome, more handsome than in his photograph. More mature-looking, too. Maybe that photo in her bag was a couple of years old, because his hair was different as well. Not different in colour. It was still a mid-brown. But in place of the longer waves and lock flopping across his forehead was a short-back-and-sides look, with spikes on top.

The style brought his blue eyes more into focus.

That was another thing that looked different. His eyes. In the photo they'd seemed a baby-blue, with a dreamy expression. In reality, his eyes were an icy blue. And not soft at all.

They glittered as he smiled wryly and swirled the

remains of his drink. He hadn't noticed her arrival as yet.

'To marriage,' he said, and lifted his glass in a toast.

'Marriage!' the blonde scorned. 'That's one seriously out-of-date institution. I'd rather drink to divorce.'

'Divorce is a blight on our society,' he said sharply. 'I won't drink to divorce.'

'Sex, then. Let's drink to sex.' And she slid her glass against his in a very suggestive fashion.

Jessie, who'd stayed surreptitiously watching him in the mirror behind the bar, saw his head turn slowly towards the blonde, a drily amused expression on his face.

'Sweetheart, I think you've picked the wrong guy to share a drink with. I'm sorry if I've given you the wrong impression, but I'm not in the market for what you're looking for tonight.'

Jessie almost fell off her stool. What was this? A man with some honour? Had Dora been right about Mr Marshall after all?

'You sure?' the blonde persisted with a sultry smile playing on her red-painted mouth.

'Positive.'

'Your loss, lover,' she said and, taking her glass of champagne, slid off her stool and sashayed over to sit at a table close to the band. She wasn't by herself for more than ten seconds, before a guy who'd been sitting further down the bar had taken *his* beer with him to join her.

Jessie glanced back into the mirror to find that her

target had finally noticed her presence, and was staring at her. When their eyes connected in the glass her heart reacted in a way which it hadn't in years. It actually jumped, then fluttered, then flipped right over.

Her eyes remained locked with his for longer than was wise, her brain screaming at her to look away, but her body took absolutely no notice.

Suddenly a man plonked himself down on the vacant stool that separated them, snapping her back to reality.

'Haven't seen you in here before, gorgeous,' the interloper said in slurred tones, his beery breath wafting over her. 'Can I buy you a drink?'

He was about forty, a very short, very drunk weasel of a man in a cheap, ill-fitting business suit that bore no resemblance to the magnificently tailored Italian number the target was wearing.

'No, thanks,' Jessie said stiffly. 'I like to buy my own drinks.'

'One of them feminists, eh? That's all right by me. Cheaper this way.'

'I also like to drink alone,' she added sharply.

The drunk laughed. 'A sexy piece like you shouldn't be doing anything alone. What's the matter, honey? Last guy do you wrong? Or ain't I young enough for you? Trust me. I've still got it where it counts. Here, let me show you…'

He was actually fumbling with his fly when two big hands grabbed him and literally lifted him off the stool.

'Let *me* show *you* something, buster,' the target said. 'The door!'

Jessie watched, open-mouthed, as her unexpected knight in shining armour carried the drunk over to where the bouncer was frowning at them both. Words were exchanged after which the bouncer escorted the weasel up the stairs personally whilst Jessie's champion headed back for the bar.

She found herself admiring more than his handsome face this time.

There was the way his broad shoulders filled out his expensive suit. The way he'd just handled the situation. And the way he was smiling at her.

That smile was pure dynamite. As well as something else that wasn't at all pure.

Suddenly, Jessie was catapulted back to earlier that evening when she'd been thinking about how pleasurable it would be to be in some gorgeous man's arms.

She started thinking about how pleasurable it would be to be in *this* man's arms. He was definitely gorgeous.

But he was also married. And sitting back down, she realised breathlessly, *not* on his old stool but the one right next to hers, the one the drunk had occupied.

Dora's words came back to haunt her, the ones that she'd said about how it wasn't fair to send someone like her to flirt; that she might tempt her target tonight to do something he might regret.

But logic argued against this concern. That blonde

had been very attractive. If he was going to be tempted, then why hadn't *she* tempted him?

Maybe he doesn't go for blondes, came back another voice, just as logical. Maybe he likes leggy women with wild black hair. Maybe he likes women who aren't quite so obvious.

There were many reasons why men were attracted to one woman over another.

And he *was* attracted to her. She could see it in his eyes. And in that heart-stopping smile.

'Th...thank you,' she stammered.

'You can buy me another Scotch and soda in gratitude if you like,' he said, and downed what was left of his drink. 'Unless you really meant what you said about preferring to drink alone.' And he smiled at her again.

Jessie's heart ground to a shuddering halt.

Get out of here now, girl, her conscience warned. This guy is not just dynamite, he's downright dangerous!

'I was just trying to get rid of him,' she heard herself saying.

'I was hoping that might be the case. So what can I get you? After all, a gentleman doesn't really expect a lady to buy his drinks for him.'

Jessie swallowed. What are you doing, girl? Stop looking at him that way. Stop it right now!

I'm just doing my job, she tried telling herself. This is what I get paid for. Flirting with my target. Seeing what kind of man he is.

Yes, but you're not supposed to be enjoying it!

'Just a diet cola, thanks.'

His straight brows lifted in the middle. 'You come into a bar for a diet cola? Now, that's a strange thing to do. You can get one of those from a vending machine.'

'Maybe I came in looking for some company,' she said leadingly, and hoped like hell he'd put his foot in his mouth right away so she could get out of there.

'I can't imagine a girl like you would have to do that too often. You must have men asking you out all the time.'

Actually, she did. But no one she'd give the time of day to. The men who asked her out had her tagged as one of two types: waitressing slut or single-mother-and-desperate, depending on when and where they met her.

Either way, Jessie always knew exactly what they wanted from her, and it wasn't witty conversation.

She always said no to their invitations.

One-night stands held no appeal for her. Sex of any kind had held no appeal for her.

Till tonight…

'Give me another Scotch and soda,' the target directed to the barman. 'And get the lady a Bacardi and cola. *Diet* cola,' he added with a quick grin her way.

She swallowed. 'What if I don't like Bacardi and cola?'

'Come, now, you and I both know that the amount of Bacardi they put in drinks in places like this is barely detectable. All you'll taste is the cola.'

'True,' she agreed.

'So was that other chap right?' he went on whilst

the barman busied himself with their drinks. 'Did your last boyfriend do you wrong? Is that why you're all alone tonight?'

She shrugged. 'Something like that.'

'Aah. A woman of mystery and intrigue. I like that. It makes for a change.'

'A change from what?'

'From women who launch into their life story as soon as you meet them.'

'Does that happen to you often?'

'Too often.'

'Did the blonde over there do that?'

'Actually, no. But then, she had other things on her mind tonight. Looks as if she finally hit the jackpot.'

Jessie flicked a glance over at where the blonde was now leaving with the man who'd joined her earlier. It didn't take a genius to guess that they were going back to her place. Or his. Or maybe even a hotel. There were several within easy walking distance of this bar.

'Most men would have jumped at the chance,' she remarked.

'I'm not most men.'

'Yes. Yes, I can see that.'

Their drinks came, giving Jessie a breather from the tension that was gripping her chest. As cool as she was sounding on the outside, inside she was seriously rattled. She liked this man. *More* than liked. She found him fascinating. And sexy. Oh, so sexy.

'What about you?' she asked, deciding to deflect the conversation on to him, make him admit he was married. Anything to lessen her worry over where their conversation might lead.

'What about me?' he returned before taking a deep swallow of his drink.

'Did your last girlfriend do *you* wrong? Is that why *you're* alone here tonight?'

He drank some more whilst he gave her question some thought. Suspense built in Jessie till she wanted to scream at him to just confess the truth. That *he* was the one in the wrong here. Regardless of how stressed he might feel with life, he should be at home with his wife and kids. She'd heard him say that divorce was a blight on society. Did he want to find himself in the middle of one?

Finally, he looked up and slanted a smile over at her. 'You know what? I'm going to take a leaf out of your book. No talking about past relationships tonight. I think sometimes I talk way too much. Come on,' he pronounced and put his drink down. 'The music's changed to something decent. Let's dance.'

Jessie stiffened, then gulped down a huge mouthful of Bacardi and cola. 'Dance?' she choked out.

He was already off his stool, already holding out his hand towards her.

'Please don't say no,' he said softly. 'It's just a dance. Mind the lady's bag, will you?' he asked the barman. 'Better put your cellphone away as well. You don't want a natty little number like that to get swiped.'

She did hesitate, she was sure she did. But within moments she'd put the phone away and was placing her hand in his and letting him lead her over to that minute dance floor.

It *is* only dancing, she told herself as he pulled her into his arms.

The trouble was, there was dancing…and dancing.

This was slow dancing. Sensual dancing. Sexy dancing. Bodies pressed so close together that she had no choice but to wind her arms up around his neck. Her breasts lifted, rubbing against the well-muscled wall of his chest. His hands moved restlessly up and down her spine till one settled in the small of her back, the other moving lower. The heat in his palms burned through the thin material of her dress, branding her. Her heartbeat quickened. The entire surface of her skin flushed with her own internal heat. She felt light-headed. Excited. Aroused.

And she wasn't the only one. She could feel his arousal as it rose between them.

When her fingertips tapped an agitated tattoo on the nape of his neck, he stopped, pulled back slightly and stared down into her eyes.

'Would you believe me if I told you that I haven't done anything like this in a long, long time?' he murmured, his voice low and thick.

'Done what?' she replied shakily.

'Picked a girl up in a bar and within no time asked her to go to a hotel with me?'

She stopped breathing. Stopped thinking. Her world had tipped on its axis and she felt every ounce of her self-control slipping. A voice was tempting her to blindly say yes. Yes, to anything he wanted. She had never in her life felt what she was feeling at this moment. Not even with Lyall.

This was something else, something far more powerful and infinitely more dangerous.

'Will you?' he said, and his smouldering gaze searched hers.

She didn't say a word. But her eyes must have told him something.

'No names,' he murmured. 'Not yet. Not till afterwards. I don't want to say anything that might spoil what we're sharing at this moment. Because I have never felt anything quite like it before. Tell me it's the same for you. Admit it. Say you want me as badly as I want you.'

She couldn't say it. But every fibre of her female body compelled her to cling to him, betraying her cravings with her body language.

'You do talk too much,' she whispered at last.

His lungs expelled a shuddering sigh. Of relief? Or was he trying to dispel some of the sexual tension that was gripping them both?

'Then you *will* come with me,' he said. 'Now. Straight away.'

They weren't questions, but orders.

He would be an incredible lover, she realised. Knowing. Dominating. Demanding. The kind she had used to fantasise about. And which she suddenly craved.

'I...I have to go to the ladies' first,' she blurted out, desperate to get away from him. Once some distance broke the spell he was casting over her, she would recover her sanity and escape.

'I suppose I could do with a visit to the gents' as well. I'll meet you back at the bar.'

She didn't meet him back at the bar. She spent less than twenty seconds in the ladies' before dashing back to the bar, collecting her bag from the barman and bolting for the exit. She ran all the way to Wynyard Station, where she jumped on the first train heading north.

It was only half an hour since she'd walked into that bar. But it felt like a lifetime.

CHAPTER FOUR

'THE phone's ringing, Mummy.' Emily tugged at Jessie's jeans. 'Mummy, are you listening to me? The phone's ringing.'

'What? Oh, yes. Thanks, sweetie.'

Jessie dropped the wet T-shirt she was holding back into the clothes basket and ran across the yard towards her back door.

Goodness knew who it would be. She'd already rung Jack first thing this morning to put in a verbal report about last night, petrified at the time that he'd know she was lying.

She'd made up her mind overnight to give Mr Marshall the benefit of the doubt and only tell Jack about the incident with the blonde, and not the conversation that had happened later. She'd already wiped that part off the video as well.

But no sooner had she told him that she'd witnessed the target turning down a proposition from an attractive blonde than Jack had stunned her by saying he wasn't surprised, that the wife herself had rung that morning in a panic to say that he could keep the money she'd already paid, but that she didn't want her husband followed any more. It had all been a mistake and a misunderstanding. He'd come home last night and explained everything and she was very happy.

At which point Jack had added smarmily that he could guess what had happened in the Marshall household last night.

'I can always tell,' he'd joked. 'The wives' voices have a certain sound about them. A combination of coyness and confidence. Our Mr Marshall really came good, I'd say. Like to have been a fly on their bedroom wall last night, I can tell you.'

That image had stayed with Jessie all morning— of her actually being a fly on that bedroom wall, watching whilst the man she'd danced with last night, the man who'd wanted her so desperately, was making love to his wife.

Jessie knew it was wicked of her to feel jealousy over a husband making love to his wife. Wicked to wish she'd been the one in his bed. Wicked, wicked, wicked!

But she couldn't seem to stop her thoughts, or her feelings. She'd hardly slept a wink all night.

Now, as she dashed inside to the strident sound of the phone, she could still see the desire in his eyes, hear the passion in his voice, feel the need of his body pressed up against hers.

Had he been telling the truth when he said this was a one-off experience? That he'd never done or felt anything like that before?

She was inclined to believe him. Possibly, he'd been more intoxicated than he looked. Or he'd been too long without sex. Silly to believe that there'd been something special between them, right from the first moment their eyes had connected.

That was the romantic in her talking. Men thought

differently to women, especially about sex. All she'd been to him was a potential one-night stand.

Maybe, after he discovered she'd done a flit, he'd been relieved. Maybe he'd rushed home in a fit of guilt and shame and genuinely made things up with his wife. Maybe he hadn't simply used the desire Jessie had engendered in him to make love to a woman he didn't feel excited by any more.

But why would he do that? For his children's sake?

Perhaps. Christmas was coming up soon. A family should be together at Christmas. He did hate divorce. She'd heard him say so. And he'd toasted marriage.

Clearly, his marriage mattered to him.

She had to stop thinking about him, Jessie decided as she snatched the receiver down off the kitchen wall. Whatever happened last night, it was over and done with. She would never see the man again. End of story. *Finis!*

'Yes,' she answered breathlessly into the phone.

'Jessie Denton?'

'Speaking.'

'It's Nicholas Hanks here, Jessie, from Adstaff.'

'Pardon? Who?' And then the penny dropped. 'Oh, yes, Adstaff. The employment agency. Sorry, it's been a while since I heard from you.'

'True, but, as I explained to you earlier this year, the market for graphic artists isn't very buoyant at the moment. Still, something came up yesterday and I thought of you immediately.'

'Really? Why me, especially?' Any initial jolt of excitement was tempered by her experiences in the past. Recruitment people were, by nature, optimists. You had to take what they said with a grain of salt sometimes.

'This particular advertising agency wants someone who can start straight away,' the recruiter rattled on. 'They don't want to interview anyone who's currently employed with another agency.'

Jessie's heart sank. There had to be dozens of unemployed graphic artists in Sydney. Once again, the odds of her securing this much-sought-after job was minimal.

'So which agency is it?' she asked, refusing to get her hopes up.

'*Wild Ideas.*'

'Oh!' Jessie groaned. 'I'd *love* to work for them.'

Her, and just about every other graphic artist in Sydney. Wild Ideas was only small compared to some advertising agencies. But it was innovative and very successful. Run by advertising pin-up boy Harry Wilde, it had a reputation for promoting any graphic artist with flair to the position of creative designer, rather than head-hunting them from other agencies.

'Yes, I thought you might,' came the drily amused reply. 'You have an interview there at ten o'clock Monday morning.'

'Gosh, that soon.' She'd have to ring the restaurant. Fortunately, Monday was their least busy day; if she rang early, they'd be able to call in one of the casuals, no trouble.

'Can you start straight away, if you have to?'

'Too right I can. But let's be honest…Nicholas, wasn't it…what are the odds of that happening?'

'Actually, you have an even-money chance. We sent over the CVs of several people on our books yesterday afternoon and they've already whittled them down to two. You're one of those two. Apparently, they're keen to fill this position, post-haste, and don't want to waste time interviewing all the would-bes if there are could-bes. I remember your portfolio very well, Jessie, so I know you have the talent required. And you interview very well. Frankly, I was very surprised you weren't snapped up for that art job I sent you along for earlier on in the year.'

Jessie sighed. 'I wasn't surprised. Regardless of what they say, some employers are dead against hiring a single mother. They don't say so straight out, but underneath they worry that you'll want time off when your kid's sick or something. I'm sure that's been part of my problem all along.'

'Jessie, your single-mother status is clearly stated on your résumé, which Wild Ideas has already seen. Yet they still specifically asked for you. Clearly, your being a single mum didn't deter them, did it? You do have your little girl in full-time care, don't you?'

'Yes. But…'

'But nothing. Your circumstances are no different from those of any other working mum, be they single or married. What will count with Wild Ideas is your creative talent, your professional attitude and your reliability. Impress them on those three levels and I feel confident that this job will be yours.'

Jessie had to struggle to control the stirrings of excitement. No way could she afford to get carried away with false optimism. She'd been there, done that, and at the end of the day was always bitterly disappointed.

'You talk as if I'm the only one going for this job,' she pointed out. 'There is another applicant, isn't there?'

'Er—yes,' came the rather reluctant reply.

'Well, presumably this person is just as well-qualified for this job as I am.'

'Mmm. Yes. And no.'

'Meaning what?'

'Look, it would be very unprofessional of me to say anything negative about the other applicant. She is a client of our agency as well.'

She. It was a woman.

'But let me give you a hint when it comes to what you wear for your interview. Nothing too bright or too way-out or too overtly sexy.'

Jessie was taken aback. 'But I never dress like that. You've met me. I'm a very conservative dresser.'

'Yes, but you might have thought that going for a job at Wild Ideas required you to present a certain…image. Trust me when I tell you that your chances of being employed there will be greatly enhanced if you dress very simply.'

'You mean, in a suit or something?'

'That might be overkill, under the circumstances. I would suggest something smart, but casual.'

'Would jeans be too casual? I have some really nice jeans. Not ones with frayed holes in them. They're dark blue and very smart. I could wear them with a white shirt and a jacket.'

'Sounds perfect.'

'And I'll put my hair up. Down, it can look a bit wild. What about make-up? Should I wear make-up?'

'Not too much.'

'Right.' Jessie speculated that the other applicant was possibly a flashy female, who tried to trade on her sex appeal. Not an uncommon event in the advertising world. Perhaps with Harry Wilde now being a married man instead of a playboy, he preferred to play it safe over who he hired these days. Maybe Nicholas was subtly advising her that the *femme fatale* type would not be looked upon favourably.

'Is there anything else I should know?' she asked.

'No. Just be your usual honest and open self and I'm sure everything will work out.'

'You've been very kind. Thank you.'

'My pleasure. I'm only sorry I haven't been able to find you a job sooner.'

'I haven't got *this* job yet.'

'You will.'

Jessie wished she could share his supreme confidence, but life had taught her not to count her chickens before they hatched.

'Have to go, Jessie. There's someone else on the line. Good luck on Monday.' And he hung up.

Jessie hung up as well, only then thinking of Emily still out in the back yard all by herself.

Her heart started thudding as a mother's heart always did when she realised she'd taken her eyes off her child for a few seconds too long.

Not that Emily was the sort of child who got herself into trouble. She was careful, and a thinker. Her pleasures were quiet ones. She wasn't a climber. Neither did she do silly things. She was absolutely *nothing* like her father. She was a hundred per cent smarter, for starters.

Still, when Jessie hurried back outside into the yard, she was very relieved to see Emily was where she spent most of her time, playing under the large fig tree in the corner. It was her cubby house, with the sections between the huge roots making perfect pretend rooms. Emily could happily play there for hours.

Her daughter had a wonderful imagination. Jessie had been the same as a child. Maybe it was an only-child thing. Or an inherited talent. Or a bit of both.

Whatever, the Denton girls loved being creative.

Jessie realised then that she wanted that job at Wild Ideas, not just for the money, but also for herself. Being a waitress had been a good stopgap, but she didn't want to do it for the rest of her life. She wanted to use her mind. She wanted the challenges—and the excitement—of the advertising world.

'Mummy, who rang our phone? Was it Dora?'

Jessie, who'd finished hanging out the washing, bent down and swept her daughter up into her arms. It was time for lunch.

'No, sweetie, not Dora. It was a man.'

Emily blinked. 'A nice man?'

'Very nice.'

'Is he going to be your boyfriend, Mummy?'

'What? Oh, no. Heavens, no! He's just a man who finds people jobs. It looks as if he might have found Mummy a job as a graphic artist. I have to go for an interview on Monday. If I get it, I'll earn a lot more money and I'll be able to buy you lots of pretty things.'

Emily didn't seem as impressed with this news as Jessie would have expected. She was frowning.

'Why don't you have a boyfriend, Mummy? You're very pretty.'

Jessie felt herself blushing. 'I...I just haven't met any man I liked enough to have as a boyfriend.'

Even as she said the words, a pair of ice-blue eyes popped into her mind, along with a charismatic smile. Her heart lurched at the memory of how close she'd come to making the same mistake her mother had made. Brother, she'd got out of that bar just in time.

'I have *you*, sweetie,' Jessie said, giving her daughter a squeeze. 'I don't need anyone or anything else.'

Which was the biggest lie Jessie had told her daughter since she'd said she liked being a waitress. Because last night's experience showed her she *did* need something else sometimes, didn't she? She needed to feel like a woman occasionally, not just a mother. She needed to have a man's arms around her once more. She needed some release from the frustration she could feel building up inside her.

Some day, she would have to find an outlet for those needs. A man, obviously. A boyfriend, as Emily suggested.

But who?

Those blue eyes jumped back into her mind.

Well, obviously not him. He was off limits. A married man.

If only she could get this job. That would bring a whole new circle of males into her world.

OK, so lots of guys in the advertising world were gay. But some weren't. Surely there had to be the right kind of boyfriend out there for her. Someone attractive and intelligent. Someone single—and a good lover.

Of course, attractive, intelligent *single* men who were good lovers were invariably full of themselves, and unwilling to commit. There would be no real future in such a relationship. She'd have to be careful not to fall for the guy. Or to start hoping for more than such a man could give.

Jessie sighed. Did she honestly need such complications in her life? Wouldn't it be better if she just went along the way she was, being a celibate single mum?

Men were trouble. Always had been. Always would be. She was much better off without one in her life. Emily was happy. *She* was happy. She'd be even happier if she got this job on Monday.

Feeling frustrated was just a temporary thing. She'd get over it. One day.

Jessie sighed again.

'Why are you always sighing today, Mummy?' Emily asked. 'Are you tired?'

'A little, sweetie.'

'Why don't you have a cup of coffee? You always do that when you're tired.'

Jessie looked into her daughter's beautiful

brown eyes and laughed. 'You know me very well, don't you?'

'Yes, Mummy,' she said in that strangely grown-up voice she used sometimes. 'I do. Oh, I can hear Dora's car! Let's go and tell her about your new job.'

'I haven't got it yet, Emily. It's only an interview.'

'You'll get it, Mummy,' she said with all the naïve confidence of a four-year-old. 'You will get the job.'

CHAPTER FIVE

THE offices of Wild Ideas were in north Sydney, on the third floor of an office block not far from North Sydney Station. A bonus for Jessie, who didn't own a car.

She arrived in the foyer of the building early, dressed in her best stone-washed jeans and a freshly starched white shirt, turned up at the collar. She carried a lightweight black jacket—in case the air-conditioning inside was brutal—as well as a black briefcase. Her shoes were sensible black pumps, well-worn but polished that morning till they shone.

Her hair was pulled back tightly and secured at the nape of her neck with a black and white printed scarf she'd borrowed from Dora. Her make-up was on the neutral side, especially around her eyes and on her mouth. The only jewelry she wore were small silver cross earrings. Plus her watch. She'd be lost without her watch.

She glanced at it now. Still only twenty-five minutes to ten. She wasn't going up to Wild Ideas yet. Only desperates arrived that early. Instead she headed for the powder room, where she spent a few minutes checking that she didn't look like a *femme fatale*.

Actually, her appearance would be considered *very* conservative in advertising circles. But she'd never been a flashy dresser, even when she could afford to be.

Finally, she gave in to her pounding heart and rode the lift up to the third floor. It had been some months since she'd been for a job interview and she felt sick with nerves and tension. Not because she didn't think she could do the job. Jessie had never been lacking in confidence in her own abilities. But after being knocked back as often as she had, she'd begun to wonder if anyone would ever see what she had to offer.

Still, this chance was the best she'd had so far. *An even-money chance.*

As Jessie exited the lift on the third floor, she wondered if the other applicant was in there now, being interviewed, impressing the boss so much that he wouldn't even bother to see her. Maybe the receptionist would say 'Thank you very much but the job's already taken'.

Jessie took a deep breath and told herself not to be so silly. Or so negative. Harry Wilde had obviously liked her résumé. Surely, he'd have the decency to give her an interview.

The reception area of Wild Ideas fitted its image. Modern and colourful, with crisp, clean lines and furniture. Red-painted walls, covered in advertising posters. Black tiled floor. Very shiny. The sofas were in cream leather, the desk and coffee-tables made of blond wood.

The receptionist was blond as well, but not overly glamorous or overly beautiful. Possibly thirty, she wore a neat black suit and a nice smile—not the sort of smile used before delivering bad news.

'Hello,' she said brightly when Jessie walked in. 'You'll be Jessie Denton.'

'Yes, that's right,' Jessie replied, her palms still distinctly sweaty. 'I'm a bit early.'

'Better than being late. Or not turning up at all,' the blonde added ruefully. 'I'll just give Karen a ring to let her know you've arrived. Karen's Mr Wilde's PA,' she explained. 'Just take a seat over there for a sec.' And she motioned towards one of the seats that lined the waiting-room walls.

'Jessie Denton's here, Karen,' she heard the receptionist say quietly into the phone. 'OK… Yes, I'll tell her.'

By the time she looked up, Jessie had sat down, leant back and crossed her legs, doing her best to appear cool and confident. Inside, she was a bundle of nerves.

'Mr Marshall hasn't finished with the other applicant yet,' the receptionist informed her. 'But he won't be long.'

'Mr *Marshall*?' Jessie choked out, her legs uncrossing as she jerked forward on the seat. 'But…but…'

'Mr Wilde is overseas at the moment,' the receptionist cut into Jessie's stammering, and before she could recover from her shock. 'Mr Marshall is in charge while he's away.'

'Oh. I see. Right.' Jessie took a deep breath and leant back again, exhaling slowly. Crazy to think that this Mr Marshall was *her* Mr Marshall from Friday night. Marshall wasn't such an unusual name. On top of that, *her* Mr Marshall was an accountant. What would an accountant be doing running an advertising agency, even temporarily?

'My name's Margaret, by the way,' the reception-ist went on breezily. 'We might as well get to know each other. I probably shouldn't be saying this but I think you're more Mr Marshall's cup of tea than the girl who's in there now.'

'Why's that?' Jessie asked.

Somewhere on the floor a door banged.

'Judge for yourself,' Margaret murmured.

Just then this amazing creature swept down a cor-ridor into the reception area.

The first thing that struck Jessie was her bright orange hair, which looked as if it had been cut with a chainsaw. A *rusty* chainsaw.

The second was the myriad gold studs and rings that adorned her starkly white face. Ears. Nose. Lips. Eyebrows. Chin.

Lord knew what other parts of her body had been pierced. Possibly a great many.

Thankfully, the girl was clothed from head to foot so Jessie could only speculate. Her style, however, was a combination of grunge and gothic and the gar-ments she sported looked as if they'd been rescued from a charity bin. The kind they used for recycled rags.

'Tell Harry Wilde to contact me when he gets back, if he's still interested,' the escapee from the Addams Family tossed over her shoulder as she marched across the floor in her ex-army boots. 'I wouldn't work for him down there if he was the last man on earth. He knows absolutely nothing about the creative soul. Nothing!'

The moment she was gone Margaret looked over at a wide-eyed Jessie and grinned.

'See what I mean? I think you're a shoo-in.'

Jessie could not believe that fate had been so kind to her. 'I sure hope so. I really want this job.' She simply couldn't go the rest of her life being a waitress.

The reception phone buzzed and Margaret picked it up. 'Yes, Karen, I'll send her down straight away. And don't worry, he'll like *this* one. Your turn,' she said with an encouraging smile to Jessie as she hung up. 'Down to the end of that corridor. Go straight in.'

Jessie gulped, then stood up. 'Er—just one thing before I go. Do you happen to know Mr Marshall's first name?'

'Sure. It's Kane. Why?'

Jessie could not believe how relieved she felt. For a moment there…

She shrugged. 'I knew a guy named Marshall once and I was a bit worried this might be the same man. Thankfully, it isn't,' she muttered, and Margaret laughed.

'We all have one of those somewhere in our past.'

True. But the trouble was this one wasn't far enough in Jessie's past. He was only a couple of nights ago, and could still make her tremble at the thought of him.

Her nerves eased a lot with the surety that the Mr

Marshall about to interview her wasn't Curtis Marshall, married man and sexily irresistible hunk. She also couldn't deny she felt good that her competition had turned out so poorly. Clearly, Nicholas from Adstaff hadn't given carrot-top the same conservative-dressing advice he'd given her. Or if he had, she'd ignored him.

The door at the end of the corridor led into the PA's office. It wasn't quite as colourful as Reception, but still very nice and spacious and modern. Karen herself was nothing like Jessie had expected Harry Wilde's PA to be. She was forty-ish. A redhead. Pleasantly plump. And sweet.

'Oh, thank you, God!' she exclaimed on seeing Jessie. 'Did you see the other one?'

'Yes. Um. I did,' Jessie admitted. 'But to be honest, people like that are not unusual in the advertising world. She probably sees herself as an artiste with a certain avant-garde image to uphold.'

'We don't hire avant-garde artistes here,' Karen said wryly. 'We hire people with lots of innovative ideas who know how to work. And work hard. Now, did Margaret happen to mention that Mr Wilde's away right now?'

'Yes, she did.'

'Good. Then you'll understand why I'm doing part of your interview. Mr Marshall is an excellent manager and motivator, but he has no background in advertising. I've been with Mr Wilde a good few years and I know what he likes in an employee. I've already had a good look at your résumé, and I was impressed. Now that I can see you in person, I'm even more impressed. If you could just show me your portfolio, please?'

Jessie pulled out her portfolio and handed it over. She'd included samples of the best work she'd done over the years, plus mock-ups of ads she would like to do, if ever given the chance.

'Mmm. This is excellent. Michele is going to be pleased with you. Michele will be your boss. She's one of our top executives. Her assistant quit last week after they had an altercation over his lack of motivation. He's been having a lot of time off. A drug problem, we think. Anyway, she needs a good graphic artist to step into his shoes straight away. She has several things that need to be finished before the Christmas break. On top of that, she'll be going off on maternity leave in the middle of next year. She's having another baby. When that happens, we're hoping you'll be able to fill in for her. I gather from Adstaff that you do have ambitions to become a creative designer yourself, is that right?'

'It's my dearest wish. The sample ads at the back of my portfolio are my own original ideas. They're not actual campaigns I worked on.'

'Really. I hadn't quite got that far.' She flipped over some more pages of the portfolio, stopping to stare hard at one of the pages. 'Is this one of yours? This white-goods magazine ad,' Karen said, holding up a page.

'Yes, that's one I made up myself.'

The page had a vibrant blue background to highlight the white goods. In the middle was a dishwasher, washing machine and dryer, surrounded by other smaller kitchen appliances, all in stainless steel. Draped across the three taller items was a very glamorous Mae-West style blonde, her evening gown white with a very low neckline, her scarlet-tipped fingers caressing the appliances. Above her were the words, 'It's not the appliances in your life but the life in your appliances,' a parody of Mae West's famous comment, 'It's not the men in your life but the life in your men.'

'It's brilliant!' Karen exclaimed.

Jessie puffed up with pride. 'Thank you.'

'We have a new account for a kitchen-appliance company which this would be perfect for. I must show it to Peter. He's handling that account. I can see Michele and Peter fighting over you. Of course, Mr Marshall will have to hire you first,' she added with a grin. 'But I'm sure that's just a formality. Come on, let's get you in there. Hopefully, he's recovered from the last applicant by now. You should have seen his face when she walked in. My fault, of course. I was the one who picked her. Her résumé was impressive, but in reality she was not suitable at all.'

'Do you mind if I ask why not? Looks can be deceiving. She might have been very talented.'

'She was. A *very* talented graphic artist. But not suitable for promotion. Harry likes his front people to have a certain look, and style. After all, they have to deal with a wide range of clients, some of whom are very conservative. Harry believes first impressions are very important. Kane agrees with him. And you, Jessie Denton, make a very good first impression.'

'But I'm only wearing jeans.'

'Yes, but they're clean and neat, and you wear them with panache. And I simply love what you've done with your hair. Very classy.'

Jessie could not have felt more confident as she was ushered into Harry Wilde's office. Her self-esteem was sky-high, her heart beating with pleasurable anticipation, not nervous tension.

Fate had been good to her, for once.

But then the man seated behind Harry Wilde's desk looked up, and Jessie's heart literally stopped.

Oh, *no*, she groaned. How could this be? The receptionist had said his name was Kane, not Curtis!

But it *was* him. No doubt about it. She wasn't about to forget what he looked like, especially when he was even dressed the same, in a suit, shirt and tie.

His ice-blue eyes locked onto hers, his dark brows lifting in surprise. Or was it shock?

'Yes, I know what you mean,' Karen said to him with a small laugh. 'A definite improvement on Ms Jaegers. This is Jessie Denton. Here's her portfolio.' She walked forward and placed the folder on the wide walnut desk. 'I've had a good look at it and it's simply fabulous. Now, can I get either of you some coffee? Or tea?'

'No, thanks,' Jessie croaked out.

'Not at the moment, Karen,' her boss said.

'OK, I'll leave you to it.'

'Re*lax*,' she mouthed to a shell-shocked Jessie as she walked past her.

And then she was gone, shutting the door behind her.

Jessie just stood there in the middle of the large, plushly furnished office, her shock slowly draining away, anxiety rushing back. Anxiety and dismay.

Fate hadn't been kind to her at all. It had dangled the most wonderful opportunity in front of her nose like a carrot, only to snatch it away at the last moment. Because *this* Mr Marshall—regardless of what his first name turned out to be—wasn't about to hire her, no matter what she did, or said.

There was no way out.

If she told him the truth about why she'd been at that bar last Friday night, he would feel both humiliated and threatened. If she didn't tell him the truth, then she had to fall back on that other even more sordid reality. That she'd fancied him like mad and been tempted by him, despite knowing he was married.

No, that wasn't right, she suddenly realised. If she kept her decoy work a secret, then she would not have *known* he was married. He didn't wear a wedding ring. She'd noticed that the other night.

In that case, how could she explain her sudden disappearing act?

Saying simply that she'd changed her mind seemed rather lame. She would come across as a tease. She supposed she could say someone in the ladies' room had warned her he was a married man and that was why she'd done a flit.

That might salvage *her* pride and reputation, but it wouldn't do much for his.

The main problem here was that *he'd* known he was a married man all along, and he'd still asked her to go to a hotel room with him.

Recalling that highly charged moment brought back to Jessie the feelings she had shared with him that night. The mutual attraction. The rush of desire. The heat.

She stared at him as a new wave of heat flowed through her body, flooding her from her toes right up into her face.

There *was* no way out of this, except out the door.

'I guess I might as well leave right now,' she choked out. 'Just give me my portfolio back, please, and I'll get going.'

CHAPTER SIX

KANE rarely felt panic, but he felt it now. She was running out on him. *Again!*

He couldn't let that happen. Not now that he'd found her. The thought that he would never see her again had haunted him all weekend.

Of course, it would help to know why she'd run out on him in the first place. The only reason he could imagine was that he must have come on too hard and too fast for her.

Now he didn't know what to think.

All he knew was that nothing had changed for him since Friday night. One look from those incredible eyes of hers and he'd been right back there on that dance floor, his body consumed by the need to sweep her off into bed.

Bed? He almost laughed at that notion. A bed would not do. This all-consuming passion he was suffering from demanded a much faster, harder surface to pin her to. A wall. A floor. This desk, even.

Kane swallowed. He was really losing it!

And he'd lose her again, if she knew what was going on his head.

'Last Friday night has no relevance whatsoever to today,' he said with astonishing composure. Lust was a very powerful motivation. 'That was pleasure. This is business. But perhaps we should get the past out

59

of the way first. Would you care to sit down and tell me why you left the way you did?'

She frowned, but stayed standing. He tried to stop his eyes from continually raking her from head to toe, but truly she was a magnificent-looking woman. And so sexy in those tight jeans, it was criminal.

'What's the point?' she said sharply, brown eyes flashing. 'I can't work for you. You must know that.'

He didn't, actually. Was she worried about sexual harassment in the workplace?

Perhaps she had just cause, given how much he craved her right now. But Kane could exercise control and patience when necessary. *And* when she wasn't touching him. The last thing he wanted to do was frighten her off. She was the first woman in a long time who had made him feel what he'd felt on Friday night. To be honest, he couldn't recall *ever* feeling quite what he'd felt on that dance floor.

Usually, he could stay in control. Usually, his brain was always there in the background, analysing the situation, making judgement calls, warning him when the momentary object of his desire was another waste of his time.

But it hadn't on that occasion.

Maybe that was why she'd obsessed about him all weekend. The way she'd made him forget everything but the moment. He hadn't known anything at all about her, except that she went into sleazy bars alone, dressed to thrill. Not a great recommendation.

Yet he'd still wanted her like crazy.

He still did.

No way was he going to let her escape from him

a second time. He wanted to experience the magic he'd felt in her arms once more. Too bad if it didn't go anywhere. He was sick and tired of thinking about the future and working his life to a plan. He'd got into a rather boring rut over the years. He'd forgotten how to be impulsive.

He wanted this woman, and he was going to have her, whether she was good for him or not.

'But you won't really be working for *me*,' he replied smoothly. 'You'll be working for Harry Wilde. I'm just the caretaker manager till Christmas, which is less than two weeks away now. After that, any boss-employee relationship between us is over.'

She still stared at him with wary eyes and he wondered why. Damn it all, she fancied him. He knew she did. She'd been with him all the way on Friday night, till she'd gone to the ladies'.

He'd been stunned when she hadn't showed up again.

'So what *did* happen on Friday night?' he asked, his teeth clenched firmly in his jaw. 'Did you just change your mind? Was that it?'

'I…I…'

Her fluster was telling. And quite enchanting. Maybe she wasn't the tease he'd been thinking she might be. Or a serial good-time girl, the kind who cruised bars at night looking for some cheap fun and excitement.

'It's not a crime to change your mind, Jessie,' he said gently. Though it had felt like it at the time. He'd been furious.

'I didn't change my mind,' she said, which totally confused him.

'What, then?'

Jessie felt she had to come up with some explanation, or look a right fool.

'A girl in the ladies' told me you were married,' she blurted out. 'I...I don't sleep with married men.'

There was no doubt her excuse startled him. His head jerked back and he blinked a couple of times. But then he did the strangest thing.

He smiled.

'Married,' he said with a low chuckle. 'How come I didn't think of that? *Married!*' And he laughed again.

'I don't think it's funny,' she snapped. She knew a lot of modern people didn't take marital vows seriously. But she did.

'Aah, but it is funny. Because I'm *not* married,' came his astonishing announcement. 'My brother is, however. My twin brother. My *identical* twin brother. He's been frequenting that particular bar every Friday night for a while, so it's understandable that someone made a mistake, thinking I was him.'

Jessie opened her mouth, then closed it again. The man she'd flirted with, and wanted so badly on Friday night, hadn't been her target at all. It had been this man, Kane Marshall, Curtis Marshall's twin brother!

As amazing as this revelation was, it did explain the small differences between the target's photograph and the man in front of her. His hairstyle. The colour of his eyes. And his whole personality. The man in the photograph had seemed softer.

There was nothing soft about Kane Marshall.

A second realisation hit Jessie with even more force. Kane Marshall was single. And available. There was absolutely no reason why she couldn't say yes if he ever asked her out.

Which he would. She could see it in his eyes.

A thrill—or was it a chill?—rippled down her spine. So much for her decision not to have a man in her life.

Of course, she hadn't anticipated at the time that she could possibly have *this* man. He was a whole different ballgame.

'You're *definitely* not married?' she asked.

'Definitely not. My divorce came through a few months ago.'

This added news didn't thrill her. She wasn't sure why. Perhaps because most of the recently divorced guys she'd met were always on the make. It was as though after casting aside their wives, sex was the *only* thing on their minds. They were always on the hunt for new prey. She'd met quite a few newly divorced men at the restaurant and they usually gave her the creeps, the way they looked at her, and the way they assumed she'd be easy meat.

Was that what Kane Marshall had thought of her on Friday night, that she was easy meat? She'd gone into that bar alone, after all. Why would a girl go into a bar alone on a Friday night, if not to pick up some guy? The only excuse she'd given him for not going to a hotel room with him was that someone had told her he was married.

Now that he knew she knew he wasn't, he had to be assuming she'd fall into bed with him next time without a qualm.

As much as the *idea* of falling into bed with him was incredibly exciting, Jessie knew that the reality might not be wise.

'No wife,' he stated firmly. 'No children. And no current girlfriend. Just so we don't have any more misunderstandings.'

Jessie blinked. That was sure laying his cards on the table. Next thing he'd be telling her if he had any communicable diseases!

'So are you quite happy to work here now?' he went on.

'Are you offering me the job?'

'Absolutely.'

'But you haven't even looked at my portfolio!'

'No need. I trust Karen's judgement regarding your creative talents. She has much more experience in this field than I do. I just wanted to see you in the flesh, to make sure you had the presence and style that Harry requires in his executives.'

Jessie frowned over his words, 'in the flesh'. Maybe his offering her this job had nothing to do with her talents and everything to do with his wanting to see *more* of her in the flesh, so to speak.

Still, if she was strictly honest with herself, she wanted the same thing. Whenever his eyes were upon her—which was all the time—she could think of nothing but being in his arms once more.

Hadn't she come to the conclusion at one stage over the weekend that she needed a man in her life? A boyfriend? A lover? Why not Kane Marshall? He wasn't married. Clearly, he fancied her as much as she fancied him. Crazy to fight an attraction as strong as this was. She would only lose.

'Even if I wasn't comparing you to the last applicant,' he went on suavely, 'I would be suitably impressed, and very happy to offer you the job. If *you're* still interested, that is.'

Jessie suspected he was asking her if she was still interested in him, as well as the job.

'Yes, of course I am,' she said, deciding it would be hypocritical to say anything else.

'Good,' he said, then delivered another of those dazzling smiles of his.

He was smooth! And incredibly confident.

He both excited and rattled her. A strange combination. She'd always been attracted to physically strong men, but Kane Marshall represented more than just physical strength. His persona carried exceptional charisma. A magnetism which perturbed her. His steely gaze had the capacity to sap her willpower. But it was his sexy smile that could do the most damage. She suspected that if they became lovers, he could make her *do* things. Wild things. Wicked things.

Her thoughts sent an erotically charged quiver rippling down her spine. Suddenly, her knees felt like jelly.

'I...I think I'd better sit down,' she said, reefing her eyes away from his and pulling up one of the upright wooden chairs adjacent to the desk. She sank down onto its solid surface, grateful not to have to look at him for a while. But eventually, she had to face him once more. When she did, her shoulders were rammed back against the chair-back, her back was as stiff as a board and her legs were tightly crossed.

Her rigid body language was wasted, however. He wasn't looking at her. His handsome face was down, and he was going through what looked like her résumé.

'I see here that you're a single mother,' he remarked before finally glancing back up at her.

Jessie's chin lifted defiantly. 'Is that a problem?'

'Absolutely not. I admire unmarried women who keep their babies,' he added with warmth in his voice and another of those winning smiles.

'I meant, is that a problem with my job?' she bit out, irritated with herself for going to mush inside again.

'I don't see why it should be. You have your little girl in day-care, it says here.'

'Yes, but there will be times when she gets sick. Or I might have to attend a school concert. Or some emergency.'

'Work conditions here at Wild Ideas are very flexible. You can work your own hours, or at home if you want. All that is required is that the work is done, meetings are attended and deadlines met. Your immediate boss is the mother of a little girl herself, with another baby on the way, so I'm sure she will be very understanding about such matters. Speaking of Michele, I think perhaps I should take you along to meet her shortly. She rang earlier with instructions to have someone sitting at the computer by her side before lunchtime. Or else.'

'You mean you want me to start straight away, *today*?' Jessie gasped.

He raised a single eyebrow at her. 'I thought you understood that. Is there any reason you *have* to leave?'

'No...no, I guess not. But I will have to ring the day-care centre and tell them I'll be a bit later than usual picking Emily up.'

'Will that worry your little girl?'

'No. But it might worry me. I'm not sure how often the trains run and how long it will take me to get there. I have to pick Emily up before six. They close at six.'

'You don't have a car?'

'No,' she admitted. 'I haven't been able to afford to run one.'

'You should be able to now. Your pay is sixty-five thousand dollars a year, with bonuses.'

All the breath was punched from Jessie's lungs. 'You're joking! Sixty-five thousand?' Before she'd had Emily, she'd only been on forty thousand.

'That's right. Your basic salary will be reviewed every six months, with rises given on performance.'

'That's incredible.'

'Don't worry. You'll have to deliver.'

'I'll deliver. Don't you worry about that.'

Their eyes met once more, with Jessie wondering if their conversation still carried a double meaning.

She hoped not. She'd hate to think that underneath his impressive surface, Kane Marshall was just another divorced creep.

'You should consider leasing a car,' he went on. 'Curtis always tells me that leasing is a much more sensible option in business. My brother is an accountant,' he added.

Unnecessarily. Jessie already knew that. But she could hardly say so. Still, it sent her wondering exactly where Kane Marshall usually worked. Karen had said he was an excellent manager and motivator. But for what company?

'If you like,' he was saying, 'I could get Karen to organise the leasing for you. All you have to do is tell me what kind of car you'd like.'

'I...I don't really know. I'll have to think about it.'

'If you tell me the make and model in the morning, it can be ready for you by the time you finish up tomorrow. Meanwhile, I'm quite happy to drive you home after work tonight. I wouldn't want you to worry about your little girl.'

Jessie stared at him. He certainly wasn't wasting any time in making his move.

'You don't have to do that,' she said. 'I do have a friend I could ring to pick Emily up if I think I can't make it.'

'A man friend?'

The question sounded casual, but Jessie could see more than curiosity in his eyes. Insane to imagine he was jealous. But it felt as if he was.

'No,' she said, and was sure he looked relieved.

'An elderly lady. My landlady, in fact. I rent a granny flat from her. But she's also a good friend.'

'It's no trouble for me to drive you home, Jessie,' he said. 'You don't live that far away. Besides, I'd like the opportunity to talk to you some more. Out of the office.'

'All right, then,' she agreed, if a bit stiffly. She wished she could get the thought out of her head that she was being weak. 'Thank you.'

'It's my pleasure.' And he smiled at her again.

Jessie suppressed a moan. Oh, he was just so gorgeous. How could she possibly say no?

Yet she hated for him to think she was easy.

Jessie was well used to the way most men thought about single mothers. They were considered desperates. Desperate for sex. Desperate for company. Desperate for some man—*any* man—to give them the emotional and financial support they obviously weren't getting from whoever had fathered their child.

In truth, there were quite a lot of single mothers who did act that way.

But Jessie wasn't normally like most single mothers. She'd always prided herself on her self-sufficiency. After Lyall, she'd never wanted to rely on any man for anything. Not even for sex.

Not till she'd met Kane Marshall.

Now he was all she could think about. Already, she was looking forward to his driving her home. Her skin actually broke into goose-pimples at the thought.

Yet she should have been concentrating on the job she'd just been given.

Jessie jumped to her feet. 'Now that that's all settled, I'd better get started, don't you think?'

He was much slower in rising, buttoning up his jacket as he did so.

His action drew her eyes to his suit. It wasn't the same pale grey number he'd worn on Friday night. This one was a darker grey. But it was just as expensive-looking and stylish. Not a wrinkle marred the line of its sleeves, or where the collar sat neatly around his solid neck.

He was a big man, she noticed once more. Not overweight. Just tall, and strong, with the broadest shoulders.

He would look good, naked. *Feel* good, too.

Oh, dear, Jessie groaned to herself. I'm in trouble here. Big, big trouble.

'This way,' he said as he walked around and gestured towards the door.

Thankfully he didn't touch her. His eyes were bad enough. The way they kept running over her.

He wasn't all that different from those other divorced creeps who'd pursued her, Jessie realised as she bolted through the door ahead of him.

The difference lay in her. Those other men hadn't made her tremble with a look. They hadn't made her forget every wise word of warning her mother had ever given her about men.

No, that wasn't true. She hadn't forgotten any of her mother's warnings. She knew what Kane Marshall was, and what he wanted.

The difference this time was that she wanted exactly the same thing he did.

CHAPTER SEVEN

JESSIE could not believe how quickly the day went, and how nice everyone was at Wild Ideas, especially her immediate boss.

In her early thirties, Michele was an attractive brunette, married, with one little girl and another baby on the way. She was warm and welcoming to Jessie, but at the same time efficient and precise. *Very* precise with her directions. She knew what she wanted—art-wise—and expected things to be done exactly as she wanted.

But Jessie was used to that. Jackson & Phelps had been a demanding company to work for. They had high standards and had trained her well.

But she much preferred working for Wild Ideas. Such a friendly atmosphere. The staff was relatively small—about twenty—and pretty well everyone had popped their heads into Michele's office at some time during the day.

Actually, calling it an office was misleading. It was more of a work station. The behind-the-scenes office layout at Wild Ideas was open plan, cut up into cubicles, some larger than others. Michele's area was quite large, but not fancy in any way. Plain pine furniture. No carpet. No doors. One window that looked out on to the main road.

Still, everything in it was clean and functional,

with state-of-the-art computer equipment, along with every piece of software imaginable. Jessie got very excited to work on the very latest G5 Macintosh, which was so much faster than her old Imac.

Just as well, because her predecessor had left things in a right mess. There was so much to sort through that when lunchtime came she ate a sandwich at her desk. Margaret from Reception dropped by and brought her some coffee, which was sweet of her. Jessie could see that they were going to become friends.

The only breaks she had were to go to the ladies' room and to make three phone calls. The first was to the restaurant to say that she was quitting. Since she was only a casual anyway, they didn't much care. They'd fill her spot within hours. The second was to the day-care centre. True to form, Emily didn't give a hoot that she would be late picking her up. Traitorous child! The third was to Dora, who was thrilled Jessie had got the job.

Unfortunately, Jessie couldn't explain about the fiasco with the Marshall brothers, not with Michele sitting right next to her.

Actually, Jessie liked it that she worked right beside Michele and wasn't off in another section on the floor, either in a corner by herself or with a whole bunch of other graphic artists. It seemed that at Wild Ideas, each creative designer had their own personal graphic artist. Sort of like their own private assistant. Jessie could see that this was a very successful way of doing things. New team leaders were being trained all the time. No wonder Harry Wilde never had to head-hunt executives from other agencies. He didn't need to.

'Time to wrap it up for today, girls. It's almost five.'

Jessie whipped her head round at Kane's voice to find him leaning against the open door frame, watching her. He looked as if he'd been there a while.

Actually, she'd surprised herself, the way she'd been able to put the man out of her mind for most of the day. But the moment their eyes met once more, all the feelings he evoked in her rushed back.

Not just heart-pounding desire. That was a given. But accompanying jabs of panic, and worry.

Her life since Emily had been born had been so simple. And straightforward. Maybe a little boring. And yes, lonely at times. But not too stressful.

If she became involved with Kane Marshall—even on just a casual basis—he would begin to make demands on her time and her space. As a single mother who now had a full-time job, Jessie knew she wouldn't have much spare time for leisure and pleasure.

'So how did our new girl work out, Michele?' Kane asked.

'Excellent,' Michele replied crisply. 'She's very good at what she does. And I suspect she'll be very good at what I do. Eventually,' she added with a cheeky wink.

Jessie didn't know what to say in reply to such fulsome praise, so she said nothing.

'We'd better get going, Jessie,' Kane asked. 'The traffic will be heavy. I'm driving Jessie home today,' he explained to Michele. 'She has to pick her daughter up by six and she's not sure about the train timetable.'

'Yes, I know. Jessie told me all about your knight-to-the-rescue act,' Michele said drily, a slightly knowing smile playing on her mouth. 'Off you go, love. And thanks for all your hard work. See you tomorrow at eight-thirty.'

'Eight-thirty?' Kane echoed. 'I thought the hours here were nine to five.'

'Jessie and I had a talk and we decided eight-thirty till four-thirty would suit us better. We're both up early with our children anyway. Might as well get them to day-care and get to work. Then we'll have more time to spend with them in the evening.'

'Whatever.' Kane shrugged his broad shoulders, his nonchalance reminding Jessie that men like Kane didn't have to worry about making time for children. All they had to think about was themselves.

Men did that very well, she reminded herself. So don't go thinking he's driving you home because he's genuinely kind. He's driving you home because he wants to get into your pants.

Jessie was appalled when this thought didn't repulse her, as it normally would. Maybe she shouldn't have stayed celibate this long. Suppressing a sigh, she turned off her computer, picked up her bag and stood up.

'Bye, Michele. Thanks for being so nice. See you in the morning.'

'She *is* a nice woman, isn't she?' Kane said as they

rode the lift down to the basement car park. He sounded surprised.

'Very,' Jessie agreed. 'Good at her job, too,' she added, determined not to let her secret thoughts and desires make her go all stiff and awkward with him again.

'Harry doesn't hire any other kind,' Kane commented.

'I hope he won't be disappointed with me when he gets back.'

'I'm sure he won't be, Jessie. This way,' he directed when the lift doors opened.

She was glad when he didn't get all handy once they were alone in the car park. She wasn't keen on guys who used any opportunity to grab at a girl.

'Here we are,' he said, stopping beside a sleek silver sedan. Inside, she noticed, it had grey leather seats and that lovely new smell. Jessie didn't know what the make was and she didn't ask. She knew next to nothing about cars. Which reminded her...

'By the way, I won't be leasing a car just yet,' she advised him as he drove expertly round the circular ramp that led to the street.

'Why not?'

'I don't like to rush into things. I like to think about them first before taking the plunge.'

'Is that a learned habit, a statement of fact, or a warning for me?'

'Do you need a warning?'

The car emerged into the late-afternoon sunshine, and very heavy traffic. Kane's very masculine mouth remained shut till they stopped at the first set of lights.

'Jessie, let's not play games with each other,' he said firmly. 'You came into that bar the other night looking for male company. If you hadn't been told I was a married man, we'd already be lovers.'

Jessie decided then and there that the time had come for the truth. Her pride demanded she not let him think she made a habit of cruising bars at night, picking up perfect strangers and agreeing to go to hotel rooms with them.

'No one in the ladies' told me you were a married man, Kane,' she confessed, her chin lifting as she turned her head his way. 'I made that up.'

'You *what*? But why? I mean… Oh, go to hell!' he muttered into the rear-vision mirror. The lights had gone green and the driver behind was honking his horn.

'Look, just drive and listen!' she told him in that tone she used on Emily when she wouldn't go to bed at night.

Once he got over his shock at her giving him orders like that, he actually obeyed. The silence gave her the opportunity to tell him the truth, starting with her working as a decoy earlier this year when she hadn't had any money. She explained how she hated it and had quit, but agreed to do it one last time so that she could buy Emily the expensive fairy doll for Christmas.

He *did* throw her a startled look when she said she'd only gone into that bar last Friday night to do a decoy job. When she revealed who her target was, his car almost careered into the wrong lane. She had to tell him to keep his eyes on the road again, after which she was able to finish her story. She even mentioned that she hadn't labelled his brother a potentially unfaithful husband because Kane had knocked back the blonde.

'Of course, I didn't know at the time,' she added, 'that it was *you* knocking back the blonde and not your brother, Curtis.'

Kane was speechless at first. Then a bit stroppy.

'Well, thank you very much for not ruining my brother's marriage! Why didn't you? Guilt?'

'*Guilt?* Why should I feel guilty?'

'Come on, doll, let's face it. If I had been some poor, unhappily married bloke, and you'd swanned into that bar making eyes at me whilst I was sloshed, I'd have had a hard job resisting you, too.'

'Don't exaggerate,' she said. 'I'm not that sexy.'

'Trust me, sweetheart, you are. You're one hell of an actress, too. I could have sworn you were genuinely turned on last Friday night, that you really wanted me to make love to you.'

This was her out, if she wanted to take it.

Jessie decided on a middle course.

'I *did* find you rather attractive,' she admitted with considerable understatement. 'But I would never have gone to a hotel room with you. Not within minutes of meeting you.'

That was her story and she was going to stick to it.

'I didn't know your name, either,' he muttered. 'But I couldn't have given a damn.'

'Yes, well, you're a man. You're a different species entirely. Women are, on the whole, a little more careful.'

'Not all women,' he ground out.

Possibly, he was remembering the blonde.

'I do realise that. I also realise that single mothers have a certain reputation for being...shall we say...easy marks? I wouldn't like you to make that mistake if you're thinking of asking me out. Which I presume you are. Because why else would you be here, driving me home?'

Another set of lights brought the car to a halt. His head turned till his eyes met hers once more. He smiled wryly.

'You seem to have me taped perfectly. What can I say? Yes, I want to ask you out. And yes, up till now, my intentions have not been entirely honourable.'

'And now?'

'I still want to take you to bed. But I also want to spend time with you out of bed. You're a very intriguing woman, Jessie Denton.'

Jessie felt herself blushing. She turned her head away to stare out at the halted traffic, which was thicker than when they'd left north Sydney. She glanced at her watch. It was almost half-past five and they were only at Chatswood. Still, once they got through this bottleneck it should be plainer sailing to Roseville. They should arrive before six. But it would be much quicker on the train.

'So will you go out with me?' he persisted.

Jessie turned back to face the road ahead. She

could feel him looking at her but refused to look his way again. Those eyes of his made her melt almost as much as his smile.

'Maybe,' she said, pleased with her cool tone.

'When?'

'Don't rush me, Kane.'

Kane. She'd called him Kane. She couldn't remember calling him that before.

'How about this Friday night?' he jumped in immediately. 'You must have had someone mind your daughter last Friday night. You could do the same this Friday night. We could go out to dinner, then on to a club, or whatever you like to do. The movies. A show. Anything.'

Going to bed with him would be nice, she thought, shocking herself again. Truly, she was in a bad way. But her pride was still greater than her need.

'I'm not sure about this Friday,' she said. 'I still don't know all that much about you. I mean, you've at least read my résumé. I don't even know what you usually do for a living, when you're not minding the store for Harry Wilde.'

'You'll find the answer to that question on your desk in the morning. Easier than trying to explain what I do. It would take all night.'

Jessie blinked over at him. He called her intriguing. He was the intriguing one.

'OK, but I still don't know much about you personally. I mean, you said you were divorced. How long were you married and why did your wife divorce you?'

'We were married for three years and *I* was the one who asked for a divorce.'

'Good heavens. Why? Was she unfaithful?' The idea seemed ludicrous to Jessie. If Kane were her husband she would never look at another man.

'Not that I know of.' The lights went green and the car crawled on through the busy intersection. 'My wife and I had a difference of opinion about the matter of having children,' he explained. 'We should have discussed it before we got married, I suppose, but… Did you see that bloke cut me off?'

She did and it was a near miss. Still, they weren't going fast enough to have a serious prang.

'Driving a four-wheel-drive, of course,' Kane ground out angrily. 'Worse than truck drivers, they are. Why any sane person would need a mini-tank to get around the city I have no idea. They should all be banned. Now, where was I? Oh, yes, my divorce. Look, when I realised that I couldn't change my wife's mind about having kids, I decided to call it quits. It was quite an amicable parting. We're still very good friends.'

Jessie couldn't help feeling disappointed that Kane was one of those selfish modern men who didn't want children. Truly, he should never have got married in the first place. That poor woman, wasting three years of her life on a man who would never give her what she wanted.

Which was a good warning for herself.

'I see,' she said, nodding.

'And what about you, Jessie?' he counter-questioned whilst she was still pondering if it was worth the risk of falling in love with Kane Marshall, just to have the pleasure of going to bed with him. 'Why aren't you still with the father of your child?'

She could have told him the long version. But she decided he probably wouldn't be interested.

'He died,' she said. 'In a snowboarding accident. Before Emily was born.'

'God, how awful!' He seemed genuinely shocked and sympathetic. 'That's tragic, Jessie. Truly, I'm very sorry. I hope his family has been supportive.'

'I never told them about the baby. Lyall was estranged from his folks, and frankly, I didn't like the sound of them. Anyway, they live over in New Zealand. I could hardly afford to fly over all the time. I thought it best to raise Emily by myself.'

'But what about your own folks?'

Jessie winced. 'Not a pretty picture there either, I'm afraid. Mum was a single mother herself. My father was a married man. She was Irish and Catholic, so getting rid of me was out of the question. Anyway, she emigrated to Australia when I was a baby, by which time she was all bitter and twisted about men. A few years ago she went back home. She wasn't at all pleased about my becoming a single mother. Said I was a fool. But I'm a very different single mother from my mum, I can tell you.'

'I don't doubt it. You're one very strong character, Jessie Denton. Very brave.'

'Brave?' Jessie gave that notion some thought. 'Not really. I was scared stiff at the time. Not to mention seriously depressed. I didn't have post-natal depression. I had pre-natal depression. But I couldn't have done anything else. Emily was my baby. And really, other than having a few money worries, it's been an incredible experience. I wouldn't change a day of it. And now that I've got a decent job, I won't even have any money worries,' she added, not wanting him to think she needed money from any man. Or that she might look at him as a possible meal ticket.

'I read on your résumé that you've been working as a waitress,' he said. 'Did you like doing that?'

Jessie shrugged. 'Not overly. But it was the only job I could get other than decoy work. And I couldn't bear doing that on a regular basis. I only did it this one last time for the money. Do you have any idea how much a Felicity Fairy doll costs?'

'Actually, yes, I do. I've been instructed to buy one for my niece for Christmas. She's about the same age as your Emily. Maybe we could go Christmas shopping together.'

She slanted him a wry smile. 'You planning on seducing me amongst the soft-toy section of Sydney's biggest department store? Save yourself the price of a dinner?'

He laughed. 'I can't see any man seducing you on the cheap, Jessie.'

'One did. *Once,*' she added tartly. 'And I ended up with Emily.'

'So I'm being punished for some other man's misdeeds, am I?'

'Let's just say I look before I leap these days. But you're out of luck. Dora bought Emily's doll for me last Saturday. So you'll have to go Felicity Fairy shopping by yourself. A word of advice, however. Do it soon or there won't be any left to buy.'

'I'll do that. We're getting close to Roseville. I might need some directions soon.'

Jessie glanced at her watch again. 'We'll only just make it in time.'

'What happens if you're late?'

'There are penalty rates for every quarter of an hour you keep them waiting after six o'clock.'

'That's rough. What if there was an accident and the traffic was backed up for miles?'

'Indeed,' she said drily. 'That's why I'll be catching the train in future. But it gives you a little inkling of the stresses and strains of being a working mother. Not much time left over for extra-curricular activities, either. Take the next corner on the left. The day-care centre is four blocks down, on the left. It's cement-rendered, painted pale blue. You can't miss it.'

'Would you go to work if you didn't have to?' he asked as he swung round the corner.

'I don't *have* to work. I could stay at home on welfare. But I don't think that's much of an example to Emily as she grows up. I think if you can work, you should. On top of that, it's nice to have some extra money. Welfare sucks, I can tell you.'

'What if you were married, and your husband earned a good income? Would you work then?'

Jessie laughed. 'I don't indulge in futile fantasies, Kane.'

'I was thinking of my brother's wife, Lisa. She's been a stay-at-home mum for over four years. I thought she was happy but she's not. I advised her this weekend to get a baby-sitter in a bit more often and join a gym. But I have a feeling that's just a temporary solution. I think she needs more.'

'She should find a good day-care centre and go back to work, even if it's only part-time. Or do some voluntary work, if she doesn't need the money. She needs adult company occasionally. And challenges outside of motherhood and wifery.'

'Yes,' Kane said. 'That's good advice. Thanks, Jessie. You might just have saved my brother's marriage for a second time. Aah, there's the place. And it's still only two minutes to six. We've made it!'

'Only just,' Jessie said, scrambling out of the car as soon as Kane slid into the kerb. 'Thanks a lot, Kane. Please don't wait. You've been very kind but you can go home now. It's only a ten-minute walk for me and Emily from here. We'll be fine. Bye. See you tomorrow.'

She didn't wait for him to argue with her, just slammed the passenger door and dashed inside.

Kane stared after her, then broke into a wry grin.

'You don't get rid of me as easy as that, honey,' he muttered.

Switching off the car engine, he climbed out from behind the wheel and walked around to the pavement, where he leant against the passenger door, folded his arms and waited patiently for Jessie to return.

CHAPTER EIGHT

SHE emerged after only two minutes, leading a little clone of herself by the hand. Black curly hair. Pale skin. Square jaw.

Jessie's expression, when she saw him waiting for her by his car, was a mixture of surprise and irritation. Her daughter's big brown eyes carried curiosity and delight.

Introductions were made rather reluctantly, with Jessie calling him Mr Marshall.

Emily gave him an odd look. Some of the delight had gone out of her eyes. 'Are you my mummy's new boss?' she asked. 'The one who made her late?'

'I am,' Kane confessed. 'But I'm going to make it up to you both by driving you home, then ordering a couple of pizzas to eat for dinner so that Mummy doesn't have to cook tonight.'

He'd opened both passenger doors invitingly whilst delivering this plan for the evening to a frowning Emily. When he glanced up at Jessie to find out her reaction, a rather strange smile was playing on her generous mouth.

'Is there a problem with that idea?' he asked, looking from mother to daughter.

'Mummy won't let me go in any car that hasn't got a proper car seat,' Emily announced primly whilst Mummy just kept on smiling. 'And Mummy won't let me eat pizzas. She says they're rubbish.'

'Aah. Headed off at the pass,' Kane muttered. 'Calls for right-flank action. OK, how about I walk home with you and Mummy? That way I'll know where you live for future reference. Then I can come back and get the car whilst you find out from your mummy what I *can* buy you both for dinner.'

'We always eat with Dora on a Monday,' the little powerhouse of information countered. 'Today is a Monday. Isn't that right, Mummy?'

'Yes, sweetie,' her mother said. With great satisfaction in her voice, Kane noted ruefully.

'Checkmate, I think,' Jessie added with a wicked gleam in her eyes.

Kane's teeth clenched hard in his jaw. He'd see those eyes glitter for a different reason one day. Or he wasn't the guy voted most likely to succeed!

'Is that the correct metaphor?' he asked, his soft voice belying his hard resolve. 'Besides, chess is just a game. This is war. I will reconsider my tactics on the way to your house.'

Slamming the car doors, he zapped the lock, slipped the keys in his trouser pocket, then faced the enemy with one of his how-to-win-friends-and-influence-people smiles.

'May I carry your bag for you, little lady?' he offered, reaching for the small backpack which Emily had been dragging along the pavement.

'I can carry my own bag, thank you very much,' she informed him pertly. Although she needed her mother's help to put it on.

Kane slanted Jessie a droll look. 'A new feminist in training?'

'No. An independent spirit. Everyone needs to be one of those these days to survive.'

'You could be right. OK, how about *you* carry the bag, Emily, but I'll carry *you*?'

Without waiting for her next objection, Kane hoicked Emily up to sit on his shoulders, one leg on each side of his head. She really was very light, even with a bag on her back.

'You wrap your arms around my neck and I'll hold your feet,' he told her. But when he grabbed her sandal-clad feet, a shower of sand sprayed down the front of his designer suit.

'What the...?'

'Emily spends a good deal of each afternoon in the sandpit,' Jessie explained without any apologies.

'Right,' Kane said through gritted teeth.

'It'll brush off easily enough,' Jessie told him blithely. 'Here... Look...'

He stiffened when she started brushing him down.

'I think the sand's all gone now,' he said curtly after a minute's torture.

She kept on doing it. 'I don't want you blaming me for ruining your lovely suit. Italian, is it?'

'Yes.' He named its designer.

She rolled her eyes at him. 'I should have guessed.'

At last, she took her hands off him.

'OK, you've been returned to your usual sartorial splendour. Let's walk.'

Kane was very relieved to walk. Still, his reaction

to her merely brushing his hands down over his chest gave him an inkling of how incredible it would be to have her touch him without clothes on.

'It's fun!' Emily's excited voice brought Kane back to the moment in hand. He'd loved riding on his father's shoulders as a child.

'It's a bit like horse-riding,' he said. 'Have you ever been horse-riding, Emily?'

'Yeah, I take her every weekend,' Jessie muttered under her breath beside him. 'When I can fit it in between the ballet and the violin lessons.'

Fortunately, Emily didn't hear her mother's sarcasm.

'No, I haven't,' she said politely. 'Mummy, can I go horse-riding?' she asked in all innocence.

'There aren't any horses in the city, sweetie,' Jessie replied. 'We'd have to drive out into the country and we'd need a car for that. We don't have a car.'

'I'll take you,' Kane said, and was rewarded with the most savage glare from Jessie.

'You don't have to do that,' she bit out.

'But I want to,' he said. 'I'd enjoy it.'

And it was true. He would enjoy it.

'When?' Emily chimed in. 'When?'

'Soon,' Kane promised.

'Not till after Christmas,' Jessie intervened abruptly. 'We're all too busy before Christmas. On top of that, Mr Marshall would have to get a proper child seat before we could go anywhere in his car. Such things take time.'

Her slightly smug smile suggested to Kane that she

thought that getting a car seat would be just too much trouble.

'Kane,' he said firmly. 'You are to call me Kane. *Not* Mr Marshall.'

'Very well. This way…*Kane.*'

She led him round a corner that brought them into a tree-lined street that was much quieter than the road the day-care centre was on. Emily had fun picking leaves off the trees, her happy chatter distracting the two adults from their verbal foreplay.

Because that was what it was. Kane knew it, even if Jessie didn't. She wanted him as much as he wanted her. She was just too cynical about men to give in to her desire and just go with the flow. She thought if she delayed the inevitable, Christmas would come, he'd leave Wild Ideas and that would be that. Out of the office and out of her life.

Kane refused to be deterred. The more difficult she was, the more he was determined to have her, not just in his bed, but in his life. His feelings might not be true love as yet, but they were more than lust. Oh, yes, much more.

Five minutes later, she stopped to open the front gate of a delightful old Federation house. It had a lovely rose garden on either side of a paved front path that led up to an enclosed front porch and a front door with stained-glass panels on either side.

Dear Dora, it seemed, was not exactly poor. Homes like this in Roseville were not cheap. Kane wondered if she rented out her granny flat to Jessie and Emily more for the company than the money.

'I'll have to put you down now, Emily,' he said

as he approached the front steps. 'Otherwise you'll hit your head on the porch roof.'

Jessie's heart turned over as she watched Kane lift Emily off his shoulders and set her gently down. The look of adoration that her child gave him made her want to hit the bastard.

Because that was what he was being. A right bastard. Using Emily to get to her.

Well, it wasn't going to work. She wasn't going to bed with him now, no matter how much she'd wanted to when she'd been brushing him down a few minutes back. The man was built, all right. Clearly, he worked out a lot.

Dora must have heard them arrive because she whisked open the front door before anyone rang the bell.

Jessie had to laugh at the look on her face when she saw Kane.

'This is Mr Marshall,' Emily piped up. 'Mummy's new boss. But he likes to be called Kane. He wanted to drive us home but he didn't have a car seat for me, so Mummy said no. But his car is lovely,' she rattled on. 'It's very shiny and silver. He's going to take me in it to go horse-riding after Christmas. He's going to have a car seat by then. He wanted to buy us pizza tonight but Mummy said no. Can he come to dinner, Dora? You always cook too much food. Mummy said so last Monday night.'

Jessie was besieged by a mixture of pride that her four-year-old daughter could talk so well, and embarrassment at the ingenuous content of her chatter.

Dora just laughed. She was used to Emily. Kane looked genuinely enchanted, which confused Jessie to no end. Was he that good an actor, or did he really like Emily?

She would have thought a man who didn't want his own children would be more impatient and less kind.

He must really want to go to bed with me an awful lot, Jessie decided, not sure if she felt flattered or infuriated.

'I'll have to pop a few extra potatoes in,' Dora said. 'It's roast lamb tonight. Do you like roast lamb, Mr Marshall?'

'Love it. And it's Kane, remember?'

'Kane,' Dora repeated. 'But I thought...' And she threw Jessie a frowning glance.

'Would you believe Kane has a twin brother named Curtis?' Jessie replied. 'An *identical* twin brother? He's married, whereas Kane is divorced.'

'Really?' Dora said, enlightenment in her eyes. 'Fancy that!'

'Yes,' Jessie agreed drily. 'Fancy that.'

'I haven't got any brothers or sisters,' Emily said with a sigh. 'That's because my daddy died.'

'Yes, your mummy told me about that, Emily,' Kane said, squatting down to her height. 'That was very sad. But you're sure to get a new daddy one day. Your mummy's a very pretty lady. Would you like a new daddy?'

Before Emily had a chance to reply, Jessie hurried over and swept her up into her arms. 'Enough idle chit-chat. We have to get Emily bathed and changed before dinner. Why don't you stay and talk with Dora, Kane, while I do that? Dora, ply our guest here with some of your cream sherry. That should keep him out of mischief.'

'I don't ever drink and drive,' Kane replied, an amused lift to the corner of his mouth. 'But I'm sure Dora and I can find plenty of subjects to talk about whilst I watch her cook.' And he gave Jessie a look which implied that by the time she returned for Dora's roast-lamb dinner, he'd know everything there was to know about her.

She and Dora had had many deep and meaningful discussions over the last year or so, and women, unlike men, usually told the truth about themselves. A clever questioner could find out anything he wanted to know.

Jessie suspected she'd just made a tactical error.

But it was too late now.

She comforted herself with the knowledge that no matter what Kane discovered, she still had her own mind, and her own will-power. He couldn't force her to do anything she didn't want to do.

The trouble was that deep down, in that hidden woman's place which she'd been ignoring for over four years, the craving to be made love to was growing.

Sexual temptation was a wicked thing. Dark and powerful and primitive. It was not swayed by reason, or pride. It was fed by need, and fanned by desire. She wanted Kane's body inside her much more than Dora's roast dinner.

She wanted him in ways that she'd never wanted Lyall.

So what are you going to do about it, Jessie? she asked herself bluntly as she went through the motions of giving her daughter a bath.

'Mummy,' Emily said as Jessie massaged the no-tears shampoo through her thick curls.

'Mmm?' Jessie murmured a bit blankly. Her mind was elsewhere, after all.

'I like Kane. He's nice.'

'Yes, yes, he is.'

'Do you like him, Mummy?'

'I…well…I…'

'He likes you.'

Jessie sighed. No point in trying to pull the wool over Emily's eyes. Or in lying. Not if she eventually gave in and went out with Kane on Friday night.

'Yes,' she said simply. 'I think perhaps he does.'

Jessie waited for the next question. But none came. Emily just sat there in silence.

Jessie bent down to see the expression on her daughter's face. But it carried that brilliantly blank look which her daughter could adopt when she wanted to hide her feelings from her mother.

'Emily Denton, what are you thinking?' Jessie demanded to know.

'Nothing.'

'Don't lie to me. Tell.'

'I was thinking about Christmas, Mummy. Does Santa *always* give you what you ask for?'

Jessie was glad of this change of subject. 'He does, if you're a good girl.'

'*I'm* a good girl.'

Jessie smiled and gave her daughter a kiss and a cuddle. 'You surely are. You have nothing to worry about, sweetie. Come Christmas Day, you're going to get absolutely *everything* you asked for.'

CHAPTER NINE

JESSIE should have predicted that Kane would charm both Dora and Emily to the degree he did. The man was a charmer through and through. By the time she and Emily returned to the main part of the house for dinner, he had Dora eating out of his hand.

As for Emily…Santa Claus himself couldn't have caused more excitement in the child. She insisted on sitting next to Kane, who treated her as no one had ever treated her before. As if she was a special little princess whose every word was precious and every wish immediately catered to.

Any worry Jessie harboured over her daughter growing too attached to a man who would only be a temporary part of her life was momentarily pushed aside when she saw how happy Emily was. When it was time for her to go to bed—way past her usual time—Emily begged Kane to read her a bedtime story. Which he duly did, and very well too.

Naturally, when the first story was finished, Emily begged for more. A family trait, Jessie decided bitterly, always wanting more.

Kane read her another story, then another, till Emily's yawns finally stopped and she fell asleep.

'She's dropped off,' Jessie said from where she'd been standing in the bedroom doorway with her arms crossed, watching Kane's performance with swiftly returning cynicism. 'You can stop reading now.'

He looked up from the book. 'But I need to find out if Willie Wombat finds his long-lost father,' he protested with a mischievous gleam in his eyes and the most charming smile.

Jessie steeled her heart and rolled her eyes. 'Fine. You take Willie Wombat out into the living room and finish the story whilst I tuck Emily in. I'll be with you shortly to see you out.'

'What, no nightcap?'

'No. It's late and I have to go to work tomorrow. You do too.'

'I'm the boss. I can come in late.'

'Well, I can't. I'm on probation for three months.'

'Who says?'

'Michele. Apparently, that's Harry Wilde's hiring rule. If a new employee can't cut the mustard in three months, he or she gets their walking papers.'

'Harry never told me that. There again, I don't think he expected me to have to do any hiring during the month he was away. Does the idea of probation worry you, Jessie?'

'No. I can cut the mustard. No problem.'

'I'll just bet you can.'

He stood up from where he'd been sitting on the side of Emily's bed, glancing over at the other bed as he made his way towards the door.

Jessie was eminently grateful that she shared a room with her daughter. Also that her own bed, like Emily's, was nicely single. It eliminated temptation.

Jessie stepped aside to let him through the doorway.

'Don't make yourself too comfortable,' she warned drily. 'I won't be long.'

He didn't answer, just gave her a searching look as he moved past.

Jessie wished she'd shut her mouth. Saying too much was almost as bad as saying too little.

She hadn't done much talking during the roast-lamb dinner. Dora and Emily had done enough. And Kane, of course. Brother, could that man talk.

The trouble was he was so darned interesting. And entertaining. Yet, in retrospect, he hadn't actually talked about himself, an unusual trait for a man. His concentration had mostly been on Emily and Dora.

Dora must have told him her whole life story during the course of the meal, from her childhood to her childless marriage to her husband's death, then her recent years of looking after her increasingly fragile widowed mother. She had even revealed how much she resented her younger brother's not having helped with their mother, something she hadn't even told Jessie.

Kane had made all the right noises at the appropriate places. He had a knack with sympathetic murmurs, that was for sure.

Emily had tried to outdo Dora, giving Kane a minute-by-minute description of everything she did every day, pausing for words of praise at intervals, which she duly got.

Jessie smiled wryly down at her daughter as she tucked the sheet around her. Cheeky little devil. A right little flirt too, fluttering her long eyelashes up at Kane all the time.

Jessie had steadfastly not fluttered or flattered or flirted with the man in any way all evening. But despite her keeping a safe distance, he'd still got to her. A quiet look here. A smile there.

Oh, yes, he'd got to her. Made her want things she hated herself for wanting. Not just sex. But more. Too much more.

He was the devil in disguise, tempting her, tormenting her. She knew she should resist him, but feared she was fighting a losing battle. All she could salvage was a bit of pride by not making her surrender too easy. Jessie suspected that Kane Marshall had always found winning much too easy. It would do him good to work for her conquest, such as it would be. Nothing special to him. Just another bit of skirt. Another notch on his gun.

Jessie wondered how many women there'd been since he'd split with his wife. She resolved to never let him know he was the first man she'd even looked at since Lyall, let alone wanted this badly.

'All finished,' she said brusquely as she marched from the bedroom into the living room. 'Let's go.'

He was sitting on the sofa, the one that ran along the wall opposite the television. It was a very roomy sofa. His suit jacket, she noted, had been removed and was draped over one of the kitchen chairs. His tie was there as well, and the top button of his business shirt was undone.

Clearly, he had seduction on his mind, not leaving.

A tremor raced through Jessie.

'You have a very intelligent little girl,' he said as he snapped shut the book he'd been flicking through, placed it on the side-table next to the sofa and stood up. 'Very sweet, too,' he added.

'Unlike her mother,' Jessie snapped, once again folding her arms across her chest.

'Oh, I suspect the mother could be even sweeter than the daughter,' he said as he walked slowly towards her, bypassing the chair with the jacket and tie. 'In the right circumstances.'

'Don't you dare touch me,' she warned when he was less than an arm-length away.

She was standing in the middle of the kitchenette, with her back not far from the kitchen sink.

He stopped and frowned at her. 'You do realise you are being ridiculous,' he said softly.

Was she?

Possibly. But she wasn't about to back down.

'I will not have sex with you with my daughter sleeping in the next room.'

His eyebrows lifted. 'Sex was not what I had in mind for now, Jessie. Just a kiss. Or two.'

'Huh! Men like you don't stop at a kiss or two.'

He frowned. 'Men like me,' he murmured. 'Now, I wonder what you mean by that? Presumably nothing very complimentary. I suspect you've already lumped me in with the type of divorced guy who wants to sow his wild oats, with no strings attached. Or perhaps the sleazebags you told me about who target single mothers because they think they're desperates. Am I right?'

'Something like that.'

'You're wrong. I'm nothing like that at all.'

'I only have your word for that.'

'I haven't been with a woman since my divorce,' he shocked her by saying. 'Natalie was the last woman I slept with.'

Jessie blinked. It was over a year since he'd left his wife! It didn't seem possible. A man like him, so handsome and virile-looking. Women would have been throwing themselves at him all the time.

'But why? Are you seriously undersexed or something?'

He laughed. 'You wish.'

'But…but…'

'Look, I guess after the failure of my marriage I became a bit wary, and very selective. Casual sex held little appeal. I wanted a real relationship with an intelligent woman who wanted the same things I wanted.'

A career woman, she interpreted that to mean. One who'd give him company and sex, but not expect him to fulfill the traditional roles as husband and father of her children.

Jessie couldn't see a single mother with a demanding four-year-old filling those requirements. Not on a permanent basis.

'Then last Friday night,' he went on, 'I was hit by a thunderbolt. You. Suddenly, I didn't care what you were or who you were. I just had to have you. Be with you. Make mad, passionate love to you.'

She looked away from his eyes, lest he see the same crazy compulsion in hers. He reached out to turn her face back to the front again, his fingers both gentle and possessive. Her arms—suddenly heavy—slipped out of their crossed mode to hang loosely by her sides.

'You want that too, Jessie,' he whispered. 'Don't deny it. I've seen the desire in your eyes. And the fear. You think I'll hurt you. You and Emily. But I won't. I promise. I'd cut out my heart before I did anything to hurt either of you. I can see how special you are together. More special than any mother and daughter I have ever known. I want only good things for you both. Trust me. I'm one of the good guys. Now kiss me, Jessie Denton.'

She didn't kiss him. Because he kissed her first, cupping her face and taking her mouth with his, not waiting long before prying her lips open and sending his tongue to meet hers. The contact was electric, firing a heat that raced through her veins and skin, spreading like a bushfire raging out of control. Her arms rose of their own accord to slide around his body, her palms cementing themselves to his back as she pulled him closer. Then closer still.

He moaned deep in his throat, the sound an echo of what was going through her own head. The yearning for even closer contact was acute, but they couldn't be any closer if they tried. They were already glued together, mouth to mouth, chest to chest, stomach to stomach, thigh to thigh.

The anticipation of how he would feel, filling her to the utmost, took Jessie's breath away. If only she wasn't wearing jeans. A skirt could have been lifted, panties thrust aside. They could have done it right there and then, standing up. She'd never done it like that, standing up. She'd never even thought about it before.

She thought about it now and literally went weak at the knees. Did he feel her falling? Was that why he pushed her back up against the sink, to stop her from falling to the floor?

Jessie instinctively shifted her legs apart, giving him better access. His hips moved against her, the friction exquisite. Soon, she was moaning with abject need and total surrender.

'Mummy!'

Emily's high wail cut through Jessie's near-orgasmic state, bringing her back to earth with a crash.

'Oh, God,' she moaned, wrenching her mouth away from his. 'Emily.'

The mother in her, she swiftly realised, was still stronger than the woman, even the wanton woman Kane had so swiftly reduced her to. In another second or two, she would have been practically screaming. Disgusted with herself, she squeezed out from behind Kane's heaving chest, leaving him to sag against the sink whilst she dashed into the bedroom.

'What is it, Emily?' she asked in a voice that mocked what was still going on inside her. So calm-sounding.

'I had a bad dream,' Emily whimpered. 'There was a bear. A big one. I was scared.'

Bears often figured in Emily's nightmares. Jessie sometimes wished there weren't so many children's stories with bears in them.

'There are no bears living in Australia,' Jessie explained gently for the umpteenth time. 'Except in the zoo. You don't have to be scared about bears.'

'Is Kane still here?' Emily asked fretfully.

'Yes. Why?'

'He won't let the bear get me. He'll chase it away.'

Jessie rolled her eyes. 'Fine. You don't have to worry about any bears then, do you? So go back to sleep now,' she crooned, gently stroking her daughter's head. 'OK?'

Emily yawned. 'OK.' She closed her eyes and was back fast asleep in no time.

Jessie envied her child that ability. Sometimes, Emily would fall asleep as soon as her head hit the pillow. Jessie had never been a good sleeper, finding it difficult to shut her mind down at night. She knew she would do more than her fair share of tossing and turning tonight.

But it was clear that to continue fighting her feelings for Kane was futile. And rather ridiculous. He was right when he'd said that. They were adults. They wanted each other. OK, so she probably wanted more from Kane than he wanted from her but that was always going to be the case. She was a woman and he was a man.

Jessie had always been a reasonably decisive person, unlike her mother, who'd muddled through most of the events that had shaped her and Jessie's lives. When she was growing up, taking charge of her own life had been one of Jessie's main goals. Mostly, she'd been successful. In hindsight, Lyall had been a big error in judgement, but the consequences of her mistake had led to great joy.

Getting involved with Kane was possibly unwise. But at the same time she was only human, not a saint.

Having tucked Emily in once more, she returned to the living room, determined not to muddle through.

She was surprised to find Kane putting on his jacket.

He turned with a troubled expression on his face. 'I'm sorry, Jessie,' he said, stuffing his tie into one of the pockets. 'I didn't mean for things to go that far. I really didn't. But you do have an unfortunate effect on me.'

Jessie frowned. 'Unfortunate?'

Kane smiled a wry smile. 'I'm not used to losing control. I pride myself on being a planner. I rarely go off at half-cock.'

She couldn't help laughing, although she smothered it so as not to risk waking Emily.

'Yes, well, if I had actually *gone* off at half-cock,' he muttered, 'I might be able to laugh too.'

'Oh,' she said, taken aback by this revelation. 'I thought…'

'No,' he growled. 'I didn't.'

'It must have been a darned close call.'

'Agonisingly so.'

'Could you wait till Friday night, do you think?'

His eyes flared wide. 'Do you mean what I think you mean?'

'I would imagine so.'

His face actually lit up. 'Wow. That's a turn-up for the books.'

'I decided you were right. I was being ridiculous.

But I want you to understand that this can't really go anywhere. I'm not the woman you're looking for, Kane. I have Emily for starters. And a full-time job now. At best, I could be your friend and part-time lover.' There! She'd taken charge and it felt good.

He didn't say a single word for a few seconds, just let his eyes search her face. She could not tell what he hoped to find.

'I can handle that,' he said at last.

Jessie wished she knew what he was thinking. And planning. He'd just told her he was a planner. Something in his voice and his face suggested his agenda wasn't quite the same as hers.

But what?

She hoped he wasn't underestimating her. Or thinking she was a push-over after all.

Time for some more taking charge.

'By the way, on Friday,' she said firmly, 'I won't be staying anywhere with you all night, so don't go thinking I will. You have from seven till midnight. I can't expect Dora to mind Emily later than that. She's an old lady.'

'I could pay for a baby-sitter,' he suggested.

'Someone I don't know? No way, José. It's Dora, or nobody.'

'Fine. I won't argue. But I think you're in danger of becoming an over-protective mother.'

'Think what you like. It won't change my attitude towards my daughter.'

'I never thought it would. But that's OK. I admire a woman who knows her own mind.'

'And I admire a man who respects a woman's wishes.'

'I'll remember that.'

Yes, but for how long? Jessie wondered.

Till Friday night, naturally. That was the aim of this game after all. Get the girl into bed. But after that, Kane might not be quite so accommodating.

Still, she would cross that bridge when she came to it.

Till then, she was going to have a hard job thinking about anything but Friday night.

CHAPTER TEN

A COPY of a book called *Winning at Work* was sitting on Jessie's desk when she got in the next morning.

'Is this from you?' she asked Michele, who was already there at her desk, beavering away.

'Nope. It was there when I got in. I imagine Kane dropped it off for you to have a look at.'

Jessie recalled he'd said something about a book.

She picked it up and turned it over, blinking at the sight of Kane's photo on the back.

'Good lord!' she exclaimed. 'He's the author!'

Michele glanced up with a surprised look on her attractive face. 'You mean you didn't know the man who drove you home yesterday was *the* Kane Marshall, management guru and motivator extraordinaire?'

'No! I've never heard of *the* Kane Marshall.' Other than his being the twin brother of Curtis Marshall, possible philanderer.

'Something tells me that's about to change,' Michele muttered under her breath.

'He actually *wrote* this?' Jessie said, still stunned.

'Sure did. I gather it's been a runaway best-seller in the USA. It hasn't come out here yet. We Aussies aren't into self-help books as much as the Americans. But we're getting there.'

'Have you read it?'

'Nope.'

Jessie stared at the bio inside the front cover. Kane had a list of professional credits a mile long. Degrees in business and marketing. *And* a degree in psychology. This was his first book, but he was apparently well-known in the business world for his weekend seminars called 'Solving Work Problems'. He was described as a gifted after-dinner speaker, with his services being highly sought after by companies as a consultant and an educator.

Jessie sighed. Any secret hope she'd been harbouring that Kane Marshall might change his mind about what kind of woman he was looking to have that real relationship with just went out the window. He was a workaholic!

'You sound tired,' Michele said. 'Late night?'

'No. Just not enough sleep.'

'Aah. Man trouble.'

'What?'

'When a mother can't sleep it has to be man trouble. And it doesn't take much to guess which man. Although I'm not sure what the problem is. Do you already have a boyfriend? Is that it?'

'Goodness, no, I haven't had a boyfriend since Emily's father.' She and Michele had chatted a bit about their backgrounds over coffee yesterday, so Michele knew about Lyall.

'Aah…' Michele nodded. 'The once-bitten, twice-shy syndrome.'

'Can you blame me? After Lyall died, I found out he wasn't just two-timing me. He was triple-timing me.'

'Not nice,' Michele agreed. 'But that was Lyall, not Kane.'

'Maybe, but in some ways they're alike. Both tall, dark and handsome, with great smiles and the gift of the gab. Those sort of guys are hard to trust.'

'So you didn't say yes when he asked you out?' Michele ventured.

Jessie sighed. 'Yes. I did. We're on for Friday night,' she confessed.

'Playing hard to get, I see. Smart girl.'

'You call that playing hard to get?' Jessie put Kane's book down on her part of the work station and pulled out her chair.

'Sure. That's five whole days since you met him.'

Jessie sank down into her chair. 'Actually, it will be a week since I met him.'

Michele's eyes widened. 'Really? You'd met him before the interview on Monday?'

'Yes. In a bar in town last Friday night. But we didn't exchange names. I—er—drank with him and danced with him, but I did a flit when he wanted more than dancing. He was as shocked as I was when I showed up here yesterday.'

'Shocked, but still pleased. He's obviously very taken with you, Jessie.'

'You think so? It's hard to tell with men. It could just be sex, you know.'

'Nothing wrong with that. Lots of relationships start with sex. Don't fall into the trap of being too cynical about men, Jessie. There are some genuinely good ones out there. I don't know Kane all that well, but what I know I like. Everyone here thinks he's great. So give him a chance. Oh, and don't forget to go thank him for the book. He'll be dying to know what you think, I'll bet. Lunch-time would be a good time, when Karen's out. She and Margaret have lunch together at a café up the road every day at one. Kane has his lunch delivered, Margaret tells me. He's an obsessive reader and usually stays at his desk. You could pop along any time after one and he'd be all alone.'

'Are you sure that's a good idea?'

'Why not? What do you think he's going to do? Ravish you on his desk?'

Jessie didn't like to admit that that was exactly what she thought he might do. Worse was the reality that she wouldn't mind one bit.

She'd already come into work wearing a skirt, instead of jeans. And no stockings.

The clear blue sky this morning had promised a hot summer's day, so her selection of a pink and white floral wrap-around skirt, a simple pink T-shirt and slip-on white sandals was really quite an appropriate outfit for work. No one could have guessed by just looking at her that whilst she'd dressed she'd secretly thrilled to the thought of how accessible she was, if by some chance Kane found the time and the place to seduce her at work.

Stupid fantasy, really. But darned exciting to think about.

By lunch-time, every nerve-ending in Jessie's body was tap-dancing. She was grateful when Michele left to do some shopping. A trip to the ladies' room assured her that her make-up was still in place. She wouldn't have been surprised if it had melted all over her face. But she looked OK. Her hair was up, secured by a long pink clip. She toyed with taking it down, then decided that would be on the obvious side. The last thing she wanted was to be obvious.

Thankfully she had a good excuse for going to his office. She didn't want to show up looking like a desperate. Even if she was fast becoming one.

Another attack of nerves sent her bolting into a toilet cubicle. Five minutes later, she was back at her desk, where she skip-read a few chapters of the book to get the gist of it whilst she stuffed down one of the two sandwiches she'd brought from home. That done, she made her way to Kane's office. It was one-twenty.

Karen's desk was blessedly empty. Fate hadn't made her stay back for some reason. Jessie's heart sank, however, when she saw the door to the inner office was half open and a woman's voice was emerging.

Don't tell me Karen is in there with him, she thought.

Jessie took a couple of steps towards the door, grinding to a halt when the woman—who didn't sound like Karen—said something about being pregnant.

'Pregnant!' Kane exclaimed in a shocked voice. 'Good God, Natalie.'

Jessie sucked in sharply. Natalie. That was his ex-wife's name.

'Don't worry, darling,' the woman said in a droll

tone. 'It's not yours. I'm only a month gone and it's at least a couple of months since we were together. Besides, if I recall rightly, you used a condom.'

Jessie's heart squeezed tight. A couple of months ago Kane had still been sleeping with his ex. Yet he'd made her think he'd been celibate since they split up over a year ago. She'd thought at the time that was unlikely. What other women had he lied to her about?

'Who's the father?' she heard Kane ask.

'Some guy I met at a party. A lawyer. I didn't even find out his last name, would you believe? But I could find it out if I want to.'

'What are you going to do about the baby?'

'I know you'll think I'm mad, but I'm going to have it.'

'You're joking!'

'No. No, Kane, I'm not.'

Jessie couldn't bear to stand there, listening to any more of this conversation. She turned and fled back down the corridor as quietly as her pounding heart would permit. Tears threatened, but she made it back to the toilet cubicle, dry-eyed. Even then, strangely, she didn't cry. She wanted to, but something inside her was damming back the tears, a big, cold, angry lump.

One part of her wanted to go back and confront him, throw his lies in his face. But another part of her argued that to do that was to finish it between them.

Could she bear that? To walk away without going to bed with him, at least once?

Jessie supposed she could. She could do just about anything once she put her mind to it.

But it would be hard, especially with his being here at work every day. She would keep running into him. And wanting him.

So, no, she wouldn't be confronting him, Jessie decided as she made her way back to her desk. Or accusing him. She would use him as he was using her. For sex.

At least this added knowledge of his character would stop her from falling in love with him. The man was a lying scumbag, like most men. An empty charmer. Just because he'd made a raging success of his professional life didn't make him a good guy, as he claimed to be.

When she thought about his choice of career it suited him very well. What was he, really, but a glorified salesman? A con artist. A seller of dreams. Such seminars as he conducted preyed on people's weaknesses, making them think they could be winners too, if only they listened to him. He'd spin her a whole world of dreams too, if she let him.

But she wasn't going to let him. Or listen to him. He could talk all the bulldust he liked. None of it was going to get to her any more.

'What are you muttering to yourself about?'

His voice behind her came out of the blue, startling her.

Jessie swallowed, then spun slowly round on her office chair, a cool smile at the ready.

'Just thinking of all the things I have to do before

Christmas,' she said, her eyes running over the man himself for the first time that day.

Yes, he *was* gorgeous. Utterly. With that air of masculine confidence which she found almost irresistible.

But she was ready for him now, ready and armed with the knowledge of his true self.

'I did offer to take you shopping,' he said with one of his winning smiles.

'So you did. And I might have to take you up on that by this time next week.'

'What about this Saturday? Emily could come with us. I promise I'll have a proper car seat by then.'

Jessie found her own smile. A slow smile. A saucy smile. 'Do you think you'll be capable of getting out of bed after Friday night?'

His blue eyes registered shock. But then he smiled back. 'Is that a challenge of some sort?'

'Let's just say it's been a while for me. I might take some satisfying.'

A flicker of a frown skittered across his face. 'Boy, when you decide to do something you do it full throttle, don't you?'

'I have a take-no-prisoners attitude to life sometimes.'

'That's what I like about you. You're so damned honest and upfront. Except when you're cruising bars looking for straying hubbies, that is,' he added ruefully.

Jessie shrugged. 'That's all in the past now that I have a decent job. And it's not as though most of those guys didn't deserve to get caught. So tell me, Kane, were you ever unfaithful to your wife?'

'What a question!'

'One you don't want to answer, I see.'

'No, I don't mind answering it. I was never unfaithful. I sowed my wild oats plenty in my younger years. Once I got married, however, I put all that behind me.'

'One of the good guys,' she said just a fraction tartly.

He frowned. 'I take it you're still not convinced.'

'Does it matter?'

'It matters to me.'

Jessie decided this conversation was running off the rails. 'By the way, thank you for your book. I was suitably impressed. And a little surprised. I didn't realise you were famous.'

'I'm not so famous,' he said modestly.

'But you will be. Your book is fabulous.' Jessie knew you could never flatter a man enough. Flattery, she could handle. And flirting. Just no falling in love.

He looked so ridiculously pleased, she felt guilty. 'But you can't possibly have read it yet.'

'Well, not properly. But I will. Before Friday night.'

'Stop talking about Friday night!' he suddenly hit out in an agitated fashion. 'I know it's only three days away, but after last night it seems like an eternity. I don't think I slept a wink.'

He did look tired, now that she came to think of it. There were dark circles under his eyes.

'I didn't sleep very well myself,' she confessed.

'Jessie, this is ridiculous. Why should we torture ourselves? Be with me tonight. Get Dora to mind Emily. She told me last night that she'd be quite happy to mind Emily any night we wanted to go out. I asked her. I even offered to pay her but she refused. She said she'd be happy to do it any time.'

Jessie felt both flustered and furious. 'You had no right to go behind my back like that.'

'No right to do what?' he countered. 'Try to organise things so that I can spend some time with a woman I'm crazy about?'

Jessie flushed at the passion in his voice. 'I told you. I don't like to be rushed.'

His sigh was ragged. 'OK. Yes, I am rushing you. I'm sorry. It's just that life is so short and when you see something that you really want, you have to reach out and grab it before something happens and it gets away from you.'

'Is that what you tell people in your book?'

'Not that I recall. This is something which has come upon me just lately. It's possibly worse today.'

'Why is it worse today?'

'Would you believe my ex-wife has just been in to see me? And guess what? She's pregnant, by some guy she doesn't even know the name of. *And* she's going to keep the baby.' Kane shook his head in utter bewilderment.

'What's wrong with that?' Jessie challenged. For pity's sake, did he expect her to have an abortion? He'd divorced her because she wanted children. The man just didn't understand how strong the maternal impulse could be. She could never have terminated *her* baby, and she hadn't even been craving one at the time.

'You don't know Natalie,' he muttered. 'She's not the single-mother type.'

'Is there a single-mother type?'

'No. I guess not. It was just so unexpected, not to mention quick. Our divorce papers only came through three months ago. You can imagine how I felt when she announced she was pregnant.'

Actually, Jessie didn't have to imagine anything. She'd been there and heard his reaction. He'd been worried sick that it was *his*.

'It's not as though you're still in love with her,' Jessie said impatiently. '*Are* you?'

'No, of course not!'

'Then her having another man's baby is irrelevant. Leave her to her life and you get on with yours.'

He stared at her for a second before his mouth broke into a wry grin. 'Yes, Dr Denton. I'll do just that. Which brings me back to tonight. What do you say, Jessie? Would you let me take you out to dinner? Just dinner.'

That was about as believable as 'the cheque's in the post'!

Jessie scooped in a deep breath whilst every pore in her screamed at her to agree. But to say yes would be the kiss of death. She'd show her weakness and then he'd have her right where he wanted her.

'I'm sorry, Kane,' she said, quite truthfully. 'I make it a policy never to go out during the week. You'll just have to wait. You can always have a lot of cold showers,' she suggested with more than a hint of malice.

Their eyes met, and held.

'I don't think there's enough cold water in the world to fix my problem,' he bit out. 'Still, I guess I'll survive. But I would suggest that if you're going to come into work each day looking good enough to eat, then for pity's sake, keep well out of my way!'

CHAPTER ELEVEN

'MUMMY'S got a boyfriend! Mummy's got a boy-friend! Mummy's got a...'

'Yes, all right, Emily,' Jessie interrupted sharply. 'I've heard you. And do stop jumping up and down on your bed. It's not a trampoline. Look, go and put a video on. I'll never be ready in time if you keep distracting me.'

Emily was off the bed and out of the room in a flash. If there was one thing that would successfully shut Emily up, it was watching one of her favourite videos.

Being left alone, however, didn't help Jessie as much as she had hoped. Her hands kept shaking for starters, and her usually decisive mind could not seem to settle on what she should wear tonight.

Kane had told her in an email yesterday—one of several he'd sent her during the last three days—that she didn't need to be dressed up. Something casual would be fine.

Jessie had been relieved at the time. Her wardrobe was ninety-five per cent casual. But most were on the cheap side.

The evening promised to be warm, so a skirt was probably a good choice. She pulled out a black and white one similar to the pink floral she'd worn to

119

work the other day, the one which Kane had said made her look good enough to eat.

Oh, dear. She shouldn't have thought about that. Her nipples tightened and a little tremor ran down the back of her legs.

A glance at her watch brought instant panic. She only had a quarter of an hour before Kane was due to pick her up at seven. She'd already showered and done her make-up since arriving home, but she was still naked under her robe, her hair was a mess and Dora would be arriving any moment with Emily's dinner.

The darling woman had promised to feed the child, as well as look after her for the night. She seemed just as excited at Jessie having a so-called boyfriend as Emily was. Jessie hadn't liked to disillusion them over Kane's true intentions—they both thought he was the ant's pants—so she let them think what they liked.

Meanwhile, Jessie just kept telling herself that to-night was nothing serious. Just fun and games.

'Fun and games,' she repeated as she opened her underwear drawer and pulled out a black satin bra and matching G-string from underneath her more sensible sets. They had been outrageously expensive when she'd bought them pre-Emily, and had rarely been worn. Motherhood had made her breasts larger, so when she put the bra on, her cups really did run-neth over.

But oh, my, she did look seriously sexy, with a cleavage deeper than the Grand Canyon. The G-string looked OK from the front. But she didn't even risk a peek at a rear view. What she didn't know couldn't depress her.

A knock on the granny-flat door was followed by Dora's voice as she opened the door and came in. 'It's just me, Jessie, with Em's dinner.'

'I'm still not ready, Dora. Can you organise things out there for a few minutes?'

'No worries. We'll be fine, won't we, Emily?'

No reply from Emily.

'Emily,' her mother shouted whilst she manoeuvred on the stretchy black cross-over top she'd bought to go with the skirt. 'Sit up at the table for Dora. I've set a place for her, Dora. And her apple juice is in her special cup in the fridge.'

'Yes, yes, stop fussing. I can manage. You get on with getting ready. Kane will be here soon, you know.'

'I know,' Jessie muttered, hurriedly wrapping the skirt around her hips and tying the sash tightly at the back. One thing motherhood hadn't improved on her figure was her waistline. It was slightly thicker now. Still, her bigger bust and hips balanced that, so the overall look was still hourglass.

Reasonably satisfied with the result—the amount of flesh she had on display in the deep V-neckline gave her a few butterflies—Jessie turned to doing something with her hair, which was a bit of a frizz, due to the humidity in the air. The only thing for it was up, of course. So up it went, brushed back from her face quite brutally and anchored to her crown with a black scrunchie.

Naturally, quite a few strands and curls escaped

but guys had always told her they liked that. They said it looked sexy. And sexy was definitely the look she was aiming for tonight.

Her jewelry she kept to a minimum. A silver chain locket necklace and silver loop earrings. Her perfume was an expensive one, a present from Dora for her birthday back in June. It was called True Love.

True irony, Jessie thought wryly as she slipped her feet into the same strappy black high heels she'd worn the previous Friday. Her only regret about her appearance was that she hadn't invested in some fake tan. No sleeves and no stockings meant that a lot of her pale flesh was on display. But she hadn't been paid yet and could have only afforded the cheap variety. Better to have no tan than to have orange streaks and oddly coloured elbows and ankles.

'Kane's here,' Dora chimed out a few seconds before he knocked on the door. She must have heard his footsteps on the concrete path which led around to the granny flat.

'Coming,' Jessie replied, amazed at how nauseous she was suddenly feeling. What had happened to the carefree girl she'd used to be?

Well, that girl was gone, Jessie realised, replaced by a nervous wreck who was scared stiff that she'd be so hopeless that Kane wouldn't want to see her again after tonight. Which might be for the best. But somehow, at this precise moment, wisdom wasn't Jessie's long suit.

Thinking about the girl she had used to be, however, reminded her that she didn't have any condoms. Still, she was sure Kane would be well prepared. A man who didn't want children would *always* be prepared.

'Kane! Kane!' Emily's excited voice reached Jessie.

Jessie hoped her daughter didn't start chanting to him about his being her mummy's boyfriend.

'Won't be a sec,' she called out from the bedroom as she hurriedly put her make-up, brush and wallet into her black patent evening bag and headed for the bedroom door.

Kane hadn't actually come inside. He'd stayed standing on the back doorstep under the light that shone down from above.

'Oh,' she said on seeing him. 'We're colour co-ordinated.'

He was wearing a black suit—casually tailored— with a white T-shirt underneath. No doubt a very expensive designer white T-shirt. Not that it mattered. On him, anything looked good.

By the look in his eyes what she was wearing was meeting with *his* approval as well. It was good that men rarely knew what a woman's clothes cost. She wouldn't mind betting that his T-shirt had cost more than her whole outfit. Minus the lingerie and the shoes, of course. They *had* been expensive.

'Doesn't Mummy look pretty?' Emily said from where Dora, by some miracle, had kept her sitting at the table, eating her dinner. Admittedly, it was spaghetti bolognaise, Emily's favourite. But Jessie had pictured her daughter hurling herself into Kane's arms the moment he arrived.

'Yes, indeed,' Kane agreed with gleaming eyes.

'Are you going to ask Mummy to marry you?'

It was just the sort of question Jessie had feared.

She groaned her embarrassment whilst Dora laughed.

Kane, the suave devil, took it in his stride. 'Would you like me to?' he said.

'Oh, yes,' Emily replied.

'Your wish is my command, princess. The trouble is I don't think your mummy's quite ready to marry *me* yet.'

'Why not?' Emily demanded to know, scowling up at her mother.

'Kane and I have only known each other a week,' Jessie said with more patience than she was feeling. 'You don't marry someone until you've known them much longer than that.'

'Two weeks?' Emily suggested, and both Dora and Kane laughed.

Jessie rolled her eyes. 'At *least* two weeks. Now, you be good for Dora tonight and go to bed when she tells you to. Thanks a bunch, Dora.'

'My pleasure, love. Just you and Kane have a good time. And don't go thinking you have to rush home. Stay out as long as you like. I'll go to sleep on your sofa.'

'I shouldn't be too late,' Jessie said firmly. More for Kane's ears than Dora's. 'Bye, sweetie.' She gave Emily a kiss. 'Love you. See you in the morning.'

'At least two weeks, eh?' Kane said as they walked together along the side-path. 'In that case, we should be engaged by Christmas.'

'Very funny,' Jessie said.

'Who says I'm joking?'

'Kane, *stop* it.'

'Stop what?'

Jessie ground to a halt beside Dora's prized hydrangeas, which were in full bloom. 'Stop being ridiculous. You and I both know you would never marry me.'

'Why not?'

'For one thing I have Emily.'

'I think Emily's fantastic. Cutest kid I've ever met.'

Jessie shook her head in exasperation. 'This is a stupid conversation and I don't want to continue it.'

'Good, because I'm sick of talking, anyway.' Before she could read his intention, he pulled her into his arms and kissed her, right there and then.

Jessie's first instinct was to struggle. What if Dora came out and around the side of the house and saw them? She even opened her mouth to protest.

Silly move.

His tongue darted inside and she didn't think about anything much after that for a full five minutes. By the time he let her come up for air, her head was swimming and her body was on the countdown to lift-off. She actually moaned in dismay when his mouth lifted. Her fingers tightened on what she thought was his back, but was actually her evening bag, resting against his back.

'Now I know what to do with you,' he said thickly as he stroked an erotic finger over her puffy lips. 'Every time you start to get stroppy tonight, I'm going to kiss you. So be warned and try to behave yourself in the restaurant. Unless, of course, you'd rather we didn't go out to eat. We could drive straight to my place if you prefer. I do have food there in my freezer and a perfectly good microwave. Wine too, and fresh fruit. I'm actually quite domesticated. I only turn into a wild beast around you.'

'I like the wild beast,' she heard herself saying in a low, husky voice. But that finger on her lips felt incredible. Before she could think better of it, her tongue-tip came out to meet it. He stared down at her mouth and then slowly, ever so slowly, inserted his finger inside.

Her stomach somersaulted.

'Suck it,' he commanded. And she did, thinking all the while that she would do anything he told her to do tonight.

The thought blew her away. This was dangerous territory she'd just entered. But more exciting than anything she'd ever experienced before. Lyall was kindergarten playtime compared to this man.

His blue eyes narrowed as he watched her blindly obey him.

His tortured groan shocked her, as did the way he reefed his finger out, as if she were a cobra, not a woman on the verge of becoming his sex slave.

'Enough,' he growled. 'You are one contrary woman, Jessie Denton,' he added. 'You run hot and cold all the time. So what is it to be tonight? You decide. The restaurant, or my place?'

Jessie was way beyond hypocrisy. She was as turned on as she knew he was. Any further delay would brand her a tease and she'd never been that.

'Your place,' she said, dropping her arms back to her sides as she took a step back from him.

He didn't reply, just grabbed her free hand and dragged her out to his car as if the hounds of hell were after them.

'Belt up,' he ordered as he fired the engine. 'And no chit-chat. It's not that far to my place at Balmoral but the traffic's heavy going into the city. I need to concentrate.'

Balmoral, she thought, her earlier dazed state slowly receding. An exclusive inner north-shore suburb with an equally exclusive beach. She'd been there once to a restaurant on its foreshores. Very up-market. Very pricy. After the recent housing boom, even the simplest apartment there would cost the earth.

She couldn't see Kane having a simple apartment. It would be a sleek bachelor pad with a view and jacuzzi. Or a penthouse, with a pool, leather furniture and a king-size animal-print-covered bed.

She was wrong on both counts. First it was a house, not an apartment. Secondly, it wasn't modern or overtly masculine. It was old—probably built in the thirties—with lots of art deco features and loads of antique furniture. The only thing she was right about was the water-view, which was magnificent from its site up on the side of a hill.

'Did you live here with your wife?' were Jessie's first words after he had led her into the cosy front sitting room. Through the windows she could see the sea down below. And the lights of the restaurant she'd once visited.

'No,' he replied. 'We had an apartment in town. I bought this when we separated. My parents live a couple of streets away. And my brother lives in the next suburb.'

Jessie thought it was nice that he'd chosen to live so close to his family.

'This is not what I expected,' she said.

He smiled. 'I know. That's one reason why I wanted to bring you here. Seeing for yourself is worth a thousand words. I keep telling you I'm not what you think, Jessie. Now, put that infernal bag down and come here…'

Jessie sucked in sharply. She should have known he'd get right down to it, once they were alone. It was what she wanted too. Inside.

But her earlier decision to come here and jump straight into bed with him had been easy when she was still in his arms, with his kisses still hot in her memory and his finger in her mouth. Not quite so easy standing here in his living room with the lights on and nothing but the sound of the sea in the background.

He frowned at her when she didn't move. 'Don't tell me you're nervous. Or that you've changed your mind,' he added darkly.

'No. No, I haven't changed my mind. But yes, I am nervous,' she confessed shakily. 'It's been so long and I…'

'How long?' he broke in.

Jessie was shocked when tears pricked at her eyes. Goodness, what was there to be crying about? 'I…I haven't been with a man since Lyall.'

She was thankful that he didn't act all surprised, or suspicious, over this statement of fact.

'I see,' he said simply, then smiled. A soft, almost loving smile. 'That's wonderful.'

She was the one who was shocked. 'Wonderful? What's wonderful about it? I've probably forgotten how to do it!'

He laughed. 'You haven't forgotten, sweetheart. You're a natural. But if you have,' he said as he walked forward and put her bag down for her, 'you have me to show you how all over again. But *my* way. Not Lyall's way, or any other man's way.'

'And what's your way?' she choked out as he took her hand and started leading her from the room.

The look he threw over his shoulder sent shivers rippling down her spine. 'The way which gives you the most pleasure, of course. I have a plan, as usual. But if at first I don't succeed, then I'll try, try again. You might be amazed at how many times I can make love in five hours.'

'It...it's already half past seven,' Jessie blurted out, trying to stop herself from totally losing it. But dear heaven, he meant to make love to her for the whole five hours?

'So I'll be a little late getting you home,' he said as he drew her through a doorway, switching on a light as he went. 'I'm sure Dora will forgive me.'

The room was, naturally, a bedroom. A huge bedroom with polished wooden floorboards, high ceilings, antique furniture and a wide brass bed covered in a silvery grey satin quilt with matching pillows. The lamps each side of the bed had brass bases with white shades and long fringes. The chandelier overhead was crystal and brass. Lace curtains covered the long windows on the wall adjacent to the bed. In the opposite wall was another door, which was open and led into an *en suite* bathroom. The light shone in just far enough for Jessie to see it was more modern than the rest of the house, being all white. Possibly a recent renovation.

It was a beautiful bedroom, only the colour of the bedding betraying that a man slept here, and not a woman.

Although, of course, women could have slept here. With Kane. His ex-wife perhaps. And others Kane had forgotten to mention.

Jessie didn't like that thought.

'What's wrong?' Kane said immediately.

'Nothing,' she lied.

'Come, now, Jessie, don't lie to me. You looked at that bed and something not very nice came into your mind. What was it?'

'I guess I didn't like to think of you having been in there with other women.'

'But I told you. There have been no other women since Natalie.'

'What about Natalie?'

'What about her?'

'You slept with her recently. I know you did. I overheard both of you in the office the other day. I went to thank you for the book at lunch-time that day and you were discussing her pregnancy and she said you weren't to worry, because it wasn't yours.'

Kane stared at her. 'Why didn't you say anything before this?'

'I...I didn't want to.'

'You just kept it to yourself and held it against me. Hell, Jessie, I wish you'd said something.'

'Would it have changed anything? You did sleep with her, didn't you?'

His grimace showed true anguish. 'Look, it was three months ago and only the once. We'd met up in her flat the night our divorce papers came through. She'd offered to cook me dinner as a kind of celebration, to show there were no hard feelings. We had too many glasses of wine over dinner and she said how about it, for old times' sake? If I hadn't been drunk and lonely it would never have happened. I can't tell you how much I regretted it afterwards. So did she, I think. It wasn't even good sex. We were both plastered. I didn't mention it because I didn't want you to think I was one of those guys who get rid of their wives and then keep sleeping with them when they feel like a bit, as a lot do. I'm sorry, Jessie. I wasn't trying to deceive you. I just wanted you to believe me when I said on that first Friday night that I wasn't in the habit of picking up women. You were a one-off, believe me. You still are. I want you, Jessie, more than any woman I've ever known. And I know you want me. Please don't keep finding excuses to push me away.'

Jessie knew he was a good talker. A clever persuader. But there was a sincerity in his voice and his eyes that touched her. Surely, he *had* to be telling the truth.

'You really haven't been with anyone else?' she asked.

'Cross my heart and hope to die.'

'I wouldn't want you to die, Kane,' she murmured, stepping forward and snaking her arms up around his neck. 'I want you very much alive.'

He groaned, his mouth crashing down to take hers in a kiss of mind-blowing hunger. Their tongues met, danced, demanded. Their bodies pressed closer, and closer. Their hips jammed together, then ground against each other.

'No, no, not that again,' he gasped as his mouth burst free from hers. 'I haven't waited the last three days for that.'

Her head was spinning but she concurred whole-heartedly. That was not what she wanted, either. She wanted him naked, and inside her. She wanted it all.

She reached round behind her back to untie the bow.

'No,' he said swiftly. 'Let me...'

Kane started undressing her as no man had ever done in her life. So slowly and sensually, his eyes smouldering with desire, his hands not quite steady. First to be disposed of was her skirt, leaving her standing there before him with nothing below her hips but that skimpy G-string.

'Arms up,' he ordered, then he took her top by its hem and began to peel it upwards over her head.

The action covered her eyes for a second or two, Jessie quivering in her momentary darkness, turned on by the thought of how she must look with her arms up, her face masked, but her body being more and more exposed to his gaze. She'd never thrilled to a sex-slave fantasy before but she did so now, imagining herself having been bought by him, being a helpless prisoner to his passion, with no other purpose than to be an instrument of pleasure.

Not her own.

Suddenly, her own pleasure seemed irrelevant. This was all for him. Her lord and master. Her soon-to-be lover.

Even when her top was thrown away, she kept her eyes shut, enjoying the sensation of being outside herself, looking in on what was happening with her mind. She heard him gasp. In admiration, she hoped.

And then his hands were on her again, still soft, but just as knowing. He took her G-string off first, which surprised her. She wobbled a bit when he picked up first one foot and then the other. She stiffened expectantly when he straightened, sucking in sharply when one of his hands stroked over her belly. Her eyes squeezed even more tightly together when it drifted lower, a startled gasp torn from her throat when both his hands slid between her thighs. But he didn't touch her there, just eased her legs apart.

'Yes, like that,' she heard him say.

And then his hands were gone, only to be felt again on her bra clasp. When it gave way and her breasts were finally naked before his eyes, she felt no embarrassment, only the most all-consuming craving to have them touched.

But he didn't touch them.

'Open your eyes,' he told her forcefully.

Of course she obeyed. How could she not? It was the voice of the master.

Opening her eyes, however, brought a wave of dizziness.

'Watch it,' he said, and grabbed her shoulders to steady her swaying body.

Once she was still, his hands moved up to dispose of the scrunchie, letting her hair tumble in wild disarray around her shoulders.

She had never been so turned on, or so compliant.

'I want you to just stand there like that,' he murmured, 'whilst I get undressed.'

Of course, she thought. What else would I do?

He stripped off his own clothes much faster than he had hers. And he took off everything, displaying the kind of body she'd imagined him to have. Muscly and hard, with not too much body hair, a broad chest and a six-pack stomach.

Jessie tried not to stare when he collected a condom from the bedside chest and drew it on.

But she did lick her very dry bottom lip.

'No, not that either,' he snapped, misinterpreting her action. 'Not yet. Later.'

Whatever you want, she almost said. Whenever you want it.

He walked around her a couple of times, just looking at her, standing there in nothing but her high heels. Only when she was at screaming point did he touch her, coming up close from behind, pushing her hair away from one shoulder and bending his head to kiss her neck, softly at first, then more hungrily.

The wild beast swiftly emerged again, and soon

he was sucking on her throat whilst his hands ran roughly up and down her arms. Her back automatically arched against him, the action lifting her breasts in wanton invitation. This time he obliged, cupping them in his hands and squeezing them together whilst his thumbpads rubbed rather cruelly over the already stiffened nipples.

Sensations shot through her like a series of lightning bolts, sizzling with electricity, leaving her burning with a fire which she knew could only be erased one way.

His mouth covered her ear, hot and heavy with his breathing.

'Don't close your legs,' he commanded on a raw whisper.

And then he took her hands in his and stretched them out in front of her, bending her forward till her fingers reached the nearest brass bedpost.

'Hold on to that,' he advised.

Very good advice. Because she might have fallen otherwise. Or fainted.

No man had ever made love to her like this before, in this position. Jessie's head whirled. But there was little time to think before he was inside her, holding her hips captive whilst he ground into her body.

She had never experienced anything so decadent before. But it felt so delicious this way. Wild and wicked and wonderfully wanton. Her mind swiftly joined her body in quest of nothing but more of the pleasure which was rippling through her entire body. She started rocking back and forth against him, tightening her insides in response to each of his forward thrusts.

'Oh, God,' he groaned. 'Yes, yes, that's it, sweetheart. That's the way.'

He let go of her hips and took hold of each of her nipples with his thumbs and forefingers, squeezing them and pulling them downwards. The combination of sensations was way beyond pleasure. It reached the outer stratosphere.

Jessie cried out, then splintered apart with the most intense orgasm she had ever had. By the time Kane followed her several seconds later, she felt as if she'd fallen into quicksand. She clung on to that bedpost for dear life, knowing that if she let go she would surely sink to the floor.

And then she *was* sinking, but somehow she didn't hit the floor. Instead, Kane scooped her up in his arms. How could he do that? her befuddled mind tried to grasp. He was behind her, deep inside her still throbbing flesh. She could still feel him there. But, no, it seemed he wasn't there any longer. She *was* being carried, and being lain down on top of his bed, his very soft, very comfortable bed. He started stroking her hair and her back and her legs, and that wave of exhaustion which had been hovering at the edges of her mind floated softly down over her. She mumbled something. It might have been 'thank you'. She yawned.

Then everything went black.

CHAPTER TWELVE

KANE returned from his trip to the bathroom to gaze down at Jessie asleep on top of his bed, smiling when he saw that she still had those sexy shoes on her feet. Carefully, slowly, he picked up each foot and removed them. She didn't stir.

He'd read her right. She liked men who took charge in the bedroom, who treated her to a bit of caveman style. Yet Kane had never acted quite like that with a female before. Natalie had been of the ilk who, ultimately, liked to be on top. To begin with, he'd liked the fact he didn't have to work hard for his sex. Time and familiarity, however, had eventually dulled his desire for her. Lack of love too, Kane realised. Resentment had built up over her unwillingness to have his children and by the end he hadn't been interested in pleasing her.

He wanted to please Jessie Denton more than any woman he'd ever met. Of course, that was because he'd fallen in love with her. Deeply. Truly. It wasn't just lust. Or fool's love, as he called it. He'd been there, done that, and he knew the difference. He wanted her, not just as his lover but also as his wife and the mother of his children. He might have only known her a week, but he was surer of that than he had been of anything in his life.

He suspected she felt pretty strongly about him,

137

too. But she was wary after her experience with that scumbag, Lyall. Cynicism was stopping her from seeing he was sincere.

Pity about her overhearing him with Natalie like that. She must have thought him a callous liar. But despite that she'd agreed to come out with him, something she hadn't done in years. His male ego had been very flattered when she'd told him he was the first man she'd been with since Emily's father. His love for her had grown at the news she didn't sleep around. As had his respect. She had character, did Jessie Denton. A tremor ran down Kane's spine as he recalled the force of her orgasm.

He couldn't wait for her to wake up. He was already hard again.

Why *should* you wait? spoke up the caveman still lurking inside him. She wouldn't want to sleep the evening through. If you want her, wake her, take her. Go to it, tiger!

Kane didn't hesitate. He hurried over to the top drawer of the bedside chest, where he'd dropped a newly opened box of condoms earlier that day. Twenty seconds later, he stretched himself out beside her still unconscious form and began trailing his fingers up and down her spine.

Jessie surfaced to consciousness with a shiver of pleasure. Yet it took quite a few seconds for awareness of where she was and what had happened earlier on to strike.

Oh, dear, she thought, grimacing into the pillow. Thankfully she was lying face down. It gave her some extra moments to compose herself before she had to admit she was awake.

Though maybe she wouldn't. Maybe she'd just lie there and pretend she wasn't really awake, just stirring in her sleep. But then that hand, which was sending shivers up and down her spine, moved into territory that jackknifed her over.

'Don't do that!' she gasped.

He smiled, then slid that devilish hand back between her legs. 'Glad to see you've rejoined the living,' he said as he teased her with a fingertip.

She flushed, then gasped when he lightly grazed over her exquisitely swollen peak. 'You're not a good guy at all,' she said breathlessly. 'You're wicked.'

His smile broadened. 'I'll take that as a compliment. Do you want to be on top this time?'

Her mouth fell open as she stared up at him. She had never been with a man who was so forthright, or so...so...

'No? That's OK. Next time, perhaps.' And he bent his head to her nearest nipple. At the same time that tantalising finger stopped what it was doing to delve further into her.

Jessie's mind was torn between two sources of pleasure. His mouth on her breast, licking, sucking, nibbling. But it was what was happening inside her which had her breathing really hard. Her belly began to tighten and she thought she would warn him.

'I...I'm going to come,' she blurted out.

He lifted his head and smiled. 'That's good. Now, are you sure you don't want to be on top?'

It must have been a rhetorical question because before she knew it, he'd hauled her up to be straddling him.

'Now take me in your hands and just ease me inside you as you sink down,' he instructed, sensing perhaps that she'd never done it like this before either. Jessie realised that she'd had a rather boring sex life up till now. Lyall had been forceful in bed but selfish, she realised. Her other boyfriends had just been ignorant. Only her natural love of being kissed and caressed and, yes, penetrated had made those sexual encounters pleasurable.

She took Kane in her hands. Just the thought of putting him inside her body with her own hands was so exciting.

Suddenly, shyness wasn't an option.

'Hey,' he said when her fingers enclosed tight around him. 'Gently does it.'

She didn't even blush. She was too focused on feeling his beautiful hardness, then inserting him deep into her eagerly accepting flesh. And ooh…it felt as good as she had known it would. No further instructions were needed, though he did take hold of her hips when she began to ride him. Probably to slow her down. The urge to go faster and faster was almost unbearable. Her need for release was intense.

'Yes!' she cried out when the first spasm hit.

He must have come, too. She vaguely recalled his own raw groan of release whilst she was moaning and groaning. When she finally collapsed across him, his arms enclosed her, very tenderly, she thought.

This time, she didn't fall asleep. She didn't feel tired at all. Just blissfully at peace. And incredibly happy.

When he eventually rolled her over and eased himself out of her body, she actually whimpered in protest. It had felt lovely with him still inside her. As he moved off the bed and away from her, the feeling of abandonment was acute. And worrisome.

How could she ever live without this again? How could she ever live without *him*?

The prospect appalled her.

He'd gone to the bathroom. She could hear him in there, whistling. The shower taps were turned on and she was imagining him in there washing himself all over when suddenly he was standing in the doorway, stark naked and dripping wet.

'OK, get yourself in here, woman,' he said. 'Refresh time.'

Jessie wanted to. Desperately. But didn't that make her a desperate? She had to stay cool, and strong.

'You and I know what will happen if I get in the shower with you,' she pointed out with what she hoped was sufficient sophistication. 'And I couldn't possibly do it again. Not this soon. Besides, I'm getting hungry. I'll need something to eat soon.'

'Funny you should say that,' he quipped, a wicked gleam in his eyes.

Jessie's mouth opened, then closed again. He meant it. He actually meant it. Worse, the idea excited her. She was getting to be as wicked as he was.

'Do you want me to come over there and carry

you?' he challenged. 'I will if you don't get that delicious butt of yours off that bed in five seconds flat.'

The thought of his carrying her naked body in his arms was almost as thrilling as her going down on him in the shower.

She stayed right where she was, and six seconds later he swept her up into his masterful and muscular arms.

'Just before I forget to tell you,' he said as he carried her into the bathroom, 'I think you are the most beautiful, sexiest, loveliest woman I have ever met.'

His words startled her. But she tried not to let them turn her head—or her heart—too much. Men like Kane were always good with words.

'Knowing you, you're sure to be thinking I'm only interested in you for sex,' he went on. 'And I have to confess,' he added as he placed her down under the hot jets of water, 'that right at this moment, sex is pretty much my main focus.'

His hands reached up to smooth her hair back from her face whilst the water soaked it through.

Jessie had often seen movies where water was used as a symbol of eroticism. Now she knew why. There was something primal about standing naked with your lover under water. The way it ran down over your body, making you aware of every exposed curve and hidden orifice. It splashed inside her mouth, beat on her nipples, pooled in her navel and ran down between her buttocks, soaking her secret places before trickling down her inner thighs.

'But it's the same for you tonight, isn't it?' he

murmured as he cradled her face with his hands and looked deep into her dilated eyes. 'We need this, you and I. Need to do everything to each other. We have to get this out of the way first or we won't be able to think of anything else. I've dreamt about you like this all week. Naked and willing in my bed, and in my shower, and in every room of my house. I won't let you wear any clothes tonight, Jessie, not even when we're eating. You're going to stay naked for me. You're going to let me touch you whenever I want to, *take* you whenever I want to. Give me permission, beautiful Jessie. Tell me that you want that, too.'

'Yes,' she heard herself say from some darkly erotic far-off place. 'Yes…'

CHAPTER THIRTEEN

'WELL? How was it last night?' Dora asked when they finally caught up with each other over mid-morning coffee. 'I was too sleepy to ask you when you got home. Sorry. I hope you didn't think I was rude to leave like that.'

Jessie had actually been grateful. She'd staggered home around one, having declined Kane's offer to walk her to the door, using the excuse that it was late enough. But she must have looked a right mess with her hair all over the place and not a scrap of make-up remaining on her face. Anyone other than a half-asleep old lady would have known on sight that she'd been having sex all night.

Jessie swallowed at the memory. Not just sex. Hot sex. Incredible sex. Sex such as she'd never known before.

'I had a very enjoyable time,' she said with an amazingly straight face. 'The food at the restaurant was fabulous. You know that place down on the beach at Balmoral?'

Dora didn't, thankfully. She said she'd never been to Balmoral, either the suburb or the beach.

Jessie invented a menu from scraps of memory of the last time she was there, all the while trying not to think of the incredible meal she *had* had last night. The food hadn't been incredible. It was just a couple of frozen dinners, washed down with white wine and finished off with a selection of melons. Incredible was the fact that they'd been naked whilst eating, and sharing one of the kitchen chairs, with her being forbidden to feed herself.

In hindsight, their various sexual encounters the previous night seemed decadent. But at the time, they'd simply been exciting.

'Where did you go afterwards?' Dora asked.

'Just back to his place for a while,' Jessie said nonchalantly.

'And?'

'He has a very nice house. Not unlike yours.'

'And?'

'It has a glorious view of the ocean and it's chock-full of antiques. Kane must be worth a fortune.'

'And?'

'And what?'

'Jessie Denton, did you or did you not go to bed with the man?'

Jessie blushed at this unexpectedly forthright question. 'Don't ask questions like that, Dora. Emily might hear.'

'Not at this distance, she won't,' Dora replied.

They were sitting at the small plastic table setting outside their communal laundry, which was a good way from where Emily was happily playing in her fig-tree cubby house.

Jessie sighed. 'Yes, I did,' she confessed.

'Good,' Dora pronounced. 'He's a really nice man.'

Jessie clenched her teeth hard in her jaw lest she

open her mouth and say something to disillusion Dora.

'And he really likes Emily,' Dora added.

'He divorced his wife because he didn't want children,' Jessie couldn't resist throwing into the conversation.

'What? Are you sure about that?'

'Positive. He told me so himself.'

'Strange. He doesn't act like a man who doesn't
like children. He's very patient, for starters. And
kind.'

'Maybe he just doesn't like babies. Emily is not a
baby.'

'True. But that's a shame. I thought he might have
been the one.'

'Which one is that?'

'The one who'll marry you and be a father to
Emily. She's very keen on that idea, you know.'

No, Jessie didn't know. 'You mean, on having a
father? She's never spoken about it to me. Emily
hasn't missed out on anything, not having a father,'
she argued defensively.

'How do you know? She's a deep little thinker,
your Emily. She sees other fathers coming to pick
up their children at the day-care centre. She might
have been wanting a father for ages, but didn't want
to say anything to upset you. She loves her mummy
a great deal but I think she'd love to have a daddy,
too. That's why Kane's been such a big hit with her.
And why she asked if you two were going to get
married last night.'

Jessie's heart turned over. It was already happening, what she'd feared all along. If she kept seeing Kane, Emily was going to get more and more attached to him and one day, poof, he'd be gone and her little girl would be broken-hearted. Her own broken heart she could cope with. She was a grown-up. But how could you explain to a four-year-old that adult relationships didn't always end in marriage? They usually just ended.

'He wants to take me and Emily out this Sunday,' Jessie said with a worried frown on her face. 'I'm going to have to call him and tell him no.' She should never have said yes in the first place. She was weak, weak, weak!

'But why, for pity's sake?'

'Because it's not fair on Emily, letting her think he really likes her. It's not Emily he wants, Dora. It's just me.'

'You don't know that. Ask him.'

'No. He'll only lie to me.'

Dora looked at her with shocked eyes. 'I knew you were cynical, Jessie. I didn't realise you were *that* cynical. For what it's worth, I think you're making a big mistake. He's a nice man and deserves a chance. Not only that, *you* deserve a chance. And Emily, too. Don't make hasty decisions. Give your relationship with Kane a bit of time. OK, so it might not work out, but if you don't try you'll never know. Life can be cruel but it can also be wonderful. You have to believe that or life isn't worth living. I was very lonely and depressed till you and Emily came along. In fact, I was in danger of being a miserable old witch of a woman, I was so full of regrets and resentments. But you brought some light into my life. You and Emily. You're a lovely girl, Jessie Denton, but where men are concerned you're way too hard. And way too distrustful. I've seen a lot of life and I'd put my money on Kane being a decent man. He might even change his mind about having children now that he's become involved with you and Emily. People can change, you know.'

Jessie didn't think that a man who divorced his wife over that single issue was likely to change. At the same time, she supposed she was being a bit hard on him. He'd really been wonderfully warm and considerate last night. He had the capacity to be a sensitive new-age guy as well; he was very capable in the kitchen. And he could give a massage like a professional. He made a great boyfriend and lover, even if not a husband and father.

She'd be out of her mind to voluntarily give him up. Just the thought of never experiencing again what she'd experienced last night made her feel sick. At the same time, she had to make some firm ground rules between them. No pretend family outings. No coming over till Emily was asleep at night. And no expecting her to stay at his place all night on the occasions they did go out.

There! That was reasonable.

Kane didn't think so when she rang him during Emily's after-lunch nap.

'You're being ridiculous again,' he growled. 'About everything. Jessie, I really like you. No, that's a lie. I love you, damn it.'

Jessie gasped into the phone.

'Yes, yes, I'm sure you don't believe me. But it's true.'

'It's you who's being ridiculous,' Jessie countered once she got over her shock. 'I know what you love, Kane Marshall, and it isn't the real me. It's the silly, weak woman I became last night. I don't know what got into me to let you do all those things. My only excuse is that I hadn't been with a man in such a long time. *And*, of course, you seemed to know just what to do to tap into my dark side.'

'Your *dark* side? I wasn't trying to tap into your dark side, sweetheart. Just your feminine side. That side you put on hold most of the time whilst you're being one tough mamma who thinks all men are lying scumbags who couldn't possibly love you or want you for anything other than sex. For pity's sake, I know you've been hurt by other men in the past. Your less than admirable father and that creep, Lyall. But that doesn't mean *all* men are bad. You don't like other people misjudging *you*, or jumping to conclusions over *your* morals, but you're only too ready to jump to conclusions over mine.'

Jessie winced. He was right. She knew he was right.

'You're a wonderful girl, Jessie,' he said more gently. 'But you really need to get that chip off your shoulder. I want you in my life. You *and* Emily. But you have to believe in me, and trust me. I don't know what else I can say to convince you that I'm sincere. Look, if you don't think you could ever love me back, then I suppose I'm just wasting my time. If last night was just you exorcising your sexual frustrations then I guess that's that, then. Just let me say that last night was the most incredible night of my life. You are everything I want in a woman and a lover, Jessie Denton.'

Jessie felt totally chastened by his speech. And moved. 'I...I thought last night was pretty incredible, too. I'm sorry I said what I said, Kane. And I'm sorry I'm such a bitch.'

He laughed. 'In a way, I like that about you. But I like the woman you were last night, too. They're both you, Jessie. And I love them both.'

'I wish you wouldn't keep saying that you love me.'

'Why?'

'Because I'm afraid of it.'

'Yes, I know that, sweetheart. But you're going to have to get used to it. I love you and I'm not going to go away.'

She was beginning to see that, his reassurance flooding through her heart like a giant wave, washing away some of those old fears, the ones where she did think no man would ever truly love and want her, not now that she had Emily. Her mother had drummed into her that no man really wanted another man's child.

But was he talking marriage here? She didn't like to ask. It was premature. And what about the matter of children? Dora could be right there. Maybe he would want children with her, if he loved her enough. If not, at least she already had Emily. And he seemed to genuinely like Emily.

'It might be nice if you told me what you feel for

me,' Kane inserted softly. 'I need some encouragement here.'

'I doubt you ever need encouragement when you want something, Kane Marshall.'

'I've never wanted something quite so unattainable before.'

'How can you say that after the way I acted last night? You said "jump" and I said "how high?"'

'That's just during sex. On a day-to-day basis, you're extremely difficult to handle. Now, am I allowed to come over today?'

'No.'

'How come I knew you were going to say that? What about tomorrow? Can I take you and Emily out, as I was going to?'

'Yes, but no sex.' This edict was more for her benefit than his. She was so tender down there, it wasn't funny.

'I wasn't expecting any. Besides, I'm knackered.'

'That's today. You'll be recovered by tomorrow.'

'You could be right. I'll be even more recovered by Monday.'

'Monday is a work day.'

'Yes, but there's always our lunch-hour. Karen always goes out and I have that lovely office—complete with that huge Chesterfield—all to myself.'

Jessie's cheeks burned at the thought. Just as well he couldn't see her. 'You don't honestly expect me to do that, do you?' she said, trying to sound shocked and not excited.

'A man can always hope.'

'Friday night is our date night,' she said primly. 'You'll have to wait till then.'

'Friday night is a definite, then? No excuses?'

'No excuses.'

'Next Friday night is the office Christmas party,' he told her in an amused tone. 'As the acting boss, I'm obliged to attend. As a new employee, I will expect you to be there too, in a sexy party dress.'

'You devil! You tricked me.'

'You should have remembered.'

'I'm not having you make love to me in your office.'

'You gave me your word. You told me you were a woman of your word.'

'That's emotional blackmail.'

'No one will notice if we slip away from time to time,' he said softly. 'My office is out of the way. And it has a lock on its door.'

'But I wouldn't be able to relax,' she protested. 'I'd be worried what people might be thinking.'

'Who cares what they think? After Christmas, I won't be the boss there any longer and no one will think a thing.'

'They'll always think you hired me because you fancied me.'

'Mmm. Could be true.'

'But it isn't! You know it isn't!'

'Yes, I know. I was only teasing. We'll be very discreet. Tell me you love me, Jessie Denton.'

'No.'

'But you know you do.'

'All I know is that you're a very arrogant man.

And far, far too sure of himself. You need pulling down a peg or two.'

'And you, missie, need a lot more loving.'

'Is that what they're calling it these days?'

'Would you rather I used a cruder term?'

'No.'

'Good, because I'm not just talking about sex. I'm talking loving in the wider context. You need everything a man who loves you can provide. You need caring for. And protection. And support. And security. You need someone there to help you when things go wrong, someone you can turn to and rely upon.'

Oh, how wonderful that would be, she thought with a deep sigh. But was it just a dream, a mad promise from a lust-crazed fool, or the offer of a man genuinely in love?

Jessie had been cynical too long to accept what Kane was offering without any wariness whatsoever.

'What you need,' Kane finished, 'is me.'

'Yes, I certainly do,' she agreed. 'You've revitalised my libido with a vengeance. But we'll both have to wait till Friday to tackle it.'

He swore. The first time he'd sworn in front of her.

'What you need, madam,' he ground out, 'is being put across my knee and having your bottom soundly smacked.'

'Ooh,' she said mockingly. 'Is that a promise or a threat?'

'You're full of bulldust, do you know that? You're scared stiff of me, that's the truth. You're scared stiff of what I can make you feel and what I can make you do. Come Friday night, you *will* tell me you love me. Right there, in that office. Even if I have to smack your bare bottom to get you to say it. And that's a promise!'

Jessie was speechless, her heart pounding at the images he evoked. And the feelings. This couldn't be love, she told herself. This was just lust. He'd totally corrupted her last night.

'That's not love,' she whispered shakily.

'What is it, then?'

'It's torture.'

'Aye, it's that too, till you surrender to it. I've surrendered to my feelings for you. So when are you going to do the same? No, don't answer that. I can be patient. Just remember I'm never going to let you go, Jessie Denton. You are mine. So get used to it.'

CHAPTER FOURTEEN

Ten o'clock Monday morning saw Kane sitting at Harry's desk, feeling quite satisfied with the way his relationship with Jessie was going. Yesterday, he'd proved to her that they didn't have to be making mad, passionate love to enjoy each other's company. He'd also showed her—at least he hoped he had— that he had the makings of a good father for Emily.

On the Saturday, he'd bought a child car seat so there'd be no objections to his driving them out to the rural outskirts of Sydney on the Sunday. After an hour's investigation on the internet, he'd found a horse-riding establishment that catered for children, and had other entertainment as well. Bouncy castles and the like.

Emily had enjoyed herself enormously, although by the time they arrived back home around six o'clock, she'd been very tired and a little out of sorts. She hadn't eaten much of the take-away pizzas Jessie had allowed him to buy this time, which Jessie said wasn't like her at all.

Kane had insisted on taking Emily's temperature— he'd heard horror stories of children coming down with meningitis lately—but her temperature proved to be normal. Jessie had said she was probably over-tired. They'd done a lot that day. After a bath, Kane had read Emily a story till she dropped off.

Afterwards, even though Jessie had let him stay, Kane had made no attempt to make love to her. He'd watched the Sunday-night movie with her—a Harrison Ford action thriller which could bear reviewing—and chatted about various topics during the ads. Books. Movies. Music. Kane had discovered she had a wide taste and knowledge of all three, which didn't really surprise him. She was a smart cookie. He'd known that from the first moment he looked into her eyes. She had intelligent eyes.

Although he'd been dying to make love to her, Kane had contented himself with a goodnight kiss. He suspected Jessie wouldn't have objected too much if he *had* seduced her, but he hadn't wanted to take the chance. She always seemed so quick to believe the worst of him.

By Friday, however, he wouldn't be capable of being so noble. He wouldn't be waiting till the party finished, either. Hell, no. Kane shuddered over the thought of how long this week would prove to be.

When the phone rang, he reached forward and snatched it up.

'Kane Marshall.'

'Kane, I have a problem.'

Kane snapped forward in his chair. It was Jessie, sounding worried.

'What is it? I thought you were here, at work.'

'I am. The day-care centre has just rung me. Emily has come down with conjunctivitis. Apparently, one of the other children had it on Friday. Anyway, because it's so contagious, they want me to go and pick her up.'

'That's fine, Jessie. You go. No problem. I'll square it with Michele.'

'That's just it. Michele's not here. She had an appointment with her obstetrician this morning, and she's relying on me to do this magazine layout by the time she gets back. I would really hate to let her down, Kane. I've tried to ring Dora but she's out, too. Lord knows where. She's usually home on a Monday. I *can* leave Emily at the centre but they'll put her in a room on her own. It's a kind of quarantine rule they have. They did this to her once before when I was working at the restaurant and she got very upset. She thought she was being punished. I...'

'I'll go get her, Jessie,' Kane immediately offered. 'Just ring them and let them know who I am and that you're giving me permission to pick Emily up. I'll take her to the doctor, too. Get her some drops for her eyes.'

'Would you, Kane? Would you really?'

Kane was amazed at the surprise in her voice. 'Yes, of course. It would be my pleasure. Poor Emily. There's nothing worse than having sore eyes. Does she have a regular doctor you take her to?'

'Not exactly. I always go to a nearby twenty-four-hour clinic. They bulk bill, but you have to be seen by whatever doctors are on call that day.'

Privately Kane resolved that little arrangement would change, once *he* was responsible for Jessie and Emily. And he aimed to be, one day. Still, that clinic would do for today.

'Right. I'll come and get her medicare card from you. Jot down the address of the clinic and I'll be on my way.'

Kane jumped to his feet and reached for his suit jacket straight away. It could only have been thirty seconds before he'd made it to Jessie's desk, where he was stunned to find her with tears running down her face.

'Jessie. Darling. What's up?' he said as he hunched down beside her chair. 'Why are you crying?'

She could not seem to speak, just buried her face in her hands.

'Jessie, talk to me. Tell me what's wrong.' He took her hands in his and lifted them to his lips.

She stared at him through soggy lashes. 'I've never known anyone like you,' she choked out. 'You can't be real.'

Relief zoomed through Kane, as well as the most ego-boosting pleasure. She wasn't unhappy. She was actually complimenting him with her tears.

But how sad that she would feel disbelief that a man would do something nice for her and her daughter.

'I'm real, all right,' he said with a soft smile. 'Just ask my mum. Now, stop being a silly billy, give me what I came for, then get back to work. You don't want everyone saying I hired a nincompoop just because I fancied her, do you?'

He liked it when a smile broke through her tears. God, but she was beautiful when she smiled. Her eyes glittered and her whole face came alive.

'We couldn't have that, could we?' she said, dashing the tears away with her fingers.

'Absolutely not.'

'OK. Here's the medicare card and the clinic's address. Now, what are you going to do with Emily after you've been to the doctor? They didn't say she was actually sick, but perhaps she should go home. I could give you the keys to the granny flat if you wouldn't mind staying with her. There's plenty of food in the fridge and the cupboards. She usually has a sleep after lunch. If she gets bored or stroppy, she likes to watch videos. She has a whole pile of them in the cabinet under the TV.'

'Sounds good to me. I'll give you a call when I get there, and I'll wait with her till you come home.'

'I don't know what to say, Kane,' she said as she drew her keys out of her handbag. 'Are you sure you can manage? I mean...you haven't much experience looking after kids on your own.'

'I happen to be an extremely devoted uncle, so you're wrong there. What do you think I did on Saturday night when you wouldn't let me come over? I minded the two terrors so that their parents could go out and relax together. Actually, I don't know what their mother complains about. They were as good as gold. Of course, I plied them with junk food and lollies till they fell asleep on the sofa in front of the TV. Then I carried them up to bed. Works every time,' he said with a quick grin.

'Now, don't you worry,' he added. 'I'm more than capable of looking after Emily. And I won't feed her junk food, or lollies. To be honest, it'll be a pleasant change from sitting at that damned desk, pretending to work. Things wind down leading up to Christmas. My entire workload this week is choosing what grog to buy for the Christmas party. *Very* challenging.'

He stood up, pocketing her keys and picking up the medicare card and piece of paper with the address. 'I'll call, OK? And don't worry.'

'I won't,' she said, looking much more composed. 'I can't tell you how grateful I am.'

Kane threw her one last smile and whirled on his heels.

Nothing made a man feel better, he decided as he strode manfully away, than being able to help the woman he loved.

Jessie worked hard and fast for the next few hours, not leaving her desk till the magazine layout looked perfect. To her, anyway.

Michele returned shortly after she'd finished, and only minutes after Kane had rung saying he was at the flat with Emily and that her conjunctivitis wasn't too bad. He'd already put one lot of drops in, they'd shared Vegemite toast and a glass of milk, followed by a banana each. Now they were settling down to watch *The Lion King*.

With her worries about her daughter waylaid, Jessie could focus on Michele's reaction to her work. When Michele started frowning, Jessie's alarm grew. Maybe the layout wasn't as good as she thought it was.

'I would never have imagined doing it this way at all,' Michele said at last, tipping her head from side to side as she studied the computer screen. 'But yes, I like it! You are very creative, Jessie. Kane's found a real gem in you. Harry's going to be delighted at your joining his staff.'

Jessie sighed her relief. 'Thank you. But…would you mind if I left now?' she asked hurriedly. 'I know it's only two o'clock, but my little girl has conjunctivitis. The day-care centre rang and wanted me to go get her straight away, but I didn't feel I could without finishing the layout first.'

'That was very professional of you, Jessie. But honestly, I would have understood. That kind of thing happens to me all the time. And yes, of course you can go. I hope your little girl is OK.'

Jessie didn't want to tell her about Kane coming to the rescue. That was her own personal business.

'I'm sure she will be,' Jessie said, standing up hurriedly and getting her things together. 'Thanks, Michele. I did work through my lunch-hour. And I'm happy to do some extra work at home to make up for the extra hour and a half.'

'Are you kidding me? You've achieved more here in less than a day than your predecessor would have done in a week!'

Jessie laughed and left.

The day outside wasn't overly hot, but it was humid, Jessie's blouse sticking to her back as she hurried to the train station. Sydney in December could be very sticky.

The train she caught was quite crowded, Jessie

lucky to get a seat. But she was still pressed up against other people, and the air-conditioning didn't seem to be working too well. Everywhere seemed crowded at the moment, even outside of peak hours. Lots of people doing Christmas shopping, she supposed.

Jessie was glad she'd finished hers. She had Emily's Felicity Fairy doll and accessories all wrapped up and hidden on a high shelf in one of Dora's wardrobes, along with a few little cheaper gifts she'd bought during the year. She'd long sent her mother's card and gift to Ireland. A lovely set of linen serviettes and holders that her mother would probably put away and never use. Truly, she was a difficult woman to buy anything for.

For Dora, she'd bought some place mats and matching coasters in a blue and white willow pattern. She hadn't spent as much money on her as her mother, but she knew Dora would appreciate the gift more, and actually use it. Dora loved that willow pattern. She had a tea set in it, a vase and a large serving plate.

It came to Jessie during the train ride home that she hadn't bought Kane anything. In truth, his rather sudden intrusion into her life had driven Christmas from her mind, which was ironic given what she'd said to Dora that night before she'd gone to the bar. Hadn't she wanted a man for Christmas, some gorgeous guy who'd give her a good time?

Kane had certainly done just that, and more. Much more.

Jessie still found it incredible that he loved her.

But he said he did and she had no real reason to doubt him. Frankly, she didn't *want* to doubt him any more. She was tired of her cynicism, tired of trying to stop herself from falling in love with him. Dora was right. Life could be cruel but it could be wonderful.

Kane was a wonderful man, despite his not wanting children of his own. Why he didn't she had no idea, but she would certainly ask him. Soon.

And if he still insists he doesn't, Jessie, where can this relationship go? You would want children with the man you loved. And you do love him, don't you? That was one of the reasons you were crying earlier. Because you knew you couldn't stop yourself loving him any longer.

You love him and you'd make any compromise just to be with him.

But maybe you're jumping the gun here, Jessie Denton.

Maybe he just wants to continue being your boyfriend and your lover. Maybe he doesn't want to live with you, or marry you. Maybe the way it is now is all he'll ever want.

Dismay clutched at Jessie's heart. It wasn't enough. Just seeing him on a Friday night. And occasionally at the weekend. Not enough at all.

But it would have to be enough. She couldn't force him to want marriage, let alone children. She couldn't force him to do anything.

Unless…

No, no, that wasn't right. She would not try to trap him with a baby. It wouldn't work, anyway. The man who'd written *Winning at Work* would never succumb to that kind of emotional blackmail. He was strong on his beliefs, be they right or wrong.

The train pulling into Roseville brought a swift end to her mental toing and froing. During her hurried walk home Jessie told herself she should stop questioning everything and just live one day at a time for a while. Things were good in her life at the moment. Kane was good for her. And he was good for Emily. Why risk what they had by wanting more? She was a fool.

'Sssh,' Kane said when she burst in through the back door. 'Emily's asleep. She nodded off during the video and I carried her into bed. But that was only ten minutes ago. Gosh, you look hot.'

'I am hot. It's terribly sticky outside.' The granny flat was nicely cool, with double insulation in the roof and fans in the high ceilings. Kane looked very cool, sitting on the sofa with his arms running along the back of the sofa and his long legs stretched out before him, crossed at the ankles. Very cool and very sexy.

Suddenly, Jessie felt even hotter.

'I'll have to have a shower and change,' she said hurriedly. 'Once Emily's asleep, usually nothing wakes her up, so we don't have to creep about. I won't be long,' she said, and fled into the bedroom.

Emily stayed blessedly asleep whilst her mother stripped off, showered then pulled on a simple cotton sundress in pink and white checks, which looked sexier on her than she realised.

*   *   *

Kane gritted his teeth when she emerged, thinking to himself that he'd better make himself scarce, or all his resolutions about not touching her till Friday were about to fly out the window. But when he rose and reached for his jacket, which was draped over a kitchen chair, her face betrayed that his leaving was the last thing she wanted.

They stared at each other for a long moment. And then she said something that floored him. His mouth literally dropped open.

'Say that again,' he blurted out, not daring to believe what he thought he'd heard.

'I love you,' she repeated, her face flushed, her eyes glistening.

Kane knew that in years to come, he would always remember that moment. A dozen different emotions warred for supremacy. Disbelief? Shock? Joy? Delight? Satisfaction? Desire?

Desire won in the end. Or was it just his own love for her? How could you not take a woman into your arms who'd just told you she loved you with such moving simplicity?

She went without any hesitation this time, not a trace of doubt in her face any more.

But he didn't kiss her straight away. He looked down into those beautiful eyes and savoured the sincerity he saw in their depths.

'When did you decide this?' he said softly.

'On the way home on the train.'

'A very good place to make decisions.'

'Much better than when I'm like this,' she told him

with a small smile. 'I can't think straight when I'm in your arms.'

'That's good to know as well.'

Her arms slid even tighter around his neck, pulling their bodies hard against each other. 'Aren't you going to kiss me?' she asked breathlessly.

'Soon.'

'You have a sadistic side to you, Kane Marshall.'

'I never claimed to be a saint.'

Neither was he a masochist. His mouth was within a millimetre of contacting hers when there was a knock on the door.

His head lifted, and they groaned together.

It was Dora, all a-flutter.

'I saw Kane's car out the front,' she said. 'Is anything wrong?'

Jessie gave her a quick run-down on the little drama with Emily. Dora looked relieved.

'I'm so glad it's nothing serious. And that Kane could help. Sorry I wasn't here, dear. But you'll never guess what's happened.'

Kane and Jessie exchanged a look that carried both amusement and exasperation.

'Why don't I make us all some coffee,' Jessie said, 'and you can tell us what's happened?'

Kane suppressed a sigh and pulled out a kitchen chair for Dora, sitting down himself once the old lady was settled.

Apparently she'd received an unexpected call from her brother that morning, the one who hadn't been much support to her during their mother's last years. Dora hadn't spoken to him for a good two years.

'If it hadn't been Christmas I wouldn't have spoken to him today, either,' she said defiantly. 'But I'm so glad I did.'

Apparently, her brother explained how he'd been inundated with business and family problems when their mum had been ill, but admitted that he knew he hadn't done enough. He'd recently had a health scare himself and had been thinking that he wanted to make it up to Dora. The upshot was he'd come and taken Dora out to lunch, over which he'd asked her to go to his place for Christmas, and for the week afterwards, right up to New Year. It seemed his business was doing very well now; he owned a couple of cafés down around the Wollongong area on the south coast. He had a huge holiday house down there, and every one of their relatives was coming.

Kane saw Jessie's face fall at this news, and guessed that she and Emily always spent Christmas with Dora. After all, she had no one else. It was just the opportunity he'd been waiting for.

'That's great, Dora,' he piped up. 'And it sure takes a load off Jessie's mind. You see, I asked her and Emily to come spend Christmas with me and my family. But she was worried sick about you, thinking you'd be all alone. Of course, you'd have been welcome to come too, but this solves everything much better.'

Dora seemed relieved and pleased at this announcement, whilst Jessie went a little quiet. After Dora bustled off to go do some more Christmas shopping, Kane was left to face a slightly cool Jessie.

'What a smooth liar you are,' she said.

Kane could feel the doubts rising in her again.

'There's nothing wrong with little white lies, Jessie,' he pointed out. 'Especially when they're partially true. I was going to ask you to spend Christmas with me.'

'*And* with your family?'

'Yes.'

'And what were you going to introduce me as?'

'What would you like me to introduce you as?'

'I don't know. You tell me.'

'How about fiancée?'

She stared at him and he sighed. 'I guess that is rushing you somewhat. How about my new girl-friend, then?'

Jessie just kept shaking her head, her expression bewildered. 'Were you seriously asking me to marry you? You weren't joking?'

'I wouldn't joke about something like that.'

'But we've only known each other ten days!'

'I know I love you and I know you love me.'

'But we don't really *know* each other.'

'I beg to differ. I know you very well. Much better than I knew Natalie when I married her, and we'd been dating for months. The problem is you don't think you know me. But you had the wrong picture of me from the start. I rather hoped I'd managed to get rid of that poor image by now, but it seems I haven't.'

'That's not true. I...I think you're wonderful. You must know that. But *marriage*? That's a very big step, Kane. For one thing, we don't agree on one very important issue. The same issue you didn't agree on with your first wife.'

'*What?* You mean *you* don't want children, either? Hell, Jessie, I thought…' A great black pit yawned open in Kane's stomach. He could not believe it. Jessie didn't want his children. The woman he loved. The woman he adored. How cruel was that?

Jessie blinked. Had she heard that right? His *ex* hadn't wanted children? But that couldn't be right. She'd said she was pregnant that day in Kane's office and that she was keeping the baby. Of course, lots of women who didn't think they wanted children changed their minds once they actually got pregnant. But if that was the case…

'Hold it there,' she said. 'Why, exactly, did you divorce Natalie?'

'Mainly because she refused to have children. But I think I also realised I didn't really love her.'

'Oh!' Jessie exclaimed with a gasp. 'I thought it was *you* who didn't want children!'

'*Me?* I love children. How on earth did you get that ridiculous idea? I thought I explained the reasons behind my divorce quite clearly.'

'You told me you disagreed with your wife over the matter of having children and I just assumed it had to be you who didn't want kids.' Jessie felt truly chastened. But secretly elated. 'I'm so sorry, Kane. My old prejudice against men again.'

He nodded, unable to feel unhappy, now that he knew Jessie wanted more children. 'An understandable mistake.'

'So you really do want children?'

'A whole tribe of them, if possible. The more the merrier.'

Jessie beamed. 'Me, too.'

'What about your career?'

'My career would never come before my kids. But hopefully I could juggle both.'

Kane's delight was as great as his despair had been. 'In that case, come here, woman, and make it up to me for thinking such dreadful things.'

She ran into his arms. This time, he actually got to kiss her for five seconds before they were interrupted.

'Mummy…'

They pulled apart to find Emily standing in the bedroom doorway, rubbing her eyes.

'Hello, sweetie,' her mother said. 'You feeling better now?'

'I'm thirsty. And my eyes are sore.'

Jessie gave a small sigh. 'I'll get you a drink of water. Kane, where are those eye drops?'

'Over here on the coffee-table. I'll get them.'

Their eyes clashed momentarily, Kane seeing that Jessie was watching him for signs of impatience.

Instead, he smiled, then hurried over to sweep Emily up into his arms. 'Did you have a good sleep, princess?'

She tipped her head on one side. 'Were you kissing Mummy just then?'

Jessie stopped breathing.

'I sure was,' Kane said. 'It was very nice, too. Do you mind my kissing Mummy?'

'No. Will you kiss me, too?'

He laughed and planted a peck on her forehead. 'There. Now let me get those eye drops into you.'

'Do you *have* to?' she wailed.

'Yes. I *have* to,' Kane returned firmly.

Jessie heaved a great sigh of happiness. Even more wonderful than everything which had happened today was having someone else put Emily's eye drops in.

CHAPTER FIFTEEN

WORK the following Friday came to a halt by lunch-time, at which point the males on the staff pitched in to transform the main office floor into party land. Several of the central cubicles were dismantled to provide a more than adequate dance floor. Desks were cleared and decorations and disco lights went up.

Peter—who apparently loved playing DJ each year—set about filling his area with his latest hi-fi gear, whistling *Jingle Bells* as he worked. Kane and Karen took charge of stocking up the temporary bar, whilst Margaret roped Jessie and Michele into help-ing her with the food, which they spread out, buffet-style, on several desks pushed together. A local ca-tering company had supplied a wide selection of cold meats, seafood and salads, with some delicious cream-topped cakes for the sweet tooths, plus loads of snacks.

Jessie thought that there was way too much to eat and drink for their small staff, but when she re-marked on this to Michele, she was informed that their office party was so popular that loads of other people in the building came, along with clients, past and present.

'And everyone's other halves usually drop in as well,' Michele added. 'Tyler's sure to be late, workaholic that he is, but he'll make an appearance at some stage, even if only to see me safely home.'

Tyler, Jessie knew by now, was Michele's husband.

'And speaking of other halves,' Michele said after a glance over at Kane, 'yours is looking very bright-eyed and bushy-tailed tonight. What *have* you been doing to him, girl?'

Absolutely nothing of what Michele was implying. There'd been no actual lovemaking, despite their spending every evening this week together. Kane didn't seem to mind stopping at a goodnight kiss. He'd even promised he wouldn't press her for more in any shape or form here at the party tonight.

'He does look yummy in black, doesn't he?' Jessie said with that swirl in her stomach that always occurred whenever she looked at the man she loved. It had been difficult controlling her own desires these past few days, but it had been more important to her to know that Kane's love was not just sexually based than to indulge in some passing pleasure.

'You haven't told anyone else here about our being engaged, have you?' she added swiftly. She didn't mind Michele knowing. They were fast becoming firm friends and she just couldn't keep her good news totally secret.

Still, it was good that Kane hadn't bought her a ring yet. That way he couldn't be annoyed with her for not wearing it at work. Jessie was still worried over what the other people at Wild Ideas might think.

'No. I haven't told anyone else,' Michele said with a sigh. 'But if you keep looking at each other the way you do, people will begin to suspect something is going on.'

Kane turned his head at that moment, and their eyes connected. His smile carried so much obvious love that Jessie could see what Michele meant.

'OK, everyone!' Kane announced to the room. 'Everything's ready for the party. Time for the girls to go and put their glad rags on. The guys too, if you've brought something more colourful to change into.' He glanced at his watch. 'At three o'clock, the doors will be thrown open and it'll be all systems go. Though speaking of systems, please make sure that your computers are safely turned off, passwords hidden and all important files discreetly locked away. I don't want Harry coming home and finding that all your wonderfully wild ideas have been stolen, or sabotaged. OK?'

'OK, boss!' they all chorused, Jessie included.

How proud of him she felt, this wonderful, gorgeous, sensible-thinking man who loved her.

Twenty minutes later, she was nervously viewing herself in the full-length mirror that hung on the back of the ladies' room door. Her cocktail dress was brand new, and very sexy. Black silk with turquoise swirls on it, it had a halter neckline, a wide, extremely tight waistband and a swishy skirt.

Her shoes were new, too. Turquoise, in the currently fashionable slip-on style, which showed off her pretty ankles and scarlet-painted toenails. This time she'd been able to afford fake tan, so her bare legs and arms glowed a nice honey colour. Her hair was down for once, and not too bushy, courtesy of the more expensive hair products she could also now buy and which tamed the frizz somewhat. She was wearing more make-up than she would usually wear in the office as well, and considerably less underwear. No bra for starters and just the briefest thong underneath.

'Wow!' Margaret said when she saw her.

'Yes, wow!' Karen agreed.

Michele just raised her eyebrows in a knowing fashion.

Kane's reaction when he saw her was not quite as enthusiastic. He wasn't too pleased, either, when Jessie was subjected to instant male attention. The men flocked around her, getting her drinks, constantly asking her to dance and pretending to be devastated when she refused.

Jessie suspected Kane was jealous, but if so, why did he keep his distance? Why didn't *he* come and ask her to dance? She wouldn't have said no to him.

Finally, after the party had been raging for over two hours, he walked over to her, his expression tight.

'Could I have a private word, Jessie?'

'Of course,' she replied, and threw her circle of admirers a bright smile. 'Won't be long.'

Kane's grip on her elbow was firm as he steered her away from the party and along the corridor towards his office. Jessie quivered inside at his forcefulness, but it was a quiver of excitement, not nerves. A few glasses of champagne had dispensed with her earlier worries, replacing them with a deliciously carefree attitude.

'I said I wasn't going to do this, remember?' she remarked blithely, all the while quite happy with the prospect of being ravished on Kane's desk.

'I haven't brought you here for sex,' Kane snapped as he banged the door shut behind them.

'Oh…'

'Look, I know you're worried about the rest of the staff thinking you weren't hired on your merits. And I've tried damned hard tonight not to embarrass you by staking my claim on you publicly. But you *are* my woman, Jessie,' he pronounced firmly. '*Mine*. And it's time everyone out there knew that.'

'Oh…'

'I've asked you to marry me and you've said yes. You should be wearing my ring.'

'But…'

'No buts. I'm tired of your buts.' With that he drew a blue velvet box out of his jacket pocket and flipped it open. 'I hope you like it.'

Jessie stared down at the solitaire diamond engagement ring, then swallowed. Oh, God, she was going to cry. 'It…it's beautiful,' she stammered.

'*You're* beautiful,' he said thickly, and taking the ring out of the box, he put the box back in his pocket, then came forward and picked up her left hand.

'I love you, Jessie Denton,' he said as he slipped it on her trembling ring finger.

Her eyes flooded, then tears spilled over, running down her cheeks. 'And I love you,' she choked out.

He wiped the tears away with his spare hand, then bent to kiss each wet cheek. 'That's nothing to cry about,' he said with a soft smile in his voice. 'At least, I hope not.'

'Oh, no,' she denied hotly. 'Never!'

With a rush of sweet emotion, Jessie wound her arms up around his neck and pulled him close. 'You mean the world to me!' she proclaimed.

His hesitation was only slight before he kissed her. Soon, there was no hesitation, only passion. His kisses were fierce, his clasp so tight around her back that her breasts were totally flattened against his chest.

His sudden wrenching away came as a shock.

'Sorry,' he ground out. 'I promised I wouldn't do that.'

She loved it that he cared enough about her to stop. But the time for testing him further was long over.

'It's all right, Kane. I *want* you to make love to me.'

'What? You mean...*here*?'

'Yes, here. Now.'

He watched, gaze smouldering as she kicked off her shoes then reached up under her skirt to peel her panties off. That done, she untied the bow at the back of her neck, letting the straps fall so that her bare breasts were exposed.

When Kane sucked in sharply, her stomach quivered and her already erect nipples tightened further.

'I'd better lock the door,' he rasped.

He did so, then took her hand and led her over to the nearby Chesterfield. There, he drew her down onto his lap, kissing her and playing with her breasts till she was breathless and shaking. Only then did he slide one hand up under her skirt.

'No,' she protested. 'No, I don't want that, Kane. I want you. With nothing between us.'

'But…'

'No buts. It's all right. It's a safe time in my cycle. And if I'm wrong, what does it matter? I love you. You love me. We're getting married. A baby would be just fine.'

Kane could not believe the impact of her words. She must really love him and trust him, if she didn't mind conceiving his baby before they were married. He could not ask for more.

How he wanted her! His lovely Jessie. His woman.

He groaned at the first contact of their naked bodies, then moaned when his flesh began to enter hers. The look on her face as she sank all the way downwards told him she felt very much what he was feeling. When her hands cradled his face and she looked deep into his eyes, it took all of his will-power not to weep.

'I love you,' she whispered, and began to rise and fall upon him in a voluptuously sensual rhythm. 'I love you,' she repeated, pressing tiny kisses all over his face at the same time.

Kane closed his eyes in defence of the emotion that ripped through him. Never in his life had he felt anything like what this woman could make him feel. He could not wait to marry her, to promise to love and cherish her till death did them part. Because nothing short of death would destroy their union.

They were as one, not just in their bodies but also in their minds. She was going to be his soul mate. His best friend. The mother of his children.

When he took her hands from around his face and held them to his lips, she stopped moving to stare at him with glazed eyes.

'I...I never thought it could be like this,' she said in a voice that betrayed some lingering bewilderment over their relationship.

'I don't think it is very often,' he returned. 'We're very lucky.'

'Yes,' she agreed. 'Very.'

'We're going to go back to the party afterwards and announce our engagement,' he commanded, taking full advantage of the moment.

Jessie nodded. 'Yes. All right. But Kane...about tomorrow night...'

Kane frowned. 'What about tomorrow night?' She and Emily were supposed to be coming to sleep over at his house. It was Christmas Eve. He'd already bought a Christmas tree. A real one. And loads of decorations, which he planned on putting up with Emily. Not to mention more presents than was wise.

But how often did a man fall in love and get an instant family, one that probably hadn't been spoiled as he intended to spoil them, if he was allowed to?

'Don't tell me you've changed your mind about coming!'

She laughed a wicked little laugh. 'I'll be coming all right. Tonight. But Kane...about tomorrow night. I know it's probably old-fashioned of me, but I won't sleep in your bed with Emily in the same house. Not until we're married.'

Kane wasn't going to argue with her. Not at this precise moment. 'Fine,' he said. 'But I give you the right to change your mind again.'

'I won't change my mind this time.'

'We'll see,' he said, taking hold of her hips and urging her to start moving again.

When she cried out in naked ecstasy, Kane suspected he was in there with a pretty good chance.

CHAPTER SIXTEEN

'LOOK, Mummy, it's a Felicity Fairy doll!' Emily squealed as she ripped off the rest of the wrapping paper. 'And her horse! And her castle!'

'What a lucky girl you are,' Jessie replied from where she was curled up in the corner of Kane's sofa, dressed in the red silk nightie and robe Kane had given her on the stroke of midnight last night. They'd been up late talking and wrapping presents for Emily.

Of course, he'd insisted on seeing Jessie in his gift, one thing had led to another and, well...at least she hadn't actually slept in his bed. This room, however, had been witness to some torrid but tender lovemaking between even more provocative present-giving: perfume, body lotion and chocolates, which he'd fed her one by one as rewards for various services rendered.

Around one o'clock, a sated Jessie had given Kane the gifts she'd bought him. A book about the teachings of the Dalai Lama, a Robbie Williams CD and a DVD of the *Lord of the Rings* trilogy. She'd gleaned his taste from their many talks. He'd been so overcome that he had to listen to the CD and watch some of the DVD before making love to her again as a thank-you.

Shortly before three, a totally spent Jessie had stumbled into the second guest room, climbed into the bed and fallen into a deep sleep, where she had remained, not moving an inch, till Emily started tugging on her hair around six, saying Santa had been and Mummy just had to get up.

After Jessie had opened a single bleary eye, Emily had rushed off, saying she would wake Kane up, too.

That had been about fifteen minutes ago.

Jessie yawned just as Kane came into the living room with two mugs of freshly brewed coffee. He was actually wearing clothes. Shorts and a T-shirt. He needed a shave but he looked good like that. Very sexy.

'I really need this,' she said as she took one of the mugs and cradled it in her hands. 'It's just as well you took me to meet your family the other night when I looked all right. I look like something the cat dragged in today.'

'You look beautiful,' he said, and bent to give her a peck on the forehead before settling next to her. 'Glowing, in fact. Being in love suits you.'

Jessie glanced down at her engagement ring then up at the man who'd given it to her. 'Being in love with *you* suits me,' she said. 'You are the most incredible man.'

'But of course!' He grinned. 'Didn't I tell you that from the start?'

She laughed. 'You're also very arrogant.'

'Not true. I just know what I want when I see it.'

'Mummy, look at this!' Emily said, holding up the prettiest pink dress. 'Isn't it beautiful? I'm going to wear it when we visit Kane's mummy and daddy. I'll look like a princess, won't I, Kane?'

'Indeed.'

Jessie's heart turned over at how happy her daughter was. Kane had brought joy to both their lives, as well as the promise of a secure future.

'So, did Santa bring you everything you asked him for?' Jessie asked her daughter.

'Oh, yes,' Emily said, surveying all her new toys and clothes and games. 'He didn't forget a thing.'

'What do you like most?' Jessie asked, knowing exactly what her daughter would say: the Felicity Fairy doll.

'I like my new daddy the most,' came her unexpected reply. 'Can I call you Daddy now, Kane?' she added, crinkling her forehead up into a frown.

'I'd like nothing better, princess. Now, come over here,' he said as he put his coffee down on a sidetable, 'and give your new daddy a hug.'

Emily smiled as only a child could smile, then ran into Kane's waiting arms.

Jessie frowned.

'Emily,' she said once her daughter was comfortable on Kane's lap, her arms tightly wound around his neck, 'did you ask Santa for a new daddy that day at the shops?'

'Yes,' came the reply 'You said if I was a good girl he would get me anything I asked for. And he did.'

Jessie blinked at Kane, who shrugged. 'The ways of the lord are very mysterious.'

She stared at him. 'I didn't know you were religious.'

'I'm not overly. But I think we might pop into a church later today, just to say thank you.'

'Can I go to church with you, Daddy?'

'But of course, princess. That's what daddies are for. To do whatever our little girls want us to do. And our big girls, too,' he added with a sexy wink Jessie's way.

'Next year,' Emily said excitedly, 'I'm going to ask Santa for a baby brother.'

'What a good idea,' Kane replied whilst Jessie tried not to choke on her coffee. 'I'm sure Santa won't have any trouble with that order. Though you have to remember that even Santa can't order the sex of a baby. That's up to God.'

'Then I'll ask God.'

'Go straight to the top. Excellent thinking. What do you think, Mummy?'

'I think we should clear away all that paper over there, then have a shower and get dressed.'

Emily pulled a face when her mother got up and went over to start picking up the mounds of Christmas paper.

'Mummies aren't as much fun as daddies,' she pronounced.

Kane smiled. 'Oh, I don't know, Emily. Your mummy has her moments. And she is a very good mummy, isn't she?'

'Oh, yes,' Emily said, and smiled over at her mother.

Jessie thought her heart would burst with happiness. She didn't know what she had done to deserve such happiness but she resolved never to take it for granted, to work hard, to always be a good wife to Kane, and an even better mother to Emily and whatever other children she might be blessed with.

Her mother was going to be surprised when she rang her later today and told her that some man did want to marry her, even with some other man's baby.

But of course Kane wasn't some man. He was a very special man.

'Daddy,' Emily whispered to Kane, 'why is Mummy crying?'

'She's crying because she's happy, princess,' he told Emily, a lump in his own throat. 'Grown-ups cry sometimes when they're happy.'

'When I cry, Mummy kisses me better.'

Kane nodded. 'What a good idea. Let's go kiss her better.'

EPILOGUE

ROBERT WILLIAM MARSHALL arrived just after midnight on Christmas Eve the following year, much to the delight of his big sister, Emily, who immediately started planning her next year's wish list, which included a pony, a boyfriend for Dora and a visit from her Nanna in Ireland, who'd been writing to her a lot since she'd become something called a Buddhist.

Within a few hours of her beautiful boy's arrival, Jessie decided work could go hang for a while. As much as she had enjoyed her time at Wild Ideas—and she'd worked till she was eight months pregnant—she felt the time had come for an extended maternity leave.

No doubt she would go back to work at some stage. Maybe she'd even start up her own boutique advertising company, run from home. When she mentioned this to Kane he was all for it, as long as he could become her partner.

When a fluttery and flushed Dora visited later that day with her new lodger on her arm—an aspiring writer in his sixties who'd never been married—Jessie and Kane exchanged knowing looks whilst Emily wondered if Santa and God had read her mind and simply got in early.

Jessie was allowed to bring the baby home on Boxing Day, which they spent at her in-laws' place.

She felt remarkably well, but it was still lovely to be waited on, and fussed over. Kane's mother could not stop picking up the baby and goo-gooing over him.

'Happy, darling?' Kane asked her when they finally went home that night and both their babies were asleep.

'Couldn't be happier,' Jessie replied.

'Care for a dance with your husband?' he said, and put on a suitable CD.

As Jessie went into her husband's arms, she remembered the first night they'd met, and danced.

Was it destiny that had brought them together?

It would be romantic to think so.

But it wouldn't be destiny that kept them together.

It would be love.

THE BOSS'S PROPOSAL

by

Cathy Williams

Cathy Williams is originally from Trinidad but has lived in England for a number of years. She currently has a house in Warwickshire which she shares with her husband Richard, her three daughters Charlotte, Olivia and Emma and their pet cat, Salem. She adores writing romantic fiction and would love one of her girls to become a writer, although at the moment she is happy enough if they do their homework and agree not to bicker with one another.

Look out for Cathy Williams's new novel, *Taken by Her Greek Boss*, available in February 2008 from Mills & Boon® Modern™.

CHAPTER ONE

'AH, YES, Miss Lockhart!' The severely coiffeured and immaculately suited middle aged woman who'd emerged from behind the smoked glass doors leading into the impressive foyer of Paxus PLC favoured her with a beaming smile. 'I'm Geraldine Hogg and I'm in charge of the typing pool.' She grasped Vicky's hand and shook it firmly. 'I have your application form here, my dear—' she waved the stapled papers at her '—and you're in for something of a surprise.'

At which, Vicky's heart sank. She didn't like surprises, and she hadn't spent half an hour battling with rush-hour traffic to find herself confronted with one. She'd applied for the post of typist at Paxus PLC because the pay offered was excellent and because working as a typist, whilst going nowhere career-wise, was just the sort of reliable job she needed while she got her house in order. Something undemanding which would give her the time she desperately needed to sort herself out.

'Now, my dear, why don't we go to my office and I'll explain all to you?' Geraldine Hogg had the sort of booming, hearty voice that Vicky associated with privately educated girls who had spent their school years getting their teeth into vigorous outdoor sports like hockey and netball. Her manner was brisk without being aggressive, and whatever so-called surprise lay ahead, Vicky felt that she would work well for the woman now ushering her through the smoked glass double doors and into a luxuriantly carpeted corridor flanked with offices.

5

'I must say, you seem rather over-qualified for the job advertised,' she said confidingly, and Vicky tried to suppress a sigh of disappointment.

'I make a very hard worker, Miss Hogg,' she ventured, half running to keep up with the enormous strides of the other woman.

She could feel her long, curly hair beginning to rebel against the clips she'd painstakingly used to restrain it and she nervously tried to shove it back into place with one hand, without missing a step. She needed this job and it wouldn't do to create the wrong impression, even though it was virtually impossible to look mature and sophisticated when her red-gold hair was congenitally disobedient and her expression, however hard she tried to look stern, was constantly ambushed by her freckles.

'Here we are!' Geraldine Hogg stopped abruptly in front of one of the doors and Vicky only just missed careering into the back of her. 'My typists are just through there.' She waved one sweeping hand at the large, open-planned area opposite her office, and Vicky peered into the room, imagining what it would be like to work there.

Her last job in Australia had been a far cry from this. There, she had been one of the personal assistants to the director of a sprawling public company.

'Come in, come in. Tea? Coffee?' She indicated a chair facing her desk and waited until Vicky had sat down before summoning a young girl through to bring them something to drink. 'I can recommend the coffee, my dear. None of this instant stuff.'

'Yes, fine, I'd love a cup,' Vicky said faintly. She felt as though she had been yanked along at dizzying speed so that she needed to recover her breath. 'White, no sugar. Thank you very much.'

'Now, I won't keep you,' Geraldine sat forward, both

elbows on the desk and gave her an intent stare. 'I'll just tell you about the little surprise I have in store for you!' She linked her fingers together and cocked her head to one side. 'First of all, let me say that I was highly impressed with your CV.' She glanced down at the highly impressive CV and flicked through it casually while Vicky's head whirled with all the dreadful permutations of this so-called surprise in store for her. 'Lots of qualifications!' She rattled off a few of them, which only served to emphasise how ridiculously over-qualified Vicky was for the job in question. 'You must have been quite an asset to the company you worked for!'

'I'd like to think so.' Vicky attempted a confident smile but was quietly glad for the interruption of the young girl bringing two cups of coffee.

'Why did you decide to leave Australia?' Sharp blue eyes scrutinised Vicky's face, but before Vicky could answer Geraldine held up one hand and said, 'No! No point answering that! I'll just fill you in on your position here. First of all, we feel that you would be wasted working as a typist...'

'Ah.' She could feel the sting of disappointed tears prick the back of her eyes. Since leaving Australia four months previously, Vicky had worked in various temporary jobs, none of which had been satisfactory, and the two permanent posts she'd applied for had both turned her down for the very reason Geraldine Hogg appeared to be giving her now. Unless she secured a proper job she would find herself running into financial problems, and she couldn't afford to start dipping into her meagre savings. Not in her situation.

'But, fortunately,' Geraldine swept on in a satisfied voice, 'we have something far better to interview you for, my dear, so there's no need for you to look quite so de-

jected. The head of our organisation will be spending a
great deal more time in this particular subsidiary and he
needs a secretary. Admittedly, you're a bit young for the
post, but your qualifications provide a good argument for
putting you forward for the job, which, incidentally, will
pay double the one you were to be interviewed for!'

'Working for the head of the organisation?' From past
experience Vicky knew that nothing came without a catch,
and this opportunity sounded just a little too good to be
true.

'I'll take you up to see him now, and while I don't,
obviously, guarantee that the job is yours, your past experience will certainly stand in your favour.'

It occurred to Vicky that none of this was happening. It
was all some bizarre dream which would end the minute
she opened her eyes. In fact, applying to the company had
had a dream-like feel about it from the start. She had seen
the advertisement in the newspaper and the name of the
company had triggered a memory somewhere in the dark
recesses of her mind. Shaun, in one of his eternal, self-
glorifying rambles, had mentioned it as one of the myriad
companies his family owned and the name had stuck because it had been the name of the road on which she had
lived with her aunt in Sydney. Just answering the advert
had taken will-power, because Shaun was possibly the one
person in the world whose memory made her recoil in
revulsion. But answer it she had, partly through curiosity
to see proof of the great Forbes Dynasty and partly because
the pay offered had been too good to refuse.

Now, she curiously looked around her as she was shown
up to the third floor. The décor was muted and luxuriant.
The central areas were open plan but fringed with small,
private offices, sheltered from prying eyes by the same
smoked glass as in the foyer. The company—which, she

recalled from the newspaper advert, had not been going
for very long—had obviously chosen the nursery supply-
ing its plants with some care, because in between the usual
lush green artificial trees that most successful companies
sported were expensive orchids and roses which couldn't
be very easy to maintain.

'Hope you don't mind the walk up,' Geraldine was saying briskly at her side. 'I can't abide elevators. Much prefer
a spot of good old-fashioned exercise. World would be a
better place if people just got off their arses, pardon my
French, and used their legs a bit more!'

Vicky, busy looking around her, puffed and panted an
agreement. Somehow she found it difficult to associate
Shaun with clean, efficient, seemingly well-run surroundings like these. She could feel her mind going down familiar paths and focused her attention on Geraldine and
what she was saying, which appeared to be a congratula-
tory monologue on the massive and successful Forbes
Holdings, of which Paxus PLC was a small but blossoming
satellite. She wondered whether any mention would be
made of Shaun, or even the brother, the one who lived in
New York, but there was no mention of either in between
the steady stream of growth, profit and share price chat.

''Course, I've worked for the family for twenty years
now. Wanted a career teaching sport, but I did the back
in, my dear, and ended up going along the secretarial road.
Not that I've regretted a minute of working here,' she confided, and just when Vicky imagined that the bracing talk
might become less factual and more personal, Geraldine
paused in front of a door and knocked authoritatively.

'Yes!'

Mysteriously, Vicky saw that the plain, down-to-earth
face had turned pink and, when Geraldine pushed open the
door and poked her head in, her voice was almost kittenish.

'Miss Lockhart here for you, sir.'

'Who?'

'Miss Lockhart.'

'Now?'

Vicky gazed, embarrassed, at the unappealing abstract painting on the wall opposite. Was this 'surprise' job offer also a surprise to the man in question, or were heads of organisations exempt from good manners?

'I did inform you a week ago...' Geraldine said, lapsing into her more autocratic voice.

'Show her in, Gerry, show her in.' At which, Geraldine pushed open the door wider and stepped back to allow Vicky through.

The man was sitting behind a huge desk, lounging in a black leather swivel chair which he had pushed away from the desk so that he could cross his legs in comfort.

Under the rapid pounding of her heart, Vicky was dimly aware of the door gently being shut behind her, and then she was left, stranded, in the middle of the large office, like a fish that had suddenly found itself floundering in the middle of a desert. Her breathing was laboured and she hardly dared move a muscle, because if she did she suspected that her shaky legs would collapse completely.

All she could see was the nightmare in front of her. The dark hair, the strong angular face, those peculiar grey eyes.

'Are you all right, Miss Lockhart?' The question was posed in an impatient voice from which could be dredged not even passing concern. 'You look as though you're about to faint and I really haven't got the time to deal with a fainting secretary.'

'I'm fine. Thank you.' Fine, she thought, considering the shock that had rocked her to the foundations. She was still standing, wasn't she? If that wasn't fine, what was?

'Then sit down.' He nodded curtly at the chair facing

him. 'I'm afraid it slipped my mind that you were supposed to be coming today... Your application form's somewhere here...bear with me for a moment...'

'That's fine!' Suddenly Vicky found her voice. 'In fact, there's no need to waste your time interviewing me. I don't think I would be suitable at all for this job.'

She just wanted to get out of the office and out of the building as fast as her legs could take her. Her skin was on fire and her temples were beginning to pound.

He didn't immediately answer. Instead, he paused in his search for the elusive CV and the pale grey eyes became suddenly watchful as they scanned her flushed face.

'Oh, really?' he said slowly. 'And why do you think that would be?' He stood up. A towering, well-built man, he strolled to the bay window behind his chair, from where he perched against the ledge, all the better to watch her.

Between the host of emotions and thoughts besieging her, Vicky tried to locate a functioning part of her brain which might come up with a good excuse for showing up at this company for a job, only to spuriously announce that she had to leave immediately. Nothing was forthcoming.

'You know, you *do* look a little nervous.' He brushed his chin reflectively with one finger while continuing to scrutinise her face with the lazy intensity of a predator eyeing up potential prey. 'Not one of these highly strung, neurotic types, are you?'

'Yes,' Vicky agreed, ready to clutch any lifeline offered that might get her out of the place, 'highly strung and very neurotic. No use to a man like you.'

'A man like me? And what kind of man might that be?'

Vicky dropped her eyes rather than reveal the answer to that particular question. The strength of the response she would give him might just blow him off his feet.

'Sit down, why don't you? You're beginning to interest

me, Miss Lockhart.' He waited until she had made her way
to the chair and flopped down, then allowed a few more
seconds to pass, during which he looked at her as though
trying to unravel the workings of her mind.

'Now, tell me why I'm beginning to feel that there's
something going on here that I know nothing about.'

'I don't know what you mean.'

'I'll let that pass.' He flashed her smile that indicated
that the subject had been dropped but by no means abandoned.

*He has a God complex, the bastard. He's always felt
that he could run my life, along with everyone else's.* She
could hear Shaun's voice, high and resentful as it always
had been whenever he spoke about his brother. Vicky's
tightly controlled mind slowly began to unravel as her eyes
locked with Max Hedley Forbes. Because that was his
name. She'd heard it often enough from Shaun's lips. A
litany of bitterness and antagonism towards a brother
whose mission in life, she'd been told often enough, had
been to undermine as many people as he could in the minimum amount of time. He'd been a monster of selfishness,
Shaun had said to her, a man who only knew how to take,
a man who rode roughshod over the rest of the human race
and most of all over his one and only brother, whose name
he'd discredited so thoroughly that even his father had
chosen to turn his back on his son.

It had never occurred to her when she applied for this
job that fate would be waiting for her just around the corner. Max Forbes lived in New York and had done for
years. She'd never thought that she would end up finding
him in an office building in Warwick, of all places. The
past squeezed her soul and she briefly closed her eyes,
giving in to the vertigo threatening to overwhelm her.

Shaun might have turned out to be a nightmare, but

nightmares were not born, they were made. The world and the people in it had shaped him, and the man coolly inspecting her now had been pivotal in the shaping of his brother. However awful Shaun had been, wasn't this man opposite her worse?

'So,' the dark, velvety voice drawled, dragging her away from her painful trip down memory lane and back to the present, 'you claim to be neurotic and highly strung, yet—' he reached forward to a stack of papers on the desk and extracted one, from which he read '—you still managed to sustain a reasonably high-powered job in Australia from which you left with glowing recommendations. Odd, wouldn't you agree? Or perhaps your neuroses were under control at that point in time?'

Vicky refrained from comment and instead contented herself with staring out of the window, which offered a view of sky and red-brick buildings.

'Has Geraldine given you any indication as to why this post has become available?' He moved around the desk and perched on it, so that he was directly facing Vicky, looking down at her.

'Not in any great detail, no,' Vicky told him, 'but honestly, there's no point launching into any explanations. The fact of the matter is...' What *was* the fact of the matter? 'The fact of the matter is that I had really set my heart on working in a typing pool...'

His lips twitched, but when he answered his voice was serious and considering.

'Of course. I quite understand that you might not want to compromise your undoubted talents by getting a good job with career prospects...'

Vicky shot him a brief look from under thick, dark lashes, momentarily disconcerted by the suggestion of humour beneath the sarcasm. 'I have an awful lot on my plate just now,' she said vaguely. 'I wouldn't want to take on anything demanding because I don't think that I would be able to do it justice.'

'What?'

'I beg your pardon?'

'*What* have you got on your plate?' His eyes scanned her CV then focused on her.

'Well,' Vicky stuttered, taken aback by the directness of the question, 'I've only recently returned from Australia and I have a lot of things to do concerning…my house and generally settling in…' This explanation skirted so broadly around the truth that she could feel the colour rise to her cheeks.

'Why did you decide to go to Australia?'

'My mother…passed away…I felt that the change would do me good…and I just happened to stay a great deal longer than I had anticipated. I landed a job in a very good company quite early on and I was promoted in the first six months. I…it was easier than coming back to England and dealing with…'

'Your loss?'

Vicky stiffened at the perceptiveness behind the question. She'd once considered Shaun to be a perceptive, sensitive person. Perhaps illusions along those lines ran in the Forbes family.

'I would appreciate it if we could terminate this interview now.' She began getting to her feet, smoothing down the dark grey skirt, nervously brushing non-existent flecks of dust from it rather than face those amazing, unsettling grey eyes. 'I'm sorry if I've wasted your time. I realise that you're a very busy man, and time is money. Had I been aware of the situation, I would have telephoned to cancel the appointment. As I said, I'm not interested in a job that's going to monopolise my free time.'

'Your references,' he said coolly, ignoring her pointed attempt to leave his office, 'from the Houghton Corporation are glowing...' He looked at her carefully while she remained in dithering uncertainty on her feet, unable to turn her back and walk out of the office but reluctant to sit back down and allow him to think that the job in question was open for debate. 'Very impressive, and all the more so because I know James Houghton very well.'

'You *know* him?' Several potential catastrophes presented themselves to her when she heard this and she weakly sat back down. It wouldn't do for Max Forbes to contact her old boss in Australia. There were too many secrets hidden away there, secrets she had no intention of disclosing.

'We went to school together a million years ago.' He pushed himself up from the desk and began prowling around the room, one minute within her line of vision, the next a disembodied voice somewhere behind her. If his tactic was to unsettle her, then he was going about it the right way. 'He's a good businessman. A recommendation from him counts for a hell of a lot.' He paused and the silence from behind her made the hairs on the back of her neck stand on end. 'Where in Australia did you live?'

'In the city. My aunt has a house there.' There was an element of danger in this line of questioning but Vicky had no idea how to retrieve the situation.

'Did much socialising?'

'With whom?' she asked cautiously. It would help, she thought, if he would return within her line of vision so that she could see the expression on his face—but then, on reflection, perhaps it wasn't a bad thing that she couldn't. After all, he would be able to see hers, and she had a great deal more to hide than he would ever have imagined in a million years.

'People from your work.' She could sense him as he walked slowly round to the side of her. His presence made her feel clammy and claustrophobic. Out of the corner of her eye, she could make him out as he lounged against the wall, hands shoved deep into his trouser pockets, head tilted slightly to one side as though carefully weighing up what she was saying. Weighing it up and, she thought with a flash of sudden foreboding, storing up every word to be used at a later date in evidence against her.

Not that there would *be* a later date, she reminded herself. Powerful though he was, he couldn't compel her to work for his company. He might grill her now because she had been stupid enough to make him think that there was more to her than met the eye, but very shortly she would be gone and he would be nothing more than a freakish reminder of how eerie coincidence could be. The thought of imminent escape steadied her nerves and she even managed to force a smile to her face.

'Off and on. I had a lot of friends in Sydney. The Australians are a very friendly lot.' She risked a sideways glance at him.

'So I've been told. My brother certainly thought so.'

'You had a brother out there?' A slow crawl of treacherous colour stole across her face and she could feel a fine perspiration begin to film above her lip.

'Shaun Forbes.' He allowed the name to register. 'My twin.'

He had never told her. She'd known Shaun for nearly a year and a half and he'd never once mentioned that the brother whose name he reviled was his identical twin. She imagined now that it must have been deeply galling to have so spectacularly failed to live up to a brother who had emerged from the womb at the same time as he had and had been given exactly the same upbringing and privileges, yet had succeeded.

Seeing Max Forbes had been a heart-stopping shock. There was enough in their physical make-up to send her spinning sickeningly back into the past and every memory she had spent so long trying to crush had reared their ugly heads with gleeful malice.

'He was quite prominent on the social scene, I gather.' His mouth twisted and he turned away and strode towards the desk.

'No. The name doesn't ring a bell.' The words almost got stuck in her throat. This was what it felt like to be toyed with by the devil, she thought. Life had not been easy since she'd returned to England. The last batch of tenants to occupy her mother's house had been cavalier in their treatment of it and, frustratingly, the estate agents who handled the rental had had nothing to say on the subject. So, on top of the uphill task of finding work and getting her finances straight, there was the little problem of the house, which needed a complete overhaul. Even the walls seemed to smell.

And then there was Chloe.

Vicky half closed her eyes and a wave of nausea rushed through her.

'I'm surprised, James spent a lot of time in his company. I might have expected that you would have seen him at some point in the offices.'

Vicky, whose vocal cords were failing to co-operate with her brain, shook her head and looked blankly at the man staring at her.

'No?' he prodded, glancing back down at her CV, and she made an inarticulate, choking sound by way of reply.

'Well, perhaps not. Shaun probably wouldn't have noticed you, anyway.'

That succeeded in clearing her head admirably. He surely couldn't have meant to insult her, but insult her he had. If only he knew that seek her out was precisely what his hideous brother had done. Charmed her with his smooth conversation and his offerings of flowers and empty flattery. Told her that she was destined to rescue him from himself, thanked her with tears in his eyes for making him want to be a better human being. And she'd fallen for all the claptrap—hook, line and sinker. It hadn't taken long before the mask had begun to disintegrate and she'd begun to see the ugliness behind the charming façade.

'Thank you very much,' she said coldly.

'Why did you decide to leave Australia if you had such a brilliant job and hectic social life?'

The question was irrelevant, considering she had no intention of working for the man, but fear of arousing yet more of his curiosity restrained her from telling him to mind his own business.

'I never intended to build my life out there. I felt that it was time to come back to England.'

Chloe. Everything had centred around Chloe.

'And you've had temp jobs since returning? The pay's pretty poor, wouldn't you agree?'

'I get by.' Lousy was the word for it.

'And you're living—?' For a minute, the piercing grey eyes left her face and perused the paper in front of him. '—just outside Warwick…rented place?'

'My mother left her house to me when she…died. It's been rented out for the past few years.'

He shoved the paper away from him, leaned back in his

chair with his hands folded behind his head and looked at her without bothering to disguise his curiosity.

'Young woman, who's just returned from abroad, and doubtless wants to refurnish house, rejects job that is vastly superior to the one for which she originally applied. Help me out there with a logical explanation? If there's one thing I can't stand, it's a mystery. I always feel that mysteries are there to be solved, and, by hook or by crook, guess what…?'

'What?' Vicky asked, mesmerised by his eyes. When she'd first met Shaun, the first thing she'd noticed had been his eyes. Those pale eyes and black hair and the chiselled, beautiful lines of his face. He was like an Adonis. If she'd had any sense, she would have seen past the outside to the man within and it wouldn't have taken her long to notice the weakness behind the good looks, the restless feverish energy of a man who needed to find his fixes outside himself, the mouth that could thin to a cruel line in a matter of seconds.

With that in mind, it sickened her that she could feel something inside her tighten alarmingly at the sight of his twin.

'I always get to the bottom of them.' He gave her a slow, dangerous smile and she shivered.

Max Forbes was so like his brother, and yet so dissimilar in ways that she couldn't quite put her finger on. If Shaun's looks had captivated because of their prettiness, his brother's hypnotised because of their power, and if Shaun had always known what to say to get the girls into bed, Vicky imagined that his brother achieved what he wanted by the very fact that he disregarded the normal little social conventions and said precisely what he wanted, despite the consequences. He had the sort of rugged, I'll-do-as-I-damn-well-want charisma that women, she suspected, would find difficult to resist. Even Geraldine Hogg had become coy in his presence.

Max Forbes looked at the small figure on the chair. She looked more like a child than a woman, with that pointed elfin face and pale, freckled skin. The picture of innocence. But his instincts were telling a different story. Something was not quite above board and his desire to find out *what* surprised him. He hadn't felt so damned *curious* about anyone for a long time. He stared at her and felt a rush of satisfied pleasure when she blushed and looked away quickly.

Oh, yes. Life had ceased to be merely an affair of making money and making love, both with a great deal of flair and, lately, not much pleasure or satisfaction. Vicky Lockhart had something to hide and the thought of discovering what sent a ripple of enjoyment through him. It was a sensation so alien that it took him a few seconds to recognise what it was.

'Oh, how very interesting,' she said politely, her brown eyes widening. The sun, streaming through the window, caught her hair and seemed to turn it to flames.

It was, he thought, a most unusual shade of red, and, connoisseur that he was, he was almost certain that it hadn't come out of a bottle. Of course, she wasn't his type. Not at all. He'd always gone for tall, full-breasted women, but still, he felt his mind wander as he imagined what that hair would look like, were it not pulled back. How long was it? Long, he imagined. Long and unruly. Nothing at all like the sleek-haired women he dated. Did the hair, he wondered, match the personality? Underneath that sweet, childish façade was there a hot, steamy, untamed woman bursting to get out? He smiled at the passing thought and was startled to find that his body had responded rather too vigorously to the image he'd mentally conjured up. Getting aroused like this made him feel like an adolescent, and he cleared his throat in a business-like fashion.

'I don't know if Geraldine mentioned the pay...' He waited for her curiosity to take the bait, then he rattled off a sum that was roughly twice what he'd had in mind for the job in question. He could see the glimmer of interest illuminate the brown eyes and her small fists clenched at the sides of the chair as though she had to steady herself.

'That's a very generous salary. She did mention that the pay would be more than the job advertised in the newspaper...'

She wanted to accept. He could see it written on her face and he waited patiently for her to nod her head.

'But, really, I'm afraid I must say no.'

It took a few seconds for that to sink in.

'What?' Not much floored him, but for a passing moment he could feel himself rendered speechless.

'I can't accept.'

He looked at the small, elfin face, the delicate mouth, the soft brown eyes fringed with impossibly long auburn lashes, and was assailed by a humiliating sensation of powerlessness. He couldn't *make* her accept his offer—he wasn't even that sure *why* he was so infuriated by her refusal; he just knew that he wanted to shake her until she agreed to work for him. The absurdity of his reaction was enough to make him shake his head and smile. He must be losing his mind. Wrapping up New York and then moving to the UK must have conspired to bring about some kind of subliminal breakdown, or else why would he now be staring at a perfect stranger and feeling this way?

He glanced down at the desk and began drumming his pen on it.

'Of course, if I can't persuade you...'

'I'm flattered that you've been prepared to try...' She stood up and gave him an awkward and, he was irritated to see, relieved smile.

'Thousands of people would kill for the job offer I've just made you.' He heard his over-hearty voice and bared his teeth in a smile of good-mannered regret. His eyes flicked to her face and he could feel himself stiffen once again at the thought of what she would look like with her hair down. Then, to his utter disgust, and completing his inexorable decline into pubescent irrationality, he glanced down at her breasts, two small bumps underneath the bulk of shirt and jacket, and wondered what they would be like. Tiny, he imagined. Small, pointed, freckled with rosy nipples. Red hair tumbling down a naked body and rose-peaked breasts just big enough to fit into his...

He virtually gulped and was obliged, as he stood up, to conceal his treacherous body by leaning forward on the desk and supporting himself on his hands.

'Are you quite sure you won't reconsider...?'

'Quite sure.' She looked at him uncertainly, then stretched out her hand, which he took and shook, paying lip service to good manners. He could tell that even that small gesture was not one she particularly wanted to make but courtesy had compelled her.

What was her story?

He made her nervous, but *why*? He didn't threaten her...or did he? He wondered whether they'd met before, but he was sure that he would have remembered. There was something unforgettable about the ethereal delicacy of that face and the teasing disarray of that remarkable hair. She *had* been to Australia, however...

'If I speak to James, I shall mention I've met you,' he murmured, walking her to the door and he felt the momentary pause in her steps.

'Of course. And do you…keep in regular touch with him?'

'I used to. He occasionally kept an eye on my wayward brother.'

'And he no longer does?'

He picked up the struggle in her voice with interest.

'My brother died a while back in a car crash, Miss Lockhart.'

Vicky nodded, and instead of proffering the usual mutterings of sympathy rested her hand on the door knob and turned it, ready to flee. She knew that she should express some kind of courteous regret at that, but honesty stopped her from doing so. She had no regrets at Shaun's fate. To forgive was divine, but it wasn't human, and she had no aspirations to divinity.

'Well, perhaps we'll meet again.' *Perhaps, indeed. Much sooner than you think.*

'I doubt it.' She smiled and pulled open the door. 'But thanks for the job offer, anyway. And good luck in finding someone for the post.'

CHAPTER TWO

THE GARDEN had been the most distressing sight to greet her upon her return to England and to the modest three-bedroom cottage that had been her mother's. She'd more or less expected to find the house in something of a state. It had seen a variety of tenants, not all of them reliable family units, and even when her mother had been alive it had been in dire need of repair. But the garden had broken her heart. A combination of young children, cigarette-smoking teenagers and, from the looks of things, adults with hobnailed boots had rendered it virtually unrecognisable.

One more thing, she thought wearily, to bring to the attention of the agency that had handled the letting, although what precisely the point of doing that would be, she had no idea. Marsha, the woman in whose hands Vicky had hurriedly but confidently left the house, had left the firm eighteen months back, and since then the house had been handled by a series of people, none of whom had done justice to it. Perhaps they'd thought that she would never return to England, or at least not quite as unexpectedly as she had in the end.

It broke her heart to think of all the time and effort that her mother had spent in the small, immaculate garden. A decade ago, it had been her salvation after the death of her husband, Vicky's father, and it had steadfastly seen her through her ups and downs, providing comfort and soothing her when her illness took hold and she no longer had the energy to go walking or attempt anything energetic.

24

She'd laid borders and hedgerows and planted wild roses and shrubbery with the imagination of someone whose every other outlet had been prematurely barred. Vicky could remember the summer evenings spent out in it, listening to the sounds of nature and appreciating the tumult of colour.

The cottage was set back at the end of a lane in a part of Warwickshire noted for its rural beauty. The small garden, now sporting an interesting array of weeds which formed a charming tangle around the occasional outcrop of lager bottles, ambled down to a white fence, beyond which stretched cultivated fields. A plot of reasonably well-maintained land bordered by trees separated the cottage from its neighbour, a rather more substantial family house to the right. To the left woodland kept the well-used roads at bay.

Vicky, sweating in her layers of clothing and grimy with the exertions of her Saturday morning garden clear-out, peered through some bush at yet another aluminium can. Robert 'call-me-Robbie' at the agency had assured her that whatever she'd found in the garden had not been there when the house and grounds had been inspected, and she knew, anyway, that she was pretty late to be lodging complaints about the state of the garden. Only recently had she managed to find the time to do anything other than superficially maintain it, a thirty-minute job whenever she found the time to spare.

This was the first time she'd really got stuck in, and that only because she'd managed to farm Chloe out to one of her playmates from school.

The thought of her five-year-old daughter automatically brought a smile to her lips.

At least she had no worries on that front. Chloe had

taken to the school and her classmates like a duck to water and that had been an enormous source of relief.

She stuck on her gardening glove, wriggled her hand into the undergrowth, half her mind still playing with the thought of her gorgeous raven-haired daughter, so different physically from her, and the other half preoccupied with the unwelcome thought that she might find one or two bugs in addition to the can, and was about to reach for the offending object when a voice said from behind her,

'Thought I might find you here. Hope I'm not interrupting anything.'

The shock of the voice sent her falling face-first into the bush, and when she emerged, after a short struggle with greenery, earth and some unfortunate spiky things, she was decidedly the worse for wear.

'What are *you* doing here?' She hadn't even rescued the can!

Max Forbes, in the bracing winter sunshine, looked horribly, impossibly *good*. The brisk wind had ruffled his dark hair so that it sprang away from his face in an endearingly boyish way that was at odds with the powerful angularity of his features, and as his trench coat blew open she spotted a casual attire of dark trousers and a thick cream jumper with a pale-coloured shirt underneath. The shock of seeing him in her garden and the impact of his presence made her take a couple of steps back.

'Be careful you don't fall into the bush again.'

'*What* are you doing here?' Now that her slow-witted brain had come to terms with his looming great masculine presence, her thought patterns suddenly shot into fifth gear, and the realisation that Chloe was out for the morning was enough to render her weak-kneed with relief.

'Actually, I've just come from your neighbours down

the road. Small world, wouldn't you say? Thompsons. Live three houses away.'

'I don't know the names of the people here, aside from the elderly couple opposite.'

'So I thought I'd drop in, see whether you'd managed to find yourself a job as yet.'

Standing opposite him, head tilted at an awkward angle because without heels she was a good ten inches shorter than him, Vicky felt small, grubby and disadvantaged. The long braid hanging down her back was an insult to anyone with a sense of style and there was mud and soil all over her face, clothes, hands—probably in her hair as well. Her sturdy wellingtons were covered in muck. When she removed the gardening gloves, she would doubtless find that they matched the state of her nails.

'It's only been three days and no luck yet. Thank you.' She refused to budge even though the cold was seeping through her jumper and waxed jacket and making her shiver. She stuck her hands in the pockets of the jacket and glared at him.

'Too bad.'

'I'm sure something will turn up.'

'Oh, I don't know. Jobs in typing pools are thin on the ground. 'Course, you'll have no trouble getting something much better paid with infinitely more prospects, but who needs *that* sort of work?'

There was a veiled amusement in his voice that only made her more addled and crosser than she already was.

'Look, why don't we go inside? I've got time for a cup of tea and you can tell me all about Australia.'

'There's nothing to tell.' A telltale pulse was beating rhythmically in the hollow of her neck and the little bud of panic that had begun to sprout the minute she'd heard his voice flowered into full bloom.

They couldn't possibly go inside. Chloe wasn't around, but signs of her were everywhere. He didn't know that she had a child and that was the way she intended it to remain. It had been the only piece of sheer luck since meeting him. She'd answered the advertisement and had sheepishly omitted to mention Chloe simply because she had gleaned from several sources that a child in the background prompted awkward questions about childcare and being a single parent; this was the road to certain rejection by any company. School and Betsy, the lady who helped her out in the evenings sometimes, meant that there were no problems on the childcare front, and she reckoned, naively, that if she ever got offered a job she would inform her employers at that point and hope that they would take her on the strength of her interview, even once they knew of Chloe's existence.

Max looked down at her and confusingly wanted to do a number of things at the same time. First, he wanted to clear out, because he had no idea what had possessed him to go there in the first place. Unfortunately, and much to his immense frustration, he also wanted to stay put, because seeing her again had somehow managed to render him even more intrigued than he'd been on their first encounter. He also wanted to brush some of that dirt off her face, if only to see what her reaction would be. In fact, the urge to do just that was so powerful that he clasped his hands behind his back and purposely looked away.

'Actually, I haven't just dropped by,' he said eventually, resenting her for putting him in a position where he was about to embark on an out-and-out lie and resenting himself for his own pathetic weakness that had brought him here to start with.

'Oh, no?' she asked warily.

'It's to do with your house, as a matter of fact.'

'What? What's to do with my house?'

'Why don't we go inside and talk about it?' He didn't think that he had ever been so bloody underhanded in his life before, and all because he hadn't been able to get this chit of a girl out of his head. She had fired up his interest, for reasons he couldn't fathom, and now here he was, behaving like some shady character in a third-rate movie. He had never, *but never*, done anything remotely like this in *his entire life* because of a woman, and he could hardly believe that he was doing it now. Conniving like a two-bit criminal.

She didn't say anything. Instead, she headed towards the house, leaning forward into the wind, which looked as though it might just lift her off her feet and sweep her away if she wasn't careful. Max followed behind by a few paces, his teeth clenched in exasperation as she told him to wait outside until she'd tidied herself up.

He raised his eyebrows in amusement. 'Why outside?'

'Because,' Vicky said coldly, 'it's my house and that's what I'm telling you to do.' Upon which she promptly shut the door in his face before he could open his mouth to protest further.

She had never moved with more speed. The house was thankfully clean, and in under three minutes she'd managed to stash away all evidence of her daughter. It took her a further five minutes to sling off the grubby clothes and replace them with a pair of faded jeans and a long-sleeved striped jumper that had seen better days. The hair would have to remain in its charming grass-ridden style.

'So,' she said, yanking open the door to surprise him leaning against it, 'what about my house?'

'Has anyone ever mentioned to you that you are completely eccentric?'

'No.' She led the way into the sitting room, which had been the first room in the house to undergo redecoration and was now in restful greens and creams and blessedly free of childish clutter. She glanced at her watch and saw that it was at least another two hours before Chloe was dropped back to the house. More than enough time to get rid of Max Forbes, whose presence was enough to bring her out in a cold sweat.

'My house,' she reminded him bluntly, once she had installed him in a chair. 'I won't sit,' she said. 'I feel filthy. Now, what about my house?'

'I can't conduct a conversation like this.' He shook his head and stood up. 'Which is a shame because I think you'd be very interested in what I have to say, but if your ill manners override your self-interest, then—' he shrugged eloquently '—at least I tried…'

Vicky looked at him doubtfully. He really shouldn't be here at all, and she knew that she should just throw him out. In fact, she should never have let him in in the first place. Hadn't this been the same old story with his brother? From the minute she'd set eyes on him, she'd known that he was bad news. He'd been too good-looking, too smooth-talking and too well connected to be interested in a girl like her, but he'd stopped at her desk where she'd been working with her head down and he'd leaned over just enough for her to feel overpowered by him. Everything she'd said, even *Please go away, I really must get on with my work* had seemed to amuse him, and he had had a way of laughing deep in his throat, a sexy laugh, while his eyes never left her face, that had made her feel uncomfortable and excited at the same time.

So if Shaun had achieved that with her, then how much

more dangerous was his brother, who had struck her as being leagues ahead of him? And if her own need to protect herself wasn't sufficient to keep her away from Max Forbes, then what about her daughter?

Dark-haired, grey-eyed, Chloe had been the spitting image of Shaun from the day of her birth. There was no way under the sun she could have been anything but a Forbes, and time had strengthened rather than lessened the resemblance.

If only theirs had been the tried and tested failed romance. If only Shaun had done the decent thing and walked away from her and his baby so that they could live their lives in peace. But, like all weak men, Shaun had needed his punch bag, and she had been his. He had rarely raised his hand to her, and then only under the influence of drink or drugs, but he hadn't needed to go down that road to gain her compliance. All he'd had to do was threaten to take Chloe away from her. It had suited him to pretend to the world that he had never fathered a child, but he'd always taken great satisfaction in reminding her in private that if his family ever discovered his progeny then they would move in to claim what they would feel was rightfully theirs. Especially, he'd been fond of saying, if they could see the uncanny resemblance she bore to the Forbes clan.

So, however painful it was to her, she'd lived in the shadow of fear. Sometimes days would pass, weeks even, and there would be no sign of him. Then he would return and demand his sexual privileges—and she had slept with him and wept bitter tears afterwards.

To have Max Forbes under her roof was to have Lucifer with the key to her front door. She'd heard enough about him to know that the existence of Chloe would be of great interest to him. Would he try and spirit her away, or take

her through the courts for custody? Ninety-nine point nine
per cent of her knew that her child was safe, but that
nought point one per cent was enough to terrify.

She'd spent years protecting her daughter from an abu-
sive man. She'd watched in helpless fear as he'd wielded
his power over them both, smilingly and ruthlessly intimidating. Vicky had lived on a knife's edge, waiting in
dreaded expectation of the worst. Now, Vicky knew she
must keep Chloe's existence a secret from Max. For all
she knew, these brothers might have more in common than
mere appearance. Much more. And she had not escaped
from one destructive cycle only to find herself hooked into
another. She would never give a man that power over her
again. Never.

Max was standing by the door, saying something, and
Vicky's attention snapped back to the present. The house.
She couldn't afford to run into problems with the house.
She had barely begun to find her feet and Chloe could do
without any more changes in her life.

'Sit down. Please. I might as well hear what you have
to say.' She nodded to the chair which he had just vacated
and he appeared to give her request some thought.

'You seem to act as though *I'm* doing *you* a favour. I
assure you, Miss Lockhart, you couldn't be further from
the truth.'

'I'm sorry. I have…things on my mind.'

'Why don't you go and change? Clean clothes might
improve your temper.'

She frowned and looked very much as though she would
have liked to argue that particular point with him, but instead she informed him that she would bring him a cup of
tea, or coffee.

That, she thought, should keep him anchored in one
place. The last thing she needed was Max Forbes prowling

through her house. At least the sitting room—the one place that was kept neat at all times, even if the rest of the cottage was in a state of disarray—contained relatively few personal bits and pieces. She'd stuffed the pictures of Chloe in the weather-beaten pine trunk behind the sofa, and the books that lined the bookshelf on either side of the fireplace were the sort of everyday reading that gave nothing away. The ornaments had mostly belonged to her mother and had been retrieved from the attic where they had been stored while the house had been rented out. It was true what they said about there being safety in anonymity.

When she returned to the sitting room with a mug of tea, it was to find him innocently perusing the newspaper which had been lying on the low, square battered pine table in front of the fireplace. She almost said *Good*, but managed to resist the temptation.

'I won't be a moment,' she told him stiffly, and, just in case he got any ideas about exploring the place, she firmly shut the sitting room door behind her. Then she looked at her watch, to make sure that time was still on her side.

Showering and changing took a matter of fifteen minutes. Self-beautification, even if the situation demanded it, was something she rarely did. Now, she just changed into a clean pair of jeans, a clean T-shirt and rebraided her hair without going to the bother of combing out all the knots, of which there would be thousands. Later, she would wash and shampoo her hair.

'Now,' she said, slipping into the room and seeing, with relief, that he was still absorbed in the newspaper, 'you were going to tell me about my house.'

'Have you heard the rumours?'

'What rumours?'

'About the supermarket. Perhaps I should say *hyper-*

market, because apparently there'll be parking for hundreds of cars. If not thousands.'

Vicky, sitting cross-legged on the large comfy chair facing him, looked at him in horror. For a minute, she actually forgot that she was supposed to be on guard. She leaned forward, elbows on thighs, mouth open.

'You're joking.'

'Horrendous, isn't it? I can't bear those sprawling supermarkets myself. I much prefer smaller, more personal places to shop. Between Fortnum and Mason's and Harrods, I've never had a problem finding what I want. Tell me, is there an equivalent here, by any chance?' Now that he had launched into his lie, he couldn't wait to distance himself from it. He glanced at her face and discovered that he couldn't tear his eyes away. Her mouth was slightly parted and sitting like that, all folded into the chair in a way he had never seen a woman do before, she looked even more appealingly vulnerable. The T-shirt was small and close fitting and lovingly outlined her small, rounded breasts. He had to remind himself that he was only there because she had posed a mystery and he hated mysteries, and not because he was attracted to her, even though his mind kept churning up some embarrassingly graphic images of her body, unencumbered by clothing.

Frustratingly, she seemed to have no interest in him whatsoever. As a man who was accustomed to women looking at him, uninterest was proving to be a powerful aphrodisiac.

'Who told you this?' she asked, after a few seconds of shocked silence.

'No one and everyone. You know how it is with rumours. No one will admit to being the one who starts it. I mean, it may be entirely without foundation and certainly, in the business I'm in, I'm sure I would have *seen* something, something rather more substantial than gossip, but—' he sighed, reluctantly focusing his attention on the bookshelf behind her '—I feel better about telling you.'

'My house won't be worth a thing if a supermarket goes up opposite!' Vicky burst out on the verge of tears. 'Not that I want to sell up, but...'

'I'm sure it's all a load of tosh,' Max said hurriedly, guiltily seeing the sheen in her eyes.

'What if it's not?' She couldn't help herself. A supermarket! No, a *hypermarket*, with parking for ten thousand cars! It was the last straw. She blinked and, of its own accord, a tear trickled down her face. Her reaction appalled and dismayed her, but there seemed nothing she could do to stifle the ridiculous leakage.

She was hardly aware of what was happening until she felt Max perch on the wide upholstered arm of the chair and he dabbed the handkerchief at her face. With a groan of despair, Vicky took it from him and did a better job of mopping herself up, then she leant her head back and closed her eyes with a deep sigh.

'Look, I should never have said what I did.' Little did she know, he thought, how sincerely he meant that. He reached out and stroked some hair away from her face, then carried on stroking her damp cheeks. Her skin was like satin and, up close, her freckles made a fascinating pattern across the bridge of her nose. His thumb slid a bit further down and, finding no deterrent, lightly brushed her mouth.

'No, it's just as well to be prepared.' She opened her eyes and looked at him. There was a gentleness in his eyes that was unexpected enough to make the breath catch in her throat.

'I could find out easily enough whether there's truth behind the rumour,' he told her softly, feeling himself harden as he carried on stroking her face. The woman was an enigma. He could hardly remember why he thought that she was hiding something. Right now, she was no more than a vulnerable girl and she was bringing out all sorts of ridiculously protective feelings he'd never known he possessed.

'Could you?' she asked urgently, her eyes flicking across his face. 'Do you think you could? It would mean a great deal to me.' In the brief silence, she became aware of his fingers on her face and she sprang away, pressing herself back into the chair and looking at him.

'I could,' he said. He strolled back to his chair and crossed his legs, then he slowly looked around him, as though taking in his surroundings for the first time. 'You know, I can't remember whether I mentioned this at the interview, but I could arrange to have building work done on this cottage at a nominal cost. The roof looks as though it could do with an overhaul and your fireplace is going.'

'But I don't work for you.' She paused and looked at him, while her hand idly rubbed her ankle tucked up on the chair. 'I don't understand why you're so keen to hire me.' There was genuine curiosity behind the question. *She* knew why she couldn't accept his offer of a job, but she had no idea why he'd continued to try and persuade her, even when it was patently obvious that she wasn't interested.

Max sighed a long, resigned sigh and watched her from under his lashes. He could still feel the softness of her skin under his. 'I'm desperate. That's the bottom line. I've been here for seven months during which time I've had a series of temps, none of whom seemed capable of thinking on their feet, and none of the applicants for the job on a permanent basis were suitable.'

'*None* of them?'

'That's right,' he said a little irritably, because there was an element of incredulous accusation in her voice that implied some kind of fault on his part.

'What was wrong with all of them?'

'Pretty much a combination of everything, actually.'

'Perhaps you're a bit too demanding,' Vicky volunteered helpfully, and her suggestion was met with a frown of instant and instinctive denial.

'I'm the least demanding boss I know. All I ask is a certain amount of initiative and common sense, along with the ability to do the usual things.'

'And how do you know *I* would have possessed the right qualities?' For the very briefest of moments, she put aside her fears of the man sitting opposite her and she could feel his personality working on her. In a minute, she told herself, she would put her defences back in place, but right now a rush of simple gratitude towards him had mellowed her. She found herself watching him intently, noticing, as she did so, how huge the differences were between him and Shaun, even though, at first glance, she'd been bowled over by their similarities. His face, she realised, was stronger, and stamped with lines of humour that had been missing from his brother's. His mouth was fuller, or perhaps that was just an optical illusion born of the fact that he just seemed more in command and more quietly self-assured than his brother. He lacked the ready smile that spoke of self-obsession and the carefully groomed look of someone to whom appearances were everything. In fact, the harder she stared at him, the less he seemed to resemble Shaun.

'Because you worked successfully for a man I have long respected,' he said simply. 'Aside from that, my first impression was favourable and I'm rarely wrong when it comes to first impressions.'

'Well, you should be,' Vicky heard herself say, her voice laced with creeping bitterness. She looked away and began toying with the end of her braid, flicking it back and forth, aware that two spots of burning colour had appeared on her cheeks.

Now, he thought, was not the time to probe deeper into that enigmatic little remark. She wasn't looking at him, in itself significant, but he could tell by the sudden flare of colour into her pale face that her reply had been instinctive and spontaneous, and that it had been prompted by *something*, some past and probably dark experience. He felt another spurt of intense curiosity, all the more destabilising because it was unaccustomed, and he had to resist the urge to barge in and whittle an explanation out of her. Women had always been an open book for him. To suddenly find himself stumped by one whose pages appeared to be firmly glued together was more than a novelty. He was discovering, to his amazement, the power of a challenge.

'Perhaps I should be,' he agreed. 'Maybe I'm more naïve than I think.'

The thought of the man sitting opposite her *ever* being naïve was almost enough to make her burst out laughing.

'Look,' he said quickly, 'I'll lay all my cards on the table. I have a gut feeling that you and I could work well together. I've suffered everything over the past few months, from misfiling to complete incomprehension when it comes to transcribing the gist of some of my more technical letters...' Something of an exaggeration, he thought to himself, but what the heck? 'Not to mention girls who can hardly think straight when they're around me...' He watched her surreptitiously to see what the impact of that comment would be, whether he might read some tacit agreement in her expression, and huffily saw that if anything her eyebrows had flickered upwards in contempt and incredulity.

'I don't think I could bear working for a man who considered himself God's gift to the female sex,' Vicky informed him coldly.

'I don't believe that's *quite* what I—'

'Someone who assumes that every woman in the room is eager and panting to climb into bed with him, someone who can't exist without a comb in his jacket pocket and a sporty car to prop up his self-image—'

'You seem to have totally misunders—'

'Swanning around, giving orders in between gazing at himself in the nearest mirror and then when all's said and done assuming that it's his right to do as he likes with whomever he wants, because he happened to be born with a passably good-looking face—'

'Hold on!'

Just at that very instant the telephone rang, and Vicky leapt up out of her chair and hurried into the hall to answer it. She was still trembling from her tirade because his passing remark had brought back a flood of memories, memories of Shaun and his serial infidelity, his addiction to proving his power over women, his swaggering, arrogant assumption that it was his right to break any female's heart if he so wanted. Her brain was still whirring around in angry circles when she heard Pat Down's voice down the line and it took her a few seconds to register that Chloe would be dropped back earlier than planned.

'I'm ever so sorry, Vicky, but my mum's been rushed to hospital with a heart attack so I shall drop her off in about ten minutes, if that's all right with you.' The voice down the line was just managing to bear up.

'Ten minutes...' Vicky repeated on a sharply indrawn breath.

'Sorry.'

'No, no, that's absolutely fine. Do you need me to hang on to Jess for you?' But no, she would take Jess with her to see her mother and she'd be by in a little under ten minutes.

Vicky hung up and flew into the sitting room like a whirlwind.

'It's time for you to go!' she ordered him frantically. 'I...I...I've suddenly remembered a very important appointment. In fact, that was the person in charge...calling to see whether I was still interested...in the job...'

'On a Saturday?' Max asked, not moving.

With a groan of desperation, Vicky grabbed his arm and began pulling him to his feet. Bad move. It appeared to make him even less inclined to vacate the sofa.

'Get up!' she finally shouted. 'Can't you see I'm in a rush?'

'And I'm trying to figure out why. No respectable company drags interviewees in on a weekend. Have you applied for something shady, perhaps? Some seedy stripping job in a nightclub somewhere?'

'Do I *look* like the sort of girl who's willing to strip in a nightclub?' she virtually screeched, hustling him to the sitting room door and attempting to shoo him out in the style of a chicken trying to get rid of a wolf from its parlour.

'Give me a minute to think about that one,' he said slowly, stopping in his tracks to her intense frustration. She glared at him and he grinned back at her.

It was the first time he had really smiled and the effect was breathtaking. Literally, it made her gasp. It changed the hard contours of his face and gave him a boyish, sexy look that was as far removed from the plastic smiles of his brother as chalk was from cheese.

'Not funny,' she said sharply.

'Take the job?'

In under five minutes there would be the sound of a car stopping outside the house, the ring of the doorbell and her daughter would come bouncing through the front door, bringing her infectious smile, her rosy cheeks and a seething nest of potential catastrophes.

She had to get rid of him.

'All right! *Now* will you please leave my house so that I can get on with…with…with my life?'

He straightened up and looked at her with a shadow of surprise. 'Starting Monday?'

'Starting Monday,' she agreed, hopping in frustration from one leg to another.

She managed to propel him to the front door, which she swiftly pulled open, breathing a sigh of relief that a small blue car wasn't hurtling down the lane in the direction of her cottage.

'Report to Personnel,' he told her, 'then come to my office and we'll take it from there.'

'Goodbye!'

'And perhaps you could do something about your eccentric line in conversation?'

'I shall see you on Monday!' She urged him out of the door and watched as he headed down the short path to the road, making sure that his car was safely out of sight before she closed it back. When it was, she slammed shut the door and leaned heavily against it, wondering what the hell she had just done.

It had been *imperative* that he left the premises before Chloe returned, she argued silently to herself, and what better method of shifting him than to agree to his proposals? Even though the logical, rational side of her brain freely accepted this as a worthwhile argument, the rest of her was appalled at the hole she had dug and into which she had recklessly jumped.

She told herself that she would turn up on Monday and work for a few weeks, then apologetically make her excuses and leave. She mentally listed some of the plus points that could be gained from her manoeuvre. This required more thought, but in the end she decided that, aside from the financial windfall to be had, she would also be able to keep an eye on him and allay his suspicious interest in her which she had sensed from the very beginning. Wasn't it a good idea for her to be in place so that she could make sure that he didn't start telephoning Australia and asking his friend about her? For starters he would learn about the pregnancy. Her connection with his brother might take longer, because she had been adamant about keeping her work life distinct from her private life and had discouraged Shaun from ever showing up at her workplace once they had started dating. But he could find out if he persevered. At least she would be on the spot to laughingly fend off any questions and deter him from snooping. She'd seen the curiosity her odd behaviour had aroused in him and she suspected that he was the sort of man to whom any intrigue was simply something to be unravelled. He could probably do *The Times* crossword in a matter of seconds.

Less palatable was the unpleasant suspicion that something about him had got under her skin. She'd learned so many lessons from Shaun, enough to put her off men for a lifetime. She would rather shoot herself than admit any kind of attraction to his brother.

In the end, though, she now had a problematic situation which she would have to deal with in whatever manner was at her disposal.

CHAPTER THREE

VICKY spent the remainder of the weekend repenting for her reckless agreement to work for Max Forbes. The reason *why* she had rushed into her hasty decision was rapidly forgotten under the onslaught of serious drawbacks. By the time Monday morning rolled around, she found herself slipping on her customary secretarial garb with a leaden heart which was only partially alleviated when, once at the office, she was informed by the personnel officer that Max only worked part-time at this particular office. When the young girl mentioned his name, her eyelids fluttered and her cheeks turned bright red. Vicky wondered sceptically whether *all* the female employees of the company responded in the same way to the mere mention of their boss. If that was the case, then she would have more to contend with than the dangerous fragility of her situation—namely overriding nausea at being surrounded by mesmerised females from nine in the morning to five-thirty at night.

No wonder he rated himself as such a potent sex symbol. She almost clicked her tongue in annoyance.

'I don't suppose he's in London *now*, is he?' she asked the personnel officer, whose name was Mandy and whose fashion statement included disconcertingly long and brightly painted blue fingernails.

'Actually, I believe he's set aside his morning to show you the ropes.'

'Oh, grand!' Vicky exclaimed with dismay, which she hid under a scarily bright smile. The smile remained plastered to her face as she was shown the now familiar route

43

up to his office, only slipping when Mandy deserted her and she found herself pushing back the door to his sanctuary.

After a break of a day and a half, during which the image of him had not left her head for longer than five minutes at a stretch, the sight of him now, in the flesh, was even more alarming than she remembered.

Had he been so *big and muscular* when she had seen him on Saturday or had he somehow grown in the interim? Even sitting behind the desk, reclining in his leather chair, his size seemed to spring out at her and reduce her to nervous, powerless pulp. He had discarded his jacket; his blue and white pin-striped shirt was cuffed to the elbows.

'Ah,' was his first word, which smacked of satisfaction, 'I wasn't too sure that you'd make it here. Good trip in? I gather you've already been through the nitty-gritty with Mandy. I've set aside a couple of hours to fill you in on some of the more straightforward bits of the job, then I'm afraid I've got to leave you to get on with it. So sit down and I'll begin briefing you on your duties.' He paused to recline comfortably in his chair. 'First of all, the coffee machine—it's in the corner of your office outside...'

Vicky, who had primly fished out a notepad and pen from her voluminous handbag, fixed him with a long, beady stare and he grinned at her.

'Just a joke.'

'I do realise that tea- and coffee-making *is* included in my job specification, but I hope it only plays a minor role.' She heard herself with a small, inner groan of disgust. The more addled he made her feel, the more unnatural her patterns of speech seemed to become, and right now she was feeling very, very addled.

'Very minor,' he agreed gravely. 'In fact, I *do* frequently make myself a cup of coffee and it's been known for me to make one for my secretary as well.' He rested his elbows on his desk and brought the tips of his fingers together so that he could survey her over them. It made her feel like a specimen in a laboratory.

'Have you maintained an office in London?' she asked politely. 'I ask because Mandy in Personnel mentioned that you split your time between here and London.'

'And New York, Madrid and Glasgow…I don't suppose you've had a chance to read any of the company literature…' He got up and strode towards a glass-fronted sleekly black bookcase that adorned one wall of the office and extracted a handful of glossy brochures, which he proceeded to hand over to her; then, instead of returning to his swivel chair, he perched on his desk, so that she had an uncomfortably close-up view of his muscular thighs, stretching taut against the fine wool fabric of his trousers.

'No, I haven't.' She idly flicked through one and her hand stopped as she saw a picture of Shaun standing next to Max and between them a man who could only have been their father. The blood in her veins started to curdle.

'My brother,' Max said shortly, following her gaze.

'The three of you founded the business?' Her voice was devoid of expression, even though she discovered that she was surprisingly curious about what his version of past events would be, because there always were the two sides to every story, but a shutter had dropped over his eyes.

'Not quite. You can look at that stuff later, perhaps take it home with you. For now, I'll fill you in on some of the projects we're working on.' He nodded at the door, inviting her to precede him out of his office and into hers which lay just through the door and which housed the filing cabinets. Like all the rest of the furniture in both the offices, the cabinets were all in black wood with chrome handles.

'Normally, my last secretary would have been responsible for taking you through this, but in this case, there's been no *last* secretary and the *last* temp didn't seem to grasp the meaning of the words "filing system", so she would have been of no use whatsoever. Anyway—' he gesticulated towards three cabinets '—the files are kept in there and should be in alphabetical order, although I'd advise you to go through the lot of them yourself. Louise found the alphabet a little exhausting. Those files over there are in the process of being looked at for whatever reason and those need updating. Your computer is over there and I'm afraid there's a stack of work for you to get your teeth into.'

'What kind of work?' Vicky idly went to the large U-shaped desk and flicked through the top file, which seemed comprised of lengthy technical documents and detailed price quotations.

'You'll naturally also be expected to handle all my business engagements and update my diary at least twice a day. Oh, yes, and meetings—I'll expect you to come along to some of the more important ones to take notes. Occasionally, there may be a social function I'll want you to attend.'

'That won't be possible,' Vicky said quickly, without thinking.

'All things in life are possible,' he told her softly, moving across to her. 'How else can anyone ever achieve anything in life, if they automatically assume that some things are not possible? *Why* will the occasional social function be out of the question? Is there any particular reason?'

'No. I just thought…that…social functions might require a more glamorous escort than your secretary…'

'Mmm. I see.' He left it there, neither pressing the point nor, she noticed, denying her claim to plainness. 'Now, files.' He moved smoothly round the desk so that he was facing the computer, switched it on and then beckoned her across to join him.

Standing next to him was an exercise in nerve-tingling embarrassment. He dwarfed her. Shaun had somehow never seemed *that* tall. Maybe he'd just been a little shorter, just as he'd been a little thinner, his features a little more blurred. Perhaps the mould, having been used once, had not quite managed to replicate itself the second time around.

'Familiar with this program?'

Vicky nodded.

'Good, then you'll have no problem finding your way around. You'll have to go through those files and update the computer, and there are one or two problems on a couple of them—discrepancies with the fees, order problems. I'm afraid you're being thrown in at the deep end but you'll have to find your way around the best you can, because the position requires a fair amount of initiative and responsibility. Tell me about your job with James?'

He strolled over to the coffee machine, and while he waited for it to kick into action he turned to face her with his arms folded.

Vicky groped her way for an adequate and truthful account of what she had done as far as work went without implying socialising of any nature. In fact, she had socialised a fair amount with James and his wife Carol, and had even babysat for them on a few occasions. 'I started off as his secretary, but I'm a pretty quick learner and, quite soon, I was being given a fair amount of responsibility. Looking after some of the smaller, more problematic customers, liaising with the service people as well as doing the usual administrative and typing stuff.'

'So you should have no problem coming to grips with all this...' He nodded vaguely at the files. 'I knew it. I took one look at you and knew that you'd be able to do the job with your eyes closed.'

'I haven't even started, as yet,' Vicky informed him warily. Heaping praise on her before she even got going was not so good, considering her long-range plan to quit the job as soon as was possible, without arousing needless suspicion.

'I think the first thing we need to sort out is my diary for the next month...' He went into his office and returned several seconds later with an electronic diary and a conventional leatherbound one, which he handed to her. 'Right. Now, let's start with tomorrow...' He pulled across one of the spare chairs from in front of the desk and strategically positioned it next to her so that, while he was no longer towering over her, he was now so close to her that with the flick of his pen on the keypad, his forearm casually but insistently brushed hers. She kept flicking sidelong, uncomfortable glances at the fine dark hairs sprinkling his powerful arms. He seemed so much more *real* than his twin, so much more *substantial*.

He began listing, very rapidly, his plans for the day, which she checked against the entries in the black diary. Some of the handwriting was poor enough to require several long seconds of tortuous interpretation and, after one particularly puzzling entry, she glanced up to find him looking at her.

'I'm beginning to understand what you meant by problems with temps,' she said with the ghost of a smile. 'If the filing system bears any resemblance to the handwriting in here, then I shall have several hours sorting out some basic stuff before I can even start to do my job.'

'Didn't I tell you?' Up close, as he was, he noticed that her skin was as flawlessly smooth as it appeared to be from a distance, and her hair, severely tied back, still managed to break free around her ears so that the tiny tendrils gave her the look of a saint whose halo had slipped to one side. Feeling his arm brush against hers, a passing touch that he could have avoided but chose not to, filled him with an almost sinful sense of excitement. He'd never known how powerful female modesty could be. Here she was, dressed in three times as much clothing as the woman he had last dated—Lord, three months ago—and yet the effect of all those clothes on him was positively suffocating. She had removed her jacket, but her blouse was buttoned up prudishly to the neck with small pearl buttons of the type worn by grannies. He could indistinctly make out the outline of her bra underneath. He wondered, and this sent a little electric shock to his groin, what it would feel like to undo those prim buttons, fingers touching skin underneath the shirt, anticipation building to a frenzy. He imagined her hands loosely tied to the bedstead with silk scarves while he undressed her, taking his time and exploring each exposed bit of skin with his tongue. He would drive her wild, enjoying her uncontrolled writhing. Naturally she would plead with him not to stop, to rip aside her bra and relieve her aching breasts with his mouth.

When he glanced her way, it was to find her looking at him as though she could read every salaciously impure thought in his head, and he flushed darkly. Good heavens! The woman was his *secretary*!

'Believe me now?' he asked roughly, sounding, he thought, the Big Bad Wolf when confronted with Little Red Riding Hood. He grinned to himself at the unconscious parallel, because right now he would have liked nothing better than to eat her up, every inch of her defensive little body, starting with her pale, slender neck and moving all the way down to the patch of hair between her thighs that would naturally be daintily shielded behind granny-style underwear.

He cleared his throat and dragged his thoughts back to meetings, calendars and business appointments. She was asking him something and he made a huge effort to concentrate and reply in a normal voice.

'I see you're in London twice this week,' she was saying, gazing down with satisfaction at the diary entries. Two business meetings in Temple, another in Uxbridge.

'So I am. Perhaps—' he frowned '—I ought to cancel those and spend a bit more time here, until you get accustomed to the running of the office.'

Vicky was quick to sit on any such suggestion. 'There's no need for that.' She realised that his recumbent arm was too close for comfort, and she discreetly but firmly edged hers away. 'In fact, having a couple of days on my own will be perfect for me to fill myself in on the files and the customers and also catch up with some of that backlog of typing.'

He could see her trying very hard to look regretful and felt a sulky and childish tug on his masculine pride that the thought of spending time along with him in the office was obviously a fate only slightly better than death, as far as she was concerned. What appealing work experience lay in store for both of them at this rate!

'Well, you can't miraculously work your way through *everything* on your own. I'm going to have to answer a few questions, presumably.' Now, he sounded piqued. The cool, self-confident, self-assured, mature and winningly charming adult seemed to have been replaced by a sulking thirteen-year-old. Where that emotion had come from he had no idea as it had never been in evidence before.

'I realise that,' Vicky said, briefly looking at him and then resuming her perusal of the file in front of her.

'Whenever I need you to help, I shall ask. I think finding my way around the business and *what you do here* is going to take the longest. I'll read up all the company literature, but Mrs Hogg—'

'Ms Hogg.'

'I beg your pardon?'

'*Ms* Hogg. Geraldine prefers good, healthy outdoor pursuits with her formidable sister to the company of men any day of the week.' He grinned and she reluctantly grinned back.

'Well, as I was saying…' What *had* she been saying? '*Ms* Hogg didn't get much of a chance to fill me in on this particular branch of your company. She mentioned that it's a fairly new concern—'

'But growing at an almost unprecedented rate,' he carried on for her, 'hence my involvement. Virtually all of our customers are new to us and have to be treated with kid gloves, aside from one or two whose mother company is based in London and whose subsidiaries coincidentally operate in this general area. I'm pretty busy for the rest of the day, but I can always pop over to your house some time after wor—'

'No!' Vicky heard the panic in her voice with alarm. The important thing was to lull any suspicions he might have of her to sleep, not stoke them into a frenzy by over-reacting to obvious situations. 'I mean, I have very…very definite views on business and pleasure.'

'Does that mean that you shed your working personality the minute you walk out of the office building?' He stared at her narrowly, head cocked insolently to one side, as though conjuring up a mental picture. 'Intriguing. As the office doors swing shut behind you, do you wrench the clips out of your hair and hitch up your neat, little tailored skirt?'

'Of course I don't,' Vicky said coolly. 'I just think that it's important to separate leisure time from work time, or else the two begin flowing into one another and somewhere down the road you realise that there's no part of your life that isn't free from work.' *Neat, little tailored skirt?* How could four small words be invested with such a derogatory meaning? He made her sound like an old age pensioner and, without thinking, she let her fingers flutter to the top button of her shirt, firmly done up, protecting her from unwanted attention. She had never been like this. There had been a time, not *that* long ago, when she'd used to wear short skirts and pretty, attractive tops, but that had been before she had learnt that prudery was the only defence against Shaun's lecherous hands. The sight of her primly buttoned up had sometimes been enough to deter him from invading her body and she had grown accustomed to the way of dressing until now, she realised with a start, most of her clothes conformed to the prissy, unadventurous image she had meticulously cultivated over time.

'But is it such a good idea to compartmentalise your life? Don't you find that a little unhealthy?' He'd pushed his chair a little way away from hers to enable him to scrutinise her face, which was now going a deep shade of pink. It occurred to her that they had successfully managed to veer away from the point of their conversation, which was namely to brief her on office business, and she struggled to find a way of bringing it back to the matter in hand. While she was busy grappling with the problem, he filled the brief silence with his sudden interest in her private life.

'Reminds me of a split personality,' he said thoughtfully, and she felt her hackles rise at the insinuation.

'I assure you I'm *perfectly normal*,' Vicky informed him

in a voice that suggested closure of the topic. She mean-ingfully peered at the file in front of her, even fetching out a piece of paper to stare at it with frowning concentration, though her eyes weren't registering much of what was written there.

'I never implied that you weren't!' he protested in an offended voice. 'I just think that it's perfectly natural for work to spill over sometimes into leisure.'

'Well, perhaps you're right,' Vicky said with a shrug. 'Are you contactable when you're in London or would you rather problems waited until you returned here?'

'You can e-mail me any time, or telephone, of course, although I'm not often in the office.' He allowed an ac-ceptable period of silence to stretch between them, then he said in a considering tone, 'Do you know, it's been my experience that women who are fanatically guarded about their private life usually have something to hide…?'

He had unknowingly hit jackpot. He could sense it in the stillness of her body, which only lasted a matter of seconds but was enough to tell an entire story of its own.

'I have nothing to hide,' she informed him icily, 'and at the risk of sounding impertinent on my first day here, I should just like to say that I resent your prying into my private life…'

'I didn't realise that I was *prying* into your private life, I *thought* that I was making a general statement…' Her tone of voice didn't appear to have put him off his stride and she saw, with dismay, the gleam lurking seductively in his eyes. 'Of course—' he dropped his eyes and in-spected his nails briefly '—you're entitled to your privacy, and if you have something that you're ashamed of…'

'I am *not* ashamed of *anything*!'

'Okay! Okay!' It was the oldest trick in the book and she knew it. He was making a show of backing away from confrontation while simultaneously appearing doubtful of her protestations of innocence.

'What could I have to be ashamed of?' she couldn't help demanding indignantly, and this was met by a theatrical shrug of his broad shoulders.

'Nothing.'

Vicky made the inarticulate sound of someone whose feathers have been severely ruffled.

'Unless,' he said as an afterthought, 'it's something to do with a man.' He flicked a quick look at her to see how this one registered but her normal serenity was well and truly back in place. 'You know, you're entitled to have whatever relationships you want, be they with married men…'

Vicky, recognising that he was fishing for information, maintained her studious silence, chewing her lip as she peered down at sheaths of paper in a business like manner.

This was what she had feared most, this willingness on his part to cheerfully overstep the mark. He had no respect for anyone's limits. If he got it into his head that jumping over them was what he wanted to do, then jump over them he would, and with a grin on his face.

'Or even married women…' He didn't seriously believe that that was a possibility but he decided to voice his thoughts anyway, if only to keep this enticing conversation on the go. As expected, she shot him a dry look and didn't bother to say anything.

'Or perhaps it's a toy boy? These things *do* happen…'

'I'm not old enough for a toy boy,' Vicky pointed out with a sigh of resignation. 'No married men, *or women, for that matter*, no toy boy, no geriatric in his seventies, no *skeletons*, in fact…' She sounded pleasingly truthful and couldn't resist a smug smile in his direction.

'Everyone has a skeleton or two,' he said quickly, and she raised her eyebrows at him.

He wasn't going to get anywhere with this one. She was now looking at him with crisp efficiency, raring to get going with whatever folder she'd been fingering for the past fifteen minutes. He admitted defeat, and for the next two hours they worked alongside one another. Instead of wasting time going through files individually, he dictated letters, briefly giving her a lowdown on each account as he covered them.

She picked things up fast. He'd spent so many months battling with various levels of incompetence that it was sheer bliss to work with someone who was capable of following his pace. Her questions were clipped and relevant, she grasped what she needed to do without requiring a lengthy process of repetition, and by the time Maria on Switchboard began putting through his calls once again he felt confident enough to leave her on her own to get on with things.

Through the office partition, he could see a sliver of her at her desk, one hand holding a pen, which she lightly tapped as she inspected whatever she had just typed onto the computer. She had shoved her hair into a bun, and ever so often she would absent-mindedly reposition her rebellious curls.

Max rolled his chair a few vital inches to the left, without altering the tenor of his conversation on the telephone, and guiltily watched her as she worked. It made him feel a bit like a lecher so, after a few minutes, he rolled himself back in front of his desk and made an effort to swivel towards the window behind him so that he no longer felt like a voyeur.

He only realised how keyed-up he was to her presence

when she politely peeped into his office forty minutes later with a question.

'I've been going through the filing cabinets,' she began, and he indicated the chair for her to sit.

'And…?'

'It appears that two files have been made of this account, and filed under separate names.' Vicky handed him the files, which boasted two different sets of handwriting. 'Problem is that the information in both doesn't correspond, even though it's all to do with the same thing. It looks as though one of your secretaries dealt with something three months ago and then misfiled the folder. When the problem recurred, her replacement started a new file and basically told the client the complete opposite of what had been said to him previously.' She stood up and leaned forward, flicking open both the files and then carefully indicating what she meant. One long strand of wayward hair escaped and skirted her neck, coiling in a perfect red-gold corkscrew curl.

'Leave it with me. I'll deal with it.'

'I don't mind…' She glanced and met his eyes, then quickly lowered hers. 'Sorry. Overstepping my brief. I suppose I was so accustomed to dealing with these types of customer problems at my last job in Australia that I could find it easy to slip back into my old ways.' She reminded herself that that would be impossible, since her time allotment for this particular job was a matter of weeks rather than years. Any slipping she would be doing would be out of the office door and into the nearest employment agency.

'I have an idea,' he said slowly, pushing himself back from his desk and tilting a bit on the chair. 'Why don't we pay a few visits to some of the more critical clients? If you meet them, then you can put a face to the voice at the end of the telephone and so can they. Have a look at my diary and fill me in on what I'm up to on…let's see…next Tuesday. We can spend a couple of hours with each and have a break for lunch at one of the better country pubs around here.'

Vicky began calculating in her head whether Brenda, her childminder, would be able to cover for her next Tuesday. Chloe would have to miss her after-school swimming lesson, but that was fine. She hated them anyway. If they managed to clear everything up no later than six in the evening, then there should be no problem at all.

She looked at him to find him staring at her with hooded interest.

'I'll get your diary,' she said hurriedly, fleeing the office before he could begin quizzing her on further evidence of her mysterious secret life. As she fished for the diary from the drawer of her desk, she wondered whether she shouldn't just head him off by fabricating something that might satisfy his masculine curiosity. It would have to be something worth secreting away, yet nowhere near the truth. Perhaps, she thought, she could invent a double life as a stripper. That would shut him up, she was sure.

As she headed back into the office, her mouth was curved into a small smile at her ludicrous but amusing secret plan.

'Share the joke?'

She raised her eyes to his but she didn't see him. What she saw, in fact, was a stage in a darkened room on which she wove with sensuous, semi-naked abandon, watched hungrily by the man sitting opposite her at the desk. Her mind was filled suddenly and sickening with an erotic image that was strong enough to blow her off her feet. She very quickly sat down, just in case, and delved blindly into the black diary on her lap, furiously flicking through the pages until her trembling fingers lighted onto the correct one.

She mumbled something about there being no joke to share, making sure that she kept her eyes firmly averted from his face, and then said crisply, 'Tuesday looks fine. If you tell me what clients you'd like to visit, then I can try and arrange them.' She was still speaking to the diary. In a minute, when her head had completely cleared of its treacherous suggestion, she would resume normal behaviour patterns.

'If we meet the first, Prior and Truman, at nine, then we can probably fit Robins in before lunch. Make sure that you leave a two-hour window for lunch, say between one and three, then a couple more and we can call it a day.'

'And which client would you like to take to lunch?' Her heart rate was getting back to its normal speed, thankfully, and she risked a look at him.

'None. I think you and I could benefit from a bit of uninterrupted time together.' He let the words sink in, then added, 'To go through any little work problems you might have encountered that you need to ask me about.' He wasn't *smiling*, she noticed, when he said this, but there was the *feeling* of a smile tugging at his mouth and she shot him a quenchingly professional look, just in case there was anything there that needed snuffing out.

Shaun had made her wise to the manipulations of the flirt. He himself had used more obvious tactics. He had often spread himself across her desk, before she'd insisted that he no longer come into her workplace, making sure that she'd had nowhere else to look but at some part of his reclining body; then, later, the big gestures of extravagant flowers and expensive dinners in the places where to be seen was to step up two notches on your street cred rating. The showy manoeuvres had lasted the length of time it had taken to get her into bed, then gradually they had dwindled, until the day had arrived when the flowers and expensive dinners became things of the past. She would always, at the back of her mind, equate pregnancy with misery, because it was then that the seriously destructive verbal abuse had really begun, the taunts that would reduce her to uncontrollable weeping, the slamming of doors and jeering that had made her want to disappear from the face of the earth.

She wondered whether Max Forbes was cut from the same cloth, just a different pattern. The more she saw of him, the more confused she was becoming, because her instincts were telling her that he was nothing like his brother, even though she was disillusioned enough to know that instincts had a nasty way of being wrong.

Then, when her irritating speculations had reached a peak, she told herself that none of it mattered a jot anyway because, whether he was like his brother or in fact a saint in the making, he was still a dangerous and unwanted intruder in her life.

'Right. Anything else?' he asked, pushing his chair back and stretching. He walked across to the door, on the back of which hung his jacket, slung negligently over the hook despite the hanger that was sitting there gathering dust. 'I've got a couple of important meetings and, as you know, I'll be out of the office tomorrow. Think you can cope?'

'I'll do my best,' Vicky told him. She could feel an unwelcome stir of excitement at the prospect of all the work that lay ahead of her. If Max Forbes thought that months of unsatisfactory temps was frustrating, then she could deliver a sermon of her own on the dissatisfaction of one very proficient temp, namely herself, who had spent the past few months photocopying, photocopying and doing yet more photocopying. In between she had managed to run errands that no one else wanted to run, do filing that had been studiously avoided for decades and transferred enough tedious information from sheets of paper to computer to make her goggle-eyed.

'You know where you can reach me. All my numbers, including the one for my flat in Fulham, are at the front of your diary.'

'I shouldn't think that anything *that* urgent will come up that requires me to get in touch with you at your home.'

'You can never tell,' he said, slinging on his jacket and patting the pocket to make sure that his cellular phone was present and correct.

Vicky, who had automatically followed him to the door, now said with wry amusement, 'You're a company director, not a highly pressurised neurosurgeon on call. Don't you think that life *might* go on if you aren't around for a couple of days?' Then she suddenly remembered that she was supposed to be working for him. When she wasn't on guard, it was all too easy to relax with him. Considering that one of the few advantages to taking this job, so she'd repeatedly told herself, was the fact that she would be keyed up and mentally alert to spot and ward off any potential danger, allowing herself to relax was not on the agenda.

'Maybe,' he admitted reluctantly, favouring her with one of those slow, specialty smiles which he seemed to do unconsciously. He opened the door and turned to look down at her. 'Maybe not. But don't worry, anyway. I'll be back soon enough.'

The words sounded like an ominous warning in the sunlit office and attached themselves to the growing line of worries complicating her life.

Or so it suddenly seemed.

CHAPTER FOUR

NEXT TUESDAY, which had seemed a million years away, arrived with stupendous speed.

During his two days out of the office, Vicky had jumped into the deep waters of bad filing, customer queries, letters to be typed, memos and phone calls and e-mails and faxes and things to sort out so that they were understandable to *her*. The time had whisked by. Every so often she would dutifully tell herself that she wouldn't be around long enough to see the benefits of some of the systems she was putting in place, but already a little voice at the back of her mind was beginning to sing a different tune.

Well, why would he find out about Chloe? He hadn't so far, and he had stopped asking difficult questions. Perhaps his nosy curiosity had all been part of his interviewing methods, to make sure that she could handle his temperament. Of course, she wouldn't stay there forever, but why not for a bit longer than she had planned? Why not? The money was brilliant, better than anything she could ever hope to earn in a million years around Warwick. Or around London, for that matter. She would be able to put a bit aside, and wouldn't that come in handy for all the building work that needed doing on her house? The place seemed to be falling down around her ears and she had to find the money to do repair work from somewhere. Hadn't she? And the work was going to be exciting. She was so sick of being given the dross as a temp; why not enjoy the sudden opportunity to have a few responsibilities? Yes, of course it was dangerous being around the man, even though he knew nothing of her personal life. But it was a danger she could handle. The fact that she was aware of it would be enough to deaden its force. She would keep him at a distance. In effect, she would use him, use him for the fabulous pay cheque at the end of the month and the fantastic chance to satisfy her need for an invigorating career, and if he started asking questions again or prying into her personal life, then she would dump the job immediately. And what was wrong with that? Hadn't she been well and truly used by that brother of his? In fact, she could look on it as a kind of game, with her in possession of all the rules. She knew, after all, all about him, but he knew nothing about her. So who was going to have the last laugh? All she needed was to be careful and she could enjoy the situation instead of being petrified.

By the following Monday, she'd made significant inroads into some of the backlog that had stockpiled on her desk, including various dusty letters which had been forgotten or ignored during the rapid succession of unsuccessful temps.

Max was out of the office more than he was in it, and when he *was* in, he spent most of his time locked in his office, on the phone or on the fax or in front of his computer, frowning at rows upon rows of numbers.

Now, as she cleared her desk in anticipation of going home, she stole a quick look at him through the smoked glass partition. Seen like this, he was less intimidating than he was in the flesh. He was reduced to a darkish shape which she could easily handle.

Not, she thought smugly, whisking her pens and pencils into the drawer and clicking it shut, that he was proving to be a problem at all. In fact, there were times when she very nearly forgot the dark connection that ran between them like an unseen, pulsating vein. She still couldn't quite manage to slot him into the harmless category that she would have liked, he was just too overwhelming for that, but at least she no longer looked at him with the terror of a rabbit caught in headlights.

And Chloe was happier and more relaxed than she had been since they returned to England.

Vicky pondered this for a minute. The only explanation she could find was that her daughter had somehow picked up her inexplicable contentment at work with her efficient, childish antennae and was happier for it.

She knocked briefly on Max's interconnecting door, while slinging on her jacket and poked her head around it to tell him that she was off.

He crooked his finger at her, beckoning her to enter, and Vicky quickly glanced at her watch, estimating how much time she could spare for a quick chat. She was accustomed to picking up Chloe from the childminder at a little after five-thirty, which didn't give her very long in terms of travel. She could, she knew, leave her there longer, but she hated doing that. It was enough of a wrench not being able to collect her directly from school at three-thirty, without prolonging her absence. And she didn't want to start taking advantage of Brenda's good nature.

'*If* you can spare the time,' he said drily, tilting back in the chair with his hands clasped behind his head.

Vicky went in, but remained standing and didn't shut the door behind her. The point was not lost on her boss, who looked at her with wry amusement.

'How are you enjoying the job so far?'

'It's early days yet.' No point committing herself to an enthusiastic response just yet. For starters, if she decided to leave in the very near future, she wanted to be able to hang on to the tried and tested excuse about it not being her cup of tea after all. And, additionally, she didn't want to give him the opportunity to imagine that he had been right all along.

'You seem to have picked it up very well, from what I've seen.'

'You've been out of the office most of the time,' Vicky pointed out.

'I've accessed some of the files you were due to update on the computer and it's all been done, and unless you've eaten the outstanding paperwork most of that has been done as well.' He sat forward and began fiddling with his fountain pen, a burgundy Mont Blanc with a solid gold trim. 'And tomorrow we've got your first introduction to clients. Nervous?'

Vicky, who couldn't reasonably look at her watch without it being obvious, fidgeted from one foot to the other and tried not to think about the dash she would have to get to her childminder by five-thirty.

'Looking forward to it.'

'I apologise for not being around a bit more to show you the ropes, considering it's early days here for you…' He began tapping the closed fountain pen on the surface of his desk and she wondered why he had bothered to ask her into his office and enquire about her levels of happiness if he was that impatient to get going. Was he under the mistaken impression that she wanted to see him?

'It's no problem.'

'You must have a lot of questions to ask.' His grey eyes swept over her, taking in her neat uniform of knee-length skirt, crisp cotton blouse and grey jacket which was now in place, obliterating all traces of femininity.

The world of fashion had a lot to answer for when it came to suits for women, he thought. It was difficult to imagine anything more conducive to killing the male imagination. He decided that his office would be far better served were she to wear something a little less military, perhaps a silky short mini skirt and a clinging wet shirt, worn braless.

He grinned inwardly at the chauvinistic irreverence of his thoughts. He personally knew several extremely high-powered female executives who would hang, draw and quarter him had they any insight into his current line of thinking. They would all be particularly disgusted, since he had always led the way when it came to equality between the sexes. He'd made it a company policy that pay reflected talent rather than gender, and females in positions of power had always been actively condoned within the various branches of his huge, global network of companies.

As far as he was concerned, the work environment was not a cat-walk and inappropriate dressing was discouraged.

Right now, however, he thought that some inappropriate dressing would do just nicely.

'No, none that I can think of offhand.'

'Sorry?' He realised sheepishly that his drifting thoughts had gone further than he thought.

'I *said*—'

'We can discuss them over dinner.'

'I beg your pardon?'

'Your questions. We can discuss them over dinner. Fewer interruptions than if we tried to sort them out here, during the day. I could pick you up around seven-thirty. How does that sound?'

'No, thank you.'

The blunt refusal was like a bucket of cold water thrown gaily over his head. The worst thing was that he shouldn't have asked her out in the first place. He might tell himself that it was business, but he knew that that couldn't have been further from the truth. He looked at her stubborn, shuttered face, her full mouth drawn into a firm, disapproving line, and felt the kick of adolescent disappointment.

Except for the fact that he wasn't an adolescent.

'Why not?' he heard himself ask. 'Don't imagine that this is anything other than work.' With a trace of satisfaction, he saw her translucent skin suffuse with pink colour and some vague notion of reestablishing his bruised male pride made him pursue the point with more tenacity than was warranted. 'Your virtue is absolutely secure with me, my dear.' Pale pink was becoming a shade darker. He noted that she was no longer looking at him but staring fixedly in the region of her shoes. 'In fact, I've always believed it vitally important that sex and work don't mix. The combination is usually lethal. I simply thought that you might feel a bit more relaxed away from the office, might find it easier to concentrate on any problems you might have without the constant interruption of telephones and people popping in and out. Naturally, if you have other, more pressing engagements…'

He glanced idly down at a sheaf of paper on the desk, letting her know, without putting it in so many words, that her reply was fairly unimportant but that he was, at the end of the day, *her boss*.

'Yes, I have actually,' Vicky told him. 'In fact, I really must be on my way…' There was a trace of guilty apology in her voice that made him clench his teeth together in frustration.

'I don't approve of clock-watching,' he said grimly. Now his jaw was beginning to ache and he slowly relaxed his muscles. He could tell that she was frazzled by his attitude but really, *what*, at this hour of the afternoon, could *possibly* be so important? He could understand that she might have plans later on in the evening, but at *five-fifteen in the afternoon*? And those plans obviously weren't innocent. If she had to scurry off to the dentist or the hairdresser or to the corner shop before it closed, then she would have said so.

He felt that spark of intense curiosity and allied with it was something more disturbing. Jealousy. *Jealousy*! It seemed that the woman was stirring up a viper's nest of unprecedented emotions. He stared at her with brooding resentment and thought that the only thing that could bring a guilty flush like that to a woman's cheeks was a man. Illicit afternoon sex. All that baloney about no skeletons in the cupboard and having nothing to hide had been pure fabrication. Did she imagine that he would care one way or another whether she was having an affair with a married man? Did she think that he was moralistic enough to sack her because she might be behaving inappropriately? Didn't the woman know that this was no longer the Victorian era?

Illicit afternoon sex. Illicit sex in the afternoon. Illicit, frantic, steamy sex in the afternoon, with the curtains drawn. Or maybe with the curtains *undrawn*. Who knew? A quiet knock on the door and she would let him in. A small, insignificant office worker with no personality to speak of and a drastically receding hairline, and upstairs they would go, to fling off their clothes and get down to the pressing business of *illicit afternoon sex*.

His mind played with the evolving scenario until he was forced to break the lengthening silence.

'Perhaps I should give you a few days' notice if I intend to keep you five minutes after you're due to leave.' His voice was laced with cold sarcasm and he unobtrusively tried to massage his jawline with his hand.

'Oh, five minutes is no problem,' Vicky said awkwardly. 'I just…you know, I'm very busy with the house…there's

always someone due to come round…plumbers…
electricians…you know…' Her voice trailed away into
awkward silence and he nodded briefly at her.

'I'll see you tomorrow. You'll have to be here by eight-
thirty if we're to get to Prior and Truman by nine.'

Vicky nodded, relieved that she had received her signal
to depart. She drove like a maniac back to her childminder's house, but even when she and Chloe were back
home, doing all the usual stuff they did in the evening, she
carried on feeling a little jumpy. As though any minute,
and without notice, she would look up and see Max
Forbes's dark, mocking face staring at her through the sitting room window. Like an avenging angel, but with nothing of the angel about him. An avenging devil.

Chloe wanted chicken nuggets for her dinner. She had
originally wanted a McDonald's, but had graciously allowed herself to be persuaded into ordinary chicken nuggets at home on the understanding that pudding, in the
form of ice cream and chocolate buttons, would be abun-
dant.

Vicky raced around the kitchen while her daughter sat
at the kitchen table and chatted about school, intermittently
drawing a family portrait that bore no resemblance to their
family, or any family for that matter, at least of the human
variety.

She hadn't bothered to get out of her working clothes
and she felt disgruntled and sticky. Out of the corner of
her eye she looked at her daughter, who was gravely intent
on her task at hand, her dark hair swinging past her satin-
smooth baby face, and felt a jolt of fear.

What was she doing? Even here, in her own house, she
half felt as though she needed to look over her shoulder,
just in case Max appeared unexpectedly, like a rabbit pop-

ping out of a hat. So what if the money was a godsend, so what if she actually was discovering that the job was as exciting as she'd thought it would be? She was still playing with fire and everyone knew what happened to foolish women who played with fire. They got burnt.

She gazed lovingly at Chloe and realised that the chicken nuggets were getting burnt.

The following morning, she made a decision. She would begin laying the groundwork for her eventual, inevitable and sooner-than-expected resignation.

She couldn't bring herself to work less hard or to do any of her jobs carelessly and thereby ensure dismissal. It just wasn't in her nature. Instead, she decided to go down the road of little hints.

He was in the office and waiting for her when she arrived with fifteen minutes to spare. He had fetched out a stack of files and, in a quarter of an hour, proceeded to fill her in on the people she would be meeting, the way their company operated and what part they played in the Forbes Corporation. In between, she made them both a cup of coffee while he perched indolently on her desk and rattled off information.

It felt comfortable. She dabbled around him, listening and taking in every word, carefully sticking a couple of pens into the briefcase which she had seen fit to buy shortly after starting the job and some paper, in case she wanted to take notes. Every so often she paused, asked a question, then proceeded with what she had been doing.

By a quarter to nine they were ready to leave, and she was fairly confident that she wouldn't find herself too much out of her depth.

What she hadn't been prepared for was how much she would enjoy the experience of being on the move with Max Forbes, meeting clients, playing a subdued but appreciated second fiddle to him. When his attention was focused elsewhere, as it was throughout the day, she could watch him with shameless interest and, with each passing minute, the respect which she'd felt for him from the very beginning became more grounded. She could now barely believe that he and Shaun had been related at all, never mind the intimate connection they had shared. Were it not for the physical resemblance, which was beginning to get a bit blurred in her mind as it was, she would have said that as two people the brothers could not have been further apart.

Lunch at a pub in the middle of the countryside, yet not incredibly far from the nearest town, was a one-hour affair which sped past. They discussed the clients they had seen, the ways in which they interacted with the property development side of the Forbes company. Max talked about New York, which was as personal as he got, and in turn Vicky chatted about living in Warwick as opposed to living on the other side of the world, without giving away too much information.

By the time they had finished with their last client at a little after three, it was pointless returning to the office.

'My car's still there,' Vicky pointed out.

'I'll give you a lift home. You can always take a taxi in to work in the morning.'

'No. That won't do.' She stared remotely out of the window, vaguely looking at the wide open spaces, dotted with the occasional house or barn conversion. They were still a little distance out of the city centre and unfortunately on the wrong side of Warwick as far as the office was concerned.

'Why won't it do?' Max asked with a hint of impatience.

'I like having my car,' Vicky said stubbornly. 'There's no public transport to speak of from my house and I don't like to think about what I'd do if something happened and I needed to get somewhere fast.'

'Something like what?' He seemed to know where he was going, and fortunately it was more or less in the direction of the office, so she was less jumpy than she might have been otherwise at the tenor of his question.

'Oh, I don't know.' She shrugged and lazily slid her eyes across to him, mentally taking in the forcefulness of his profile, the harsh cut of his features, the dark, springy hair that seemed as defiant as hers when it came to being controlled. Even though his, unlike hers, was a less obvious colour. Chloe would have that very same thick, black hair, offset by those amazing grey eyes. She felt another twinge of uneasiness, which she stifled, at least momentarily.

'I could fall over and break something...'

'In that case, you wouldn't be able to drive for help.'

'Or I could burn myself badly with a saucepan of hot milk...'

'Mm. Casualty, but still no car would be needed. You'd have to call for help.'

'Okay. I could discover at eight in the evening that I've run out of instant coffee and I desperately need to go out and buy some more from the corner shop...'

'So now you tell me that you're addicted to coffee.' There was sudden rich humour in his voice and it made her flush with excited pleasure and look quickly away from his curving mouth. 'Mood swings, you know—bouts of sudden depression, quite unpredictable...'

'Who? What?'

'Coffee addicts...' He chuckled and she automatically grinned in response.

'Do you know,' she murmured, 'I've spent years wondering about those strange personality defects of mine?

Thank you so much for sorting it out for me. Coffee addiction. Tomorrow I'm a changed person.'

This time he laughed, a deep-throated, appreciative laugh, and she felt another quick stab of pleasure.

'Okay,' he conceded, 'we'll head back to the office, but why don't we play truant and have a bit of time out rather than go back to work?'

'Play truant? A bit of time out?' She wasn't looking at him but she was smiling, weirdly relaxed and happy, despite all those misgivings which kept popping up with nagging regularity. In a little while, she would erect her defences once more. But, for the minute, sitting alongside him in his powerful car, after an unexpectedly enjoyable day, she felt too lazy to get worked up. 'Surely,' she continued, 'those are not the words of an empire builder? If they are, then I reckon I could go out and build one or two empires myself.' Cold winter sunshine glinted across the countryside, giving everything a hard edge.

'Everyone needs a bit of truancy now and again, especially when in the right company,' he murmured, more to himself than to her, so that she had to strain to hear him, and even then she couldn't be sure that she had heard correctly. 'I have an idea.'

'What?' She turned to look at him.

'I live a matter of minutes away from the office. We could go there, and before you start protesting, I'm merely suggesting it because I've had quite a bit of building work done on my place and, if you decide to stay with the firm, you'd be entitled to reduced costs. You could get an idea of the standard of work the company is capable of.'

'I haven't decided whether I'm staying or not,' Vicky said feebly, uncomfortably aware that she was raising the point because she knew she had to and not because she wanted to.

'What do you mean by that?' he asked sharply, and Vicky felt the cut of his eyes flick over to her.

She squirmed a bit in the seat and cleared her throat. 'Well, I *am* on probation...' she began, sliding away from the argument looming ahead on the horizon. 'You might very well find that I'm not suitable for the job and...and...well, I want to give it a bit of time before I make my mind up as well,' she trailed on evasively.

'Why?' he demanded. 'Are there problems that you haven't told me about? Some aspect of the work proving too difficult?'

'No! I was just speaking...hypothetically.' She cleared her throat again in an attempt to establish control over her unconvincing arguments.

While they had been talking and her attention had been distracted, he'd driven quickly and expertly back to his house and, before she could protest, he was pulling up the drive and killing the engine.

His house was in one of the many rural retreats that nestled alongside the city centre, within twenty minutes' driving distance, yet with a remote feel that came from being surrounded by open land. The front garden was set back from the road and hidden behind a luxuriant hedge that had been trimmed with awe-inspiring precision.

'I...I d-didn't realise you were bringing me to your house,' Vicky stammered, stepping out of the car and glancing at her watch.

'Oh. I thought I mentioned it.' He was unlocking the front door, his back to her, and she frowned at him, wondering why she felt as though she had been skilfully manoeuvred. He pushed open the door and stood aside to let her pass. Hesitantly, she brushed past him, feeling the hairs on her arm stand on end at the slight contact, then she was inside a compact hallway, with rich wooden flooring. The banister curved upwards to rooms that were left to her imagination but, as far as she could see, the ones on the ground floor had been decorated with flair and taste.

'Not my own,' he confessed, following her appreciative gaze around her. 'Two ladies armed with some of the weightiest books I have ever seen managed to persuade me that all of this—' he spread his arm in a sweeping gesture to encompass the house '—was precisely what I wanted.'

'And was it?' She stepped a little more confidently into the hall, and continued to survey the clever subdued oat-meal colours that lent startling emphasis to the paintings hanging on the walls and the depth of the maple flooring. Through some of the half-opened doors, which promised a house bigger and more complex than it appeared from the outside, she could see that the pale canvas theme continued throughout, with splashes of deep green or vibrant terracotta bringing bursts of intermittent colour.

'Well, I like it, so it would appear so.' He laughed under his breath and she smiled in response.

'I must say, I have absolutely no eye for interior design either,' she admitted, 'so two ladies with large books would do quite nicely for me as well.'

'It could be arranged,' he murmured, heading off out of the hall and expecting her to follow. Which she did.

She found herself in a kitchen which was expensively furnished with all the latest gadgets in evidence. None of them looked as though they had been touched. Only the semi-blackened kettle on the Aga hinted that someone actually used the kitchen, and the kitchen table, she was pleased to see, seemed to have an air of history about it.

'I take it you don't cook,' she said. 'Everything looks brand-new.'

'Everything *is* brand-new. The decorators only cleared off about a week ago. Coffee?'

She was so accustomed to making coffee for him at work that the sudden role reversal, and the even more disturbing hint of intimacy in the situation, made her flush.

'Perhaps a quick cup.' Before any silence could develop between them, she began speaking rapidly, almost eating up her words, asking him about the building work that had been done, how long it had taken, whether he was pleased with the house, if there was anything else that required doing. She would have happily rattled on about the condition of her split ends if it had succeeded in masking her awareness of where she was. In Max Forbes's house. Alone. No computer, fax machine or ringing telephone to assert the appropriate differences between them.

To her further unease, he began loosening his tie, tugging at it with one hand while he poured hot water into two mugs with the other. Her eyes clamped onto his long fingers as they pulled at the tie and she had to blink a few times to clear her head. He was saying something about walls that had needed breaking down and the chaos of the dust everywhere, despite all the precautions and plastic sheets that the builders had used. He had finished making the coffee, had removed his tie altogether and tossed it carelessly over the back of one of the kitchen chairs and now faced her across the central isle counter.

'So that would be something you'd have to get used to.'

'Used to? Sorry. I wasn't listening.' She went red and Max did his best to hang on to his temper. Having coerced the woman over his doorstep, using tactics which he had never had to deploy before, he was infuriated to discover that her reaction spoke of the wariness of someone suddenly caught in a trap. She hadn't wanted to come, she didn't care for the fact that she had now found herself here and her forced good manners were threatening to bring out the worst in him.

'I *said*,' he repeated very slowly, 'that saying goodbye to your privacy would be something you would have to get used to.'

'*Saying goodbye to my privacy?* What are you talking about?' She slammed the mug onto the counter surface with shaking hands and some spilt over the sides and slopped onto the counter. 'I may be your secretary, *for the time being*, but that doesn't mean that I have to relinquish my privacy! If those are the kind of demands you've made on the women who have worked for you in the past, then I'm not surprised they left after a few hours!'

'*What* are you talking about?'

In the sudden silence, Vicky realised that he wasn't so much angry at her outburst as perplexed by it. Ah, she thought with a sinking feeling as she realised that whatever his original remark had been she had failed to hear it, absorbed as she had been in her own thoughts.

'What were *you* talking about?' she hedged. She took a long sip of her coffee and eyed him over the rim of the mug.

'If you would make more of an effort to listen to what I'm saying, then you wouldn't fly off the handle because you've caught the tail end and stupidly jumped to the wrong conclusions.'

Vicky bristled at his tone but, since he had a point, she thought it tactful to maintain a discreet silence on the subject.

'I'm sorry,' she said stiffly. 'My mind was miles away.'

'Where? Miles away where?'

He could feel himself itching to launch into an argument, anything to prise something more out of her than secretarial courtesy. True, she lapsed into strong emotion now and again, but then only for the briefest lengths of time and her retreat into that shuttered tower of hers was swift and complete whenever that happened. There was something wary and secretive about her, and his yearning to crack her open like a fruit was beginning to get a little out of control. His sleeping patterns had altered. Often, he would get up for no particular reason at some ungodly hour and even if he did his damnedest to concentrate his whirring mind on business or work or even, God help him, other women, his thoughts would return tirelessly to the small, pale-faced witch facing him now with her cup of coffee, eyes slightly narrowed, like a wild animal that has learnt to be cautious with strangers.

Even more frustrating was the fact that his once ceaseless social life had whittled down to business meetings, client dinners and the occasional meal on his own at the local Italian. The thought of another woman, another of his simple, easy-to-please-just-add-two-tablespoons-of-compliments-and-some-expensive-meals-out women, made him go glassy-eyed with boredom.

He blamed *her*.

'I wasn't thinking of anything in particular,' Vicky said noncommittally, drinking the remainder of her coffee quickly.

Max forced himself to smile, or was it grimace? He couldn't be sure. At any rate, whatever expression emerged felt unnatural.

'The only thing, I've noticed, that gives a woman that abstracted look is the thought of a man.' Fishing. Again. And not very subtly either, he thought. Some of his remarks made him cringe. Where the hell had all his debonair self-assurance gone? He could see her looking at him with a withering expression and his mouth tightened.

'Not *all* women, actually,' Vicky told him politely.

She shoved the empty mug a few inches into the centre of the counter, a little prelude to her request to be driven to the office so that she could collect her car. '*Some* of us do sometimes find our tiny minds cluttered up with something other than thoughts of a man.'

Okay, he thought, I deserved that, but did she have to look quite so…self-righteous? His mind leap frogged into an altogether different tableau, one where self-righteousness played no part, one that involved more emotion than she probably knew how to handle. In fact, a variation on one of the many tableaux that had recently been complicating his previously unfettered life.

'Touché,' he said, flushing darkly. 'Well, I can see that you're ready to go. By the way, that rumour about a supermarket being built near your house—it was just a rumour after all. They've bought a site on the other side of town instead.'

'That's a relief—'

'And, in case you're interested,' Max continued, 'I was talking about the building work you might want to have done on your house at some point. If you're even considering the possibility, I'd suggest you get in touch with Mandy and let her know. Organising all the various people can be a nightmare, even though they all answer to this company.' Who on earth did she think she was kidding? No matter how much she tried to hide it, there was a man somewhere in her life. What he couldn't understand was why she felt compelled to conceal the fact. The mere thought of a man touching that body he constantly fantasised about made him want to grind his teeth.

'You're moving too fast!' she said lightly, walking ahead of him to the front door. She looked over her shoulder and smiled. 'And, from your point of view, I haven't been with the company for two minutes! Shouldn't I have to work a lot longer before I can qualify for any discounted building work from the company?'

God, how he wanted to take that small, delicate face between his hands and crush her mouth with his lips until she couldn't breathe, until every secret was squeezed out of her head. They had stopped at the front door but before she could open it, he leaned against it and stared at her. The tantalising thought that he could just reach out and feel the touch of her lips, run his hands along her smooth neck, made his eyes darken. The prospect of turning fantasy into reality stretched his nerves to breaking point. He could see her pupils dilate as she looked back at him in wordless silence.

'No,' he heard himself say, 'so just set the date.'

She murmured something vague and looked away so that all he could see were her long eyelashes drooping against her cheeks. Her eyelashes, despite the burnished gold of her hair, were dark and thick. He couldn't help himself. He reached out and touched her cheek and she raised her eyes immediately.

'What are you doing?' She flinched back and he abruptly withdrew his hand, which, he was disgusted to see, was shaking from the fleeting contact.

'There was ink on your cheek,' he said smoothly, pushing himself away from the door and opening it for her to precede him out of the house. She rubbed the spot vigorously, not meeting his eyes. 'I want you to type up those letters I dictated in the car today,' he said in a hard voice. His feelings had betrayed him. He had acted as though his body had a mind of its own, and his mouth was tight with anger, at himself and incidentally with her simply for *providing such ludicrous temptation.* 'I'll need them,' he said, opening her door for her and walking around to the driver's seat, 'by lunchtime tomorrow. And cancel my

meetings for next Monday. I'll be in New York for three
days. Problems with Eva, one of the subsidiaries.' He
glanced at her as he pulled out of the drive. 'It would be
useful if I had a secretary there.'

'If you like, I can arrange for Tina, Roger's secretary,
to accompany you. I know she likes overseas trips.'

His eyes, fixed on the road, were wintry when he answered. 'Leave it. I'll see what can be arranged over there.'
And he would bide his time. He had never been a man
noted for his patience. He was learning fast.

CHAPTER FIVE

THE following Monday, no sooner had she sat at her desk and switched on the computer terminal than Vicky's internal line buzzed her.

Mandy from Personnel. She had arranged for one of their company architects to have a look at her house and ascertain the cost of any building work needing to be done.

A choking fit ensued as Vicky swallowed a mouthful of coffee down the wrong way, a reaction to her shock at this sudden development.

'Building work?' she asked giddily.

'You mentioned to the big man that you wanted to take advantage of our company policy of subsidised building work for employees?'

'In passing, perhaps...I didn't mean to imply that speed was of the element...'

'You'll learn,' Mandy said dryly from down the end of the telephone. 'Max Forbes doesn't sit on things. He can make a decision in less time than it takes me to make a cup of instant coffee.' There was admiration in her voice. 'And he's obviously decided that your house is in immediate need of repair work. You poor thing. Coming all the way here from Australia to find your house falling about around your ears.'

'Falling about around my ears...?' Vicky repeated in parrot like fashion.

'That's the problem with lodgers,' Mandy continued confidentially. 'My sister rented her house out for a year and it was a mess when she moved back in. Cigarette burns

everywhere and the oven had to be chucked out completely. Anyway, Andy Griggs, the architect, is terrific.
So...' There was the sound of clicking in the background,
'I'm looking at a week today, twelve-thirty. You can meet
with him in your lunch hour, unless you'd rather arrange
it for the evening?'

'No!' Vicky said hastily. 'Lunchtime would suit me a
lot better!' What was going on? She didn't *want* any building work done to her house! In fact, if her memory served
her clearly, she was in the process of trying to tactfully
terminate her employment at the company because the
smell of trouble was getting stronger with each passing
day. 'No, what I mean is...I don't *want*...any building
work...'

'I know,' Mandy said sympathetically. Click, click,
click. Things were ominously being punched in, in the
background. 'Who does? At least you work, so you can
be out of the house when they're there. You'll just get
back to a sinkful of tea-stained mugs and ladders and
work-benches everywhere. So, I've pencilled you in for
next Monday. Andy'll meet you at your place, and you
shouldn't be longer than a hour...'

'Next Monday.' Her external line was blinking furiously. In ten minutes the post would be delivered and she
wouldn't be able to raise her head above water until mid-
afternoon at least. She would sort all this building non-
sense out later.

Except by the time the thought of architects, builders
and Mandy's phone call resurfaced, Vicky was on her way
to the childminder to collect Chloe, who was waiting for
her with an armful of painting work done at school, which,
from experience, Vicky knew would have to be housed at
least for a few days until they could be discreetly relegated
to the bin.

In her mind, she played guiltily with the thought of bashing the kitchen and the small dining room into one, so that she could have a decent-sized kitchen, big enough for a sensible eating area, maybe even some kind of bar arrangement as well where she could stick a couple of stools. Chloe would like that. It would remind her of the ice-cream bar they'd used to go to once a week in Sydney, where the tall stools were as much of an attraction as the fifty-one different types of ice-cream.

And then, if there was a bit more free wall space, she could have a notice board or two and Chloe's infantile works of art would see the light of day for a bit longer than they did at the moment.

She pushed the nasty, treacherous little thought away and entered into the gist of her daughter's conversation, which today revolved around a stuffed human project in the small class she was attending. Bradley, the name that cropped up most frequently in her daughter's conversation, had apparently hijacked the efforts of the class by accidentally sitting on one of the vital body parts that was destined to be the stuffed figure's head. At this, Chloe laughed until tears came to her eyes and Vicky allowed herself a few moments of unadulterated pleasure, listening to her daughter's uninhibited conversation and bubbling laughter.

'Now we'll have to make a new head,' Chloe confided, 'Miss Jenkins took the buttons off but the smiley mouth took us *ages* to do and we'll have to do a new one.'

'What buttons?'

'The buttons for the *eyes*, Mum!' Chloe said impatiently. 'I'm hungry. What's for tea?'

'Something nourishing and full of goodness,' Vicky said, slowing down to pull into her drive, and her daughter's face fell. She grinned to herself. 'Chicken casserole with potatoes and carrots.'

'Can I have ketchup with it?'

'No reason why not.'

Her thoughts continued to drift like flotsam and jetsam. The bedrooms. There were the bedrooms. Yes, they were absolutely fine, but really, just say building work *did* take place—which it wouldn't, of course—then wouldn't it be nice to knock a couple of those bedrooms together so that she could have a good-sized room for herself with the luxury of an en suite bathroom? Maybe even a dressing room? Nothing big, but big enough for her to actually see her jumpers and maintain the odd crease-free shirt for work.

And Chloe's room would benefit from having those dated fitted cupboards removed and replaced by a free-standing one in some cheerful, modern colour that her daughter would like.

'I can't eat that many carrots, Mum.'

Vicky glanced down to discover that there was a small mountain of orange on her daughter's plate and she hurriedly rectified the situation and tried to gather her thoughts into a less wayward direction.

In the morning, she would phone Mandy and explain that there had been some hideous mistake, that she wasn't at all interested in having any building work done—at least, not at that moment in time. She would stop letting her thoughts drift in pleasing circles that involved bigger bedrooms and bar counters in kitchens. Instead, she would think of wallpaper, paint effects and possibly getting rid of some of the heavier furniture.

By the following morning, her thoughts had turned full circle and she'd managed to persuade herself that she would meet with the architect after all.

Wouldn't it, she thought reasonably, draw attention to herself if she summarily turned down the whole thing without even assessing the cost? If she met with Andy Griggs, then she could say quite truthfully, no doubt—that it was all going to be too expensive, but that she would consider it at a later date. Who could be suspicious of sensible economic belt-tightening? If she met with the architect, she would also be able to put her mind at rest and find out for herself exactly what could and couldn't be done with the house. She loved the location but she had become accustomed to lighter, airier houses in Australia and she found the closed-in rooms claustrophobic and a little depressing. He might make one or two good suggestions which she could put into practice later on down the road. Once she'd left the company and had saved enough money to do it on her own.

All told, she decided that it was altogether better to go ahead with plans as they stood.

Her carefree frame of mind, now she had persuaded herself that she would see Andy Griggs, gave in fully to the temptation to mentally redesign the house from the bottom brick upwards. She found that there was no aspect of it she couldn't, in her head, alter. She was in high spirits when the telephone shrieked just as she was about to leave work for the day.

The minute she picked up the receiver something told her that Max Forbes would be at the other end. Some inner instinct that sent her pulses racing. It had been peaceful these last two days. Her only communication with her boss had been via e-mail and fax and the work had gone smoothly at this end.

Now, as she heard the deep velvet voice down the end of the line, she realised that something intangible had been missing from the office. Excitement. A certain thrill of anticipation. A heightened state of awareness in which her senses were always, in his presence, on full alert.

'Vicky. Max here. Glad I caught you before you left.'

Vicky played with the cord of the telephone, wondering what could have warranted a phone call when fax and e-mail could easily provide sufficient communication between them and neither sent her nervous system into overdrive.

'How is it going in New York?' she asked politely. 'I've dealt with all your e-mails and sent both of those faxes off to Roger's and Walnut House, as you requested.'

'Yes, yes. Fine. Good. Look, the reason I'm calling is that the problem out here is bigger than I had first thought.' He paused. 'Quite an unpleasant situation has arisen, as a matter of fact.' His voice, when he said that, was cold, and she shivered at the prospect of Max Forbes on the trail of whoever had made the *situation unpleasant*. She had now seen enough of him at work to realise that there was a core of steel running through him that made him a formidable adversary.

'Is there something you'd like me to do from this end?' Vicky asked anxiously.

'For starters, you can cancel my meetings for the next week. Get Anderson to chair the ones that can't wait, but the rest will have to be rescheduled.'

Vicky had already flicked out some notepaper, and even while he spoke was rapidly cataloguing in her head which of his meetings would need to be handed over to Ralph Anderson.

'Anything else?'

'Yes. I need you over here—and that's not a question, it's an order. Heads are going to roll over here and everything will have to be meticulously documented. I'm meeting with lawyers this afternoon to see where we stand, but there's a hell of a lot to get down in writing and a lot of it is highly confidential. I can't trust a temp out here to do the job, provided I can get one to do it well enough, and what's going on is too sensitive for any of the secretaries in the company to deal with the information. I take it,' he said, 'that there won't be a problem with that?'

She could hear the hard edge to the question. He was not going to allow her to wriggle out of this, and however much she told herself that she would clear off as soon as possible, she was reluctant to leave under a black cloud. She needed a good reference if she was to apply for any-thing worth doing at a later date and clock-watching never got an employee anywhere.

'How long would you need me for?' she asked, heart thudding at the prospect of asking Brenda to have Chloe and her daughter's tears at the thought of her mother going abroad without her. They had never been separated and it was a precedent she had no wish to set.

'Three days at the outside, probably less. Don't worry,' he said coolly, 'I fully appreciate that foreign travel is not something you're interested in, but this time there's no choice. You can book Concorde over. You know where I'm staying. Get a room there as well. I'll make sure there's no problem in that area.'

Vicky sighed inaudibly. 'Will that be all?'

'E-mail me with your time of arrival and expect to be working the minute your feet touch the ground.'

'Of course,' she said with a hint of sarcasm. 'I wouldn't dare expect otherwise.'

The adrenaline was still surging through her blood-stream when, one hour later, she found herself asking Brenda whether she could keep Chloe for the following night, at the most two.

'I'll pay you, of course,' she said, over a cup of coffee, and Brenda looked at her intently.

'Never you mind the money, Vicky. Just so long as this job doesn't start taking over your life. I've seen some of these career women and they spend their lives in a state of permanent exhaustion. Not,' she added thoughtfully, 'that it seems to be doing you any harm at all.'

'What do you mean?' In the corner of the room Chloe and Brenda's little girl Alice, who was one year older, were playing a vigorous game of Barbies. From the sidelines, Ken watched with blank-eyed interest.

'I haven't seen you look so...so *well*...for months. Skin radiant, eyes sparkling. Whatever work this boss is feeding you, it agrees with your system.'

'He's *feeding me*?' Vicky said, laughing, half at the antics of the Barbie dolls, who now appeared to be engaged in physical warfare despite their attire of bikinis and high-heeled pumps, and half at Brenda's mistaken notions. 'Too much work, heaps of responsibility and no end of sarcastic comments, not to mention nosy prying and pointed innuendoes.'

Brenda laughed in response. 'Well, watch out. A girl could get addicted to a diet like that.'

But it was settled, as was the flight to New York which she'd booked that afternoon, and she felt the first stirrings of excitement when she arrived at Heathrow with her small flight bag and was shown all the respect and subservience obviously given to anyone who had enough money to fly by the most expensive method in the world.

Only when she booked into the hotel in New York, after an enjoyable and uneventful flight in surroundings that were speedy but cramped, did the excitement give way to apprehension.

It dawned on her more fully now that she was going to

be here with Max Forbes for at least two days, maybe three, and this time there would be no five o'clock ending and eight-thirty start.

He had arranged to meet her in the hotel bar, to brief her on what was going on, and she felt a tremor of nerves as she slipped on her smart oatmeal-coloured trouser suit, with a long-sleeved cream polo top underneath the tailored jacket, and bundled her hair into some form of chignon. The person staring back at her in the mirror looked impeccably professional but still managed to give the impression that the wearer of those smart clothes might well have been happier in a pair of jeans and an oversized shirt.

He was already there and waiting for her when she walked into the bar. She spotted him immediately at a table in the corner, swirling a drink around in one hand. She hadn't seen him look so tired before. As if to confirm the impression, he rubbed his eyes wearily with his thumbs before asking her what she wanted to drink and summoning across a waiter to take the order.

'You look awful,' Vicky blurted out, and he smiled with wry amusement.

'And it's very nice to see you too. Glad you could make it. Did you have to do a lot of rearranging?'

'I managed.' She shrugged and sat back to allow the waiter to place her glass of cold white wine in front of her. 'What's going on? Would you like to brief me now or would you rather we wait until morning, when I'll have my laptop and can take more substantial notes?'

She sipped some of her wine and felt herself relax fractionally.

'No, I'll give you the lowdown now. Have you eaten, by the way?' He didn't give her time to answer. Instead, he beckoned the waiter across and told him to bring two of the prawn salads and some bread. 'To cut a long story short, a few days ago I received a rather disturbing call from one of my accountants for Eva. To give you a bit of background, Eva's one of the smaller subsidiaries which my father took a personal interest in because it dealt with his hobby-horse, namely computer games. As you know, computer games have come a long way and Eva's profits have risen steadily and fairly dramatically over the past five years.' He gulped back a mouthful of his drink and then banged his glass on the table, as though giving vent to some frustrating but powerful emotion. 'In the past year, sizeable amounts have, apparently, gone missing. It transpires that the chairman of the company, a man I have known for years, has been slowly but surely embezzling money in the form of bogus clients, forged signatures, etc, etc.' He rubbed his eyes tiredly again and then leaned heavily back into his chair and half closed his eyes. 'I've spent the past two days locked up in a room with the accountant, and today three high-powered lawyers, working out how to deal with the problem. So far, he's unaware. We feel that our best bet is to surprise him with the evidence, just in case he attempts to tamper with it and add to his crimes.'

'Will he go to prison?' Vicky was horrified.

'I don't know,' Max said simply. 'Fraud deserves punishment but, if he's sacked, then that will be punishment enough as far as I'm concerned. He'll be forced to take early retirement and his reputation within the computer industry will be over. Aside from that,' he sighed, 'he has a family. I'm godfather to one of his children!' He sat back as food was brought to their table. Typically, there was lots of it, and it was clearly of restaurant standard, despite the fact that they were in the hotel bar. 'It's a bloody nightmare, but you understand why it was imperative that an external secretary was brought in to deal with what's going on. It's not a big company and tongues wag.' They both dug into their salads. The prawns were as large as crabs and there was enough salad on the oversized plates to satisfy the most ravenous of appetites. 'The fewer people who know about this, the more successful our damage limitation will be. In a field like this, shares could fall at the merest mention of wrong-doing.'

'So what will you do?'

'What do you think I should do?'

'Don't tell me you would take the opinion of a lowly secretary seriously,' she said in an attempt to defuse his mood, although his reply was unexpectedly serious.

'I'm always ready to listen to suggestions.' His tone of voice left no doubt as to his sincerity.

'Well.' She paused and considered what she had been told. 'He would obviously have to leave immediately, and someone would have to ensure that his career would be effectively over. You're right, fraud would be punishable by a long prison stretch. But if I knew this man's family, I suppose I would be tempted to dismiss him with all the necessary warnings and look on it as a salutary experience.'

'Very soft-hearted.'

'Only when it comes to certain things,' Vicky informed him briefly.

'Care to tell me what brings out the hard edge in you?'.

'No.' She could feel his eyes roving over her as she bent to concentrate on her salad. 'What is the format for tomorrow?' As a conversation-stopper it was obvious, but it worked. The remaining hour was spent discussing various aspects of the problem and what would be expected of her in terms of her work. By the time she left to head back up to her room, she felt exhausted. Her head was spinning from the permutations of the problem confronting them, and she was uneasily aware that with this trip to New York she was taking yet another step towards being enmeshed in a job she knew could not last.

The following two days were the most invigorating and exciting of her career. Fact had proved stranger than fiction, as it usually does. The man involved in the embezzlement was not quite the cold-blooded fraudster she had expected. When summoned into the boardroom before lawyers and two independent accountants, he quickly confessed everything.

Sitting in the background, her fingers flew over her notepad as she took down everything that was said in her impeccable shorthand—a dying skill for which she was now immeasurably grateful. Although he was speaking into a tape recorder, she didn't think that she could bear to transcribe the emotional breakdown from a tape.

Harry Shoring wept—loud, wrenching sobs born of guilt, fear and remorse.

He had, he confessed, originally seen the embezzlement as a stop-gap measure. He had intended to pay back every penny of what he'd taken but the whole thing had snowballed. His daughter, it turned out, had been involved in a car accident and the insurance had gone only so far to covering the cost of the surgery and the hospitals, but more had needed doing. Much, much more, or else his child would have been left a cripple for the rest of her life. He'd faced the prospect of forking out for radical new treatment which might restore the use of her legs and, when his own money had run out, he'd turned to the company for what he had seen would be a loan. A loan no one else knew about.

Throughout the long hours spent listening to his account, Max sat in silence, asking only the briefest of questions, even though it was to him that Harry's watery eyes

most frequently turned. His face betrayed nothing whatsoever. He made no notes whatsoever, leaving that to the
rest of the assembled crew, but she had no doubt that every
single word spoken was being absorbed and dealt with by
that sharp, clever mind of his.

By the end of the second day, and after some discussions with the accountant and the chief lawyer, Harry
Shoring was told that he would not face the prospect of a
prison sentence. Max would, he said himself, repay every
penny of the debt from his own personal fortune, an offer
which was met with a gasp of gratitude from the older
man, but in return Harry would have to leave the firm
immediately and his pension would be altered to compensate for the embezzlement.

'What about Jessie?' he asked tearfully. 'She's been
coming along so well...my poor little baby...only fourteen...'

'I'll make sure that all health costs are covered until
progress is complete.'

The solution was unbelievably generous and compas-
sionate, Vicky thought two hours later as she sat in the
hotel conference room putting the finishing touches to various bits of documentation that would require signatures.

Her mind played back Max's words and expressions
over those past two days and something strong and disturbing quivered inside her. A confusing and uninvited notion that her secrecy about Chloe was somehow an act of
betrayal, that she should tell him about her daughter.
Hadn't she seen enough of him now to know that he
wouldn't abuse the knowledge? The thought hovered
above her like a storm cloud filled with threat. The temptation to blurt it all out was very nearly irresistible, but
something held her back. Thick, sluggish fear, lodged inside her like a vice, stilled the little voice, reasoned to her

that any confession, in the short term, would ruin this important trip to New York, told her to keep her dangerous secret to herself. After all, her daughter played no part in her working life and never would. He would never find out, not if she remained careful. And wasn't the old adage *better safe than sorry* the most priceless of advice? She ignored her gut feeling that her reasoning was built on very shaky foundations and stifled her inner protests.

Instead, she finished her stack of typing and breathed a sigh of relief. Tomorrow she would be catching the day flight back to Heathrow and would be in time to collect Chloe from school. They had spoken twice a day and she'd been amused to discover that her daughter had not spent hours sobbing over her mother's absence. Chloe, she thought, was growing up. She'd missed her daughter, but Vicky had to admit that the past two days had been rather wonderful. The fleeting window of freedom had made her see how difficult her life had been as a single-parent family. She'd forgotten what it was like to have a night of undisturbed sleep and to awaken in the morning without having to plunge into insistent childish conversation. For a few seconds, she thought how wonderful it must be to have help in the form of a partner. In her own head, Vicky had equated partnership with the likes of Shaun, but now she thought that four hands, two heads and the security of sharing must be rather nice.

She wondered what kind of father Max would make and, in the solitude of the enormous conference room, she flushed and glanced around her, as though afraid that unseen eyes might pick a hole in her head and yank out the wayward thought.

She was so consumed by the uninvited image that when she heard his voice from the door, she imagined, for a couple of seconds, that she must be dreaming, but when she turned around he was lounging in the doorframe, casually dressed in a pair of olive-green trousers and a short-sleeved shirt that emphasised his superb build.

'I've just finished,' Vicky said, in case he'd come to find out why she was taking so long. There had been a lot more to type out than she had first expected.

'Good. In that case you can run along and have a bath, get on your glad rags and join me for dinner.' He smiled slowly at her and raked his fingers through his hair. 'Unless you have other plans?'

'No other plans,' Vicky mumbled, switching off the computer and making a big deal of rustling her bits of paper to hide her confusion. He continued to lounge oppressively by the door, watching her antics, which made her feel like a gerbil pointlessly gadding about on a wheel in a cage.

'I'll meet you in the bar in—' he glanced down at his watch '—forty minutes, and we'll take a cab to the restaurant.'

'With everyone else?'

'Everyone else has a family to go home to,' Max said drily, 'and after the hours they've put in over the past few days, they'll be only too glad to get back to a bit of normality. Just you and me to celebrate the best outcome that could have been achieved, given the circumstances.'

At which he gave her a mocking half salute and departed, leaving Vicky to hastily gather her paperwork, dash up to her bedroom, have a quick bath and then devote the remainder of the time left to surveying her wardrobe, which was scantily inadequate.

She finally appeared in the hotel bar ten minutes late in a pair of black trousers, the other half of her one and only trouser suit, and a beige long-sleeved woollen top which had been flung in her case as an afterthought, and for which she was now grateful as the other three tops she had brought with her were suitable for work only. They were businesslike shirts, smartly tailored and ludicrously inappropriate for doing anything apart from sitting in front of a computer or taking notes at meetings.

Max was waiting for her in the bar. He saw her before she saw him and had a few seconds during which he appreciatively took in the trousers, her slim hips and waist and the top which fitted like a glove. He still found it incredible that she could do this to him, make him feel like a teenager all over again, but he was accepting it in the manner of someone accepting the inexplicable but unavoidable. He was even, he realised, becoming tuned in to her thoughts from the changing expressions on her face. Over the past two days he had found himself watching her, knowing when she agreed with what was being said and when she didn't. More amazingly, he had begun unconsciously looking to her for approval of some of his decisions, although he wasn't about to heed the advice of any woman or be swayed in his thoughts simply because of the way Vicky's eyes shifted to him, or the way her mouth tightened in unspoken disagreement.

He could feel that shadow of anxiety hovering around her as they left the hotel bar and headed for the restaurant. It was one of his favourites. Upbeat and stylish with classy food but without the accompanying atmosphere of snobbish elitism that so many restaurants liked to cultivate. Unlike all the women he had dated in the past, she would not be impressed by a stuffy, expensive, snobbish place. She would wrinkle that small, perfect nose in mild distaste even though she wouldn't make any comment. And why not admit it, he thought, he wanted to impress her. He wanted to show her what a well-travelled, worldly-wise, sophisticated yet unpretentious kind of guy he was.

Which meant putting her at ease. Which meant, he thought with the usual frustration he felt when he was alone with her, talking about work. Which was no problem, and over the superb starters they chatted about the outcome of the fraud fiasco. Harry Shoring, spared the prospect of prison, had been weak with gratitude, and had agreed to leave the company immediately with his reputation intact although only so long as he took early retirement and remained retired. Any hint of his recommencing work in another company and, Max had said, he would have no alternative but to spill the beans.

'Are you pleased?' Vicky asked, finishing her cold white wine and allowing her glass to be refilled.

'We couldn't have been more understanding,' Max said bluntly.

'*You* couldn't have been more understanding. After all, you *will* be virtually taking over as his financial backbone until medical treatment on his daughter can't go any further.'

Max, seeing the frank and open admiration on her face, didn't know whether to feel flattered or impatient. The generous gesture had been made without thinking. His father's friend, whatever he had done, had a sick child and was broke. Max had money—*not* helping Harry was not an alternative. No, he didn't want her admiration for his altruistic gesture. He wanted much, much more than that, and right now he was a million miles away from it. But at least she had shed that air of nervous suspicion, even if, he suspected with wry self-irony, it was the wine rather than his witty, seamless conversation that was responsible.

'It was nothing,' Max said with a dismissive shrug of his broad shoulders.

'Oh, but it *is*,' she insisted, watching as he topped up her glass. 'It may be nothing to *you*, but lots of men would have just turned their backs and walked away from the situation without feeling any sense of responsibility.'

Adulation for a simple act of humanity, he wanted to tell her, was *not* what he was after. Her cheeks were beginning to look a little flushed, and he saw, with some surprise, that most of the second bottle of wine he had ordered had gone and she was now toying with the food on her plate. She had shoved the few remaining bits of vegetables into a face-like shape, which made him grin to himself, because there was something endearingly child-like about it when her approach to life was always so coolly efficient and businesslike.

'Nice face,' he remarked gravely. 'Anyone in particular?' He tilted his head to one side in a question and tried not to burst out laughing when she went bright red and hurriedly closed her knife and fork, looking around her to see whether anyone had been observing her little activity.

'Perhaps we ought to leave,' he suggested. 'And don't look so tortured.' He leaned forward and whispered conspiratorially, *'No one was watching you. It's not that kind of place.'* When she smiled sheepishly back at him, he felt his heart do something odd and his breathing thickened slightly.

They had to get out of here. She was driving him crazy. He couldn't wait to pay the bill, leaving an outrageously generous tip because he couldn't wait for the head waiter to find him some change, and he was so excruciatingly aware of her sitting next to him in the cab that he could almost feel his skin tingling. She'd had too much to drink and the effect was devastating to his senses.

'Oh, walk with me to my room,' she sighed, supporting herself on his arm when he attempted to point her in the direction of the elevator, mumbling something about having one last drink on his own at the bar before retiring.

She'd braided her hair into a French plait and she played with it as it hung over one shoulder.

'Okay,' he said reluctantly, 'but you should get a good night's sleep. You must be exhausted.'

Her eyes danced. 'Never felt livelier.' Her hand, he noticed as they rode the elevator to her floor in silence, was still on his arm, a slight but insistent pressure that was having a noticeable effect on his body parts, one in particular.

He virtually pulled her to her room, watching as she fumbled with the credit card-style key and finally removing it from her and opening the door himself, then he stood politely back so that she could enter. Enter and turn to face him.

'I had a fantastic evening,' she breathed, looking at him then walking through into the small sitting room of the bedroom suite so that he inevitably followed. She turned abruptly and approached him. 'Did you?'

'Fantastic.' He cleared his voice.

'Then why do you look so edgy?' she teased.

Her lips were still curved into a smile when he bent his head and covered them with his own. It was like tasting nectar for the first time and after a moment's pause, she returned his kiss. Returned it with all the passion he was feeling himself, arching her body into his, pressing so that she could be in no doubt as to the urgency of his response.

He groaned hoarsely. Somehow they found themselves to the sofa. Her breasts. He had to see them, taste them, lick them. He wanted to touch every inch of the body that had filled his mind for longer than he cared to think.

When she pulled up her jumper, exposing her small, ripe breasts with their erotic lace covering, he drew his breath in sharply. Through the lace, he could see the pink, protruding tip of her nipple and he licked it, but the delicacy of this was too much for him. He felt as though he couldn't wait.

With urgent hands, he tugged the bra down so that her breasts spilled out, small, firm breasts with big nipples that were dark and engorged.

With a moan, she pushed his head down and he could feel her body shudder as he suckled at one, then the other, taking as much of her into his mouth as he could while his feverish hands prised open her legs and massaged her thighs.

Another time, he thought, and there *would* be another, he would take his time, turn lovemaking into a work of art. But for now, he was too explosively hungry for her to wait.

CHAPTER SIX

VICKY made very sure that she was out of her office when Max returned to work after New York. She knew that he would be coming in to the office at nine-thirty because of the e-mail he'd sent her the previous day. Nevertheless, from the cowardly sanctuary of the Ladies, she could still feel her heart thumping at a mile a minute.

She would give him fifteen minutes, a never-ending stretch of time during which she pointlessly stared at her reflection in the mirror and attempted to look busy with a make-up compact, just in case someone else entered the large, plush cloakroom and wondered what small, red-haired Vicky Lockhart was doing there, her cheeks flushed with colour, her eyes over-bright. It was a relatively small, friendly company, and during the short space of time that she'd been working there she could say with reasonable accuracy that she was on nodding acquaintance with most of the staff. If anyone came upon her now, staring sightlessly in the mirror, hands shaking, lips dry and an expression of gut-wrenching dread on her face, they would rush her to the nearest hospital. Or, at any rate, the nearest Sanatorium. At the very least, they would ask lots of concerned, prying questions for which she had no answers.

She only knew that her mind had spent the past few days preoccupied with one thing and one thing only.

Or perhaps *one person* would be more to the point.

When she thought of Max Forbes, her brain seemed to close down completely, leaving her at the cruel whim of memories that made her body begin to ache.

She gripped the chrome tap and stared hard and purposefully into the sink, willing the onslaught of thoughts to go away, but it was no good.

The worst, most humiliating thought of all was the realisation that none of it would have happened if she had not invited him into her bedroom. True, she'd had more than her usual amount to drink, but she knew, inside herself, that blaming a few glasses of wine for what had happened between them would be an act of cowardice. The plain, unadorned truth was that she had felt relaxed enough with him in that restaurant to open up. She'd stopped putting up barriers and had succumbed to the power of his raw masculinity and the sexy charm that she'd fought desperately against from the very first minute she'd laid eyes on him.

She turned on the tap and rinsed her face with ice-cold water, but beneath the water she could still feel her cheeks burning. Not only had she proceeded to force the man into her room, or at least put him in a position where to say goodnight and leave would risk appearing rude, she'd then done the unthinkable.

Her body had been on fire. During the meal, she'd felt herself get more and more turned on every time his eyes fell on her. By the time they'd reached her bedroom, her imagination had been in full flow and she'd been in no mood to put the brakes on.

She'd felt sexy and alluring and vampish. The memory of it was enough to make her shudder with mortification. Amazing what a few glasses of good wine and an active imagination could do to a girl, she now thought bitterly. She had slowly begun to pull up her jumper, her fingers playing with the soft fabric, while he'd stood in silence and watched, his eyes dark with desire at what she was so readily and eagerly offering him. No strings attached. On a plate. With a silver spoon. And all condiments included. What man wouldn't have been burning up with enthusiasm for such an abandoned offering? She'd opened the floodgates by kissing him, and doing a strip tease, in a ridiculously sensuous fashion which had probably had him sniggering all the way back to his bedroom.

But he hadn't been sniggering then. She'd seen the darkening intent in his eyes with a flare of wild excitement. When their mouths had met, she'd felt as though the moment had been one she'd been waiting for all her life and the greed of his responses had fuelled in her a heady sense of power. When he'd pulled down her bra, the air had felt wonderfully cool on her hot skin and her nipples had puckered in response and pulling back had been out of the question. She had, and the thought of it now made her groan with shame, shoved him down to her breasts. There had been just one thing in her head at that point, and that was the burning need to have her desire sated. She *needed* to feel his mouth on her nipples, sucking, drawing them in, nibbling and licking the pulsing, protruding bud.

Her legs, opened and waiting for his urgent exploring hand, had been a wet cavern of delight. He'd massaged her thighs while she had placed both her hands behind her head, eyes shut, body arched upwards to receive his ravaging mouth.

From outside, the light had filtered into the room and spread an interesting array of shadows around them, so that everything seemed other-worldly. She could remember watching in drugged fascination as he'd stripped off his clothes. His hands hadn't been able to undo his shirt-buttons quickly enough and in the end, he had ripped it off. Only a few hours before, he'd been the archetypal boss with his demure, efficient secretary. She'd taken notes, her legs neatly crossed beneath the prim, unrevealing skirt. No one would ever have guessed that only a few hours later she would have shed all her inhibitions and thrown herself at her boss with the urgency and feverish passion of a woman who had spent her entire adult life in a sexual desert.

Vicky inspected her face in the bathroom mirror for guilt and shame. She would have to make sure that she eliminated both before she ventured back into her office. She'd made an utter fool of herself but she wasn't about to lose every shred of dignity in the process.

She would have to make a show of pretending that the whole sorry episode had not made any indelible mark on her. She smiled ruefully at her reflection at the thought of that whopping lie. The fact was that her moment of abandon had cost her dearly. She straightened, fished into the make-up compact and began applying a little mascara, controlling her shaking fingers with effort.

Even in the throes of her love affair with Shaun, before revulsion had set in, she'd never felt such a burst of dangerous, white-hot craving. She'd not been able to get enough of Max. When his mouth had left her breasts and moistly made its way down the flat planes of her stomach, the throbbing between her legs had made her squirm. The first touch of his tongue flicking gently at her pulsing womanhood had made her moan loudly and thrash against the bed, then she'd begun to move against his mouth, her body twisting up and down and from side to side while he gripped her hips and plunged his tongue deeper and deeper into her welcoming, honey-sweet essence. Her orgasm had been a wild, shuddering release that had seemed to vibrate into infinity, and still their lovemaking had continued. He'd waited for her body to sag then, slowly but surely, like a maestro fine-tuning an instrument, he'd aroused her all over again, and this time she'd been the one to explore his body, until his desperate need for her had made him push her down onto his huge erection.

At no point and at all points, they could have stopped themselves from reaching the final destination.

But they hadn't and there was no point killing herself with regrets. It had happened and now she would just have to suffer the consequences.

She finished with the mascara, and dabbed a little lipstick on. Blusher she would leave. There was enough natural colour in her cheeks to make anyone think she had overdone it with the artificial stuff anyway.

She was stuffing the compact into her bag and wondering whether she should head back, when the cloakroom door was pushed open and Catherine, secretary to one of the company directors, let out a little squeal of relief.

'I've been looking for you *everywhere*,' she said anxiously. 'What on earth have you *done to him*?'

'*Done* to him? Done to *whom*?' Vicky said, feigning ignorance.

'Your boss! He got in ten minutes ago and stormed into Jeremy's office like a tiger in need of a victim, then he ordered me to *smoke you out*. Those were his precise words, Vicky. *Smoke you out.*' The excitement of what could possibly be going on had replaced the urgency of her mission. Catherine now looked as though she would be more than willing to listen to any number of juicy explanations, however impatient Max had been to get hold of Vicky. '*So what's going on?* I haven't seen him that thunderous for…forever, and *I've* been here since the company got going! *What* have you gone and done?'

'I'd better go, Catherine. No point *you* getting into trouble as well by staying here too long.' Which did the trick. Catherine jumped and practically shoved Vicky out of the cloakroom so that she found herself propelled into her office with a lot less preparation time than she had hoped for.

Forbiddingly, he was waiting for her in his office, and the dividing door was open so that she was subjected to the full force of his scowling face as he beckoned her into the chair in front of his desk. Vicky sat down, crossed her legs and adopted a bland expression. At least, that was what she'd aimed for. Her mouth felt as though the muscles had seized up, which probably meant that she was displaying something more akin to a deranged grimace.

'What's *this* all about?' He held a sheet of paper in one hand, which he then proceeded to dangle dismissively before letting it flutter down to the desk. Vicky followed its progress downwards, mesmerised, before finding her voice.

'I thought it best… I realise that…I'm afraid that due to my own stupidity…' She didn't dare look him directly in the eyes so instead she shifted her focus to an indeterminate point somewhere beyond his left shoulder. He'd tilted his head to one side and now appeared to be settling down to wait for her to finish her sentence.

'I just think that what happened in New York has jeopardised my position here, that's all,' she concluded, when she realised that she was going to find no help whatsoever from his quarter. He began drumming his fingers on the desk, an aggravating, steady sound that did nothing for her already shredded nerves.

'And don't act as though you don't know what I'm talking about!' she muttered when he still hadn't said anything. 'I don't think that a boss-secretary relationship is feasible when the boss has slept with the secretary! Do you?' Or even, she thought guiltily, when the secretary has slept with the boss. The steadily drumming fingers slowed their rhythm without actually stopping. The sound was driving her mad.

'It happened,' he said softly, leaning back into the chair and folding his hands behind his head so that he could stare at her through narrowed eyes. 'These things do, believe it or not. People have too much to drink...'

'I knew it! You're blaming me! I wondered when you would get down to that.'

'I wasn't blaming *anyone*. I was merely saying that human nature is not always strong. We both made a mistake—' he paused, allowing her to digest that '—but that doesn't mean that we have to let one slip-up throw everything out of proportion. Unless, of course, you feel that you wouldn't be able to put the incident behind you...in which case, I would more than understand if you walked out of this office right now.'

'What do you mean, *not able to put the incident behind me*?' Vicky asked suspiciously.

'I'm merely saying that you may feel yourself more involved with me than you care to admit...'

Vicky emitted a shriek of near-hysterical laughter which she hoped was sufficient to inform him of the absurdity of his suggestion. In case it wasn't, she clarified coldly, 'It was a mistake, as you said. Nothing more.'

'So where's the problem? We put it behind us, we get on with life. I don't want to lose a brilliant secretary and I don't suppose you're that willing to throw away a damn good pay packet, so let's make a deal. We put it down to experience and it's never mentioned again. Believe me, I feel as exposed as you do. I don't approve of any boss having sex with his secretary and, aside from that, I opened myself up to any number of scenarios which I'm experienced enough to spot and avoid. What if you'd cried *sexual harassment*? It's a measure of my trust in you and my belief that we can carry on working together that I'm asking you to stay at all.'

'And what if we find that it doesn't work that way?' She noticed that he hadn't even euphemistically used the phrase *making love*. They had *had sex*: regrettable, but not earth-shattering.

'If it doesn't work that way, then...' He shrugged and fixed his cool, grey eyes on her. 'We call it a day.'

Choosing between the devil and the deep blue sea were equally unimpressive options, she was fast discovering.

Walking out would tell its own story. And what if he got it into his head to follow her? If only because of the secretarial skills she knew he valued? He obviously had no qualms about just *showing up* on her doorstep. What if he just *showed up* and Chloe happened to be around?

On the other hand, to remain was to open a Pandora's box. Making love to Max had stirred her emotions into a chaotic, seething mass. She didn't know what she felt, she just knew that fear was involved—and not just fear of what Max could do to her should he ever find out the truth of her situation, but fear of what she could do to herself simply by spending time with him. She was finding it easier and easier to let her defences slip. One day she would make a fatal error.

'I'll give it a couple of weeks,' she said now, sitting on the fence because she couldn't think of where else to go. 'But I'll only stay on one condition,' she continued inflexibly, 'and the condition is that if I decide, for whatever reason, that I'm unable to work for you, then you leave me alone. You don't try and persuade me to stay, you just respect my decision.'

'Of course,' Max said, magnanimous in victory. He felt himself sag with relief. He hadn't known what he would do if she'd stuck to her decision to resign. In fact, it was true to say that he hadn't known a number of things until she'd come along and turned his world upside down, because there was no use pretending otherwise. He felt like a man clinging onto a piece of driftwood in the middle of a stormy sea, with no real clue as to where he was going or when his ordeal would end.

'Fine,' she said quietly, looking away from him while he continued to stare at her. He wondered how much or how little their lovemaking had meant to her. Certainly, her averted profile wasn't giving much away, and he was overcome by a primal urge to force her to submit to him, to confess that he had made the earth move for her, to acknowledge that she'd never been as aroused by anyone in her life as she'd been aroused by him. In fact, he was assailed by a ridiculous, puerile desire to hear her tell him that he was the best.

He irritably began tapping his fountain pen on the desk, while his mind threw its leash and travelled joyously down memory lane, rearing up at the volcanic turn-on the sight of her naked body had been for him. Every bit of her uncovered had been a revelation without compare. The taste of her nipples still lingered on his tongue, making him feel worryingly unsteady. Sleeping with her, instead of diminishing his fantasies, had succeeded in making them proliferate. Right now, at this very moment, he could quite easily have locked the outside office door, whatever the hell anyone who came along might think, and taken her. Stripped her of her neat little grey outfit, a libido-quencher of the highest order, and laid her on his desk, naked and exquisitely open to his mouth and hands. He would have liked to have suckled on her delicious breasts at this very moment, with the fax machine going outside, the light on his phone informing him that he'd calls waiting and the computer terminal begging to be downloaded of its important messages. He couldn't think of anything more erotic than letting the world of high finance wait until their needs were satisfied. He cleared his throat and hastily rummaged pointlessly through some of the paperwork lying in his open briefcase. With great effort, he managed to get his mind to operate on a more relevant level and, with even greater effort, he succeeded in speaking to her about work and what had been happening in the office since he had been away.

She was leaving when he thought to ask, 'What did Andy Griggs have to say about your house?'

Vicky, with one hand on the doorknob, turned to face him. Andy Griggs had slipped her mind. 'I'm seeing him this evening. I had to cancel our previous appointment,' she said, 'but of course I shan't go ahead with anything, not until I know one way or another…'

Max felt an unsteadying combination of impotence, panic and anger. 'Naturally,' he said calmly, making himself smile and giving a rueful but utterly understanding shrug of his broad shoulders. 'Have you decided what you would like to have done anyway?'

'Well…' Vicky hesitated. 'I…I *have* noticed, ever since this all came up, that the house is in desperate need of renovation. I never gave it much thought when I first got back to England. I was too busy sorting out other aspects of my life. But last weekend I had a walk around the place and—' she sighed '—things need changing. The rooms need rearranging. It worked when it was rented out because most of the time the tenants were students, so four small bedrooms was an attraction, but now I think I'd like to make the master bedroom much bigger, perhaps with a little sitting area, and I could do something about having a pl—' She'd very nearly said *playroom*, but in time she swallowed the word down, although the near-slip had jolted her. 'A place to work. I could put my computer in there…' She gave her head a little shake and smiled apologetically. She hadn't meant to say so much. As usual, she had ended up rambling on. 'I have no idea why I'm planning all this,' she said firmly, 'There's a good chance I won't remain with the company—' she looked down when she said that, because the reasons for her departure were close enough to the surface of her mind to make her tremble '—and, even if I do, I haven't got the money.'

'Money isn't a problem.'

'Not for you perhaps.' She pulled open the door, not wanting to become embroiled in a conversation that was only serving to remind her of yet something else she would be giving up when she left. 'Will that be all? I think I should be able to cover most of this by this afternoon and the rest I'll do first thing in the morning, if that's all right with you.'

'Fine. I'll be out of the office this afternoon.' He paused. 'I take it there won't be any surprises waiting for me tomorrow morning when I get in?'

Vicky flushed but didn't say anything and, after a few seconds, he gave her a curt nod of the head, which she read as her dismissal, and she went back into her office, breathing a sigh of relief that she was out of his presence, even though things had not gone according to plan. The plan had *been* that she would now be on her way to yet another employment agency, clutching her CV and prepared to do a typing test. Instead, here she still was, ensconced in her leather swivel chair, and she was edgily aware that a part of her was relieved that she wouldn't be leaving. It was, in fact, the same part that had encouraged her to remove her jumper a few nights previously and to offer herself to the man she kept reminding herself she needed to escape from. And it was the same part that responded to his wit, his humour, the part that had, she acknowledged shakily, become addicted to his every mood, every shift in his expression, every change in his voice. Her fingers continued to fly across the computer keys and her eyes scanned the document she was typing, but her mind played its dangerous games somewhere else. Somewhere in a land of No Return, where her heart seemed to have wandered when she wasn't looking.

She was so absorbed in her thoughts that she jumped when he strode into her section an hour later, slinging on his jacket and checking his pockets in an unconscious and automatic gesture which she had grown to expect. She stopped with her hands hovering fractionally over the keyboard. She could feel nervous perspiration prickling under her arms and above her lip. She even thought she could feel the rush of blood through her veins. Hot, boiling blood, surging like a toxin. She'd fallen in love with him and it was like feeding off poison. He had to repeat three times that he would see her in the morning before she came to her senses and nodded, not daring to open her mouth because she knew her voice would give her away. Her eyes drank him up, though. She felt like a guilty sinner, gorging on temptation as she took in the lean hungry power of his body—the body she had touched!—the angles of his face, the full, sensual lower lip that promised so much more than fulfilling sex.

When the door slammed behind him, she could feel her body slump, and it was blessed relief to finally leave the office at a little before five so that she could rush to her daughter and try and regain some of her lost sanity. Chloe would be a tonic, with her incessant chatter and her innocent preoccupation with her school day. It wouldn't leave room in her head for Max.

Unfortunately thoughts of him plagued her all through

her daughter's tea, and by the time she had settled Chloe upstairs and opened the door to the architect she felt wrung out.

It didn't help that the expression on his face as he was shown through the house made her realise, dejectedly, that the house really *was* in need of a serious overhaul and that it was now out of the question that any such overhaul would be forthcoming.

'You do realise,' he said thoughtfully, rocking on his heels and tapping his lips with his pen, 'that you have damp.' He led her across to one of the offending walls in the sitting room, fiddled around with a gadget and then held it up for her to see. 'If something isn't done about it fairly soon, the walls are going to deteriorate. Your idea about knocking through a couple of rooms would be a good way of clearing up the problem because we can do some damp-proofing at the same time.' Over a cup of coffee, he continued to elaborate on her ideas, tossing in more enticing ones of his own, which Vicky listened to with a sinking heart.

'I haven't got money for all of that,' she finally confessed bluntly. 'I mean, I might just have to do a superficial job, at least for the time being. A paint job here and there, some wallpaper, maybe get some new furniture.'

'Won't take care of the damp.'

'Well, what can you do about that?' She frowned irritably, thinking that she hadn't eaten her dinner as yet and her stomach was beginning to feel hollow. 'You must be able to patch it up somehow.'

'Patch-up jobs never really do the trick,' he said gently. For an earnest, middle-aged architect he certainly had a winning salesman's technique, she thought drily.

'Well, I shall think about everything you've said.'

'And I'll send my detailed report through shortly,' he

told her, getting to his feet and handing her the cup of
coffee. 'I say go the whole way,' he advised, walking
ahead of her to the front door and throwing one last professional and withering glance around the hall. 'It'll cost
you a fraction of what you would have to pay if you looked
outside the company, and you wouldn't have to wait
months before work could begin.'

Vicky opened the door swiftly before she could be further undermined by this subversive talk.

'In fact,' he said, pausing to look at her thoughtfully,
'I've been told that the go-ahead for this particular project
could be as early as next week. Just think, in less than four
weeks you could turn this into the house of your dreams.'
The brown eyes crinkled at her and she laughed.

'Go away before you win me over completely! I'll think
about it.'

Which she did, as she made herself some beans on toast
and untied her hair, running her fingers through its length,
idly thinking that she really ought to go and get it all
chopped off into a tailored hairstyle more suitable for a
mum.

Andy Griggs did a good line in persuasion, she thought.
He hadn't been pushy, but his assessment of the house and
what it needed had been professional and honest. It was
hardly his fault that some of his suggestions were so tempting that she had to stop herself salivating at the mouth at
the thought of them. At one point, he'd even managed to
persuade her that altering her staircase completely would
transform the overall aspect of the house, and she'd in-
anely found herself agreeing. He would send his detailed
analysis through, she thought, and she would promptly put
it somewhere safe and out of sight. In a drawer somewhere. From which she might occasionally extract it, if
only for the purpose of drooling. She certainly couldn't
see her way to chancing upon enough money to turn the

project into reality, especially if the costs were non-subsidised, but who could tell what might happen in the future? There was always the Lottery. Should she ever decide to play it.

She was washing her plate and glass, with the radio playing quietly in the background, when the doorbell went.

He must have forgotten something, she thought irritably, because at a little before nine she was already beginning to wind down to her usual night-time routine of the news on television, followed by her book, followed by sleep. Or maybe he'd read the longing in her eyes at all his renovating proposals and in an act of pure sadism had written up all his plans in record time and intended to present her with them while she appeared vulnerable.

She smiled at the thought of that and was still smiling when she pulled open the front door and saw Max Forbes standing on her doorstep, still in his working clothes, although he'd removed his tie and undone the top button of his shirt. The breeze had ruffled his dark hair and the darkness outside made his face appear more angular than usual.

What was he doing here?

She had to resist the temptation to peer behind her towards the stairwell, to make sure that Chloe hadn't heard the ring of the doorbell and was drowsily making her way down the stairs.

A series of futile *whys* pounded in her head like the blows of a hammer. *Why* had she ever applied to the wretched company for a job? *Why* had she stupidly accepted the job with him when it had been offered? *Why* had she somehow found herself persuaded to stay on, even though her common sense had repeatedly lectured her on the foolhardiness of her actions? And, most searingly brutal of all, *why, why, why* had she yielded to him in every possible way? Made love with him? Fallen in love with him?

'Oh, hello,' she said. 'What are you doing here?' Her hair, curling down her back, was an unwelcome reminder of her femininity, as was the clinging short-sleeved top which she had flung on minutes before Andy Griggs had rang her doorbell, and the tight faded jeans.

'I was in the area and decided to come along and see how you had fared with Andy.' He leant against the door-frame, supporting himself with his arm, invading her space so that she stepped back a few inches, though not enough to give him any room to enter.

'You were in the area *again*? You seem to be in this area an awful lot.'

'Warwick is a small place.' He shrugged. 'Some friends live near here and asked me over for a drink. I think they want to make a match with their daughter. She's dull, rambling and conversationally unexciting. So, what did Andy say?'

'Well, he had a lot of good ideas.' Vicky gave in, though she still continued to block any possible sign of entry. 'I told him that I'd give the whole thing a great deal of thought and then get back to him.'

'But you won't commit yourself to anything because of what happened between us,' he prodded. 'One of the reasons I had to see you was to ask you something that's been on my mind for the past couple of hours. Do you feel unsafe when you're around me? If you do, then you might as well move on. Do you think that if we're alone together for more than five minutes I might grab you? Just because we happened to make love together once?'

'Of course not,' Vicky said tightly.

'Sure?' he asked softly, and she wondered whether he was trying to massage his own masculine ego by forcing her to admit that yes, he bothered her, and yes, she didn't think straight when she was around him.

'Quite sure. Now if that was all…'

'Actually, not quite all.' He produced some folded paper which he must have been holding the whole time but which she had failed to notice. 'This document you typed to Dobson is completely off track.'

'It is?' She reached out for it, embarrassed to have been picked up on an error, even though she had been particularly careful with this one because of the nature of the client.

'Have you got a PC with a printer? You'll have to make all the alterations on it now because I'm going to have to get back to the office and fax it off so that they have it sitting with them by five-thirty tomorrow morning when Bill's leaving for the Far East to consult with their sister firm over there about the operations.'

'Have you altered it on hard copy? If you have, you can leave it with me and I'll make sure it arrives on his desk by tomorrow morning.'

'Sorry.' He shook his head ruefully. 'I've added a couple of extra paragraphs, so we're going to have to go through this one together. Looks like I'm going to have to come in.'

CHAPTER SEVEN

MAX looked at the unwilling set of her face and the stiffness of her shoulders and managed to sustain his implacable smile with effort. He knew that he shouldn't be here at all, but that was a road he had no intention of going down. It led to too many frustrating questions.

'Is there a problem?' he asked politely, cocking his head to one side and shoving his hands deeper into his trouser pockets. 'I won't stay very long. Just long enough to get this damn thing done, and it goes without saying that I wouldn't have bothered coming here in the first place if you hadn't typed the wrong information in the first place.' He saw her colour deepen and felt a twinge of sheepish guilt. It galled him to realise that the changes he wanted to make were simply a handy excuse for showing up unannounced on her doorstep.

Somehow, somewhere, he couldn't get it out of his head that she was concealing a lover somewhere, and he vaguely thought that appearing out of the blue might smoke the man out.

'Well,' she hedged, looking up at him and chewing her bottom lip in a nervous gesture. 'I *was* about to go to bed...'

'At this hour?' He looked at his watch with overdone amazement. 'I've heard of quiet lives, but isn't nine o'clock taking things a little far?' He grinned, and wondered whether her intention of going to bed at an hour when most children over the age of thirteen were still up had anything to do with the mystery man, whose presence now seemed large, looming and gut-clenchingly real. Was he upstairs lying in the bed, sprawled and waiting? 'Don't tell me that you need your beauty sleep.' He tried to peer around her up the staircase, which was shrouded in darkness and she followed the line of his eyes with an irritated click of her tongue.

'Well, if you're quite sure that this won't take too long,' she told him, standing back to allow him access. Chloe was safely ensconced upstairs, sound asleep. There was almost no chance that she would suddenly awaken and come downstairs. Her sleeping habits had always been predictable. When she got into bed, she went to sleep, and only roused when the first fingers of light were beginning to worm their way past the closed curtains and into the bedroom. She wasn't one of those children who randomly prowled at odd hours in search of a warmer bed or a cup of juice or something to eat.

Nevertheless, she could feel her eyes anxiously flicker up the stairs as she led him away from all possible danger points and into the relative safety of the kitchen.

'I'm sorry about the mess,' she said perfunctorily, making a space on the kitchen table for him to spread the paperwork. The kitchen was small, but it was the brightest room in the house. No chance of subdued lighting creating any kind of atmosphere or playing havoc with her common sense. 'I've just finished eating.'

'Oh, really? What?' He made himself at home in one of the chairs, dumped the papers on the table and adjusted himself so that he could watch her as she self-consciously wiped the kitchen counter and put the kettle on to boil.

'Just some beans on toast.'

'I'm ravenous,' he told her casually. 'I dropped by the office on the way back from my meeting to collect this letter and then I came straight here to go through the corrections. Haven't had anything to eat since lunchtime.'

Vicky paused, turned to face him and met his candid gaze with a flicker of impatience. 'Are you hinting for something to eat?'

'Well, I *would* have had more than enough time to dine out this evening with…to have a meal if I hadn't been compelled to rush over here and get this matter sorted out post haste.'

'I'm afraid there's nothing fancy in the fridge.' She wondered what he would say if she offered him some fish fingers with potato shapes, or turkey dinosaurs with spaghetti hoops. 'I could fix you a cheese sandwich.'

'Beans on toast would be better.' He stretched out his long legs in front of him, crossing them at the ankles and clasped his hands behind his head. 'Haven't had that since…since I was a child, come to think of it.'

Vicky moved to the cupboard and began opening a can of baked beans, the contents of which she proceeded to dump into the saucepan which she'd used for heating her own only half an hour before. Then she stuck two slices of bread into the toaster and turned to face him, leaning against the counter, arms folded.

'What do your girlfriends cook for you?' she asked innocently, her eyes wide open. Girlfriends, she thought, as opposed to drunken one-night stands with employees. Girlfriends who did normal, girlfriendy things like cook meals instead of one-night stands who were in the position of being ordered to cancel their plans for the evening, prepare some food, and then, for that after-dinner treat, sit down and go through a load of work which would have to be typed until heaven only knew what time in the morning.

'Not beans on toast,' he said succinctly, and Vicky ploughed on with fatalistic intensity.

'What, then?'

'If I recall, a couple of them tried to prepare elaborate three-course meals…'

'Tried?'

'My kitchen isn't equipped for the preparation of elaborate three-course meals. God, that smells good. Any chance of some grated cheese over the top?'

The bread popped up and she liberally spread butter on it, then poured the entire tin of beans over both slices and finished the ensemble with a generous helping of grated cheese which melted into the beans. She stuck the plate in front of him and watched as he rearranged himself so that he could dig in. Anyone would think that he was enjoying a piece of the finest steak.

'If I recall, you have an extremely well-equipped kitchen.'

'Oh, that was before I had the new kitchen installed. Have you anything to drink? A cup of tea, perhaps? White, two sugars.'

'Sure that'll be all? I can always rustle up some plum crumble for afters,' Vicky informed him with sweetly biting sarcasm, unable to resist. He looked at her, fork poised *en route* to mouth, and she added quickly, 'It was a joke.'

'Plum crumble. A fading memory.'

'Oh, for goodness' sake! If your girlfriends can whip up gourmet meals, they're perfectly equipped to rustle up beans on toast and plum crumble. Please stop acting as though it requires talent.'

'A good plum crumble requires a great deal of talent,' he contradicted. 'And my *girlfriends* don't *rustle up* beans on toast for me, or *anything* else, for that matter, because I don't encourage that sort of thing.'

Vicky looked at him, mouth open, as though he had suddenly taken leave of his senses. 'You don't encourage that sort of thing?' she asked, confused. 'What's the point of having that kitchen if you never use it?' Comprehension dawned in her eyes. 'Oh, *I* get it. *You* are the one to do the cooking!' She imagined him whipping up an impressive array of food in under ten minutes and clad only in an apron. It was a sexist thought but irresistible. If *she* were the woman in his life, she would insist that he prepare her a meal, wearing nothing but a white apron, and she would fondle him as he cooked, distracting him with the tantalising flicker of her fingers on his body. She blinked away the sexy thought.

'Don't be absurd.' He finished eating with a gratified sigh of pleasure and stood up with the plate, heading to the sink and washing it without waiting for her to intercept him. 'I don't like women cooking for me, just in case it gives them ideas…'

'What kind of ideas?' Vicky asked, at a loss.

'Ideas of permanence.'

'Oh, *those* kind of ideas.' She nodded wisely. 'Very clever of you. What man in his right mind would want a woman to get ideas of permanence? When he can enjoy fruits of a relationship with no commitment or strings attached?'

Max turned very slowly to face her, and he slung the tea towel over his shoulder. Incongruously, it made him look all the more dangerously masculine. 'I don't think this has much to do with the purpose of my visit, do you?' he asked softly, and Vicky felt herself flush with shame. She'd reluctantly let him come in through lack of choice, even though she realised the necessity of getting him out as quickly as possible, and yet here she was, indulging in pointless conversation just because her curiosity was niggling away at her.

'Right.' She briskly wiped her hands on a towel, sat down at the kitchen table and shuffled the papers around to face her. The first set of corrections, which were done insultingly in bright red pen, made her frown. 'Are you *sure* these haven't been typed correctly? I mean you're just rephrasing what was said in the original draft.'

'I've added bits in,' Max informed her testily.

'Relevant bits?'

'Are you questioning me?'

'No, of course not, I just wondered...' Her voice trailed off into silence as she quickly inspected the rest of the documents. With a spot of rapid typing, she would be able to get this lot done in under forty-five minutes. 'My computer's in the utility,' she said, standing up and flicking through the paper. 'Give me a few minutes and I should be able to have this all typed up for you.' When he stood up, she eyed him sceptically. 'I shouldn't bother,' she said, 'The utility's a bit on the cramped side.'

'Why do you store your PC in your utility?' He ignored her request to stay put, and followed her through the kitchen door, briefly out into the cold, and then into a separate shed which housed a washing machine, a tumble drier, various clothes lines which were coiled in disarray on the floor, a sink and a stack of wellingtons shoved in the corner. Vicky switched on an electric heater, pulled a chair in front of the beaten-up desk on which the computer sat, beady-eyed and waiting.

'I keep meaning to move it,' Vicky admitted, switching on and watching the flat black screen jump into life. 'When I got back from Australia, this was the first thing I bought, thinking that I could work from home if need be, and I wasn't home when it came, so my neighbour got them to stick it in here and the thought of moving the whole lot out and into one of the bedrooms was so exhausting that—' She peered at the screen, licked her lips and clicked to open a new file and rapidly began to type '—I left it here. Besides, I like it in here.'

'You *like* your utility?'

'There's no need to sound so surprised,' she said tartly, glancing up from her typing to glare at him briefly. 'Everyone has a special place. *You* must have a special place. Haven't you?'

'No,' he said bluntly. 'If you discount my bed.'

'Well, *this* is my special place,' Vicky informed him, looking at the screen. 'I used to have picnics here when I was a kid. Made it kind of exciting because it wasn't attached to the house and Mum and Dad didn't mind me using it in winter because they could stick the heater in and warm it up. And whenever Mum did the ironing in here, I made sure that one of my picnics was in operation.' Vicky smiled at the sudden memory. 'She spent half her time tripping over my dolls.'

'Happy childhood stuff, that.' She hadn't realised but he'd moved directly over her, and he now leaned down, encircling her with his arms so that his head was on a level with hers, and he could read the document as she typed it. She could feel his warm breath against her neck and her thought processes thickened in response. Her breasts were beginning to ache. Would he see her nipples hardening behind the fine, stretchy cotton of the T-shirt? She wanted to glance down and evaluate what her wretched body was doing, but didn't dare.

Instead she frowned in concentration at what she was doing and tried to work even faster. On either side of her chair, his arms were like two steel bands, trapping her in. If she moved five inches in either direction, flesh would meet flesh. The thought sent another wave of light-headed giddiness racing through her.

'No, no. Those figures don't look quite right. Go back to the last page.' When she did, he reached out and traced the offending lines on the computer screen, his arm way too close to her for comfort, but shifting her body would only put her into contact with his other arm. Vicky tried to look knowledgeable, but in fact she barely heard when he instructed her to carry on. She just knew that reaching the last page couldn't come too soon.

When she was finished, she saved the lot and then asked him whether he would mind switching on the printer. He moved away and she felt her body go limp before she straightened up and began printing.

'Well done,' he said, as page after page was printed and he collected the lot, standing to one side with his hip resting gently against the washing machine, pushing his fingers through his dark hair as he narrowly inspected what she'd just written. If he made the mistake of telling her that there were one or two things still to correct, she felt she might fling the computer at his handsome head. It wasn't fair that he could waltz into her private life like this and shake the hell out of it. She needed all the personal space she could find to come to terms with what he had done to her, and showing up on her doorstep unannounced wasn't helping matters along.

'Is everything in order?' Vicky asked, vacating the chair rather than face the possibility of another trapped situation. She waited, and when he finally nodded switched off the computer terminal and then, for the sake of safety, pulled out the plugs. 'Just in case,' she informed him, when she realised that he was watching her with an odd expression. 'It's an old house.'

'Which brings me to Andy. What did he have to say?'

He slipped the papers into the thin leather case and followed her out of the utility and back through the kitchen door, which Vicky locked behind them.

'Just that work needs to be done on the place. There's some damp.' She reflected that the tone of voice used by the architect when he had said this implied *rampant* damp rather than just the odd patch here and there. 'He's going to send a report through with all his suggestions and costings in a few days' time and—' she shrugged, folding her arms '—I'll have a look at it.' She looked at him, refusing to invite further debate on the subject. Things had gone quite smoothly, considering. She'd managed to school her features into a professional, unflappable mask and, more to the point, her daughter had remained obediently asleep upstairs, but it was best not to tempt fate. She had a nasty habit of kicking you in the teeth when you did that.

'I take it that you don't feel the inclination to expand on that,' he said, turning to face her with the leather case tucked under one arm.

'It's late.'

'It's—' he looked pointedly and for an aggravatingly long time at his watch '—a little after nine-thirty.'

'That's what I mean. It's late.'

'I can't believe you consider nine-thirty *late*.'

Vicky shuffled on her feet and gave up the attempt to outstare him. 'I've never been a night bird,' she mumbled vaguely, and he, even more aggravatingly, raised his eyebrows in amused cynicism at this non response.

'Would you say that it's too late for a nightcap?' he asked, adding smoothly, 'Of coffee? I wasn't implying a stiff drink.' His eyes caught hers and she could see the follow-up to that mirrored in the peculiar grey eyes. *We both know where alcohol can take us.* Or, at least, she was certain that that was what she read there before he lowered his eyes.

'A quick cup.' she fought against irritation. Her personal involvement with him, her feelings for him, were not appropriate, and she would have to fight against allowing that to seep out into her voice. It occurred to her that she could take the craven way out of the whole situation and put him in a position where he would have no alternative but to sack her. Gross impertinence, whatever that comprised, would do the trick, she was sure, but she quailed at the idea. Aside from anything else, it would not do to have a poor reference from him. He was an important person in the area, as she was finding out on a daily basis, and she knew that, if he wanted, he could easily scupper her chances of landing a good job locally.

'Of course. I wouldn't dream of keeping you from your nightly routine,' he murmured politely.

'I didn't say that my *nightly routine* involved going to bed at nine. I do *get out*, you know.' She turned on the tap to fill the kettle with a ferocity that had the water splashing out at her.

'Oh, do you? Where? Are there many night spots around here? I must say, I tend to head back to London for night life.'

'Depends on what kind of night life you're looking for.' She hoped she sounded calm and mysterious and in possession of a night life, instead of evasive because a night life was something she had given up on a long time ago. Even when she'd lived in Australia fear of reprisal from Shaun had altered her social habits, so that, in the end, she had tended to stay put with her daughter, inviting the occasional girlfriend over to her aunt's house for supper, but avoiding anything that indicated fun.

Fun, she'd been told, was not to be on her agenda.

Shaun had not wanted her, but the thought that someone else might had driven him into a frenzy. He'd liked controlling her life, dropping in when it suited him, watching her with sadistic amusement as she scurried nervously around, fully aware that one wrong word might just be enough to threaten the quality of her life. Looking back at it, she was amazed that she'd allowed herself to live for so long in the grip of perpetual fear, but at the time she'd really imagined that there was no way out. She'd never questioned that he would take Chloe away from her if she didn't do as he said. She'd witnessed his rages and his unpredictable behaviour and she'd always known that he was more than capable of it. Now, she could reason that the law would have stopped him, but back then the law had played second fiddle to fear.

'I suppose so.' He reached out for the mug of coffee and their fingers briefly brushed. 'What kind of night life would *you* be looking for? You're a young girl. Still clubbing?'

'Oh good grief. I haven't been clubbing since…since for ever.' She almost smiled at the thought of going to a night club with a young daughter in tow.

'Why not?'

'Because…I don't enjoy that sort of thing,' she said vaguely, which anyway was the truth.

'So you…?'

'Go to the movies, all the usual stuff. Drink your coffee or it'll go cold.' By way of example, she swallowed some large mouthfuls of hers and laid the mug on the counter with finality. She was exasperated to see that he refused to take the hint, sipping at his as though he had all the time in the world to kill.

'You're distracting me, standing there tapping one foot and fiddling with your fingers.'

Vicky, who hadn't realised that she was doing either of those things, promptly stopped both. Annoyingly, her mind seized on the word *distracted* and she wondered what he'd meant. Did he mean that he couldn't take his eyes off her? Hardly, she thought with a trace of wry realism. Shaun had been fond of reminding her that, were it not for the striking colour of her hair, she would have faded into the background; she lacked spark.

He drained his cup, stood up and headed out of the kitchen with an abruptness that had her scurrying off behind him after a few seconds of disorientation.

'Right. Thanks for your help, Vicky,' he told her in a clipped voice. 'Grudging though it was.'

'I'm sorry. I didn't mean to appear grudging.' Even when she said that, she knew that she *sounded* grudging. 'It's just that I'm one of those boring creatures of routine, and having my routine put out of joint makes me go into a funny mood.'

'I'll remember that for the future,' he said drily. He pulled open the front door and at that split instant two things happened.

A sharp gust of wind blew into the hall, lifting her hair and then rushing past her to the kitchen door, which had been left open.

The slam of the kitchen door reverberated in the house like the sudden, startling clap of thunder, and there was an answering cry from up the stairs.

Vicky's blood froze in her veins. For a second or two she truly thought that she might have been turned to ice, then she was galvanised into action. It was as though her brain, temporarily disabled, had suddenly shot into overdrive and in the space of a few seconds had processed all the horrific possibilities that could arise for the sound of that childish voice crying out from a bedroom upstairs.

'What the…?' He stepped back into the hall and she placed the palms of her hands flat on his chest in a vain attempt to prevent him coming in any further. 'What's going on here?' he said sharply, his eyes narrowing on the empty staircase.

As if on cue, Chloe yelled, 'Mummy! Where are you?'

Vicky turned on her feet and raced up the stairs, taking them two at a time, her heart beating like a steam-engine in her chest. She was out of breath by the time she made it up to the bedroom. She shot in, shutting the door behind her, because she was pretty sure that Max would now be back in the house, waiting for her to return and offer some explanation, if not heading up the staircase in a mission to find out what was going on.

'Shh!' she hissed, edging over to the bed where her daughter was sitting up, bolt upright, yawning and rubbing her eyes. 'The wind blew the kitchen door shut, honey.'

'Oh. I thought it was thunder.'

'You need to go back to sleep. Tomorrow's school.' She stroked the forehead and plastered a soothing smile on her face. It made her feel one-dimensional. 'And you know Mrs Edwards doesn't like sleepyheads in her class!' If she sounded any more hearty, she thought, she would end up alarming her daughter instead of reassuring her. She held the little face between her hands.

'Can I come downstairs for something to drink?'

'No, honey.'

'Why not?'

'Because there's nothing in the fridge. Must go to the supermarket tomorrow.'

'Can I check for myself?'

'Too dark, Clo.'

'Pleeeaaaasssssseeee…?'

Instead of uttering a few calm words that would send

her drowsy daughter back off to the Land of Nod, it appeared, Vicky thought, that she had succeeded in rousing her completely. In a minute Chloe would be out of the bed and ready for fun and games.

'Tell you what,' Vicky said, 'I'll go and have a look and bring you up a milk shake. I might just be able to rummage up some milk, I think.'

'When?'

'In a minute.'

That explanation seemed to do the trick, because Chloe subsided in a satisfied heap back onto the bed and within minutes her eyes were closed and her breathing was regular.

Very quietly, Vicky tiptoed out of the bedroom, closing the door gently behind her, then she flew down the stairs, half hoping that Max would have somehow left the house, ignoring his understandable curiosity, respecting her need for privacy. Her hopes, such as they were, were dashed by the sight of him looming darkly in the hallway, front door ominously closed, a grim expression on his face.

'Care to tell me what's going on?'

'I'd rather not, actually,' Vicky said, holding herself erect and willing herself to feel angrily invaded instead of guilty and terrified. Max Forbes would be able to sniff out the scent of guilt and terror and as soon as he did that he would be on her case like a ton of bricks. She decided that giving him some of the truth might be the best idea. 'Or rather, not at this moment. Please.'

'Because it's way past your bedtime?' His mouth twisted cynically and she flinched from the brutal disbelief in his eyes. 'And of course, you weren't lying, were you? You *do* go to bed early because that's what having a child does to a woman, isn't it? Screws up her sleeping habits? How old is he? Five, six, seven, older?'

'It's a she, not a he,' Vicky said wearily. 'And I'll explain it all to you tomorrow, if you'll just go away now.'

'Not,' he said coldly, 'on your life. You lied about her at your interview and as your employer I have every right to know what other lies you've told.'

'I haven't told any other lies,' Vicky said uncomfortably.

'I think *I'll* be the judge of that.' He took a few steps further into the hall and Vicky couldn't resist it. She glanced towards the staircase, which was thankfully empty, then she turned to face him, her hands balled into tight fists, her mouth set in a stubborn line.

'All right,' she muttered through clenched teeth, 'I'll tell you what you want to know. In the sitting room. And then when I've finished I want you to leave. Is that clear?'

He ignored the command in her voice, as she had known he would, but at least he followed her into the sitting room. Somehow, pouring out her personal life, highly edited though the version would be, in a cold, dark hallway, was not what Vicky wanted.

He sprawled on the chair, filling it out in a way that made it seem diminutive and inadequate, and Vicky quietly closed the door behind her. Then she perched on the arm of the chair facing him, her fingers laced together on her knees, her mind whirling with the frantic need to get rid of him as soon as possible. All her initial fears, which had somehow been sidelined over the past few weeks, rose up and threatened to engulf her. In a stroke, he could bring her life crashing down around her ears. He could take Chloe away from her if he ever discovered the child's identity. He could certainly ensure that her working life in the area was ended. He was a man of influence and power, and that could speak in tongues she couldn't even begin to understand. She forced herself to think rationally. He had no idea that Chloe was his niece and there was no reason why he should ever find out.

For a split instant, she felt a twinge of guilt that she was wilfully depriving her daughter of a blood relative, but then the instinct for survival took over and she drew a deep breath.

'Okay. I have a child. She's five years old and I know that I should have told you about her, but I was scared.'

'Scared of *what*?' The curl of his lips informed her that he was not prepared to be sympathetic.

'You have no idea what it's like…'

'No? Then why don't you enlighten me?'

The expression on his face made her feel like a whingeing damsel in a Victorian melodrama. 'It's very hard being a single-parent family,' Vicky said quietly. 'It's fine for you to sit there and offer comments about the situation, but you have no idea how difficult it is being on your own with a child.'

'Where's the father?'

'He's dead. He died in a car crash.'

'Australian, was he?'

'He lived there, yes. I lied about my daughter because I felt that having a child would be held against me when it came to getting a job. Most employers shy away the minute they hear that there's a young child on the scene. They foresee lots of broken appointments and late arrivals and days off. I was going to tell you, but I suppose I just kept putting it off because I knew you'd react the way you did.' She sighed. 'You're right and I was wrong. I should never have taken the job with you in the first place.' That much, at any rate, was heartfelt.

'I can't believe that you resorted to all this subterfuge to conceal the fact that you have a child. It doesn't make any sense.' He frowned and stared at her narrowly until she looked away. 'I can understand the patterns now,' he mused slowly, 'the need to leave work on the dot, the evasiveness when it came to working late or overtime. All that slots into place. What *I'm* having a problem with is the *why*. *Why* lie in the first place? The majority of women working for me are married, with kids. We're not talking about an old-fashioned, chauvinistic, medieval establishment here. We're not talking about the sort of place where gossips would ferret out an unmarried mother and send her to the gallows for punishment.' He gave a dry, hard laugh. 'So why don't you tell me the full story? *What else is there?*'

'There's nothing else,' Vicky said, standing up. 'If you feel that you can't work with me now, then I'll understand.' She brushed a few non-existent specks of dust off her jeans and then edged behind her chair, gripping the back of it with her hands. Why did he think that she was still hiding something? Could he read what was going on in her mind from the expression on her face? Did he have X-ray eyes? She felt as though her nervous system had been put through a shredder.

'And there's another thing,' he said pensively, stroking his chin with one long finger and making no attempt to budge.

'What? What's another thing?' She could barely conceal the jumpiness in her voice, even though she knew that the more jumpy she sounded, the more penetrating would be his scrutiny of what she had told him.

'The myriad times you mention that you *might just leave the company*. Why do you do that, I wonder?'

Vicky, for her part, wondered desperately why he didn't leave her house. All that musing and speculation was making the hairs on the back of her neck stand on end.

'Are you one of these women who needs constant re-assurances?'

'*One of these women who needs constant reassurances?* Oh, please!'

'Then why are you always threatening to walk out? There's no need to feel insecure. You've told me your dark little secret—' he allowed a few nasty seconds to elapse, just to remind her that he was quite aware of the holes in her storyline '—and I don't think your status will affect your job.' He stood up and she very nearly groaned with relief. 'So I expect to see you in the morning,' he added, walking towards the sitting room door and resting his hand lightly on the door handle, 'and you needn't worry,' he said seriously, 'that I'll make any unreasonable demands on you. I'm not an ogre. I do appreciate that working women with children cannot be as accommodating as single, child-free women. But—' his eyes narrowed on her '—I would have appreciated the truth from the beginning, and what I *don't* expect is to discover that any more lies have been told. Got it? You're in a job that sometimes requires the utmost confidentiality. A loose-tongued liar is the last person I need working for me.'

'I'm not a loose-tongued liar! I made *one* mistake, told *one* lie, for which I apologise. I don't make a habit of running around lying to anyone and everyone. But if you feel that way, then I'm more than happy to quit!' She looked at him with mutinous determination and he appeared to think the matter over.

'One chance, Vicky, because you're so damn good at what you do. But that's it.'

Vicky murmured something fairly inaudible. She had just lived through the most harrowing couple of hours since she had returned to England. Her vocal cords were apparently giving up through sheer stress.

He abandoned his condemnation of her and assumed a lighter tone. 'I can understand why the thought of renovations to this house hold so much appeal. I expect you've been thinking along the lines of playrooms and places to store toys?'

He fully opened the door, and Vicky saw Chloe before Max, who was still looking at her. She was standing at the bottom of the staircase, nicely caught in a pool of light, her dark hair tousled from sleeping, her right hand clutching the moth-eaten teddy that had been her faithful companion since birth.

Max, following the startled widening of her eyes, turned around, and whatever he had been saying died on his lips.

'You promised to bring me up a milk shake, Mum,' Chloe said. 'I'm thirsty.'

CHAPTER EIGHT

THERE was a sense of doomed inevitability about the whole thing. In the space of a second or two, Vicky accepted that fate had just been playing games with her ever since she had accepted the job, waiting for this very moment to evolve so that she could have the last laugh.

She watched the scenario unfolding in front of her and realised that there was nothing more that she could do.

Chloe, who had barely noticed the presence of another adult in the room, now became aware of Max standing to one side, stepping out of the shadows, and her eyes opened wide in shock and puzzlement.

'Shaun?' she whispered uncertainly. She scuttled over to Vicky, her eyes fixed on Max, and clutched the proffered hand. Vicky reached down and swept her daughter into her arms, wrapping her protectively into her, with one hand cupping the back of Chloe's dark head. She knew that her hands were trembling. 'Mummy, what's Shaun doing here?'

'It's not Shaun,' Vicky whispered, aware that Max's eyes were boring into her, demanding answers. 'How about that milk shake?'

'She called me *Shaun*.' Max regained his power of speech, but before he could launch into a series of questions Vicky looked at him sharply and held up one finger for him to keep quiet, then she walked away towards the kitchen, still hanging on to Chloe, although she was now aware that her daughter's head had popped up and was doubtless surveying the unnerving vision in front of her with childish curiosity and apprehension.

Disconcertingly, Max had followed in her wake. Vicky had a vision of them both avidly looking at one another, and the weight of all the explanations lurking in the not-too-distant future made her feel sick and weary. She switched on the kitchen light and, still not looking at Max, she sat Chloe on the kitchen counter and proceeded to pour milk into a glass, add some chocolate powder and stir, really as though everything was fine and her life hadn't been suddenly turned on its head. It was the calm before the storm. She felt like breaking into hysterical laughter and had to fight the urge, because calm was what was needed. A calm hand, a steady head and a cool determination.

'Okay, honey,' she whispered unsteadily to her daughter, whose attention she now had to fight to retrieve. 'You can have your milk shake in bed and Mummy will explain everything to you in the morning.'

'Has Shaun come back from Heaven to visit us?'

'No, darling. Of course not. This man here just *looks* like him, that's all.' *Heaven? Shaun Forbes?* She walked past Max and proceeded up the stairs with her daughter. 'There's no need to follow us,' she addressed the figure behind her in a cold voice. 'I *will* come back down.'

'You'd better.'

Don't you dare threaten me, she wanted to say, but fear made her keep quiet, relieved at least that he'd turned and was heading back down.

'But who *is* he?' Chloe asked unsteadily, as she was deposited onto the bed and handed her glass of milk shake. 'Why does he look like Shaun?' She drank a mouthful of milk shake and watched her mother over the rim of the glass. Vicky tried to imagine what must be going through her daughter's head. Surprise, bewilderment, all muddled up because she was still sleepy. Certainly no excitement. Her father had made no effort to try and cultivate a relationship with her and, consequently, Chloe had seen him as virtually a stranger, one who brought her the occasional present, depending on his mood and whether any money happened to be available at the time. From the very beginning he'd insisted on being called Shaun by her which, as it turned out, couldn't have been better, because *daddy* implied an affectionate intimacy which was patently lacking in their relationship. Later on, indifference had given way to a certain amount of wariness, because she'd been able to see the effect he had on her mother, even though Vicky had done her utmost to protect her daughter from her father's nastier sides.

'They're related,' Vicky said, smoothing the dark hair with her hand. She kept her voice as low, as soporific and as expressionless as possible, and she kept up the stroking until Chloe's eyes began to flicker shut, then she carefully removed the glass of milk shake and placed it very quietly on the bedside table. 'I'll talk to you about it in the morning.' Right now, *morning* seemed a long way away. In fact most things, including normality, seemed a long way away, with Max Forbes prowling around downstairs, waiting for her to reappear so that he could start firing questions at her. The questions, she thought sickly, making a hushed departure from her daughter's room and gently closing the door behind her, weren't as terrifying as the prospect of what would come swiftly in their wake. Therein lay a whole murky morass of possible avenues, none of which she cared to contemplate.

At the top of the stairs she paused, took a deep breath and then headed down the stairs and into the sitting room, where Max was waiting for her, as she knew he would be, lounging by the window with his hands stuck into his pockets. He waited in perfect silence as she sidled across to the nearest chair and sat down. Waited and watched until she could feel her body perspiring and her nerves stretching tighter and tighter, pulling her to breaking point.

He was waiting for her to start babbling, she thought. He probably figured that she would babble herself right into a corner, from which he could then proceed to bar her exit and do precisely as he pleased.

She cracked, though managed to hang on to a fairly steady voice. 'I suppose you want an explanation of what just went on.' When he didn't say anything, she carried on with rising anger, 'Well, standing there in silence isn't going to get either of us anywhere!'

Instead of responding with a verbal outburst, he strode towards the door and closed it, then he strolled towards her, so that she was reluctantly forced to stare up at him. She winced when her eyes met his. Judging from the expression on his face, whatever deductions he had reached showed that he was halfway there to providing his own correct explanation.

'The door's shut,' he said silkily, 'and you can consider yourself trapped here until you tell me what's going on. And don't even think about skirting over the details. I want you to start at the beginning, leaving nothing out, and then—' he moved across to the sofa, sat down, crossed one ankle over his thigh and looked at her '—I shall decide what to do with you.'

'*What to do with me?* You can't do anything with me!' She sounded a lot braver than she felt and her fingers were twining together nervously.

'Of course I can.' He shot her a patient, rueful look that didn't disguise the cold, hard, reptilian determination in his eyes. 'But we won't go into any of that just yet.'

Vicky felt a quiver of dread race along her spine. She cleared her throat, but when she opened her mouth to speak she could barely enunciate what she wanted to say.

'Start at the beginning,' he told her in the same kind voice that was designed to turn her into a nervous wreck. 'Which—' he leaned forward and surveyed her musingly, his head tilted to one side '—I take it involved my brother, Shaun? That was the name your daughter uttered, wasn't it? *Shaun?* With that look of stunned recognition in her eyes?' The veneer of kindness was disappearing, as she had known it would sooner or later. '*Not,*' he added softly, 'that I wouldn't have guessed her identity. She could be my brother's clone. Same hair, same colouring, same eyes... Little secrets *do* have a way of slipping out sooner or later, don't they?' He bared his teeth in a smile while she continued to look at him with mesmerised apprehension. 'Or perhaps,' he continued languidly, 'slipping out is a bit of a misnomer...because that would imply a mistake, wouldn't it? When there must be a name for the deliberate exposure of a so-called secret...wouldn't you say? What word would I be searching for here, do you think?' He stood up and strolled towards the window, idly flicking back the curtain and peering outside for a few seconds before reverting back to his inspection of her face. His movements were lazy and unhurried. Here was a man, she thought, with all the time in the world to pin her to the wall and crucify her. She swallowed hard.

'What are you talking about?' she mumbled.

'Tut, tut, tut. Please. No games.' Another threatening baring of the teeth, then he sat back down. 'Just the truth. When did you decide to hunt me down so that you could— hey, presto—turn over your trump card and take me for every penny I've got?'

'Hunt you down?' Vicky shook her head in utter confusion. 'Fleece you? *What* are you talking about?'

'Stop it! Now!' He sat forward and punched one clenched fist into the palm of his hand with such force that she jumped. 'What happened? Did you meet my brother out in Australia and decide that he was a good match? A good match, that is, until you discovered that his outgoings usually exceeded his incomings by several thousands per month? Or maybe even when you found that out you still decided that there was enough there to make it worthwhile, but only a child could have got the commitment... Is that when you decided to become pregnant? Backfired, though, didn't it...because he didn't marry you, did he?'

'You've got this all wrong.' Her mind tried to grapple with all the misconceptions being hurled at her but it was lagging behind. As fast as he tossed one accusation at her, and before she'd had time to deal with it, he was moving on to something else, some other nightmarish misunderstanding. From one correct assumption, he'd woven his own theories, and was now in the process of shooting her down with them.

'No,' she began a little more forcefully, 'that's not what happened at all...'

'I gather. But things must really have looked grim when Shaun died. No wedlock, no cash... What was there for a poor girl to do but hot-foot it over here to England and check out what further sources of finance were available?'

'Look, this has gone far enough!' She stood up, trembling, but her legs were unsteady and she slumped back onto the chair.

'I don't think so. Actually, I don't think we've even begun as yet.' There was grim resolution stamped on his face. Not in a million years would anyone have ever guessed that the man sitting opposite her possessed anything resembling a sense of humour. That he had made her giggle, made her blush, had touched her and turned her body to fire. Now the opposite was happening. With every word, her body was turning to ice.

'You played it cool, though. I have to admit it. My hat's off to you, and I'm as sceptical as they go when it comes to a gold-digger.'

'I am not a *gold*-digger!' She spat the words out. With anger and frustration she watched his dark eyebrows raise in incredulous disbelief.

'No? So are you telling me that it was sheer coincidence that you managed to wangle a job working for your ex-lover's brother?'

'I didn't *wangle* a job,' Vicky muttered miserably. 'I just—'

'Just what? Happened to be walking past a company that carried the Forbes name? And decided to apply for a job? Without it ever occurring to you that the similarity of the names might indicate something?'

'You don't understand. I saw the name and yes, I was curious...'

'And a little curiosity got your brain churning, didn't it? You must have thought you'd hit jackpot when you saw me! Now all you had to do was reel me in, slowly but surely, and you took your time. No rushing in and producing the child like a magician pulling a rabbit out of a hat...'

'*Chloe. The child's* name is *Chloe.*' His phraseology sparked off a memory that bit into her like acid. Shaun had called his daughter *the child.* It had enraged her then, and just hearing the same, dehumanising words come from his brother's mouth enraged her now. 'And, for your information,' she said vehemently, standing up and discovering that her wobbly legs could actually support her now, 'the thought of getting money from your brother or any other member of his wretched family was the last thing on my mind!' She walked over to where he was sitting and loomed over him like an angry, red-haired, avenging angel.

'And you expect me to believe that?' His lips twisted into a sneer of disbelief and, without pausing to think, she raised her hand and slapped him hard on the face, hard enough for his head to swing back and for her hand to feel as though every bone in it had been broken. The display of violence surprised her as much as it surprised him but, before she could step back, his hand had shot out, grasping hers by the wrist and yanking her forward so that she had to catch herself from toppling on top of him.

'You knew exactly what you were doing. Why don't you admit it? Why else did you accept the job offer unless to ingratiate yourself with me, until an opportune moment came for you to reveal your little secret? Damn you!' His grey eyes were blazingly furious and Vicky shrank back with a small cry of dismay and fright. For the first time it really hit home that his armoury of weapons, should he choose to deploy them, was extensive.

As if reading her mind, he gave her hand another fierce jerk and then said in a dangerously soft voice, 'Well, my dear, I'm a completely different kettle of fish to my brother. When you decided to play with me, you decided to play with fire—and fire burns. Do you understand what I could do to you? I could drag you through the courts and demand partial custody of the...of my...my brother's child. In fact, I could probably swing to take her away from you. After all, money talks, and she would be in line for a very large fortune.'

Vicky felt the colour drain from her face. 'You c-couldn't,' she stammered. 'You wouldn't...'

He looked at her for a few seconds, holding her terrified

gaze, then he released her hand as though touching it was distasteful. Vicky took a few steps back, her eyes still clamped on his face, searching to discover whether he had meant what he'd said. *Surely not?* The law wouldn't hand over custody of her child to this man, anyway, although the money element was enough to keep a seed of doubt planted in some corner of her mind.

'Why not?' he shrugged, then rubbed the side of his face again, where she had hit him. She sincerely hoped that she'd broken a few of his teeth in the process, but if she had he was successfully hiding the fact.

'What do you mean, *why not?*' Vicky asked in an appalled whisper. 'Chloe's the beginning, the middle and the end of my whole life! If you try and take her away…' Her voice began to waver and, without warning, she broke down. No warm-up of sniffles, no watery eyes as a prelude—she just collapsed into tears, loud, distraught, uncontrollable sobbing that was imbued with all the grief that she'd experienced over the past few years, starting with her mother's death.

'Oh, for God's sake,' Max muttered, standing up, 'I don't intend to take your child away from you. It was a threat.' He thrust a handkerchief into her hand and Vicky clutched it gratefully, pressing it to her eyes. 'How the hell do you think I feel?' he all but yelled, striding restlessly around the room, his fingers raking through his dark hair. With her face pressed against the handkerchief and her head downturned, she could still feel the energy emanating out of him like an electric current.

'One minute I have a good secretary, the next minute I discover that the good secretary is the mother of my niece! And you stand there, sobbing and pleading with me to believe that there was no hint of a hidden agenda anywhere on the dinner menu?'

Vicky lifted puffy, red eyes to him and said, 'Yes.'

'*Yes? Yes?* Is that *all* you have to say on the matter? You just *expect* me to take you at your word and write it all off to *quirky coincidence*?' He paused in front of her. His dark hair was a mess and his searching eyes made her look away hurriedly.

'Yes,' she repeated weakly. 'I mean, that's what *I've* written it all off to.' She sighed deeply and then proceeded to do origami with the handkerchief, folding it and unfolding it until he finally snatched it off her and shoved it back into his pocket.

'Sit down,' he commanded, 'and explain.'

'Only if you're prepared to listen to me.'

'I'll try.'

It was better than nothing, even though his expression, while not seething with hostility as it had been a couple of minutes ago, was still cynical enough to make her want to abandon her explanations before she'd even begun.

'I met your brother in Australia when I was nineteen. I...' She stumbled in the face of the uphill task facing her. How could she summarise six years of her life in the space of fifteen minutes when every day of every month of all those years was filled with emotional detail? She took a deep breath. 'I'd gone to Australia to live with my aunt— well, you know all of this, but when my mother died, I just couldn't face staying on in England. My mum and I had always planned to go on a joint holiday to visit Aunt Ruth and, well, it seemed as though the moment had come when Mum was no longer around. I couldn't bear being in the house but I couldn't bear the thought of selling it, either. That's why I rented it out. Mum's funeral was on the Tuesday and by the following Tuesday I was on a plane leaving England for what I thought would be six months. I ended up staying for nearly six years.'

'And why was that?' The timbre of his deep voice almost made her start.

'Lots of reasons.' She shrugged and avoided his silver eyes. 'The weather was good. Aunt Ruth was so thrilled to see me that she managed to persuade me to apply for an extension on my visa and then, when that came through, it seemed as though destiny wanted me to stay. And then I landed the job working as a personal assistant to the director of a public relations company. It was a huge responsibility and I adored it, even though I knew that James mainly hired me because of my English accent. He missed England. He used to say that having me around was like having his own private rose garden in the office.' Her lips softened into a smile of fond memory and Max scowled. He could feel his fingers pushing against the fabric of the chair from the effort of controlling his rampant rage and jealousy. Knowing that his brother had slept with her, fathered a child by her, fuelled a sense of obliterating anger. He wanted to shout and rip the house down. He could barely breathe properly, and here she was, smiling at the mention of her ex-boss. Another lover, perhaps? One more trophy? He struggled to maintain some balance, although his jaws ached.

'How nice,' he said tightly. 'And was he another one of your lovers, alongside my brother?'

'That's a horrible thing to say!'

'Is it?' He could feel himself wanting to hurt her and steeled himself against the temptation. 'I took you at face value and now here I am, confronted by a woman who had a child by my brother, slept with me and has God knows how many more skeletons locked away in her closet somewhere.'

'There *are* no more skeletons. I know you think…you feel—'

'*Think* what? *Feel* what?'

'Angry with me. Disappointed…'

Max tried to modulate the decibel level of his voice when he next spoke. It wouldn't do to have the neighbours flying over to the house because of the noise. '*Angry? Disappointed?* Yes, those two will do for starters.'

Vicky looked uncertainly at him, scared at the under-lying savagery she sensed and, worse, understood. She knew that she'd done far more than disappoint him. She knew that she'd destroyed his trust for ever and the thought of that made her feel sick.

'I met your brother while I was working for James.' She leaned back into the chair and closed her eyes. 'And I'll admit that for a while, I was…I suppose, infatuated with him. I had just gone through a very bad patch, I was still trying to recover from Mum's death and Shaun was like a tonic. Always on a high. Happy. I was completely taken in with his live-for-today attitude. It was just what I needed.' She risked a look at Max from under her lashes. He was sitting very still. Only the muscle in his jaw showed that he was hearing a word she said.

'We started dating and it was fun, for a while. I'd never experienced life in the fast lane, and Shaun was very much someone who lived in the fast lane. Sports cars, late-night parties, exotic friends. It was all very exciting for a while.'

Her words were drifting in and out of his head. The *for a while* lifted his spirits temporarily, because it promised that worse was to come, but he found that he couldn't focus on anything she was saying. Not really. He was too busy thinking about her in bed with Shaun, too busy feel-ing betrayed by her casual deception, too busy agonising over the fact that nothing she could say or do, however horrendous, could kill his fast-growing feelings to-wards her.

'What was that?'

'I asked what…what *you* thought of your brother,' Vicky said timidly. She had sometimes wondered whether she hadn't misjudged Shaun, or whether there hadn't been something in *her* that had driven him to turn into a monster when he found himself in her company. Maybe it hadn't been *him* at all. Maybe the fault had lain with *her*.

'Wild. Reckless. Prone to excess. I'm surprised you found him so appealing. Did you enjoy living on a knife's edge?'

'I suppose I must have. For a while.'

'You keep saying that. *For a while* this, *for a while* that. What does that *mean*?' He shot her a brooding, glowering look and then abruptly stood up and resumed his restless pacing around the room, as though the confines of the chair were stifling him.

'It *means* that after a few months I…I began to see another side to your brother. A much…darker side.'

Max stopped pacing and turned to look at her. 'What *darker side*?'

'Did you communicate with Shaun?'

'Oh, yes. Christmas cards.' His mouth twisted bitterly. 'My attempts to communicate with my brother ended when we were about…sixteen. From there on in we might just as well have been strangers.'

'Then perhaps you don't know that Shaun—'

'Dabbled with drugs?' he asked intuitively, watching the contours of her expressive face. 'Of course I knew. It was one of the reasons he was sent to Australia. His opportunity to wipe the slate clean and start over. I tried to talk some sense into him before he went, tried to make him see that he was damaging himself by taking drugs, but Shaun stopped listening to me, like I say, when we were still kids. I found out what he was up to through our father, whose only contact was through mutual friends over there. I take it the straight and narrow path didn't last long?'

'No.' Having waded through the factual aspect of her relationship with Shaun, she now screeched to a halt. The personal stuff was still too raw for her to expose in a storybook fashion, as though nothing she was describing had actually happened to *her* or damaged her the way it had.

'So what happened?'

For the first time since she had embarked on her explanation, Vicky stood up and watched him from behind her chair with a shuttered, stubborn expression.

'I'd rather not wade through all of that,' she muttered.

'Why not?'

'Because it's irrelevant.'

'I happen to find it highly relevant.'

'Why? Aside from assuaging your curiosity, why do you care about the nuts and bolts of what happened between me and your brother?'

Max could feel his anger, previously abated, spring back into life with a vengeance and he gritted his teeth together. 'You were the last to know my brother, to see him, and, whatever happened in our pasts to sour our relationship, I'd still like to try and find out what was in his mind when he died.'

'Well, I can't oblige,' she muttered, flushing. 'What matters now is how we deal with this...situation...'

Max's voice was cold when he spoke. 'You're out of a job. That's the first step to *dealing with this situation*. You do realise that, don't you?' He didn't give her time to answer his rhetorical question. 'And I won't be supporting my niece financially from a convenient distance. Close up and personal. That's the role I intend to play.' His mouth was a grim line.

'I never said—'

'You don't need to. Whatever you claim your motives were, whether or not you intended me to find out about her, I suspect that the thought of money winging its way through your front door would compensate for the loss of your job.' He stood up and walked slowly around the room, pausing to glance at the occasional ornament or book lying on the shelf, while she watched him in appalled fascination. He had stripped her of her job, which was absolutely fine as far as she was concerned, but she could feel him gnawing away at her dignity, moving in leisurely, threatening circles, giving her only enough breathing space to be terrified of what might come next.

'I can survive happily without your money,' Vicky bit out sharply. 'And, just for the record, your brother gave me nothing towards his daughter. I've managed on my own for years and I can carry on managing.' She could feel tears pricking against her eyelids and she blinked them rapidly away.

'All the right sentiments.' He turned to face her. 'They might sound good coming from someone else.' He trailed his finger along a shelf, in the manner of someone checking for dust. 'So here's our little problem. Out of the blue, I have a niece, someone who deserves to carry the family name. I don't intend to run away from my responsibilities, such as they are, which means an investment of time as well as money, and, please—' he held up one hand to cut off the heated protest forming on her lips '—spare me the aggrieved pride. As far as I can see it, everything has a solution and here's mine. My niece inherits the family name and so, on an incidental basis, do you. I'm proposing to marry you.'

In the stunned silence that ensued, Vicky's expression went from shock to incredulity and finally to hilarity. She burst out laughing. She laughed so much that she found herself gasping for breath. Her eyes were streaming and in the absence of a handkerchief, she dabbed them ineffectively with the bottom of her shirt..

'I fail to see the joke,' he said tightly, which set her off again and when the hoots of laughter had finally subsided into little hiccups, she sobered up enough to say,

'Of course I won't marry you.' There had been nothing funny about his proposal. Her reaction had been one of delayed shock at finding her foundations rocked, but the thought of marrying him, when she of all people knew that heartache of relationships that exist without love, filled her with a deep, unaccountable sadness. She also knew that any liking, affection, the most remote of warm feelings towards another human being, could tarnish rapidly under the glare of a forced situation, a relationship created for the wrong reasons and endured for the sake of something or, in this case, someone. 'We don't love one another,' she said, and another stab shot through her, but this time the bitter stab of unrequited love. 'So what would be the point?'

'The point would be legitimising my niece; the point would be to create a stable environment for her.'

'The point would be that we'd be miserable, and misery doesn't make for stability.'

'How do you know that? If I recall, we were compatible enough…on more than one count.'

'That was then, before all of this…blew up.' She didn't want to be reminded of precisely how compatible they had been, and it went beyond sex and physical attraction. Despite her wariness, and despite all the voices in her head that had daily lectured to her on the unsuitability of the man, she'd found herself drawn to his personality, seduced by his mind. She'd surrendered all her defences for the transient pleasure of enjoying his humour and his intelligence, which made his ferocious hostility now all the more painful. 'You lead a fast bachelor life. You can't just take a wife and a child on board at the snap of your fingers! Don't you understand what a handicap that would be for you?' She watched the hard set of his features and felt a simmering anger. 'Your own brother couldn't even countenance the thought of having his life churned up by the arrival of his own flesh and blood.' She hadn't wanted to drag a rational conversation back into the personal battle-field that was her past with Shaun, but somehow she couldn't help herself. 'Oh, he *saw* his daughter, when it suited him, but she was never allowed to call him *Dad*. He didn't like what that word did for his fast-living image.' She laughed shortly.

'I'm not my brother,' Max told her with deliberate, cool emphasis, 'despite the similarities.'

'I won't marry you. If you want to see Chloe now and again, then feel free, but that's it.' Another spark of inspiration came to her. 'Aside from all the reasons I've given, do you realise that you might not even get along with her? How many children have you played with recently?'

'I don't see what that has to do with anything,' he muttered, flushing darkly.

'I guess that means *none*. You might *hate* children.'

'I think I'd know whether I did or not.'

'How? If you've never had any contact with them?' Now it was her turn to fire staccato questions at him. 'They can be clingy. They can whine and nag and they're no good around expensive clothes and furnishings. They constantly need juice, and mealtimes can be a battlefield. And I haven't even started yet...'

'I'm sure—'

'That you could manage? That's a *very* sweeping assumption!'

'So would you suggest that I get to know Chloe?'

'That might help.'

'What does she like?'

'What do *most* kids like? Junk food. Mickey Mouse. Outdoor fun.' She almost smirked at the thought of Max Forbes, impeccably dressed and leader of men, having outdoor fun with Mickey Mouse while consuming some chicken nuggets from a box. Did he even know who Mickey Mouse *was*?

'So let's take her to Disneyland. I'll get the hotel and flights booked and let you know the where and when.' He strolled towards the door while she remained open-mouthed and gaping at this neat turnaround of events. He shrugged at her expression and opened the sitting room door. 'Don't look so stunned. You put the idea into my head. You could almost say it was *your* idea. And don't get up. I'll see myself out.'

CHAPTER NINE

HE WAS determined. That much Vicky could acknowledge. He had given her four days in which to sort out her life, and now ten days in Disneyland: a holiday guaranteed to win the hearts of most children under the age of ninety. Even before they'd boarded the plane at Gatwick airport, she'd felt powerless in the face of her daughter's excitement.

Chloe had digested the fact that the man bearing a striking resemblance to her father, the man providing this sudden and hugely expensive treat, was her uncle. But, even so, on the trip over, as they'd sat next to one another, Chloe mistakenly lapsed into calling Max 'Shaun' a couple of times. Vicky, sitting in the aisle seat across from her, had winced as she coolly but firmly corrected the error.

Over her daughter's head, Max had caught her eye and said innocently, 'Never mind about that. She's only a baby. Can't help making the odd mistake and, face it, Shaun and I *were* twins.'

'Yes, but…' Vicky persisted.

'He's nicer than Shaun,' Chloe pointed out thoughtfully, 'don't you think, Mum? Shaun could be *scary*.'

'I think you've smudged just *there* on your colouring,' Vicky said by way of distracting her daughter, but she was aware of Max, still staring at her, ears no doubted pricked up and alert to continue Chloe's conversation.

'Haven't,' Chloe said, concentrating on a non-existent smudge.

155

'Well, you might,' Vicky said inconsequentially, 'so you'd better make sure you give it all your attention.'

That had been the day before. One whole flight followed by a meal at the hotel, during which she'd barely managed to get a word in edgewise.

Yes, Max Forbes was definitely a determined man. He was obviously determined to make an impact on his niece and he'd succeeded in a matter of a few hours—proving, Vicky thought with grudging admiration, how fickle children were. He'd won Chloe over with an unforeseen ability to enthuse over all things Disney, to express an interest in Barbie and the advantages of having a Barbie Ferrari bought for her for her next birthday, and topped it off with an uncanny knack of making sure that his colouring on the plane had been inferior to hers. Over a hamburger and fries meal, he had winningly offered to relieve her of her tomatoes and lettuce, and, by the end of the short evening, he'd left one child eager to see him in the morning and one mother who felt as if the ground under her feet had turned to quicksand.

'We'll have to get going early in the morning,' he'd murmured to her as they'd left the restaurant.

An exhausted Chloe was draped over Vicky's shoulder, so her pace of walking was painstakingly slow. No swift escape from the disturbing presence at her side. Unfortunately. Because the more she saw of him with her daughter, the deeper in love she fell. She had watched covertly, looking for signs of the mask slipping, but there had been none. He seemed delighted with Chloe, and she wondered, briefly, whether his joy with her as well as his feelings of responsibility towards her were tied up with his own feelings for the brother now lost to him for ever. She wondered if he was trying, through Chloe, to make amends for family differences that would never now be put to rest.

More to the point, Vicky wondered—and agonised—that if Chloe continued to be enraptured with him, she would find herself well and truly trapped in a situation she'd never foreseen.

'How early?'

'Before eight. If we're to get on the good rides. Which park do you want to go to first?'

'Park?'

'Didn't you read the guidebook I gave you?'

'Not much,' Vicky admitted, breathing a sigh of relief as the elevator doors opened. They were staying in the same hotel, but fortunately on different floors, an inconvenience for which the hotel had apologised and for which she was deeply grateful. The doors closed on them.

'You seemed to be absorbed in it when you weren't playing with Chloe.'

Absorbed on the one page, she thought, refusing to meet his eyes. Too busy concentrating on the man standing next to her to get any reading done.

'Here, give her to me. I'll take her the rest of the way.' He removed the barely stirring child to him before Vicky could protest. 'I'll meet you at seven-thirty for breakfast.' He stroked the dark head on his shoulder, then stood back to allow Vicky to pass as the doors slid open onto the luxuriously carpeted corridor.

The hotel was mightily expensive, with two sprawling halves which both shared a fabulously child-friendly pool, complete with fake sand.

'I suppose so.'

'And then we can go to the Magic Kingdom first. Get there before the crowds start amassing.'

They arrived at the bedroom door and Vicky stuck in her credit card-style key and pushed open the door before turning to him.

'You can hand her over now.'

He swept past her, through to one of the double beds which had been turned back and laid Chloe on it; then he proceeded to look critically around the room. 'Not as big as I'd expected,' he told her, folding his arms.

'More than big enough for the both of us.' Vicky stayed firmly positioned by the door, in the manner of someone willing an uninvited guest to depart.

Max moved slowly towards her, then, when he was about to leave, said casually, 'What did Chloe mean when she said that I was *nicer than Shaun*? Did he hit her?'

'No,' Vicky answered, startled by this abrupt shift in the conversation.

'What about *you*? Did he ever hit *you*?'

She hesitated just fractionally too long before responding with an unconvincing, 'No.'

'Why did you put up with it?'

Vicky looked over her shoulder, but Chloe was sleeping with unladylike abandon on the double bed.

She'd kept the lights turned off so that her daughter would not wake up, but she now wished that she hadn't, because the darkness imbued their conversation with a level of confidential intimacy that frightened her.

'When did it start? Were you pregnant at the time?'

'He wasn't a serial beater,' she said in a low voice. 'In fact, he only really lashed out at me twice. The first time was when I told him that I was pregnant and the second time was when I told him to stay away from me, after Chloe had been born. But aside from that he was—'

'The perfect partner?'

'Does it make any difference now?'

'It wouldn't if the past didn't play such an influential part in our lives. You can't imagine that by refusing to discuss it it all goes away, like a bad dream.'

'I'm not implying that that's how I feel…'

'Then talk to me, Vicky.'

'Why? Because you're on a mission to bond with my daughter and you think that you might as well bond with me as part of the deal?'

'Because,' he said levelly, 'I want to know.'

Because, she thought bitterly, *you anticipate a long time of seeing me ahead of you if you're to maintain contact with your niece, in which case you might as well smooth the way between the two of us.*

'Why didn't you tell him to leave you alone?'

'Because he threatened me,' she said flatly. 'Because he said that his daughter belonged to him and, if I didn't play along, he would make sure that his powerful family knew of her identity and they would move in to take her away from me. Fool that I was, I believed him.'

She heard Max's indrawn breath and steeled herself not to respond.

'It was always Shaun's way to prey off people weaker than he was. He liked to be in a situation he could control,' he murmured, more to himself than to her. 'You were young and vulnerable and he took advantage of the fact.'

'But I'm not young and vulnerable any longer,' she reminded him stiffly.

'Which is just as well. The young and vulnerable hold no charm for me whatsoever.'

With which he'd left her, awake and wondering what he'd meant by that remark. Had he been trying to tell her that *she* held a certain amount of charm for him? Or had it been a general statement which he had made without thinking? Or maybe he'd just been trying to point out yet one more difference between him and his brother. The permutations were endless, and by the time she'd finally fallen asleep she'd been nursing a mild headache from the sheer workings of her tired brain.

They both arrived at the hotel breakfast bar the following morning to find Max waiting for them, casually attired in a pair of deep green Bermuda pants and an open-necked, short-sleeved shirt in a dull cream and green check. Outside the heat would be building already. The weatherman—if the local weatherman was to be believed—had predicted a high of early eighties and had confidently assured her that the sky would remain blue and cloudless.

'Busy day ahead,' he addressed Chloe. 'Busy, busy day ahead. Lots of characters to meet, lots of exciting rides to go on. Have you even been to a fun park before? With rides and roller coasters?'

'No,' Chloe said. 'But I *have* seen a clown.'

Max nodded gravely. 'Yes, that would be impressive as well, I'm sure.'

'And I *have*,' Chloe said, gaining momentum, 'been in that pretend racing car outside the supermarket Mum takes me to at home.'

'Oh, *that* racing car. Goes fast, does it?'

'Well, it's just *pretend*,' Chloe told him gently. 'It doesn't really go *anywhere*. Does it, Mum?'

'No, honey.' Vicky looked thoughtful and said in an equally gentle voice, 'But perhaps Uncle Max thinks that these pretend cars actually shoot off and go places.'

'Thank you for explaining that to me, *Mummy*,' he said, raising one eyebrow with amusement. 'I'll bear that in mind for future reference.'

She heard the laughter in his voice and maintained a composed face.

'So which rides do you want to go on?' he asked Chloe, taking a bite of croissant so that his mouth was instantly covered in buttered crumbs. The sight mesmerised Vicky, who imagined how enjoyable it would be to lick each crumb off. Individually. It would take hours. Or at least seconds, because her tongue would not be able to resist searching his out. That would be the hardest part of seeing him. The seeing and the wanting but the not being able to touch. The agony as she was forced to play the happy, jolly, pally game when her body hungered to be touched by him in a way that was very far removed from pally.

'All of them!' Chloe's face was slowly but surely becoming submerged in maple syrup, despite Vicky's best efforts at keeping it at bay.

'Even the Tower of Terror?' He made his voice go spooky and took another bite of his croissant, this time absent-mindedly licking one finger clean before wiping his mouth with his linen napkin. He had no idea how eerily alike he was to his niece. It was uncanny the way nature could take a shade of hair and a colour of eye and replicate both so precisely in another human being. Even the spacing between the eyes and the shape of the mouth was all Forbes.

'What's that?'

'You mean your mother didn't read the description out to you?'

'No, she didn't.' Two pairs of grey eyes bearing the same expression stared at her, and she couldn't help a smile.

'She's too young for that particular ride, Max. *You* can go on it on your own.'

'I shall have to,' he said indolently, returning his gaze to his niece's besotted face. 'However terrifying a ride is, nothing terrifies the great Max Forbes!'

'Nothing?' Chloe asked, delighted, and Vicky heaved a loud, conspicuous sigh.

'Well. Spiders. Obviously.'

'*I'm* not scared of spiders. Am I, Mum?' Chloe glanced across at her mother, allowing her face to be dabbed with a napkin in the process. This, Vicky thought, was the relationship she should have had with Shaun. They should have delighted in each other's company. Instead, his rare visits to see his daughter had been an ordeal of moodiness, shouting and, after fifteen minutes of fatherly affection, a rapid downhill run to indifference and finally irritation. He'd brought her gifts inappropriate to her age, then had become sulky when she failed to be delighted with them, while Vicky had hovered miserably in the background, not quite knowing what to do and wishing he would just leave. There had never been one pore in his entire body that had possessed anything of the ease with which Max was now enchanting his niece.

'Not the ones in books, at any rate,' Vicky said, smiling.

'I'm not scared of anything,' Chloe assured him, abandoning the remnants of her breakfast in favour of conversation, 'I'm like you! Can I go on the Tower of Terror? Please? Say yes! Say yes!'

'Absolutely not,' Vicky responded immediately. 'It's a…' She plucked the guidebook from her bag, opened it at the relevant page, and read, verbatim, '"…*terrifying plummet, guaranteed to scare the most hardened.*" Anyway, there's a height limit and you don't measure up, short stuff. Apart from which, that particular ride isn't at the Magic Kingdom, so you'll have to settle for something a lot less adventurous.'

Later, as they entered the fantasy world of the Magic Kingdom, Max said to her, 'And what about you? Ever been to a place like this?'

'Not quite.' She paused and looked around her. Ahead was the fairytale Disney palace, pale spires rising up to the sky. It was early, but already beginning to get crowded. 'In fact, I never went abroad until I was an adult. Not all of us benefitted from a privileged background, financially.' But her voice was lacking in acrimony. 'I *did* go to Alton Towers, though, when I was fifteen, and from what I remember it wasn't *quite* like this.'

Chloe, desperate to get going, tugged her hand. She was in a state of high excitement. Vicky thought that her daughter might just spontaneously combust from it if she didn't go on a ride quickly. Were there medical services on site for desperate ride-deprived children? She put the question to Max and they both laughed companionably. She could already feel her resolution to remain as distant and as objective as possible beginning to crumble.

This was what it was all about. Being dragged along by a child, with the sun shining and your heart bursting with love for the man by your side. Had it not been for several clouds on that particular horizon, she would have said that happiness was very nearly within her grasp.

Even thoughts of Shaun, when she *did* think about him, had lost their power over her. He'd melted away into a vague shadow, eclipsed by the dynamic presence of his very much alive brother. Had that always been the way? she wondered. She could almost feel a pang of sympathy for him now, an emotion that would have been unthinkable three or four months previously. His ghost had let her go, or maybe it was the other way around.

The morning was spent on rides, little, delightful rides, for which the queues were not as lengthy as the guidebook had led her to believe. The three of them sat in the little cars, with Chloe between them, and anyone seeing them would have thought that they were the archetypal nuclear family, needing only the dog and the family saloon car to complete them. They would have done a double-take, had they heard the convoluted history behind them.

And was it her imagination, or had all that hungry, masculine lust bitten the dust? Ever since he'd found out about Chloe, the sexual interest he'd had in her had died. He was behaving with such wonderful ease, was chatting to her in such a friendly and unthreatening fashion, that she wanted to burst into tears. Instead, she forced wide, bright smiles onto her face until the muscles in her jaw began to ache from the strain of it. Over lunch, she watched him from under her lashes, watched the way his attention was focused on his niece, winning her over. When he looked at *her*, he wasn't seeing her as a woman, he was seeing her as Chloe's mother. With all the cards on the table, she couldn't have hoped for a better situation, nor could she have expected to be feeling as desolate as she was now.

'You're getting red,' he said, as they headed towards the MGM studios.

'Thank you,' Vicky snapped shortly. An unsightly blush added more unwanted colour to her cheeks and further worsened her temper.

'And you've gone into a sulk.'

'I have *not* gone into a *sulk*.'

'What are you thinking?'

'I'm thinking that Chloe's having a wonderful time,' she lied, looking at her daughter, who was ahead of them by a few paces. 'I've never been able to afford many treats for her.'

'That needn't be a problem from now on.'

'Because she's got an uncle with a bottomless wallet to oblige her? In case you're interested, money causes as many problems as it solves, and I don't believe in flinging it at children willy-nilly.'

'Stop spoiling for an argument.' He looked sideways at

the angry tilt of her head, the tight mouth, and felt an irrational desire to smooth it all away with his fingers. He wanted to stroke her face and produce a smile, like a magician pulling a rabbit out of a hat. His feelings for his niece, unexpected as they were, had been remarkably easy to find, but for a man who'd never had a problem with women her damned mother was proving to be a brick wall. He'd made a decision to back away from her, to win her over without suffocating her with an arrogant need to get what he wanted, and he was baffled that she was so tangibly failing to respond. Even when he'd managed to bring a smile to her face her eyes had slithered away from his and found sanctuary in her daughter.

'I am not *spoiling for an argument*. Why would I want to argue with you?' She glanced at him and tossed her head, like a beautiful wild filly rearing up angrily against restraint.

Had it not been for Chloe skipping ahead, looking back every so often to make sure that she was still within the fold, he would have been seriously tempted to drag Vicky back to the hotel room and restrain her in any way he could. Which would have had her bolting off in the opposite direction. He couldn't win, could he?

'You tell me,' he said through gritted teeth. 'Do you resent me because your daughter and I get along? Are you jealous?'

'That's ridiculous!'

'Is it?' He didn't want to. At least, he knew he shouldn't, but he pulled off the band securing the end of her plait and wove his hand into her hair, relishing the soft fall around his fingers and tightening his grip when he felt her automatically try and pull away from him.

'What are you doing?' she breathed.

He dodged the question. There was no acceptably polite

way of telling her that he was fighting the urge to do something very physical and very satisfying with her.

'I am trying to get your attention.'

'Well, you're not setting about it the right way.' She gave her head a gentle tug, but abandoned the effort when Chloe turned around. Instead she forced herself to smile, and when her daughter pranced to them and held her mother's hand she was reduced to having his hand in her hair, caressing her head. What was he playing at? She heard herself chatting to Chloe, valiantly keeping up the pretence that her body wasn't on fire, as his fingers softened and finally his hand dropped to curl around her waist.

He could feel her body tense. He could also smell the expectancy there and it thrilled and frustrated him at the same time. It was as though he knew the numbers to the combination lock, but not the right sequence and, however much he jostled with the digits, he never quite managed to get it right. The gentle brush of her slight body against his thigh was a sweet, agonising reminder of how capable she was of tormenting him, without even realising it.

She had a quality of stubbornness about her and, even though he could work out its origin, he still found it exasperating. It was as if her gentleness had hardened through experience into bull-headed pride, which had a nerve-racking tendency to shift into place just when he thought that he was getting through to her. He glanced down and hungrily eyed the gentle bounce of her small breasts, two mounds pushing against her light salmon T-shirt. Under normal circumstances, their one act of love-making, which had been the most satisfying he'd ever experienced, would have naturally led to more, but she'd dug her heels in and was continuing to dig her heels in.

By the time they had made it to the MGM studios, his

imagination had taken his frustration to new, unrewarding heights.

After some exhaustive queues for rides which Chloe seemed desperate to experience, they found themselves standing in front of the Tower of Terror, a massive brown house designed to look terrifyingly spooky. It succeeded.

'Bigger than I thought,' Max murmured dubiously. 'And no good for you, little one.' He patted the top of Chloe's head and she shot him a woebegone smile of acceptance.

'But feel free to go ahead yourself,' Vicky said, positioning herself opposite him just in case his errant hand decided to stray again. With Chloe there, she was compelled not to make a scene, which was the last thing she wanted to do anyway, when the feel of his skin against hers was sinfully exciting.

'I wouldn't dream of abandoning you two ladies…'

'Go ahead. We'll wait here for you.'

'The queue's too long.'

'Oh, that's all right. Never mind us. We'll grab an ice-cream and watch the world go by, won't we, Chlo?' She gave him a nasty grin and arched her eyebrows in feigned surprise, as though struck by a sudden thought. 'You're not *scared*, are you? Not when you told us that you were only scared of *spiders*?'

Max looked down at her and uncomfortably tugged at the collar of his polo shirt, as though it had unexpectedly shrunk two sizes and was now a tight fit. 'Why don't *you* have a go, if you're so daring?'

'Ah, so you *are* scared.' Vicky folded her arms and shot him a triumphant, lofty smile. This little nick of vulnerability was unbearably endearing, little did he realise. She noticed that he was looking positively sheepish and resisted the impulse to burst out laughing. 'I think I might just take you up on your offer, if you don't mind waiting for me...' Chloe's eyes went round with admiration.

'You wait,' he murmured into her ear, before she headed off to join the curling line of people waiting for the ride of their lives. 'When you stumble back here, white-faced and shaking...'

'Coward,' she murmured back with laughter in her voice, and she looked to find him grinning wickedly at her. Whatever ride she went on, she decided that it couldn't destabilise her more than the man standing in front of her. What man in all creation could make all her senses feel as though she was hurtling through space and could wreak havoc with her nervous system in a matter of seconds?

Forty-five minutes later, she discovered that when it came to matters of the heart she was hopeless, but when it came to rides she was utterly lacking in fear, and for the next week she exhaustively tried them all while Max and Chloe experimented with interactive playgrounds for preschool children and rides that a three-month-old baby would feel at home on. Much to her glee. The one simulator ride he ventured on rendered him ashen-faced and speechless, and he was obliged to recover over a bag of chocolate chip cookies shared with his niece. He was good-natured in defeat and willingly allowed her to scamper off on mile-high roller coasters and death-defying water slides, while he tamely crammed his large masculine frame into ride-along cars and teapots and carousel horses with Chloe.

She discovered that they had settled into a habit of sorts, and one which suited her perfectly. They explored parks by day, a tiring business which left no time for personal chit-chat, had a spot of lunch, then went their separate ways in the early afternoon. Vicky had no idea what he hived off to do at two-thirty in the afternoon, but she suspected that he worked, having noticed that, despite the fact that the holiday had been designed for bonding with his niece, he'd still travelled over with his laptop computer. In the evenings, they both ate with Chloe, and then Vicky retired at a reasonable hour to bath her daughter, settle her and have an early night herself. The days were long and sleeping was no problem.

It came as a shock when she awakened on the Tuesday morning to the realisation that the holiday was virtually at an end. One full day left and they would be leaving the following night. She would have to start packing her stuff in the evening.

She couldn't believe that all the warnings in her head about caution and wariness had been for nought. Aside from the occasional reminder to herself that he could hurt her, she'd allowed herself to succumb to the magic of the place, just as Chloe had, without a thought for common sense. Aside from that one fleeting instance when he had touched her, with the safeguard of Chloe to let him get away with it, he had been the model of good behaviour. If anything, it had not reassured her of his worthwhile intentions but added to the growing list of reasons why she had fallen in love with him in the first place. Hostility was always a safer defence against surrender, but she'd failed to consider that it takes two to wage a war and, in the absence of a willingly antagonistic partner, she'd found herself suspending her despair and giving in to the moment.

He made it easy for her to laugh. He didn't give her the time or opportunity to dwell on her own personal problems and she'd discovered that it was remarkably easy to put off dealing with the complications of her life, of which he was a major one, until a later date. Some mysterious *later date*, when she would be forced to wake up and confront issues and handle the grief that she was busily creating for herself simply by enjoying him without the boundaries she knew were essential.

But she still imagined that she could somehow put off reality for the next two days, until he said to her, as they prepared to go their separate ways for the afternoon, 'We need to talk.'

Vicky took in the implacable expression on his face, browner now that it had been less than a fortnight ago, and felt a slither of foreboding crawl up her spine. 'How can we?' She shrugged helplessly, reluctant to let reality intrude on the last day but one. 'Chloe—'

'—has been fixed up with a babysitter for this evening. She's coming at seven-thirty. I arranged it through the hotel and, before you start throwing up your hands in anxiety, their babysitting service is very professional. They're all trained in childcare; I asked lots of questions before booking one. So we can have a meal and a…chat. It's time to sort out what we're going to do about the situation.'

Why did that have such an ominous ring about it?

Vicky wanted to ask *Already?* but she knew the dangers of even thinking along those lines, never mind voicing them. She also knew that he was right. If what he had set out to do with this trip was prove himself as a sound figure in Chloe's life, and a reliable, easy-to-digest one in hers, then he'd succeeded—if anything, rather well. He'd left her with no arguments to voice.

Chloe was asleep by the time the fresh-faced babysitter arrived, complete with a bag of 'things to do', which would not be used, and Vicky was more or less ready to go. Mentally bracing herself, and feeling a little strange in her first dressy outfit of the holiday—a small pale-coloured flowered dress in silky material, falling softly to mid-thigh, and a pair of wedge-heeled cream sandals that lent a couple of inches to her height. For the first time she felt nervous at the prospect of seeing him without the convenient distractions of Chloe and rides and people around them.

He was waiting for her at the bar, and it was a shock to see him, as well, more formally dressed. He was still wearing short sleeves, but his trousers were dark, and his bronzed skin gave him the appearance of someone of Italian descent. As she walked towards the table his eyes travelled once over her, then fell to his drink. He sat back in the chair, waiting until she had sat down, then called the waiter over to order a drink for her. In the silence that followed, Vicky nervously tucked her hair behind her ears, willing herself to feel the ease she'd felt with him over the past few days, but failing to find it.

'So—' he swallowed a long mouthful of his whisky and soda, then reclined back in the chair and watched her through brooding eyes '—glad you came after all?'

'It's been fun,' Vicky said, feeling like a candidate at an interview. She nervously accepted a glass of wine from the waiter and sipped from it. 'Tiring. Chloe's been ready for bed every night by seven. In England, I have to persuade her to climb under the duvet before quarter to eight.' She smiled at the thought of her daughter being cajoled into the dreaded bed.

'She's…a wonderful child. All credit to you.' He tilted his glass to her in a mock salute. 'From the sounds of it, you accomplished the near-impossible against all odds.'

'It wasn't as difficult as you make it sound,' Vicky informed him, gulping back rather more of her wine than she had set out to do and nearly choking in the process. 'I'm no saint, just one of millions of women who find themselves in a situation where they have no choice.'

'But you had my brother to contend with as well. My

brother with his threats and verbal abuse. And no money to cushion the future.'

'I never thought that my future needed cushioning,' Vicky lied valiantly. 'And I know where this is going. A long summary of my unfortunate past, followed by a swift recap of all the reasons why you should get what you want.' She'd known for a while that she had to recapture some of that lost hostility if she were to avoid complete emotional demolition. Now, she clawed and scrambled her way towards it, pretending not to see the hardening of his features. 'Well, it won't work.' She swigged back the remainder of her wine and it flared through her head like a bolt of white heat, then she banged the glass onto the table, extracting a few curious glances from the people sitting closest to them. 'You can see Chloe, of course you can, but within limits. Perhaps every other weekend. I don't want her life disrupted!'

'Don't you mean that you don't want *your* life disrupted? Don't you think that she deserves to know as much about her father's family as possible? Why deny her the heritage that's hers?'

'She's only a child! She doesn't know a thing about her heritage and doesn't care less!'

'But she won't be a child in ten years' time, will she?' he said venomously, leaning into her, his body rigid with anger. 'I wish to God,' he bit out furiously, 'that you'd fill me in on what your problem is! I'm offering you safety, financial security, an arrangement that's virtually foolproof and the best possible solution for the three of us!' He slammed his fist on the table and the couple closest to them got up and moved, giving them some very suspicious backward glances, 'What more do you need to be convinced?'

'I don't want *an arrangement*! I want...thunder and lightning...and fireworks...and magic!'

'Like you had with my brother?' he jeered. '*Those* kinds of *fireworks*?'

Vicky's face drained of colour and she stood up on shaky legs. 'I think I've heard enough.' She gathered up her bag and tried to gather up her lost self-control as well.

'Sit back down!' He lowered his voice to a demanding growl as the area around them cleared hurriedly. 'Running away won't solve anything!'

'There's nothing to solve!' She was bending towards him, her long hair hanging over one shoulder, her breasts heaving with emotion.

'Marry me and your problems will be over!' It was an order, not a request, hurled at her by a man whose eyes were flaring like shards of silver glass, his whole body taut with the desire to bend her to his indomitable will.

And he expected her to capitulate?

'Marry you and my problems would be about to begin!' She straightened, still shaking like a leaf. 'I'm going to pack. And you can do your own thing tomorrow. Chloe and I will stay here by the pool.'

'Listen to me' he commanded urgently, standing up, his long strides easily keeping up with her as she strode out of the bar.

'Why should I?' she threw at him. 'Because you're rich? Important? A Forbes?'

'Because there's something I need to tell you…'

'What?'

'You're being bloody stubborn,' he muttered.

'And *that's* what you want to tell me?'

'What's so wrong with being taken care of?'

'For the sake of maintaining your heritage?'

'Just answer the question!'

'I don't need you!' she told him, and herself, fiercely. 'I don't want to be *taken care of*. I'm more than capable of taking care of myself and my daughter! We're not *charity cases*!'

'I never implied that you were!'

'Then what *is* it you're implying?'

'I'm willing to give you—'

'I'm not interested.'

'Fine.' For a few electric seconds they stared in the darkness at one another, then he turned on his heel and walked away. Vicky followed him with her eyes until he disappeared around the hotel wall, then she too made her way slowly back to her room, not quite understanding why and how everything had gone so badly wrong, but knowing, somewhere, that open warfare was for the best.

CHAPTER TEN

WHY was it for the best?

She noticed that she'd somehow arrived at the gift shop, which was a grand affair with an alluring display case for every Disney product known to man. Or so it seemed. Instead of beating a hasty retreat, she found herself dawdling in front of the sweatshirts, ambling over to the array of postcards, indulging her train of thought.

Why, she thought, was open warfare for the best? Who was she protecting? Chloe? Not a bit of it. Chloe had accepted Max Forbes with the open enthusiasm of a child. Vicky was, she admitted, protecting herself, but how long could she go through life making herself pay for what had happened in the past? Where was the use condemning herself to a lonely future because she measured every man against Shaun and instantly backed away?

Max Forbes was nothing like his brother, aside from his physical resemblance, and even then there was something more finely honed about his face. It was as though nature had taken exquisite time with Max and then had done a rush job with his twin brother.

She strolled over to the stationery counter and absentmindedly registered that Mickey and Minnie were everywhere. On mugs, cups, paper, pencils. Spooky.

So what if he didn't love her? Was that the end of the world? Wasn't it better to have him in her life as a friend, rather than enemy? Because he *was* going to be in her life, one way or another. He wasn't going to just disappear and leave her to get on with things the way she always had.

She'd seen the affection in his eyes when he looked at Chloe, the curiosity of the world-weary man chancing upon something new and magical, the innocence of childhood. When he looked at his niece and saw the striking resemblance to him, he must feel a strong pull on his heart strings. How could he not?

So she could never have her ideal. Well, she wouldn't be the first in the universe, would she? And Chloe would have two parents rather than just her; a family, a sense of belonging.

A plump girl with amazingly white teeth and a broad smile walked across and asked her whether she could help, at which Vicky jumped and hurriedly grabbed a Pluto picture frame from the shelf and a box of writing paper which sported an intricate array of Disney characters leaping around the edges. Chloe would love it, even though letters, at this point in time, were solely addressed to her mother. With Max in her life she would now have two recipients for her three-line letters with their careful handwriting.

She left the gift shop and, instead of heading up to the bedroom to rescue the babysitter from her duties, made her way to the informal coffee shop that overlooked the pool for a cappuccino. As seemed to be the case in Florida, a simple cup of coffee was accompanied by something edible, in this case a vast butter biscuit dusted with powdery sugar. The actual cup of coffee was huge, and she realised that she should have specified a small cup.

The coffee shop was half empty, with a handful of couples sitting at tables in front of large dishes of ice cream. Most were poring over guidebooks, planning the remainder of their holiday with military precision. The décor was bright and jaunty. Not conducive to solitary meditation. But Vicky's mind, having broken its reins, was now unstoppable. It poured over the past and then leapt into the future and poured over that. There were so many permutations of what could happen that she felt dizzy, but the glaringly obvious thing was that she wanted Max in her life—she wanted his rich humour, his unexpected kindness, his wit, even the glimpses of ruthless cynicism that could have the other secretaries in the office running for cover. She loved every angle, every facet, every small nook and cranny of this man, and the thought of fighting him for evermore would end up destroying her.

She took a few more sips from her mug, managing to reduce the volume by very little, nibbled some more biscuit, like a mouse tentatively working its way around the outside of a piece of cheese, and then she stood up and dusted herself down.

Max would either be in the bar or in his bedroom. Presumably.

He wasn't in the bar. The prospect of going to his bedroom was a little daunting, especially when she wasn't quite sure what she was going to say once she found him, but her moment of brief hesitation was replaced by resolve and five minutes later she was knocking on his door. Her whole body was keyed to his response. She could feel every nerve stretching inside her.

When he pulled open the door, she was shocked by his face. He looked as though he had spent a night on the tiles. His hair was sticking out at odd angles and there was nothing cool and assured about his features. They were drawn, but his glittering silver eyes were as hard and shuttered as she had expected.

'What do you want?' he asked, standing in front of her, and her heart sank. She was beginning to forget what she wanted, and she realised that she hadn't even worked out what the heck she was going to say.

'I thought we might have a talk,' she said in a brave

little voice, looking up at him and fighting not to wilt at his expression.

'About what? Haven't you said it all? I must have been a damn fool to ever think I could batter down your defences. You've shut yourself away in your bitter little castle, and you're not going to let anyone get in, are you? Least of all the brother of the man who you think ruined your life.'

'He *did* ruin my life!'

'But that's in the past, isn't it? Or can't you accept that? Maybe you've grown so accustomed to being a victim that you've started to enjoy it. Oh, what the hell... I don't even know why I'm bothering to have this pointless conversation with you. Go to bed.' He half turned, preparing to shut the door.

'No!' she cried. 'Don't!'

'Don't *what*?' His eyes raked mercilessly over her.

'Don't shut me out. Please! Please?'

'Give me one good reason why I shouldn't. Isn't that what you've done to me?'

That expression of vulnerability brought a wave of tenderness over her that made her legs tremble. She hadn't thought that she was shutting him out. She'd been protecting herself in the only way she knew how, protecting herself against the possibility of ever being hurt again.

'Won't you let me in?' she asked quietly, reaching out and placing her hand flat on his chest.

She felt his body tense but she kept her hand there, needing the warmth of his skin through his shirt; then he turned away and rasped, 'Shut the door behind you.'

He stalked across to the small couch in the corner of the room and, her heart beating wildly, Vicky closed the door and walked across to his bed, and perched on the edge, crossing her feet at the ankles and loosely entwining her fingers on her lap.

She could hear the steady background hum of the air-conditioning system, which somehow only managed to intensify the silence between them.

He wiped his hands across his eyes and then looked at her, waiting for her to speak. She'd entered his territory and now it was going to be up to her to speak her mind, never mind the degree of receptiveness in the audience.

'I didn't mean to shut you out,' she began hesitantly. 'I didn't think I had, anyway. I mean, I came over here at your suggestion and you can't say that I've tried to monopolise Chloe's attention. In fact, I've hardly seen her at all these past few days!' Her automatic position of self-defence cranked into gear, but when she looked at him she discovered that it wasn't working with him.

'We're not talking about Chloe.'

'No,' Vicky murmured inaudibly. She drew a deep breath. 'I suppose...I suppose you're right. I went through a bad time with Shaun and I've let it influence my life. When I saw you...you brought everything back. I...it was like being hit by a roller coaster at full speed...I felt like my past was catching up with me again...and I was scared. Terrified, in fact,' she amended truthfully, reliving what she'd felt when she'd first set eyes on that familiar, yet not familiar face. 'I thought you were going to be just like Shaun. It didn't take long for me to realise...' Her voice wittered away into silence as she sensed dangerous ground ahead. Her fingers plucked at her skirt.

'*What?* For you to realise *what*?' There was a watchfulness about him that hadn't been there a few minutes previously and that was almost as alarming as his bitterness.

'For me to realise...that you weren't anything like

Shaun. Your brother was cruel, sadistic and addicted to getting his own way.' She couldn't sit still any longer and she stood up and walked jerkily towards the window and looked out, not seeing anything.

'And what was *I*?' he asked with mild curiosity. She could feel him staring at her and her stomach responded by going into knots.

'Nothing like your brother,' was as far as she would go on that one, and for the moment he seemed to accept her staccato answer. 'I should have left as soon as I could. I had planned to, but…'

'But what?'

'But I…enjoyed the job. I'd spent months doing menial work to pay the bills and, even though I knew it was dangerous working for you in case you ever found out the truth about me, it was tempting to carry on doing it for a little bit longer, enjoying the challenge of a job where I had to actually think. Never mind the money, which was very useful. I was finally in a position where I could afford to spend a bit on Chloe and on the house. I was putting money aside. I told myself that soon I'd leave…and then…'

'Your past jumped up to bite you on the hand when you were least expecting it. Another shock to your system, no doubt.' His voice was laced with jeering cynicism and for a brief second her eyes flashed angrily at him. He was deliberately making this hard for her, but what could she do about that?

'Yes,' she answered meekly, and he shot her a darkly challenging look before glancing away.

'So tell me why you've come,' he said, mildly curious now, not giving an inch. 'To prove right the old adage that confession is good for the soul? Nothing further to add to the litany of past regrets?'

'To tell you that I've been a fool,' she said with a shuddering sigh, and this time there was something different when he looked at her, although his voice was casual when he spoke.

'Oh, yes? And why would that be?'

'Because…' Her voice faltered now that she had hit the thin ice patch and risked falling in. What would he do if she confessed that she was in love with him? Would he laugh? Look embarrassed? Launch into an immediate retraction of his offer of marriage with the threat of real emotion entering into the equation, messing up his tidy little convenient proposition? None of these possible scenarios did anything for her self-confidence.

'Because…what?'

'I've thought about what you offered…' she began again, veering away from one patch of thin ice towards another. 'You know…your proposal…'

'What makes you think that that still stands?' he asked indifferently, though his eyes were still narrowed and watchful on her.

'I'm sorry…I thought…'

'But let's just say, *hypothetically*, that I was still prepared to enter into an arrangement with you.'

'Well, talking hypothetically,' Vicky volunteered nervously, 'I've realised that I would be prepared to go through with such an arrangement. I've looked at the way you are with Chloe…unless it was all one big act…'

'I don't pretend things I don't feel,' he responded grimly, and she wanted to scream at him, *Well, what do you feel about me? Aside from the occasional burst of lust? Anything at all?*

'In that case, I think it might be a good idea. I know it's not an ideal situation…' She smiled wistfully, imagining what the ideal situation would be. 'But it could work…'

'And I've been thinking as well.' His voice was serious, and she knew what he was going to say even before the words were out. It was like having a bucket of freezing water poured over her. 'I can't marry you, Vicky.'

'No. Well. Fair enough.' A great well of despair washed over her. 'I…that's fine… It was stupid of me to have resurrected that old proposal anyway. When we get back to London we can work something out…I know Chloe would be heartbroken if she didn't see you again…' Her feet, which were desperate to get her to the door, seemed to have been nailed to the floorboards. Amazing. She almost groaned with the frustration of it.

'Don't you want to know *why* I've changed my mind?'

'No…really…it's enough that you have…' She heard the misery in her voice and cringed.

'I've been doing some thinking of my own,' he said quietly, leaning forward and resting his elbows on his knees. He swept his fingers through his hair, but continued to stare at the ground until she eventually sidled a bit closer to him—because, if she didn't, she wasn't sure she would be able to catch a word he was saying. Not that he'd begun to say anything at all.

She felt a little braver now that he wasn't staring at her and reducing her thought processes to pulp. 'There's no need to explain anything to me. I mean it.'

'There is.' He favoured her with a brief glance, then he resumed his peculiar inspection of the carpet, as though he was looking for something he had misplaced there. His vocabulary, from the looks of it, she thought, which appeared to have deserted him completely.

The seconds dragged into one minute, two minutes, five minutes, until she said edgily, 'Well, explain away, then.'

Her remark was greeted with another quick look, too quick for her to read the expression in his grey eyes.

'If you've been watching my interaction with your daughter, then I've been watching yours, looking at the way you two reach out automatically for one another, the way Chloe looks across to you every so often for support…and you were right. Marriage and family is about more than arrangements and practicalities. It's more than a business proposition, two people adding up the pros and cons for living under the same roof, sharing the same house and then trying to work out whether it'll be worth the effort.'

His words jabbed into her like the blades of a knife, and every jab was accompanied by a sharp twist.

'I've always been sceptical about love; I've seen too many friends start out with hope and end up with ashes, and your relationship with Shaun was just another example of why emotion never gets anyone anywhere. Or so I thought. The fact is, emotion is all we have, and without that marriage is a sham, a hell on earth. It takes more than a lack of argument to make a good marriage, just like virtue isn't necessarily a lack of obvious vice.' He sighed deeply and raised his eyes to hers. 'Hence my change of mind.'

Vicky's head felt as though it was stuffed with cotton wool. The inside of her mouth wasn't faring much better either.

'Are you trying to tell me that you don't love me?' she said in a high, flippant voice, to defuse the situation which was threatening to overwhelm her. *Remind me,* she thought, *never to ask someone for honesty. Much better to avoid it at all costs.*

Instead of finding answering relief in his eyes, he didn't say anything.

'I'm not saying anything of the sort.'

His words dropped into the silence like bombshells. First of all she thought that she'd perhaps heard incorrectly, then it occurred to her that she'd misinterpreted what he had said. Hadn't there been a double negative in there somewhere? Lastly, she figured that perhaps it was just an elaborate counter-bluff, maybe containing a pun, although his face was unsmiling. A wash of unaccustomed colour stained his cheeks, but he was still holding her gaze, waiting for her to say something.

'Then what *are* you saying?' she asked into the oppressive silence. More requests for honesty, she thought numbly, could only end in tears. Hers.

'I'm telling you that I love you and I can't put you through a marriage that's one-sided. I thought,' he carried on, now addressing his fingers, 'that I could show you how much…how much I…well, you know what I'm saying here…' His flush deepened and his voice was unsteady, as though every word was an effort. 'I…but it hasn't worked…and…'

'So you're saying that *you love me*?' She could feel the wild stirrings of hope pushing through her woolly-headed brain, and as fast as she tried to shove it back it resprouted. Her heart was thundering inside her.

'I'm saying that I love you, Victoria Lockhart.' This time his voice was steady and his eyes never left her face.

She smiled slowly and went to sit alongside him on the sofa. 'Would you mind very much telling me that over and over again, because I'm finding it difficult to take in?'

He carried on looking at her, and suddenly the humour was back in his eyes.

'Now, why would I do that?' he drawled, sitting back on the chair so that he could have an all-encompassing view of her. From the expression on his face, it was a view he liked.

'Because I seem to have spent my life searching for you and I need you to tell me that my love for you is returned. You forget, I'm a woman whose self-esteem has taken some battering in her life...' Her self-esteem had never felt better. When she thought of Shaun and the emotional mess she'd been, she had the unreal feeling that she was thinking of a different person altogether.

'Well, there might be a bit of a price to pay...'

'What kind of price?' She looked at him with wide-eyed innocence, but there was a wicked smile on her face that matched his.

He leaned forward, curled his hand around the nape of her neck and pulled her to him, then he proceeded to kiss her thoroughly, only stopping to say into her hungry mouth, 'The marrying kind of price...' His tongue dipped back into her mouth and she laughingly struggled her way out of the heady embrace.

'There's no need,' she said, pink-faced but serious. Her hands pressed against his chest and she could feel the movement of his heart beating against his ribs. He reached to clasp both hands in her hair, on either side of her face, while the soft pads of his thumbs stroked her temples, her eyes, her cheekbones. Her small breasts ached for the same soft, seductive caress. 'I know that your sense of duty and responsibility prompted you to propose originally, but...'

'If only you knew,' he murmured, now stroking the slender column of her neck, then travelling inexorably downwards to cup her jutting breasts.

'If only I knew...what?' Her words ended on a gasp as he unbuttoned her and scooped her breasts out of their lacy bondage, rubbing his thumbs erotically over the raised tips.

'When I proposed to you,' he said, stilling his fingers

so that he could capture every ounce of her attention, 'I meant it. I *wanted* to marry you. I was determined to claw my way to your love if I had to die in the process. And now, my darling...' His fingers resumed their expert manipulation of her breasts, sending a convulsive shudder through her body. 'I don't intend to let you go. Ever.' He dipped his head to trail the tip of his tongue delicately around her nipple, circling, touching, flicking, until her unsteady breathing became small moans of pleasure. 'I *want* to marry you, just like I *want* Chloe to be a daughter to me, like she's a daughter to you...' He suckled on her breast, just long enough to make her slide a few centimetres down the sofa, long enough for his hand to gently curve around her thigh, massaging the willing flesh and edging upwards.

'And then, who knows?' He looked up at her and his grey eyes were dark with passion and tenderness. 'More babies?' He nuzzled her and she could feel him smiling into her breasts. 'If you thought you'd found the archetypal tycoon, then, my darling, you were wrong, because the prospect of domesticity has never seemed so good...'

'Are you telling me that I've tamed a tiger?' She watched his dark head against her body and was thrillingly, sinfully happy.

'Not,' he said, shifting his body so that he could unzip his trousers, 'completely. In one very important aspect, my love, you'll never be able to tame me...'

IN HER BOSS'S BED

by

Maggie Cox

The day **Maggie Cox** saw the film version of
Wuthering Heights, with a beautiful Merle Oberon
and a very handsome Laurence Olivier, was the day
that she became hooked on romance. From that
day onwards she spent a lot of time dreaming up
her own romances, secretly hoping that one day
she might become published and get paid for doing
what she loves most! Now that her dream is being
realised, she wakes up every morning and counts her
blessings. She is married to a gorgeous man, is the
mother of two wonderful sons and her two other
great passions in life – besides her family and read-
ing/writing – are music and films.

Don't miss Maggie Cox's exciting new novel
The Rich Man's Love-Child
out in March 2008 from
Mills & Boon® Modern™.

To my wonderful brother Billy,
loved but not lost.
I will hold you in my heart for ever.

CHAPTER ONE

THE voice in her head seemed to come from far away, and had a sense of urgency about it. Irritated at the interruption to her dream, Morgen mentally willed it away, longing for the dream to come back. But to no avail. It was gone, like leaves scattered by the wind. As the fog in her head began to clear it became painfully apparent that she had pins and needles in her hands—the same hands that her head was resting on, on her desk.

'Oh, my God!'

Lifting her head, she briskly rubbed her palms together, then flexed her fingers, her heart racing slightly as the blood began to circulate again. It started racing even more when she saw the stony-faced expression of the man standing on the other side of the desk, disapproval bracketing a mouth that looked as if it smiled just about as often as Morgen had dinner at the Savoy.

She started to rise to her feet. 'I'm sorry, I—'

'Was wasting the firm's time? By my calculations it's at least another hour until lunch, and I've been told that most of the staff in this office grab a sandwich and eat it at their desk. Obviously you have *other*, less strenuous ideas for using your desk, Miss…?'

Hateful man! For a couple of moments Morgen struggled to get a handle on her anger, not to mention humiliation, but then, taking a deep breath and tucking her hair behind her ear, she straightened her shoulders and rallied. How dared he cast aspersions on her character by insinuating that she fell asleep at her desk on a regular basis? And who, in God's name, was he anyway?

'My falling asleep like that has never happened before, Mr…?'

'You first.' He ran an impatient hand through hair the colour of rich dark caramel, and Morgen couldn't help noticing that he looked in urgent need of both a haircut and a shave. Besides that, there was an edge about him that made her stomach knot. This was a man who would never suffer the indignity of being ignored, she concluded, not in this life. And it wasn't just because of those jaw-dropping good looks, either.

'McKenzie. Morgen McKenzie.'

'And—apart from being employed by this firm to do apparently not very much—you work for Derek Holden, is that right?'

Swallowing with difficulty, Morgen felt the slight burn of heat in her cheeks. 'I'm his assistant, yes.'

'Then where the hell is he? I had a meeting booked with him in the conference room at ten-thirty. I got an earlier flight back from the States to make sure I was here on time, I'm jet-lagged, in dire need of a shower and something to eat, and there's no sign of your boss anywhere. Care to tell me where you think he is, Miss McKenzie?'

Right now, what she actually *cared* to tell Mr High-and-Mighty-I'm-so-much-better-than-you standing in front of her was probably unprintable, but she was equally angry with Derek. Why hadn't he briefed her on the fact he had a ten-thirty appointment with this man, whoever he was? She'd checked the diary thoroughly before she'd left last night, as she always did, and there had been no meeting in the conference room at ten-thirty pencilled in then. What the devil was he playing at?

Her heart sank at yet another painful reminder of her boss's slow and steady decline. Once a smart up-and-coming young architect, since his divorce Derek Holden had turned more and more to the bottle in search of comfort. In the past six months Morgen had seen him turn into a sad, shambling wreck of his former self. It was a good job that she was quick-witted and smart herself, because she had saved his bacon on more than one occasion—taking over work that was definitely not in the province of a mere personal assistant. She concluded that Derek must have known about the meeting for a while but had forgotten to tell her about it.

Now, as her fingers turned over the wide pages of the desk diary, hovering over the blank space next to ten-thirty, Morgen frowned down at it, rapidly scanning her brain for the best excuse for his absence she could possibly come up with. Sensing the man's irritation grow more acute as the seconds ticked by, she reflected that this handsome Goliath in front of her was going to take a heck of a lot of convincing.

'Unfortunately Derek has been taken ill,' she explained smoothly, assuring herself she wasn't too far off the mark. He usually didn't show up until around ten most days anyway, but because it was now almost eleven-fifteen she assumed he must be feeling even more the worse for wear than usual. He probably wouldn't show up today at all—which might be for the best, considering the glowering face before her.

'Really? Then why in hell's name didn't someone let me know?' The deep, resonant bellow almost made Morgen jump out of her skin. 'Why didn't *you* let me know, Miss McKenzie? Isn't that what you're paid to do?'

'If you'd care to tell me who you are, I might be able to—'

'Conall O'Brien. Obviously you weren't even aware that your boss and I had a meeting, were you? Care to explain why?'

Her head hurt at the relentless barrage of questions, but her pulse nearly careened to a halt like a car coming upon a sudden hairpin bend when he said his name. Conall O'Brien. The charismatic head of O'Brien and Stoughton Associates—premier architects with offices in London, Sydney and New York. Although Morgen had worked for the London office for just over a year now, she had never set eyes on the man himself. However, his awesome reputation preceded him.

It was well known that he took no prisoners and showed little leniency to anyone having personal problems—a fact that had been made abundantly clear to her already. He absolutely hated tardiness and expected one hundred and ten per cent from the people who worked for him. He mostly worked out of the New York office, and occasionally Sydney, but she had never known him to come to London in all that time—he had always sent a representative. How on earth could Derek have forgotten to brief her on something so important? His love for the bottle might have finally put both their jobs in jeopardy.

A single mother with a six-year-old daughter and a mortgage to pay, Morgen couldn't afford to lose her job right now. Her day had started badly, because she'd been up all night nursing Neesha's cold. Then falling asleep at her desk due to exhaustion—could this day get any worse? she wondered. While she was contemplating this, eyes the colour of a freezing Atlantic Ocean in a squall bored unmercifully into hers, and Morgen knew she had a long way to go to redeem herself in front of this man.

'I know this doesn't look good, but Mr Holden has been working terribly hard lately. Yesterday he definitely looked under the weather. I'm not surprised he isn't in today.'

'Never mind that. Why weren't you aware that we had a meeting? Dammit, it was arranged only last week. Presumably you and your boss do communicate?'

To Morgen's alarm he shrugged off his trench coat and threw it on a chair beside the window that reflected the impressive high-rise vista of the city of London. He was dressed from head to foot in bespoke tailoring that screamed quality and money. The suit was a deep dark blue with a very faint pinstripe, matched with a royal blue shirt and silk tie, and its wearer exuded the kind of power that mostly only those born to wealth and privilege could effortlessly carry off. Coupled with that watchful intelligence in those 'I'm not missing a damn thing' arctic blue eyes, and those intimidatingly broad shoulders, he clearly wasn't a man to be trifled with. Though right now Morgen wasn't trifling at all. She was fighting for her life in deadly earnest.

'Of course we communicate. Derek—Mr Holden obviously meant to tell me to put it in the diary, but because he was so busy he unfortunately forgot. I can assure you it's very unlike him, Mr O'Brien. Why don't I pour you a cup of coffee and maybe send out for some food, if you're hungry? And in the meantime I could ring Mr Holden at home and tell him you're here. He could jump in a taxi and be here in about twenty minutes or so, I'm sure.'

'From that comment I take it that he's not exactly at death's door, then?'

Feeling her face burn, Morgen dissembled. 'I'm afraid I don't have any details at present.'

'So go get the coffee, then get me Holden on the phone—I'll talk to him myself. Don't worry about food—I've got a lunch appointment at one, so it will keep.'

Pulling out a chair from the wall, he dropped down into it opposite Morgen's desk, his impressive frame all but dwarfing it. Yet she would swear there wasn't so much as an ounce of superfluous flesh on that awesome physique. Intensely aware of every single thing about the man, she didn't miss the yawn he swiftly suppressed or the faint look of weariness that briefly glimmered in those quick-witted blue eyes.

She couldn't help but be relieved when she escaped from the room into Derek's office, to pour some coffee from the percolator that was always kept on simmer. As far as Morgen was concerned the air around Conall O'Brien was far too rarefied for her liking, and she wondered how the people in his office coped with the man. When Conall said 'jump', did they all jump automatically? Probably…either that or risk being fired.

Crouching down in front of the cabinet where she kept the best crockery, only used when Derek was in conference with VIPs, Morgen cursed softly as several empty whisky bottles fell out onto the thick grey carpet and rolled towards her feet. As she quickly started to gather them up the door opened quietly behind her, and she found herself in the humiliating position of being caught red-handed.

'Very unlike your boss to "forget" our appointment, you say, Miss McKenzie?' His voice dripping with icy disdain, Conall fixed his unforgiving gaze on Morgen. 'I guess if I had a belly full of whisky I'd be inclined to forget my commitments as well…wouldn't you agree?'

Her startled green eyes widened as she glanced up at him, and her stomach turned decidedly queasy at the fact that poor Derek's unhappy drinking problem was no longer exclusively their little secret. 'If you'd—if you'd like to wait outside I'll just get rid of these and make your coffee.'

'Leave them.'

'It's all right. It will only take a minute, then I'll—'

'Leave the damn bottles, Miss McKenzie, and get that feckless boss of yours on the phone, pronto!'

Morgen's knees were shaking as she got to her feet. Her lips pursed, she turned away from the accusing glare of a pair of wintry blue eyes and went to reach for the phone on Derek's desk.

'Wait a minute.'

'What?'

'On second thoughts, right now I need a caffeine fix more urgently than I need to tell your dear Mr Holden his services are no longer required.'

Her heart sinking, Morgen replaced the phone shakily back in its cream-coloured rest. 'You don't mean that.'

'What?' A briefly amused quirk of perfectly sculpted lips brought the first glimpse of a smile, but Morgen steeled herself against falling into such a trap. He wasn't going to lure her into any sense of false security so easily. 'You don't believe I need a caffeine fix?'

'It's not that. I just—I mean, you can't fire Derek! He's a good man. Honestly…he'd do anything for anybody. His wife left him recently, and he hasn't coped with it very well. I've no doubt he'll turn things around, given the chance.'

'Spoken like a loyal and true assistant. Is that *all* you

do for your boss, Miss McKenzie? Help him in the office?'

The insinuation was so blatantly obvious that for a moment Morgen was dumbstruck. Then, with trembling hands, she drew the black lapels of her suit jacket together over her blouse and, with all the dignity she could muster, raised her gaze to look Mr High-and-Mighty O'Brien straight in the eye.

'I don't care for your crude implications, Mr O'Brien. If you knew Derek Holden then you'd know that he only had eyes for Nicky, his wife. And if you knew me then you'd also know that I make it an absolute rule never to get involved with anyone at work.'

'Never?' The brief smile suddenly became teasingly wider, revealing perfectly white teeth against his tan, and Morgen had to concentrate hard so that she could think.

Folding her arms across her chest, she deliberately didn't smile back. *How dared he? How bloody well dared he make casual sexual insinuations when she was in fear of losing her job as well as her boss?* But then she guessed that not many people would dare stand up to this man without fearing the consequences. Well, perhaps he'd met his match in her. Because, as much as she needed this job—and God only knew how much—she wasn't about to cower in a corner because this man had the power to intimidate.

'Absolutely never, Mr O'Brien. Now, if you'd care to wait in the outer office, I'll get you that coffee you're apparently so desperately in need of.'

For a long tension-filled moment, during which Morgen would swear the only thought in his mind was to give her the sack on the spot, Conall treated her to one of his hard, unrelenting stares, then surprisingly turned away to move towards the door.

'Strong and black, Miss McKenzie—no sugar. You don't mind if I use your office to do some work?'

'Go ahead.'

Feeling like a deflated balloon, she almost sagged against the desk when he'd gone. When she next saw Derek…she couldn't decide whether she'd read him the Riot Act or simply wring his neck.

Conall drew out a sheaf of papers from his briefcase and rubbed at the pain throbbing in his temple. If he didn't catch up with some sleep soon they'd have to carry him out of there on a stretcher. It wasn't because he was un-accustomed to a long working day, or even working seven days a week—it was all grist to the mill as far as he was concerned. That was how he'd built up the busi-ness when his father had retired to 'let his son take the reins'. But, having had non-stop meetings five days run-ning and then two consecutive long-haul flights—one from California to New York, where he'd touched base at the office, then from New York on to London—his body needed sleep like a prisoner on Death Row needed to stay awake.

Taking another mouthful of the strong black coffee Morgen had brought him, he stopped reading the writing on the page in front of him and thought about the woman he'd just met. Where he lived they used the expression 'hot'. As far as her figure and her face went, Morgen McKenzie was on fire. Even though his rage at her boss's ineptitude, as well as finding her asleep at her desk, had almost made him lose it big time, his hormones wouldn't have been in prime working order if he hadn't reacted to the beautiful girl in front of him. And, God knows, he'd reacted.

When he'd discovered her on her knees in Holden's

office, trying to hide the blatant evidence of the man's drinking problem, it had taken just one dazzling glance from those big green eyes of hers to almost make him forget what he was there for. It hadn't helped matters either when the vee of her blouse had gaped a little, unwittingly giving him a very sexy glimpse of her gorgeous cleavage, white lace bra and all. He'd received a sexual charge so acute that for a moment his thoughts had been scrambled to the four corners of the earth.

Of course he couldn't help being angry that she'd been asleep at her desk. He had a reputation for being hard but fair to his employees, and could be generous to a fault to the people who deserved it, but he absolutely deplored slackers—workers who didn't pull their weight. One look at Morgen and he'd hazarded a guess that the lady had been burning the candle at both ends—no wonder she was tired! With looks like hers she doubtless had a queue of admirers going round the block—what reason would she have to stay home and mope when she could be out on the town every night? Never mind the effect it had on her performance at work. The thought made his blood boil. Who would blame him if he gave her her walking papers along with her boss?

Conall sighed and rubbed a hand round his beard-roughened jaw. Trouble was, Derek Holden had been a rising star amongst the young architects in the UK office. Up until recently Conall had only received the best reports. One of the main reasons for his visit—apart from appeasing his mother—was to find out what had been going wrong. Of course he wasn't about to reveal as much to the provocative Miss McKenzie. He decided he'd let her stew for a little while—keep her guessing as to whether she or her boss were about to lose their jobs. That at least ought to get some proper work out of her.

'Can I get you some more coffee?'

She breezed into the room, a flush on her pretty face that was immediately arresting and her dark hair floating loose from its fastening. Conall sensed straight away that she'd been up to something.

'Who were you phoning?' he asked smoothly, using the time to make another leisurely inventory of her face and figure. 'Could it be the hapless Mr Holden, by any chance?'

Guilt was written all over her face as plain as day, and Conall wondered if her feelings were always so transparent.

'If I'd spoken to Derek I would have told you,' she replied testily. 'If you must know I rang my mother—to let her know that I'd probably be home late.'

'You live with your mother?' Now she had really surprised him. Conall studied her features with renewed interest, momentarily mesmerised by her sexily shaped mouth with its highly desirable plump lower lip. He put down his coffee cup and made a discreet adjustment to his sitting position.

'She's staying with me at the moment because she hasn't been very well.'

Morgen hesitated to reveal that the real reason her mother was staying with her was that she was looking after Neesha, her daughter, who had been poorly these last few days. Her stomach tightened at the thought of her little girl suffering in any way, but she couldn't afford to take time off when Derek was absent from the office more often than he was in. Especially not now, when she had the big boss breathing down her neck, probably looking for any reason—however trivial—to sack her. She didn't want him automatically assuming, as so many employers did, that if she had a child she would be somehow less reliable or committed to her job. The truth of the matter was that she was even *more* reliable and committed to her job because she had responsibilities at home.

Frustration bit along her nerves. She wished he wouldn't look at her so closely, as if she was some sort of interesting foreign object beneath a microscope. Ever since that remark earlier, about what she did for Derek, she'd been feeling extremely self-conscious. If only he would go! Why was he hanging around in her office when he could surely hang around with the VIPs upstairs? Was he laying some sort of trap to catch poor Derek out?

'I'm sorry to hear that, but if you think I'm going to be more lenient with you because you've got troubles at home, then I'm afraid you're going to be disappointed, Miss McKenzie.'

Was he going to sack her? A wave of anger washed over her at the thought. It was so unfair! She hadn't had one day off since she'd started this job, and she stayed until at least six or six-thirty most nights. Just her luck to doze off at her desk and for him to walk in right at that moment! She'd even given up several Saturdays to accompany Derek to site meetings and take notes, but what would Mr Big-Shot know about that? No, he'd simply taken one look at her and assumed the worst. Well, she wasn't going to go down without a fight, that was for sure!

'Are you threatening me, Mr O'Brien?'

'I found you asleep at your desk, Miss McKenzie. In my book that's a sacking offence.'

His jaw was very square and very hard-looking, and right now Morgen wanted to punch it and knock him off his chair.

'And does the concept ''innocent until proven guilty''

ring any bells with you?' She was shaking so hard that she was barely able to get the words out.

Conall leaned forward to lay his sheaf of papers on her desk, then leaned back again with his hands behind his head as if amused.

'What's to prove? There is no doubt in my mind that you were asleep when I walked into the room. Unlucky for you the last time I had my eyes tested I was assured I had twenty-twenty vision.'

'There was a perfectly good reason that I fell asleep— and it was for all of five minutes, if that!'

She heaved a breath that strained at the buttons on her blouse and Conall became transfixed by the sight. He wanted to ask her to have pity. It seemed the lady just had to take a breath and lust took the place of the cool professionalism he usually maintained. His gaze drifted back to her face and those flashing green eyes of hers. He had no intention of sacking her, but he wasn't averse to playing a little cat and mouse either.

'Okay. Convince me.'

He was just so smug and self-righteous sitting there that suddenly Morgen lost the urge to prove anything. Let him think what he damn well liked, for all she cared! There were other jobs besides this one. She'd just have to temp for a little while until she found something more permanent. Though the thought didn't hold much appeal, and she was genuinely upset at the idea of leaving Derek in the lurch. Particularly now, when he needed all the support he could get. Still...

'I've changed my mind.' Smoothing down her skirt with a trembling hand, she turned on her heel and stalked back into Derek's office with her head held high.

Stunned, Conall pushed himself to his feet, loosened

his tie and followed her. He found her pulling files from a tall mahogany cabinet and laying them out on the desk.

'I said convince me, Miss McKenzie.'

'Go to hell! And if that's a sacking offence too, then I've well and truly been given my marching orders, haven't I?'

'It would mean so little to you, losing your job?' Frowning, Conall watched her stalk to and fro from the cabinet, somehow deflated that he had pushed her too far. If that wasn't bad enough, there was a little niggle in the centre of his chest that told him he might just be wrong about Morgen McKenzie. That being the case, he didn't want to lose someone who might turn out to be a valuable employee.

'There you go again, making assumptions about situations you know nothing about!' She stopped her agitated stalking and dropped her hands to her hips. 'My job is very important to me, Mr O'Brien, and if you'd care to ask around in the office you'd more than likely find out that I do it well—at least, I haven't had any complaints so far. Unfortunately Derek isn't here right now to corroborate the fact. Perhaps when he does come in you can ask him.'

'And do you really believe his good opinion is honestly worth having?' Raising his eyebrow, Conall waited with interest for her answer.

'If you're referring to the bottles…' Morgen's eyes drifted towards the now closed cabinet and a tinge of pink highlighted her beautiful cheekbones. 'The fact that he's got a problem with drink doesn't make him a bad person, or a man whose opinion doesn't count. He's won awards for this company, Mr O'Brien, as I'm sure you must be aware. He's a talented architect with a bright future. Right now he needs help and support. He doesn't deserve to lose his job because his world suddenly fell apart when his wife walked out.'

'And what about what this firm deserves, hmm?' Rubbing at the smooth tanned skin between his brows, Conall frowned. 'We have our reputation to think of…clients who expect a first-class service. If that level of service starts to suffer because of individuals like Derek Holden, who can't cut it when their personal lives start to encroach on their work, then I'm sorry—but we're not in the business of extending patience indefinitely. If he can't get his act together pretty soon then there are plenty of other ambitious young architects waiting to fill his shoes.'

Several thoughts jumped into Morgen's head at once, but one inched ahead of all the rest. The man was ruthless…unbending. He didn't care if Derek was suffering the torments of hell. All Conall O'Brien cared about was that right now Derek wasn't 'cutting it'—ergo, he wasn't making any money for the firm. It would serve him right if she walked out right now in protest. Nobody was indispensable, that was true, but he was going to have a hell of a time making sense of things without her around to explain them. Especially when all the other secretaries were run off their feet as well. She was tempted to do it, too.

Seeing the conflict in her troubled green eyes, Conall feigned a look of boredom, wondering what she'd do if he called her bluff.

'So, Miss McKenzie…are you staying or going?'

'I won't let Derek down.' She was fidgeting with her hands, and her angry glance slid away from Conall's unflinching stare. Her emphatic statement made it quite clear that it was Derek she owed her allegiance to—not him or the firm.

He wanted to admire her loyalty—no matter how misplaced, in his opinion. After all, hadn't her boss let her down too, leaving her to face the music while he drowned his sorrows at home? But Conall found he couldn't. It irked him immensely that she insisted on trying to protect a man who clearly didn't deserve it.

'Good. Now that we've established that you don't want to make yourself unemployed, perhaps we can get some work done around here?'

The expression on Morgen's face told him she wanted to throw something at him. The fact only hardened his resolve to deal with the situation in his own inimitable way—the way that had turned his father's business into the successful firm it was today. Conall gestured at the unopened files on the desk. 'Are these current projects?' When she nodded mutely, he slipped behind the desk and sat down in the big leather chair that Derek Holden usually occupied. 'Bring me some more coffee and I'll take a look while I'm here.'

Biting back 'I'm not your servant,' Morgen swallowed her pride and reluctantly returned to the outer office to fetch his cup. As she poured coffee with a shaking hand, she couldn't help wondering for how long she and her boss would keep their jobs now that their dictatorial senior partner had made his ominous presence felt.

CHAPTER TWO

THE ringing of the phone on her desk made her jump. She snatched it up guiltily, wondering if Conall was straining an ear to keep tabs on her movements. Glancing at the door to Derek's office, and seeing it closed, she breathed a sigh of relief.

'Morgen McKenzie.'

'It's Derek.'

'For goodness' sake! Where are you?' Cupping the mouthpiece with her hand, she turned her head again, to make doubly sure the door to the other office was shut.

'I'm at home. Where do you think I bloody am?'

As Morgen had expected, he sounded irritable and hung-over. Her stomach knotted with deep apprehension.

'Do you know who you missed an appointment with this morning?'

'Don't play games with me, Morgen, I'm not in the mood. Whoever it was I'm sure it will keep. Thankfully, you always come up with the perfect excuse to explain my absences. That's what makes you such a priceless assistant.'

'And that's supposed to be a good quality? Lying?'

'What?'

She heard the chink of glass, then something heavy thud to the floor. Instinct and experience told her that he had already been drinking this morning and probably still was. If Conall caught so much a whiff of the fact they'd both be for the high jump.

'Your meeting was with Conall O'Brien, Derek. Does the name ring any bells?'

'Oh, sh—!'

'My sentiments exactly. However, that doesn't do either of us any good. He's still here in your office, waiting to see you. First impressions predispose me to believe that he's prepared to wait quite a while until you show up.' Though he had mentioned to Morgen that he had a one o'clock lunch appointment, she remembered. Glancing down at her watch, she saw that it was a little after twelve-thirty. Thank God the man would be leaving soon—but, more importantly, how soon would he be back?

'Have pity, Morgen! I'm in no fit state to deal with that man. I can't possible—possibly come in today. You'll have to tell him I'm ill or something.'

Gritting her teeth, Morgen glared at the phone. 'I've already told him that, Derek, but quite frankly I don't think he believed me.' Now wasn't the time to reveal that Conall had wandered into his office the very moment Derek's empty whisky bottles had rolled out onto the floor in front of him. If he knew that he'd been rumbled—by the head of the firm, no less—there was no telling what Derek might do in his present state of mind. 'You'll just have to try and come in. Make some coffee, then grab a quick shower. I'll order you a taxi and meet you downstairs in the lobby.'

He sighed noisily in response. 'I can't do it. I feel like death, if you must know. You're asking me to do the im-impossible.'

Damn Nicky Holden for leaving him in the lurch! But what was the use of blaming his wife? It was Derek's reaction to the whole sorry mess that was making things worse. Who would have thought that a successful, confident, bright young man who designed major projects worth millions of pounds would fall apart like a house of cards because his marriage hadn't worked out? Morgen could only wonder. It wasn't that she was unsympathetic. She had been through a similar scenario herself, and been five months pregnant to boot when her husband Simon had walked out. The difference being that she just hadn't had the option of falling apart. Not when she had a baby to take care of and a widowed mother who constantly looked to her for support.

Sighing now, she scraped her hand through her hair and completely dislodged the little tortoiseshell comb that held it in place. The dark silky strands of her shoulder-length hair escaped to slip round her face.

'There's only one thing for it, then. I'll come to you and help you sort yourself out. I'll be with you just as soon as I can order a cab. For God's sake, stay put—and, Derek…?'

'Yes, Morgen?'

'Don't drink any more. If you want to make yourself useful put the kettle on and have a bite to eat. Got that?'

At the other end of the phone the receiver clattered down without a reply.

Morgen was just grabbing her coat off the chrome coat tree when the door swung open and Conall strode back into the room. His sudden appearance put the fear of God into Morgen, and she hated the fact he could so easily intimidate her. His arms folded across that impressively wide chest of his, he eyed her consideringly, like a big cat about to play with a mouse. Damn, damn, damn! Wasn't she allowed any luck today? It seemed not.

'Going to lunch already, Miss McKenzie?'

'I've got an appointment. I'll only be about an hour, if that. I was just...I was just coming to tell you.'

'Were you, indeed?'

Was the man always so untrusting? Morgen huffed an exasperated breath and tried valiantly to meet his gaze. No easy undertaking when those cold blue eyes looked as if they would spear shards of ice into her body at any moment.

'I know you don't believe me, but I really have to be somewhere right now. I promise I won't be long, and if you need me to stay late tonight I'll be only too happy to do so.' It almost killed her to say it when she knew Neesha was probably pining for her. Her little girl loved her nana, but it was Morgen she wanted when she was feeling poorly. Still, she would do all she could right now to keep her job. She only prayed that Neesha would be feeling much better by the time she got home.

'Would you be going to meet your boss, by any chance?' Intently studying the suddenly surprised green eyes, Conall knew he had struck gold. Loyalty in general he admired—but subterfuge to dig her boss out of a hole? Well, that was a whole different ballgame in his book. He didn't know whether to be more furious with Morgen, for thinking she could pull the wool over his eyes, or the errant Derek, who had let himself slide from grace so ignominiously.

Worrying at her lip, Morgen swept back her hair with her hand. It drew Conall's appreciative male gaze to the luxurious glossiness of it.

'He's going to come into work. He just needs to freshen up a little and sort himself out.'

'And you're going to help him? What are you going to do? Hold his hand while he gets into the shower?' The very idea of this raven-haired temptress and a shower did things to Conall's libido that could be constituted as sexual torment.

Morgen didn't think it would do her case any good to confess that it wouldn't be the first time she'd gone to Derek's house with rescue in mind. She was practically as familiar with the layout of the once swish Westminster apartment, with its stunning Thamesside view, as she was with her own small terraced house in Lambeth. Only the inside of Derek's once lovely home was no longer quite so lovely, due to neglect. Even his cleaner had quit, telling Morgen that she was tired of disposing of empty bottles of booze at every turn.

'Like I said before, he just needs a little bit of support through this difficult time. We can't just abandon him.'

'We?' Conall's eyebrows shot up to his hairline.

'The firm…me. Don't you want him to get better?'

She frowned, like a little girl who didn't understand some particular adult peculiarity, and something told Conall that she was too damn caring for her own good. However, it wasn't enough to make him restrain his temper. 'I'm running a business here, Miss McKenzie, not a care home.'

He saw her blanch. Did Derek Holden in his alcohol-ridden state know that his beautiful raven-haired assistant was championing his cause while he was away? Probably…no doubt the man was using that very fact to what he hoped would be great advantage.

'Don't bother calling a cab; I've got a car downstairs. I'm coming with you…to see if I can't help to talk some sense into him. Lead the way.'

'But what about your one o'clock meeting?'

'I've already postponed it. Now, let's go and discover what kind of condition your boss is in.'

*   *   *

Derek's already pallid face turned deathly white when he saw the visitor Morgen had brought with her. Stumbling back inside the wide hallway, with its once shiny parquet floor, he drove his hand through his dishevelled brown hair, desperate to regain some composure but failing miserably.

The air smelt old and stale, as if nobody had opened a window for a very long time. Morgen took one look at her boss and wished she had a magic wand so that she could put all that ailed him right in an instant. Turn back the clock to the time before Nicky had walked out on him, when he'd been a man who was very clearly steering his own ship, carving out a name for himself in what could be a highly competitive cut-throat business and acquitting himself with distinction.

'Hello, Derek. Why don't I make us all some coffee? Have you eaten?'

When he mumbled incoherently in reply Morgen slipped past him, reluctantly leaving him to deal with Conall alone. In the huge fitted kitchen, where there was every modern convenience known to man but not so much as one clear work surface to stand a cup on because dirty crockery was everywhere, Morgen rolled up her sleeves and got stuck into some of the mountain of washing up. She doubted there was a clean mug or cup in the whole place, never mind a clean percolator, and she couldn't make coffee without it. From experience she knew that Derek wouldn't give house-room to the instant stuff. At least, he wouldn't if he were sober...

Finding herself too interested in the now raised voices, Morgen turned on the hot tap to full flow to drown out the sound and grimly occupied herself with the task in hand. She knew instinctively it was little use praying that Conall would go easy on Derek—in terms of possibility

that would be akin to expecting a boa constrictor to go
easy on a mouse. Going easy on him would probably not
get them very far, anyway. She'd tried the softly, softly
approach herself, and Derek had merely laughed and told
her that he definitely had his drinking under control and
not to worry.

Five minutes later, sensing movement behind her, she
turned to find Conall in the doorway minus his jacket and
tie. He was a big man—strong and fit—and looked as if
he could take on a whole army and emerge victorious.
With his hair slightly disarrayed, and his hard jaw unshaven, there was something dangerously compelling
about him that couldn't be ignored, despite her silent vow
that his good looks cut no ice with her.

'He's going in the shower. Can you have that coffee
ready when he comes out?' His keen-eyed gaze moved
curiously round the room as he spoke, and when he
brought it back to Morgen he was shaking his head as if
he couldn't quite believe the sight that confronted him.

'If we pay the guy enough to live in a place like this,
why the hell doesn't he employ a cleaner?'

'He did.' Touching her cheek unknowingly, Morgen
left a small trail of soapy suds on her skin. 'She walked
out.'

'Why should that surprise me?'

About to turn away and return to see how Derek was
faring, Conall found himself walking towards Morgen at
the sink instead. Without a word, he reached down to
gently stroke away the suds from her face. Up close, he
saw that her green eyes were flecked with intriguing ha-
zel lights and her dark lashes were long and luxurious—
without the benefit of mascara, as far as he could detect.
Her scent enveloped him for a moment—something
warm and sensual, like a sunny day on the Cote D'Azur

where he occasionally liked to holiday. His stomach muscles clenched iron-hard in response and a throb of heat went straight to his groin.

'You had some soap on your face.'

'Thanks.'

She turned away, clearly flustered. Smiling to himself, Conall walked back to the doorway. He liked the fact that he could ruffle her feathers. Truth to tell, he liked it a lot.

'How are you feeling now?'

Studying the pale, heavy-eyed features of the man before him, Conall wondered if there was really any point in dragging him back to the office for a meeting today. The hour in his office had given him enough time to brief himself on the current details of the big Docklands project Derek was presently in charge of, and he'd already rung the site manager and arranged a four o'clock meeting with the contractors and the client. He'd give Derek a day's grace to get his act together, and tomorrow morning first thing they'd have a meeting of their own, when Conall would lay out the options as he saw them before him.

Basically, the man had to agree to professional help or walk. There were already outrageous sums of money being wasted on this project through one discrepancy or another, as far as he could see, and Conall was damn sure his firm weren't going to help his client lose any more. Apart from that, they had an international reputation to protect—and protect it he would.

'Some more coffee would be good.' Feebly, Derek smiled and held out his mug.

Morgen relieved him of it and turned back into the kitchen. As she poured strong black coffee near enough to the brim her stomach rumbled, reminding her that she hadn't eaten a thing since dinner last night. Right on cue, her head started to throb. Too much coffee, not enough sleep and no food were not the best of combinations to aid health and vitality, she thought wryly, wondering when she'd find time to even eat the tuna sandwich her mother had put in her bag that morning. She prayed it would be soon, or she wouldn't be much help to anyone.

Poor Derek. 'Dreadful' didn't even begin to describe how he looked. 'Walking dead' was possibly more apt. Like a made-up extra in one of those old Hammer Horrors. There was no way he'd be any use in the office today; surely Conall could see that?

Hovering in the doorway while Derek manfully drank down his coffee, Morgen felt her nerves bounce badly every time her gaze connected with Conall O'Brien's. There was no doubt he was a formidable man, but he'd actually been much more lenient with Derek than she'd expected. She could have sworn she'd even glimpsed sympathy in his eyes every now and then as Derek had fumbled and stuttered an explanation as to how he had got himself into such a sorry state—but perhaps her senses had been deceiving her. Conall and sympathy just seemed to be the complete antithesis of each other. The man clearly judged having personal problems as some kind of major weakness.

Finally, glancing at his watch, he reached for his jacket on the back of the sofa and addressed Morgen directly. 'We'd better get back. I think Derek would be best served by sleeping off some of his excesses for the afternoon and coming into the office tomorrow instead. I've booked a four o'clock meeting with the contractors at Docklands, and you can come with me and provide back-up—fill me in on anything I'm not familiar with. You okay with that, Miss McKenzie?'

Normally Morgen wouldn't be fazed by such a prospect—she often accompanied Derek to site meetings—but this one was a biggie, and Derek had left the firm wide open to criticism by his absence and unwillingness to return phone calls. Consequently, as his assistant, Morgen had taken most of the flak. She'd been fending off irate telephone calls for days now, and she was certain it would become quickly evident to the gimlet-eyed senior partner of O'Brien and Stoughton Associates that a lot less had been accomplished on the project than he had a right to expect.

Suddenly a cuddle and a bedtime story with her lovely Neesha seemed even further away than it had this morning. Something told Morgen that this particular meeting would stretch well into the evening.

'That's fine with me, Mr O'Brien.'

'Leave the booze alone, Holden, and get an early night. If you want to keep your job, be in the office at nine tomorrow morning and we'll talk.'

Getting unsteadily to his feet, Derek threw a panic-stricken glance at Morgen as he followed them out into the hall to the front door. He was like a little lost boy, she thought, looking for her to save him. She turned away at the too familiar feeling, resenting it suddenly, but Conall didn't miss the brief warm smile of consolation she flashed back at the man.

He imagined what it would feel like to be on the receiving end of one of those gorgeous smiles himself. Pretty damn good, he reflected as she breezed past him out onto the stairwell, leaving a trail of her mesmerising scent. As she marched ahead of him back to the car his gaze locked onto those trim sexy calves in pale stockings and low heels and he knew he had a bad case of lust at first sight. The problem, as he saw it, was: what did he intend to do about it?

'I'm going back to my sister's place to get a shower and a shave. Can you hold the fort until I get back?'

Her backbone stiffening, Morgen flashed Conall an irritated glance. What did he think she'd been doing for the past six months while Derek slid further and further down the slippery slope of depression? Hiding in a cupboard?

'I'm sure I'll manage somehow.' Ripping her gaze away from his unwanted scrutiny, she wished she wasn't so acutely aware of the intimate confines of the luxurious car, with its cream leather upholstery and connotations of wealth and power.

'Why did his wife leave him?'

Conall's question took Morgen completely by surprise. Her hand was on the door handle beside her, but she withdrew it onto her lap, tucking her hair behind her ear as she spoke.

'He said she couldn't cope with his success. She was trying to forge her own career as a singer and felt that Derek didn't support her enough. They came from very different backgrounds, and in the end I suppose they just wanted different things. The differences just became too much to withstand—for Nicky anyway.'

Shrugging, she stared down at her own ringless hands, fighting off the unexpected sense of failure that suddenly descended on her out of nowhere. She didn't want to think about Simon, her ex-husband, but her last two sentences might have been describing their own disastrous union—brief though it had been. He had been an ex-pupil of Eton, one of the foremost public schools in the country, then gone on to medical school. When Morgen had met him he'd just been promoted to a registrar's job at Guy's Hospital, and his charm and total self-confidence had swept her away.

His parents were wealthy and his father, an eminent heart surgeon, had been knighted in the Queen's honours list. Morgen hadn't exactly received the red carpet treatment from his family, and straight from the off she'd known she wasn't good enough for their darling Simon. How could she be? She'd gone to a mixed comprehensive in South London, then trained as a secretary at a local technical college. Her father had been a bricklayer and her mother a school secretary. It went without saying that her family had hardly moved in the same illustrious circles the Vaughan-Smiths had frequented.

'These things happen.' Not taking his eyes from her, Conall wondered what she was thinking. 'He'll have to get over it soon. Especially if he wants to keep his job.'

'Derek isn't deliberately sabotaging his future. The man is in a lot of pain, for goodness' sake!'

Fielding off the frosty stare that accompanied Morgen's words, Conall knew she was probably thinking he was a hard bastard—someone who didn't give a damn about the people who worked for him as long as they helped the firm turn a profit. The truth was that he cared passionately about bringing out the best in people, and was only too happy to share the fruits of his own success with them when they did. However, that didn't mean he couldn't be tough when he had to be…ruthless, even.

As far as he could see Derek Holden had wallowed in his own self-pity long enough. If something were not done about that soon, it wouldn't just be the man's job that went down the pan, it would be his life. O'Brien and

Stoughton could easily hire another architect, but Derek couldn't be brought back from the dead.

'I'm well aware that the man needs help—professional help. In the meantime I'll be taking over things for a little while. You'll be working directly for me, Miss McKenzie. Think you can handle that?'

He couldn't help needling her, if only to see her react. Her captivating face instantly revealed her unhappiness. Her emotions were laid bare, and Conall realised it wasn't easy for her to don the civil mask of control that professionalism required. Not when in reality she was in turmoil. Inexplicably he felt himself warm to her in a way he hadn't warmed to a woman in a long time. And the prospect of being 'hands on' in the office while Derek took a necessary sabbatical—with Morgen as his assistant—suddenly appealed much more than it probably had a right to. As soon as he got back to his sister's flat in Highgate Conall would telephone the New York office and let them know he was extending his stay in the UK indefinitely.

'I can handle anything you care to throw at me, Mr O'Brien. Why don't you try me and see? Part of my secretarial course curriculum was how to deal with difficult people. In fact I specialised in it! See you back at the office.' And with that Morgen slipped out of the car, slamming the door behind her.

Conall laid his head back on the cream rest and mused that her hostility was probably a bonus. It would make it all the sweeter when she finally decided it was worth her while to be nice to him. Priding himself on knowing women as well as he did, and having personal experience that wealth and status in life were powerful aphrodisiacs—especially when it came to attraction—Conall didn't doubt that that would soon be the case...

CHAPTER THREE

AT THREE-THIRTY that afternoon Morgen made her way to the ladies' washroom to freshen up. Staring at her reflection in the bank of mirrors, she frowned at the soft bluish shadows beneath her eyes. She'd be lying to herself if she didn't acknowledge she looked just about as tired as she felt, but her spirits were lifted a little despite the tension of the morning because she'd heard from her mother that Neesha was more or less back to her old self today.

Reflecting on that fact now, she let her shoulders drop a little with relief. That meant that her daughter could go back to school tomorrow and her mother could go back home. Relationships were strained between them at the best of times, but none more so than when Morgen asked her to take care of Neesha for her when she was sick. Lorna McKenzie did not approve of women working full-time when their children were small. Truth to tell, Morgen might have shared the same conviction if Simon hadn't walked out on her less than a year into their marriage, drastically diminishing her options.

For a man who'd initially been over the moon to hear she was pregnant, he'd soon changed his tune as his wife's pregnancy had advanced. He dealt with sick people all the time, but he had professed he was unable to cope when Morgen was wretched with morning sickness. That, coupled with her lack of desire to socialise with his friends and never seeing eye-to-eye with his parents, had been good enough grounds for him to end the marriage as far as he was concerned. Besides, he really hadn't liked the idea of being 'tied down,' he'd explained as he was leaving. His career came first, and he really hadn't been sure whether fatherhood was for him after all. He was willing to help support her and the baby, but only until Morgen could return to work full time, at which time his future contributions would be for the child only.

'The child.' Simon still rarely referred to his daughter by her given name. She didn't see him from one month to the next anyway. By now Simon had made Specialist Registrar, and was on the fast track to becoming a consultant. He worked long hours and in his free time liked to play sport and socialise with his well-connected friends. As far as Neesha's grandparents went, Elizabeth and Terence Vaughan-Smith wanted nothing to do with their grandchild—they hadn't agreed with the marriage in the first place, so why should they acknowledge a child of that union?

Morgen stared hard into her own eyes and bit back the overwhelming desire to cry.

'Don't you dare, Morgen McKenzie!' she whispered harshly through gritted teeth, returning her pale rose lipstick to her make-up bag. 'You didn't cave in when the bastard walked out on you; you're not caving in now!' Her defences were low because she was tired, that was all. But her heart ached just the same for Neesha, because her father and his family had more or less rejected her.

Oh, well. Such was life. She wasn't the only one who'd had hard times and she certainly wouldn't be the last. Look at poor Derek. What would become of him if he were unable to turn his addiction around? At the thought of her boss she glanced down at her silver-linked wristwatch, noted the time, then grabbed up her bag from beside the sink.

Hell's bells! She didn't dare be late for Conall O'Brien—not when they had a four o'clock meeting to get to at Docklands. The man already thought she was lazy and incompetent—why make life even more difficult for herself by compounding that impression?

As she hurried back along the thickly carpeted corridor to her office, Morgen prayed she'd get there before Conall. She wasn't craving his approval, but neither was she courting his disapproval—and if he started to have a go at her, the mood she was in she'd probably tell him to stick his job where the sun didn't shine, and then where would she and Neesha be?

But luck, it seemed, wasn't on her side today. Standing by the window, gazing down at the London traffic through the slats in the blind, Conall turned as she entered, causing Morgen's heart to flutter like a moth flying too close to a flame. Newly showered and shaved, and wearing another impeccably tailored suit—this one a dark charcoal-grey matched with a pristine white shirt and burgundy-coloured tie—he looked like a man who meant business. He was clean-shaven, tanned and gorgeous, with piercing blue eyes that had her cornered the instant she set foot in the room, and it seemed that the world tilted more than a little when Morgen gazed back at him. The sensation made her strangely angry, not to mention defensive as hell.

'I haven't kept you waiting, have I? I literally just popped out to the washroom for a minute. Are you ready to go?'

'You look tired, Miss McKenzie. Are you sure you're up to this?'

Now he was casting aspersions on the way she looked, as well as her ability to do her job! Striding across the room, Morgen deliberately ignored him. Instead she gathered up the papers and plans on her desk, slid them into a large manila envelope, tucked it under her arm and walked back to the door.

'Shall we go, Mr O'Brien? It's already twenty to four. I just hope the traffic is in our favour.'

She'd tied back her hair, Conall noticed, almost as if trying to regain some lost control. The idea intrigued him, made him wonder if there were areas of her life where she willingly gave up the desire to stay in control. Like when she was in bed with a lover, for instance?

Although personally he preferred her beautiful hair left unconfined, however she wore it she would command attention—because Morgen McKenzie was not a woman who could pass unremarked. Her fitted suit accentuated a figure that veered more towards the voluptuous than the fashionably thin, but because she was tall as well—at least five eight, by his calculations—she could wear a black polythene sack and still look amazing. But he hadn't missed the dark circles beneath her lovely eyes either, and he was sure she was ready to kill him for noticing. Was his first impression of her right? Was she a party girl burning the candle at both ends most nights after work? And—more to the point—did she have a man in her life?

'That's what I like to see—enthusiasm for the job. It's going to be a long afternoon, by all accounts. I've already spoken with the client. Have you met Stephen Ritchie before?'

'We've only spoken on the phone,' Morgen replied, tension edging into her shoulders as she reflected on the irate telephone calls of the past week, not to mention the threats to sue the firm. All in all, Mr Ritchie did not sound like the kind of man she was eager to meet.

'Well, it's no exaggeration to say he's baying for our

blood—or Derek's blood, at least. We're going to have to jump through hoops to come out on top. Think we can save the day, Miss McKenzie?'

He paused in the doorway, crowding her with his impressive physique. His expression seemed to increase in intensity, causing a sudden outbreak of goosebumps beneath Morgen's clothes. Trouble was, the sexy fragrance of his cologne—along with the highly alluring and more subtle scent of the man himself—kept drifting in and out of her nostrils, making it hard to think. Unable to wrench her gaze away from his, Morgen sucked in a shaky breath. His seductive blue gaze had become a perilous ocean, and she was in mortal danger of becoming irrevocably lost at sea.

'I wish you would stop using my name as a means to taunt me, *Mr* O'Brien. I don't like being intimidated.'

'Is that what I'm doing? Intimidating you?' Frowning, Conall let his gaze sweep her features with genuine surprise.

Morgen couldn't find the words to answer him—not even a simple yes or no. Her senses were too besieged by his nearness.

'Would you prefer it if I called you Morgen?' he asked evenly, his voice dropping down a sensual octave or two.

Taken aback by his unexpected concern, she stepped hurriedly ahead of him into the corridor to cover her confusion. 'That is my given name.'

'Then Morgen it is.'

Easily falling into step beside her, Conall mused how well her name suited her. Morgan Le Fay sprang to mind—the legendary dark-haired enchantress in the tale of King Arthur. There was certainly something bewitching about her, that was for sure.

'Got everything we need, Morgen?' he asked conversationally, referring to the large manila envelope under her arm.

Her green eyes briefly met his. 'I've got everything you need, Mr O'Brien.'

Sweet heaven, he couldn't argue with that... 'Call me Conall,' he said brightly, just about getting the words out past the sudden aching dryness in his throat.

It was raining when they reached the site, where two new luxury apartment blocks were being erected. The rain had quickly turned the dry sand of the ground into a river of mud, and as Morgen donned the compulsory hard hat the site foreman gave her she wished she had had the foresight to bring some Wellington boots. Derek normally kept his in the boot of his car, and she had enough experience as his assistant to know that she should have done the same. As for Conall, he didn't seem to notice the fact that his black hand-made Italian shoes were quickly sinking into a quagmire of mud and sand.

After shaking hands with the stocky foreman, and introducing both himself and Morgen, he followed the man to the nearby planning office that had been erected to monitor progress on the site.

Inside, three other men—one of them suited—were seated round the long rectangular table. The smell of brewing coffee and cigarette smoke immediately enveloped Morgen's senses as they entered. All the men glanced at her with wary gazes, as though an alien had suddenly wandered in amongst them. Clearly some men still had old-fashioned views about women on a building site, she thought irritably, concluding it was about time they got over it.

'Miss McKenzie is my assistant and will be taking notes,' Conall explained, before pulling out a chair for her to sit down. 'Unfortunately Derek Holden is on sick leave, so I will be taking over the project until his return.'

From the first few minutes, as plans were laid out on the table and one of the men got up to pour the coffee into waiting mugs, it was evident who was in charge and why. Conall O'Brien's expertise in smoothing ruffled feathers and executing the necessary action to bring things back on course was a master-class in skill, diplomacy and people management bar none. Morgen saw and heard Stephen Ritchie's initially hostile reception to Conall melt like snow beneath a sun lamp.

Previously sluggish and tired, she straightened her back, sat up and listened in awe as the man finally had both the client and the contractors shaking hands and inviting him for drinks later on in the week.

Back in the car at ten to seven in the evening, Morgen swept a shaky hand through her hair and sighed as if she'd been let out of prison. The business of the day taken care of, she was more than a little anxious to get back to her little girl, and then for a hot bath and a stiff drink. Stealing a glance at the man beside her in the driver's seat, she was amazed that Conall O'Brien was showing no signs of fatigue or jet-lag whatsoever. Instead he was smiling as his big hands curved round the steering wheel, as if all was right with his world and everything in it.

'I thought that went well. How about you?'

The fact that he'd asked her opinion when it was glaringly obvious that things had gone more than well—he'd practically had them eating sugar out of his hand, for goodness' sake!—threw Morgen for a moment.

'I thought it was an exercise in damage limitation *par excellence*. Remind me to get you on my side when I'm next negotiating my car insurance.'

'Most people are driven by fear, Morgen. As soon as you come to realise that you're halfway there. You've got to get past your own ego to soothe theirs, and once you can do that—you're home free. You can get practically anything you want.'

She said nothing. The fact that he was willing to get past his own ego to soothe someone else's fears was enough food for thought for one day, she decided—even if there was an ulterior motive.

'I'm not rushing you, Mr O'Brien, but—'

'Conall.' There was mischief in his gaze, and it momentarily banished every coherent thought from her head.

'Fine. I don't want to rush you, but I'd really like to get home if we're finished for the day now. If you could drop me off back at the office I'll pick up my car and go.'

'Going out somewhere tonight?' he asked, expertly steering the big car smoothly away from the kerb.

'No.' Her answer was accompanied by a loud sigh. 'Definitely not. All I want to do right now is cuddle up on the sofa with my favourite person and relax in front of the TV.'

Her *favourite* person? Jealousy sliced through Conall's gut like a knife heated over a red-hot blaze. So there was a man in her life after all? He'd been stupid to hope there wasn't.

It was because he hadn't been in a relationship for a while, he reflected moodily as he drove through London's crawling traffic. A man had needs, and the delicious Miss McKenzie was a provocative reminder that his weren't being met. There was something singular about her that completely tantalised him. Hooked him up and reeled him in. Something in that slightly aloof façade of hers which could just as suddenly reveal her anxieties as candidly as a child's that made him want to get to know her better. Okay, so he badly wanted to get her into bed too. It was just his bad luck that she was already spoken for.

'What about you?'

'Excuse me?' Stealing a glance, he saw that she seemed to be waiting for him to speak.

'Have you any plans for this evening?'

Yeah. After he'd popped one of his sister Teresa's home-cooked meals in the microwave to heat he intended pouring himself a large glass of wine, then catching up with everything that had been happening in the New York office in his absence.

Unfortunately he did not have a *favourite* person to cuddle up to on the couch and watch TV with. It was just a shame that Teresa had been called away on business just before he'd caught his flight to Heathrow and would be gone indefinitely. She'd left her keys with a neighbour for him, but right now he could do with some company. He supposed after his transatlantic phone call he could ring his mother and speak to her, but he really didn't feel like listening to one of her lectures telling him it was high time he came back home to England for good.

'I'll probably be working.'

Shrugging, Conall made the necessary right turn, then reached out to switch on the radio. As a beautifully articulated voice announced the seven o'clock news from the BBC, he couldn't deny he was suddenly ridiculously glad to be home again—even if he was staying at his sister's and not a home of his own. There were definitely *some* things about the mother country that he missed.

'Mummy, why did Nana make you angry?' Her brown eyes pensive, the little girl with bobbed dark hair slid into bed and waited anxiously for an answer.

Morgen bitterly regretted that she'd given way to temper where her mother was concerned. But all she'd needed after a day fraught with tension—because of the arrival of Conall O'Brien, the sorry state they'd found her boss in and the anxiety of the site meeting—was for Lorna McKenzie to verbally demolish her as soon as she walked through the door.

Fingering the vee of her blouse, Morgen reached out to drop a tender kiss on Neesha's pink cheek, happy beyond measure that the child appeared to be so much better than she had been for the past few days.

'Nana and me just had a little difference of opinion, sweetheart. Sometimes it's hard for her to understand that I need to go out to work to support us both. But if there was any other way I could arrange things differently, believe me, I would.'

'Nana thinks you drove Daddy away because you were too stubborn. She thinks if you were nicer to him he would have stayed.' Neesha was biting her lip, and her expression was all eyes.

Feeling as if she had a lead weight in her stomach, Morgen clasped her daughter's small plump hand in her own and forced a smile.

'Nana had no right saying such a thing to you, honey. She doesn't want to accept that your daddy was scared about being a father. She thinks there must have been something I could have done to make him stay.'

No matter how 'nice' she might have been to Simon, he wouldn't have stayed. She knew that for a fact. Now there was a lump in her throat too. Not because she pined for him, but because she could see the confusion on her child's face. Why had her daddy abandoned her? How was a child supposed to understand that? Oh, how could her mother have been so selfish and stupid to say such things to her?

'Some people just aren't cut out to be parents, darling. It's a hard fact of life, but true, I'm afraid.'

'Then why did you and Daddy have me?'

'We made you because we wanted a baby—even if Daddy got scared later on and couldn't stay. And when I held you in my arms that very first time I thought you were the most beautiful, most perfect, most amazing little person that I'd ever seen in all my life, and I loved you with all my heart and always will.'

Clutching the child to her breast, Morgen breathed in the fresh clean smell of her hair, the impossibly soft black silky strands tickling her nose while the heat and softness of the sweet little body pressed fiercely against her own.

'I love you too, Mummy. You're the best mummy in the whole world *and* the prettiest. When I grow up I want to look just like you!'

Gently tucking her back down into her bed, with its quilted pink counterpane, Morgen smiled. 'You're good for my morale, you know that?'

'What's that?'

'Morale means your confidence—the way you think about yourself. You make me feel good when you say such sweet things to me. That's what I mean.'

'Good. I want you to feel good. I hate it when Nana makes you sad. I'll say goodnight now, Mummy, I'm feeling rather tired.'

'Okay, gorgeous. You snuggle down now, in your cosy bed, and I'll see you in the morning. You don't mind going back to school tomorrow?'

'I'm looking forward to it. I miss my friends.'

'I'm sure they've missed you too, poppet. Goodnight, angel, God bless.'

Back in the living room, Morgen stooped to pick up a purple stuffed elephant and an anatomically unlikely Barbie doll from the carpet, along with two dog-eared storybooks that were Neesha's favourites. Straightening the soft velvet cushions on the couch, she flopped down wearily, at the same time reaching for the remote and flicking on the television.

The choice of viewing was pretty dismal. Between a documentary on car crime, an awful soap whose soundtrack instantly depressed, football and one of those mindless reality TV programmes where members of the public were only too eager to humiliate themselves in front of the viewing masses, there was nothing to remotely tempt her. Pushing herself to her feet again, Morgen rifled through the bottom drawer beneath the television for a video.

When her hand settled on a much-loved romantic comedy, she knew that if the trials and tribulations of the perfect couple onscreen couldn't capture her attention then nothing would. Slipping the film into the VCR, then making a quick detour into the kitchen for a bag of crisps and some cheese, Morgen tucked her feet beneath her on the couch and settled back to enjoy the film.

When ten minutes had passed, and she realised she'd barely registered any of the action unfolding before her because her mind was unwittingly preoccupied with Conall O'Brien, she frowned deeply, then turned up the volume on the film to drive any further troublesome thoughts away. There was nothing about him she liked, she decided. Just because he was too handsome for his own good and was impressive under fire didn't mean that she was going to join his fan club. Along with his assets he was autocratic and domineering, and clearly possessed of a heart made of stone or something equally unbreakable. Thank God he was in the UK on a purely temporary basis, as far as she knew, and as soon as either Derek was back or they found a suitable replacement, Conall O'Brien would be back on a plane to America.

'Amen to that,' she said aloud, munching a handful of crisps. But even the impeccable credentials of the gorgeous hero onscreen, endearingly pleading his case to the equally gorgeous but wary heroine, for once didn't have the power to distract her from thoughts of the man she was certain she disliked intensely.

'Get those letters done and on my desk for signature in an hour, Miss McKenzie.'

Morgen's gaze moved from the stack of paper Conall had dropped onto her desk up to his broad shoulders in yet another classy suit as he strode back into Derek's office and slammed the door. She shook her head from side to side and grimaced.

'Whatever happened to "Would you prefer it if I called you Morgen"?' she queried beneath her breath.

Obviously he'd had a change of heart overnight. Perhaps he'd worked too hard and too long and jet-lag had finally caught up with him? Hah! The man didn't need an excuse to be ill-mannered. She'd bet her last penny it came naturally to him.

'Enough, already!'

Irritated beyond belief at the way he was getting to her, Morgen sifted through the impossibly untidy writing on the stacked pages before her, automatically prioritising them in order of importance. Twenty-four letters, some running to at least two pages apiece—was he trying to break some kind of record?—were not going to get typed up in an hour, no matter if her fingers were on fire. That said, she liked a challenge. Slipping off the black jacket she wore over a sleeveless pink top, she settled herself more comfortably in her seat, then swivelled round at the curved desk to face the computer at the other end.

Okay, so Conall hadn't imagined it—this intense, completely incomprehensible instant attraction to Derek Holden's raven-haired assistant. Just now, when he'd dropped those letters onto her desk and seen that voluptuous body of hers lovingly filling out a little black suit that, hard as it might try, did nothing to conceal those sexy curves, the wildly inappropriate desire that had stabbed through his body had completely staggered him. He'd had to retreat quickly to recover himself.

Now he stared out of the window at the familiar dome of St Paul's cathedral and completely missed the view. Last night when he'd been unable to get to sleep he'd naturally blamed the jet-lag. But if he was absolutely honest sleep had eluded him because he'd been plagued by erotic thoughts about Morgen McKenzie that had simply refused to go away.

'Damn!'

Curse words came easier than explanations right now. He had a lot to do today too. The phone hadn't stopped ringing since he'd set foot in the office at eight. News of his arrival had travelled fast, and the world and his wife wanted a piece of him just now…and that included his mother. He'd promised faithfully to drop by tonight for dinner, but already he was regretting it. He wouldn't be able to escape her reprimands about staying away for so long, and neither would he be able to avoid the usual unwanted references to him and his father.

Scribbling a reminder on a pad to get Morgen to send some flowers to his mother's address in Marylebone, Conall pulled open the door and decided there was no time like the present. She was seated at the computer, her slim straight back towards him, so Conall swung round to the front, where she could see him.

'A dozen long-stemmed yellow roses to that address, please. By lunchtime, if you can.'

'Any message?' Regarding him coolly above her computer screen, nonetheless Morgen felt her body grow uncomfortably hot beneath his sweeping blue glance.

'Sorry, can't make tonight after all. Ring you soon. Love, Conall.'

Glancing at the name and address on the sheet of paper he'd handed her, Morgen moved her head gently in a semi-nod. Victoria Kendall. Was she a girlfriend, fiancée, significant other? For the first time she considered the possibility of him being married. The thought elicited strangely mixed feelings, but right this minute she refused to delve too deeply as to why. Even if she had been remotely attracted to him—and she most definitely wasn't—Conall O'Brien was as way out of her league as Simon had been, even more so, perhaps. And look how that liaison had ended.

'I'll get onto it right away, Mr O'Brien.'

'Good. By the way, I trust you had a pleasant evening with your "favourite" person?'

For a moment Morgen didn't have a clue what he meant. Then she remembered what she'd said in the car last night, and her brow knitted in confusion at the suggestion of anger in his tone.

'I did, thanks.'

'I imagine a woman like you has a lot of *favourite* people?'

What the hell was that supposed to mean? Tossing her head, Morgen strove to keep an even tone. 'If you're implying something not quite complimentary, then I'd be pleased if you kept your thoughts to yourself. If you don't mind.'

'Why so secretive? Who is this *favourite* person of yours you clearly don't want to discuss?'

A muscle throbbed at the side of Conall's temple as he studied her, revealing that despite the controlled, polished, suave appearance he liked to project he was perhaps not at present as in control as he liked. Morgen wondered at that.

'I'm not trying to be secretive, for goodness' sake! And even if I were, aren't I allowed a private life?'

'Without a doubt.' Conall's response was clipped. 'I was merely expressing an interest. Aren't I ''allowed'' to do that?'

Her whole body tensing beneath his dogged determination to somehow extract the truth out of her, Morgen sighed irritably. Perhaps if she told him she'd spent the evening alone with her daughter that would be an end to his interrogation once and for all?

'The person I spent the night with is Nee—'

'Morning, all. Got any coffee going, Morgen? I'm going to need it.'

They both glanced round at the slightly rumpled figure of Derek Holden as he came ambling through the door, and it was all Conall could do not to curse his timing out loud.

CHAPTER FOUR

THE door swung open. After nearly two hours ensconced in his office, Derek preceded Conall out through the door, his slightly bewildered expression reminding Morgen of a prisoner suddenly released from confinement after a long period and wondering what exactly he was supposed to do with himself. Scratching his head, he gave her a lop-sided schoolboy grin. That grin concealed a multitude of torment, she didn't doubt. It squeezed Morgen's heart and she smiled back unreservedly.

'Well, Morgen, it looks like you've got yourself a new boss for the next six weeks. It seems I'm to take an enforced sabbatical—get myself straightened out. Think you can cope without me?'

Listening to his comments, Conall had to refrain from rolling his eyes. As far as he could glean Morgen had been holding the fort for several weeks now, while Derek showed up sporadically at best. Considering the pressure she must have been under to conceal her boss's 'little problem' as far as she could, as well as tackling the considerable workload, he had to admit a grudging admiration for her being able to pull it off. It was only in the past couple of weeks that it had really come to the attention of the associates upstairs, and then only because Stephen Ritchie had personally been on the phone to them about all the times Derek had let them down by not showing up on site. Alarm bells had started ringing and investigations had been made.

'You just get yourself better soon. Eat well and get

some rest,' Morgen advised. 'We'll manage here just
fine.'

Realising that she had included Conall in that statement, she flushed with embarrassment. She knew that
yesterday he'd mentioned he would be taking things over
for a while, but that could mean just until he found someone else to step in for Derek. It didn't mean the man
himself would be staying around indefinitely. At least,
she hoped not. Her gaze slid away from both men as she
deliberately returned her attention to the screen in front
of her.

Conall accompanied Derek to the door, and after a final
few words bade him goodbye. When he turned back to
survey Morgen behind her desk he popped open the buttons of his suit jacket and pulled the knot of his tie away
from his collar. Stopping to pour a cup of water from the
cooler, he took a long, thirsty draught, then jettisoned the
polystyrene cup expertly into the bin. Beneath his out-
wardly calm exterior he was secretly stewing on that last
remark of Morgen's just before Derek showed up and
interrupted them. 'The person I spent the *night* with,'
she'd said. Right now he hardly trusted himself to speak
to her, he was so irrationally angry.

'How are you getting along with those letters?' he
asked.

'Fine. You haven't just left him to his own devices,
have you?' Morgen demanded anxiously. She parried the
flash of irritation in those perfectly blue eyes and stared
right back at him to show she wasn't going to back down.

'Does that maternal streak of yours come out for every
man, Miss McKenzie? Or is that particular trait reserved
purely for the Derek Holdens of this world?'

'You're deliberately misinterpreting me—but then why
should that surprise me? For your information, I'm not

mothering Derek at all. I'm simply acting out of concern for a man who has been very good to me as a boss. He may have had his own troubles to deal with, but he's always treated me well and with respect. Which is more than I can say for some of the men I've worked for!'

Conall flushed slightly beneath his tan at the barely disguised reprimand. Did she think he didn't treat her well? That stung. As for Derek…well, clearly Morgen thought the man some kind of plaster saint! The throb of jealousy presently zinging its way through his system wasn't pretty.

'I'm sorry to hear that.'

He was about as sorry as an elephant who'd trod on an ant, Morgen decided. 'Perhaps when it comes to treating staff decently you couldn't go far wrong if you took a leaf out of Derek's book.'

In a pig's eye, Conall reflected with heat. But part of him couldn't deny that he felt irritatingly guilty at her reprimand. He'd always thought of himself as fair, but firm—could he help it if the woman seemed to rub him up the wrong way? He winced at his own poorly chosen analogy. Still, it wouldn't do to let her imagine he was party to any such weakness as guilt.

'It'll be a cold day in hell before I take a leaf out of the book of a man who lets a woman leaving him reduce him to a drunken, shambolic wreck!' he ground out harshly. 'The man should have a bit more self-respect.'

Feeling all the colour drain out of her face, her fingers gripping the desk, Morgen wondered how she would restrain herself from walking out there and then. But just because Conall was clearly disparaging of a man like Derek, who had suffered emotionally after his wife's abandonment of him, it didn't mean that Morgen should take his comments personally and resign. She might not *like* what Conall had said, but from now on she would apply a much cooler head to the situation, and somehow remain aloof from the feelings of rage the man engendered inside her.

But, just the same, she'd be damned if she'd let him have the last word.

'You're so sure of yourself, aren't you?' Her green eyes sparkling with fury, she gripped the desk even tighter. 'You've probably never had a woman you cared for walk out on you. Beggar or king, it hurts, you know…to be abandoned by someone you love. Perhaps when it does eventually happen to you you might have a little bit more compassion for the rest of the human race!'

'Not likely, Miss McKenzie. I wouldn't let a woman get close enough to hurt me like that…though I'm not averse to getting close in other ways…'

Although his gaze never so much as wavered from her face Morgen received the disturbing impression that his contemplation of her was definitely bordering on the X-rated. Squirming in her seat, she wondered how he'd react if she told him that if he continued his inappropriate comments she'd report him for harassment. But even as the thought occurred she knew she would do no such thing. Who would take any notice of her when he was the boss?

But even as she thought that Morgen knew she couldn't lie to herself. When Conall O'Brien levelled his smoky looks at her, like him or not, the sensual nature that she had long buried since Simon walked out actually revelled in the attention, God help her. And now she was faced with the possibility of working for this man for the next six weeks!

Not wanting to fight any more, she swallowed down

her uneasiness and decided to make another attempt at reaching her implacable new boss on Derek's behalf.

'If you just leave Derek to his own devices he'll simply drink himself to death and that will be that! Don't you recognise the signs? The man thinks he's got nothing to lose since Nicky walked out. He's not thinking straight. How could he be? Couldn't you find it in your heart to help him in some way?' She hesitated to say *if you have one*...

'I hate to see you stress yourself out over this, Morgen. Confidentially, Derek's been booked into a very expensive and very exclusive drying-out clinic in the country, paid for by the firm. He'll have his every need catered for—except, of course, his need for alcohol. I've also arranged to receive weekly reports as to how he's faring. That put your mind at rest?'

Linking her hands together on the desk in front of her, Morgen exhaled a slow, difficult breath. All along he'd arranged treatment for Derek, and yet he'd let her rant on as if the last thing she could expect was for a man like Conall to help him. 'If you want to know the truth,' she admitted quietly, 'it does. I've had sleepless nights, worrying about what might happen to him.'

'And now your fears are hopefully laid to rest. He'll be in good hands.'

His reply was terse, dismissive. What could she expect when she'd been so outspoken in Derek's defence? Rude, really. She certainly hadn't pulled her punches. Reaching the door of Derek's office, Conall turned back at the last moment to glance thoughtfully her way.

'You should have talked to someone about your concerns for his welfare. That's what we have a human resources advisor for.'

'What, and have his dirty laundry aired all around the

office?' In spite of her vow to keep a cool head, she twisted her mouth scathingly. 'I don't know what it's like in the New York office, but here the gossips would have had a field-day. It's a shame, but people are only too eager to make their minds up about someone without knowing all the facts. Guilty until proven innocent. They would have had poor Derek hung, drawn and quartered before he had time to blink. Never mind his reasons for turning to drink in the first place. The man was in immense emotional pain. Right now they probably think you've given him the sack. By lunchtime the news will be all over the building.'

She was right, of course. He should have thought of it himself, Conall admitted silently. Hadn't he behaved in a similar fashion when he had had Morgen 'guilty as charged,' having discovered her asleep at her desk, without even knowing the first thing about her? It pained him to think that she had such a poor opinion of both him and her colleagues, despite the fact that he personally believed a lot of Derek Holden's emotional pain was self-inflicted and therefore didn't warrant such concern from her.

'Perhaps we ought to arrange some kind of informal meeting—make it official that Derek is on sick leave but expected to return in a few weeks' time? If it comes from me that ought to put a stop to any further speculation about him possibly losing his job.'

Directing the mouse on her computer pad to 'print,' Morgen inclined her head in immediate agreement. 'I could organise something for four o'clock this afternoon in the communal staffroom. Would that be okay?'

'I'll leave it in your capable hands. By the way, can you also organise me some lunch?' Conall's features relaxed into an unexpected smile. 'I'm going to be making a start on clearing some of Mr Holden's backlog. A sandwich at my desk will suffice. Something with chicken will do fine. Thanks.'

Morgen bet he could be almost charming when he tried, if that 'knock your socks off at twenty paces' smile of his was any indication. But she didn't want to be charmed by him, did she? His superior, arrogant manner she could handle, but his charm was another thing entirely...

Morgen sneezed, then sneezed again. As she slammed the driver's door shut a wave of heat descended, making her suddenly dizzy.

'Damn, damn, damn!' Shaking her head, she silently cursed the fates for giving her Neesha's cold. It really was the very last thing she needed, today of all days, when Conall was chairing a board meeting in the VIP suite and she was supposed to be taking notes. It was warm in there at the best of times, and if she got any hotter than she was at this moment it would be frankly unbearable.

Leaving the underground car park and making her way out onto the main road opposite the offices of O'Brien and Stoughton Associates, she had stepped off the pavement to get to the other side when suddenly a car whooshed by, practically taking the polish off her fingernails. At the same time a steely hand clamped her arm to yank her none too gently back onto the pavement. Before Morgen could recover herself Conall jerked her round to face him, jaw clenched and steely blue gaze swirling with anger.

'Have you got a death wish or something? Why the hell didn't you look where you were going?'

His heart was still beating much too fast. He hadn't

been able to believe it when he'd suddenly spotted Morgen, stepping out into the busy main road with a car bearing down on her at around thirty miles an hour. Seeing it swerve at the last minute to avoid her, he'd had to sprint to pull her back before the car that came after mowed her down. Now she was staring at him, her cheeks flushed and her pretty green eyes watery and confused.

Oh, Lord! She wasn't going to cry, was she? Conall prided himself on being as tough as the next strong, red-blooded male, but to be honest he was a sucker for weeping women, sick children and hurt animals. Frankly, all three were capable of hitting him where it hurt.

'Hey.' His voice turning gruff, he drew his knuckles gently down her cheek. A single tear gathered at the corner of one eye and slid down her flushed skin. 'I didn't mean to frighten you.'

Feeling as if there wasn't enough air to breathe, Morgen dug into her bag for a tissue, her insides quaking—more because Conall had touched her than because of her dramatic near-miss. Apart from realising that she had almost got herself killed, she was scared and confused that one man's touch could disorientate her so.

The roar of the traffic all but drowned out her shaky reply. 'You didn't frighten me. I was distracted for a moment, that's all. I should have been paying more attention to what I was doing. Thanks for coming to my rescue.' The thought occurred that if he hadn't her little daughter might well be motherless by now. That sparked off another tear, then another, until she was biting her lip to try and keep them at bay.

'Come on, let's go and get some coffee and talk a while.'

Slipping his hand beneath her elbow, Conall guided

her into a small Italian coffee bar just a little way down the road. Meanwhile Morgen was dabbing a little desperately at her tears—hardly able to believe that she was disgracing herself so badly, and in front of the one person she couldn't afford to show vulnerability to. He already had the opinion she was a shirker and not up to the job—now he would think she was a complete flake too.

A few minutes later, her senses assailed by the steamy fragrant aroma of coffee and newly baked rolls, Morgen sat facing Conall. His large frame dwarfed the chair, as usual, and his concentration was focused one hundred per cent on her—despite the steady stream of office workers dropping in for their early-morning refreshment. Her hand shook a little as she raised the creamy café latte to her lips, and the big man opposite frowned.

'Now, what's brought all this on? Maybe I can help?'

He really wanted to, Conall realised with an upsurge of longing. The distinct impression had been growing on him over the past few days that Morgen mostly went it alone, helping others without question and consequently neglecting herself. Just yesterday he'd wandered in on her comforting a distraught junior secretary whom he'd later found out had boyfriend trouble. He wondered if the 'favourite' person she had mentioned—Neil, or whatever his name was—really gave her enough support.

Then the thought of her boyfriend made him clench his jaw in irritation because, dammit, as far as Conall was concerned that was an obstacle he really didn't want to have to surmount.

'I'm fine, honestly. I've just picked up a cold and I haven't been sleeping very well.' Her glance was nervous and slid quickly away to avert further close examination.

Conall looked down into his coffee, then back again into her wary green eyes. 'I don't buy that as the only reason you're upset. What's been worrying you, Morgen? If it's anything to do with work I'm probably the best person you can talk to. The people who work for me are this firm's greatest asset. Therefore their wellbeing is my concern too.'

Put like that, his explanation sounded more than reasonable...seductive, even. But Morgen knew she couldn't confide in Conall. Apart from being only too aware that he was the owner and senior partner of the firm she worked for, she was already acquainted with the fact that he despised weakness of any kind. And, when it came right down to it, why would a man like him want to bother with an ordinary little secretary like her anyway? She'd already had one humiliating experience with Simon, and knew that huge differences in money and status could be a problem in relationships. She certainly didn't want to set herself up for a similar rejection again.

'I thought you didn't approve of people's personal problems encroaching on their work, Mr O'Brien?'

'Conall,' he said irritably, raking his fingers through his hair, then suffered immediate remorse because he had been taunting her with 'Miss McKenzie' from the beginning.

Had he done it subconsciously, in an attempt to put up a barrier between Morgen and himself? To keep their relationship strictly professional and somehow curtail the violent attraction that coursed through his veins every time he looked at her? He generally made it a strict rule that he didn't get involved with women at work. Those kinds of complications could and frequently did get messy, in his experience.

'You don't have a very high opinion of me, do you?' he added.

'You do what you have to do, I suppose. It doesn't

mean I have to like it.' Shrugging one shoulder, Morgen took refuge behind her coffee cup.

'You don't think I care about the people who work for me?'

She coloured. 'I didn't say that.'

'But you don't think I'm particularly sympathetic?'

Feeling as if she'd just blundered into a hedge of stinging nettles, Morgen wished she hadn't started this conversation. 'Your reputation precedes you, Mr O'Br—'

His brows drew together in an irritable scowl. 'If you call me that again, I'll fire you.'

Her heart thumped heavily.

'Like I said before, I'm running a business…' The rest was left unsaid. Conall couldn't understand why her comment had suddenly made him so uncomfortable. Had he become too hard-nosed for his own good? He was a success, wasn't he? His firm was a success. And he genuinely believed people liked working for him. So why should Morgen McKenzie's good opinion of him matter so much?

'I know that can't be easy.' Mentally fielding another wave of heat, Morgen cautiously considered him from beneath her lashes. 'But we're all human, you know? And life isn't a straight road with simple answers. Like I said before, I'm sure Derek didn't deliberately sabotage his career by turning to drink.'

'But we're not talking about Derek right now.' He rubbed his hand round the back of his shirt collar, then leant back in his chair and sighed. 'I'm sorry you don't feel that you can trust me enough to tell me what's bothering you. Perhaps we should talk about that? Not now—' He took a brief glance at his watch '—but as soon as we can arrange a little time together.'

The whole idea filled Morgen with intense trepidation.

It was testing enough having to work with this man, never mind arranging 'a little time together' to talk about why she felt she couldn't trust him.

'There's really no need. And, anyway, I've just got a cold. Nothing in particular is bothering me right now...' *Except you.* 'I'll be fine in a minute or two.' With an apologetic little shrug, she took another sip of the delicious coffee, feeling slightly calmer now, even though her skin still prickled with heat.

'Perhaps you ought to go straight home after the board meeting? I'll drive you myself.'

'No!'

The vehemence with which she voiced her reply made Conall's brows draw suspiciously together. Damn it all, the woman looked frightened. What was she trying to hide? A no-good feckless boyfriend who was unemployed, perhaps? Was that why Morgen looked so tired? Because she was supporting a man who relied on her to keep him? Anger briefly seared his gut, then he scolded himself for jumping to conclusions, making assumptions without knowing the facts—something Morgen had already had good reason to accuse him of. He suddenly saw there was ample reason for her not to trust him, and it was seriously beginning to get to him.

She didn't want him to drive her home. She didn't want him to see the small rundown street in which her poky two-bedroomed terraced house was situated. Not that she was ashamed of it—not when she had spent years lovingly turning it into a cosy, inviting little home for herself and Neesha. But it was surely way down the desirability league from what a man like Conall was used to. And if she so much as saw embarrassment or pity in his eyes he'd have her notice on his desk quicker than he could say Savile Row.

'I'll be fine to see out the day, then I'll drive myself home. Thanks all the same.'

Sensing it was futile to argue, Conall drank his coffee down in one long draught, then pushed to his feet. 'We ought to be getting back. I've got a full schedule today. Feeling any better now?'

'Much,' Morgen lied, her legs decidedly shaky as she followed him out through the door and into the street.

It was a long meeting—far longer than Conall would have liked. It seemed his fellow associates were making the most of his presence in the UK, and there had been several additions to the already crammed agenda.

Glancing at Morgen several times throughout the afternoon, Conall noticed the fine sheen of perspiration on her smooth brow when she swept back her fringe once or twice, and he thought that those arresting green eyes of hers appeared a little glassy and over-bright—as if she was running a fever. But they were already halfway through their discussion and there was nothing he could do about her condition right then—she was furiously taking down notes, and at that point the subject in hand was the lucrative Docklands project that Derek had been in charge of. Besides Derek, and lately Conall himself, no one else knew the project better than Morgen. Bringing in one of the other PAs to take over probably wouldn't be a very good idea from that point of view alone.

However, Conall proceeded to keep a close eye on his newly acquired assistant. When the break came for coffee, and people were milling around the refreshments that had been arranged in the adjoining room, leaving him and Morgen alone, he went over to talk to her.

'How are you feeling?'

He leant across her, saturating her senses with his seductively masculine scent, scrambling her brain even more than her temperature was already doing. Returning her gaze quickly to the pages of shorthand she had steadily been compiling throughout the meeting, Morgen decided avoiding those searching blue eyes was far safer than meeting them head-on.

'I'm fine. Thank you for asking.'

'You look a little flushed, if I may say so.'

'It's warm in here…don't you—don't you think?'

Momentarily forgetting her vow to keep visual contact to a minimum, Morgen found her glance suddenly trapped by his, like a ray of sunlight trapped a dust mote. No matter how hard she tried she couldn't look away for several debilitating seconds.

Breaking the spell, Conall moved first.

'I'll open a window.'

He opened a couple, deliberately taking his time, praying the rush of cool fresh air would help calm down his heightened libido. Conall knew the heat of desire as much as any normal, healthy red-blooded male, but when he looked into Morgen McKenzie's bewitching green eyes, with their sweeping black lashes, desire moved up to a whole other level. If he weren't careful this yearning to have her in his bed would become an obsession.

'That's better. Thanks.' She ran a hand round the back of her collar, where her hair was tied back, and Conall couldn't help noticing the curling tendrils of ebony silk that drifted loose around her nape. He shoved his hand into his trouser pocket to stop himself from reaching out to touch—to discover for himself if it was as invitingly soft as it appeared.

'Want me to get you some sandwiches and a cup of coffee?'

'No, thanks, I'm not hungry. Water is fine.' As if to highlight her preference, Morgen poured herself a glass of water from the jug in front of her on the table and took a sip. Her hand was not quite steady, and Conall frowned at the idea that she was finding the meeting an ordeal.

'Shouldn't be too much longer now.' Glancing down at his watch, he picked up the sheet of paper with the agenda printed on it from beside Morgen's shorthand pad. 'Five more items. I'll keep them as short as I can, and when we're done here I'll take you home.'

Conall saw the word 'no' start to form on her exquisite lips and squared his massive shoulders. There was no point in being the boss if you couldn't use it to your advantage in times of need. And right now Conall needed to know that he was driving Morgen home. He wasn't being totally selfish either. Anybody could see the woman was running a temperature. She'd nearly walked out in front of a speeding car earlier; the last thing Conall wanted on his conscience was her having an accident on the way home because she was too ill to concentrate.

Shifting uncomfortably in her seat, Morgen sighed wearily. 'I told you before—I appreciate your concern but I don't need you to drive me home. Now, please, think no more of it.'

But at five-forty-five precisely Morgen found herself being guided towards the car park and helped into the passenger seat of a luxurious sedan by a solicitous but steely-eyed Conall, who wasn't taking no for an answer—at least not today, and not from her. Resignedly, she gave him directions, and spent practically the entire journey in mutinous silence.

Why was he so insistent on taking her home? He was taking his responsibilities as her boss a little too seriously, Morgen decided. Expanding parameters he had no business expanding. Even Derek—bless him—as generous as he could be, would never have thought to drive her home because she was feeling under the weather. No, if he'd deemed it necessary at all, Derek would have got someone else to do it. But not this man.

Morgen stole a furtive glance at his handsome chiselled profile as he drove, and her insides fluttered with anxiety. As soon as they pulled up outside the house she'd make sure she had her key ready, thank him, then hurry away before he had a chance to insist on seeing her to the door—because she had a horrible feeling he was going to do just that. If she'd learned one thing about Conall O'Brien so far it was that he took his work and his responsibilities deadly seriously—no half-measures. Everything was done with absolute dedication and thoroughness. He was the epitome of the old adage 'if a job's worth doing, it's worth doing well.' Not that Morgen could fault that. It was just that right now she didn't particularly want him to apply it to her.

But by the time they pulled up outside the cheerful red door, in a street where doors were predominantly painted black or, even worse, grey, Morgen was feeling too ill to care what Conall would or would not do. She certainly didn't have the strength to worry about whether he thought the street she lived in looked rundown and poor, or whether the cars that were parked outside were several registrations older than his. All she wanted right now was her bed, and if she didn't make it as far as that then the couch would have to suffice. Thank God Neesha was at her mother's tonight, sleeping over, because she would hardly be capable of caring for her child the way she was feeling.

'Thank you, I—'

'Give me your key.'

'What?'

His expression as implacable as granite, Conall turned towards her and put out his hand.

'Your door key. I'm taking you inside, Morgen. I'm going to make sure you take some fever medication, then I'm going to make sure you get into bed. It doesn't take a scientist to see that you're burning up. I might even phone your doctor and ask him to pay you a visit.'

'Now, wait a minute, I—'

But it wasn't easy to be indignant when you felt as if your head was going to become personally acquainted with the pavement at any second, Morgen realised. Nodding with a mixture of fatigue and resignation, she dug into her bag for her keys and dropped them into his opened palm.

'There's a good girl.'

'I resent that!' Pulling him back by the sleeve of his expensive suit, Morgen glared, despite the spinning sensation in her head. 'I'm not a girl—I'm a woman!'

Conall's blue eyes darkened perceptibly.

'Sweetheart, from the minute I laid eyes on you there was never any doubt in my mind about that. Now, let's get you inside before you collapse where you sit.'

CHAPTER FIVE

AFTER negotiating a bright but narrow hallway, lined as far as he could see with prints of herbs and flowers, Conall felt his senses beset by the uplifting notes of rose and vanilla—two fragrances he knew well because of his sister Teresa's penchant for scented candles.

Morgen's house was an Aladdin's cave of sensory delights, he realised as he followed her into the living room. Much like the woman herself. Proportionally the room might have been small, but what it lacked in square footage it more than made up for in comfort. It was a room that a person could seriously look forward to coming home to, Conall decided, feeling a tug of something almost unfamiliar.

He'd thought he'd long ago put to rest the urge or the need to put down roots. To have a place and a person you loved to be there for you when you returned home from work at the end of the day was not something he'd considered for a very long time. Besides…for him it would never work. He hated to admit it, but he was too much like his father for that.

'What a lovely room.'

Although the main colour scheme was pale yellow and gold, there were splashes of bold vibrant colour in evidence everywhere. Soft red velvet and silk throws were draped across two big couches, and piles of cushions in a kaleidoscope of hues and textures spilled across every available seating space. Above the Victorian fireplace, that had clearly been lovingly and painstakingly restored, there was a huge, vivid framed print of a beautiful pre-Raphaelite model with skin as pale as milk and hair a rich and luxuriant auburn decorated with a wreath of white roses. Conall studied it briefly before switching his perusal to Morgen, suddenly alarmed that she looked barely able to stand on her feet.

'Thank you.'

Although feverish, she heard the genuine appreciation in Conall's tone, and something warm crowded into the empty space in her heart. Here was a man who had a reputation as an architect *par excellence*, who she knew had designed and built houses for the rich and famous—houses that were featured in the glossiest up-market magazines—dream houses—and yet there he stood, in the middle of her humble little living room, and professed he thought it 'lovely'. Right then, she almost cried.

'Why don't you sit down, kick off your shoes and let me get you some aspirin and a glass of water? If you don't sit down soon you look like you're going to fall down.'

She was in no position to argue. Dropping down onto the couch before Conall had even finished speaking, she kicked off her sensible leather loafers, flexed her toes and shook her hair loose from its knot.

For a moment Conall just stared at the glossy raven mass that slipped around her shoulders, then he moved abruptly to the door, once again engineering some safe distance between himself and her—because his desire to reach out and touch was almost too compelling to be ignored.

'The kitchen's just down the hall—the last door at the end. You'll find some medicine in the cupboard above the fridge.'

In the small compact kitchen, with its clean pine furniture and terracotta-tiled floor, Conall easily located the medicine, filled a glass with water, then stood momentarily transfixed by the childish drawings displayed on the front of the fridge, held in place by several colourful magnets.

He was particularly drawn to the one with a bold title in bright red felt-tip: 'My Mummy.' The surprisingly well-executed picture was of a tall slim lady with long flowing black hair, cat-like green eyes and a lush red mouth. For a long moment Conall just stood, absorbing the shock—acclimatising himself to the realisation that Morgen had a child. She was a mother. It had to follow, then, that the child had a father...Morgen's boyfriend? This Neil character? Or was the child the offspring of a previous relationship? He knew he had no right to be jealous or angry, but just then none of his feelings made any sense.

Swallowing hard, Conall made his way back down the narrow hallway to the living room, the thick sea-green carpet deadening the sound of his footfall. When he found Morgen lying on the couch, her head resting on a bank of velvet cushions, her eyes closed, his chest tightened inexplicably, and he found he needed a minute to accustom himself to the idea that a relationship with her—apart from a professional one, of course—was now totally out of the question. As much as he desired her—and even the thought made his heart pump faster—he wouldn't try to break up an already established relationship, especially not one where there was a child concerned.

As if sensing his presence, Morgen opened her eyes.

'You found it. Thanks.' Struggling to sit up, she accepted the two white tablets into her palm, then swallowed them one at a time with two big gulps of water.

'You keep a very tidy house,' Conall drawled softly. 'It makes it easy to find things. Why didn't you tell me you had a child?'

The swimming sensation in her head increased. The kitchen—of course... He must have seen Neesha's drawings on the fridge. Oh, well. Focusing her tired gaze on Conall's serious but undeniably handsome face, Morgen decided she might as well be frank with him. Under the circumstances, what else could she be? Too bad if he didn't like it. She hadn't asked him to drive her home in the first place, and she certainly hadn't invited him in.

'You never asked me, so it never came up.' Her tongue came out to wet the rosy seam of her lips, and Conall absorbed the wholly innocent little action with a fortitude even he hadn't thought he was capable of. Unbuttoning his jacket, he sat down, making himself comfortable on the second couch, every cell in his body thrumming with tension—because he wanted her. Even though she was flushed with fever, even though she had a child, even though she probably had a steady relationship...none of it deflected his passionate attraction one jot.

'Her name's Neesha. She's six years old. I didn't mention it because I didn't want to give you another excuse to imagine my commitment to work was less than it should be. That first morning, when you found me asleep at my desk? I'd been up the night before, nursing my daughter's cold; that's why I was so tired. It's well known that some bosses don't like female staff having family commitments. You'd already threatened me with the sack once, and I need this job. Now you know.'

Conall's blue eyes sharpened as he absorbed what she'd just told him. 'Neesha? Presumably she's the "favourite person" you mentioned the other day?'

Sighing wearily, Morgen pushed her fingers through

her curtain of dark hair, making Conall's own fingers itch to do the same. But he knew there was a wealth of resentment in that sigh that told him she didn't exactly enjoy explaining the circumstances of her life to him. And why should she?

'Of course. Who else would I mean?'

'Where's her father? At work?'

'I wouldn't know. We're lucky if we see him three or four times a year, if that.' A mirthless laugh broke free from her lips. 'Or perhaps I should say unlucky?'

'You're separated?' Conall couldn't deny the swift stab of hope that took a speedboat ride through his bloodstream.

'Divorced...five years ago. I'm a single parent. Now you know everything about me.' Her green eyes flashed resentment again, but this time Conall felt better equipped to deal with it.

He smiled. 'Not everything. Why did you break up?'

She made a little sound of exasperation, and if she'd been standing Conall guessed she would have shown him the door. Far be it from him to take advantage, but he was glad she was too indisposed to contemplate it. Though if he were truly the gentleman his mother had raised him to be without a doubt he would have chosen a better time to pursue this particular line of questioning.

'That's private.'

Hugging her arms around her middle, Morgen wished that he would just get up and go. Why was he hanging around, plaguing her with all these questions, when all she wanted to do was curl up on the couch and go to sleep? Simon had been a first-class bastard, but she wasn't about to reveal as much to her boss. Besides, knowing how men stuck together about these things, Conall would probably think the fault had been hers, and

Morgen had had enough judgements already to make her wary of exposing herself to more.

'Having children is hardly a sacking offence, Morgen. As long as my staff realise they do have a certain level of commitment to work, and don't take advantage, then as far as I'm concerned taking time off to take care of their kids when they're ill or be there to see a school play isn't a problem. I'm not a family man myself, but I know it's short-sighted not to acknowledge that people have another life outside work. If that's something I've been guilty of in the past, then clearly it's time for a change. Where is your daughter now, by the way?'

'At my mum's. She stays over there one night in the week.'

Despite not wanting to display vulnerability of any kind to this man, Morgen couldn't help but draw her legs beneath her and let her head slip back down onto the cushions. She was so tired. If falling asleep were an Olympic sport, she'd win it hands down. Conall would just have to see himself out. If he expected to see her at work in the morning she'd need at least twelve hours to try and shake this thing. She was glad, though, she acknowledged sleepily, that he'd said what he had about family. It made him seem much more approachable, somehow—less the high-powered charismatic architect and more like an ordinary human being.

By the time Conall got back on his feet, dragged his fingers through his hair and loosened his tie-knot, it was evident that Morgen was well and truly asleep. Scanning the room, he pulled a soft plaid wool throw from a padded Victorian armchair and draped it gently across her slumbering figure. He remembered she'd protested vehemently about being called a girl earlier, but right now, looking down into her flushed, almost angelic face, she reminded Conall of a small child that needed taking care of.

Why the very idea didn't have his feet burning a hole in the rug to get out of the door, he could only wonder. He'd only really ever dated career women: strong, capable, ambitious individuals who knew what they wanted out of life and stopped at nothing to get it. If a little warmth had been lacking in their make-up sometimes, tearing up the sheets as an extra-curricular activity after work had easily made up for the deficit—if indeed that was what it was.

'We work hard and we play hard,' a male colleague— proud to be over thirty and still single—had asserted over drinks one night. But even then Conall had experienced surprising discomfort at the generally accepted ethos. Having a reputation as a bit of a playboy wasn't all it was cracked up to be, he'd found. There was something about being able to have anything you wanted—including beautiful women—that didn't always sit right. He wasn't hankering after having a family, or anything ludicrous like that, but maybe it would be kind of nice to have one special woman in his life instead of several? As long as she didn't cling and expect him to marry her.

'You go through girlfriends as often as you change your shirt,' his sister Teresa had once scolded him, and he'd asked her why he should have any remorse about the fact when they were all consenting adults who knew what they were getting into from the start. He always made it clear from the outset that it was a short-term thing, with no strings, and the women mostly agreed. One or two had clung a little, he recalled with regret, but in the main everyone was happy. Everyone got what they wanted. Didn't they?

His chest felt curiously hollow as he continued to study

the sleeping Morgen. Clearly she hadn't got what she'd wanted, if she was divorced. Once upon a time had she believed in happy ever after? Conall found it disturbed him to think that her girlhood dreams had been crushed by a man. Despite his own aversion to the married state, inexplicably it made him feel as if the whole of his sex had let her down.

Good grief! Where was this leading? Shaking his head in disbelief, he glanced at the clock on the mantelpiece. Almost simultaneously his stomach grumbled. He hadn't eaten anything since this morning—he'd given the sandwiches at the meeting the go-by in order to stay and talk to Morgen. Trouble was, he was loath to leave her and go in search of food when she might need him. The idea that she was unwell and would have to manage on her own in the night seriously bothered him. If only he'd thought to ask her for her mother's phone number before she'd fallen asleep, instead of wearing her out with his questions. At least he could have rung her and told her that Morgen was ill. Now what was he supposed to do?

In the end he made his way back into the kitchen, telling himself that surely Morgen wouldn't mind if he made himself a sandwich. He'd pay her back by taking her out to dinner. Warming to the idea, he spread two slices of wholemeal bread with some low-fat spread he found in the fridge, then added a couple of messily cut slices of cheddar cheese. Okay, so he wasn't known for his culinary expertise, but he was hungry—what could be better than staples like bread and cheese? Now, if only Morgen had a handy bottle of good red wine, Conall thought wryly, he'd be in seventh heaven...

Stirring in her sleep, she felt every bone and every muscle she possessed seem to collectively groan in agony.

Something woolly was tickling her cheek, and Morgen blinked her eyes open in the semi-dark and pushed it away, panicking suddenly because she didn't remember covering herself with a throw before she'd fallen asleep. Conall? When had he left? And, more to the point, what had her parting words been? She could only pray she hadn't said something stupid. Something she might regret.

Pushing up into a sitting position, she peeled her tongue from the roof of her mouth and grimaced at the taste. Gasping for a drink, she swung her legs to the floor, wishing she didn't feel so dizzy and hot, trying to remember what she was supposed to be doing, because she couldn't somehow get to grips with co-ordinating her brain and her limbs at the same time.

'Steady. Let me help you.'

The low rumble of Conall's voice coming at her out of the darkened room made Morgen almost faint with shock. She stared as his hand came down on her shoulder and gave it a reassuring squeeze. What was he doing here? And what was the time, for goodness' sake? He'd removed his jacket and tie, she noticed, and a silky lock of his hair flopped across his forehead as he bent down to her.

'Where do you want to go?' he asked concernedly.

Morgen licked her dry lips and wished her limbs would stop shaking. 'To the bathroom. I can—I can manage.'

'You're burning up.' Automatically his hand moved to her forehead, swept back her fringe and assessed her temperature. 'As soon as I get you back from the bathroom, I suggest you get straight into bed. You'll have to show me where your room is.'

Struggling to her feet, Morgen felt like a newborn foal, trying to get to grips with the use of its legs. When she stumbled Conall was there to steady her and hold her, and she could have cried because she was feeling so weak and really did seem to need his help.

'You shouldn't be here,' she whispered forlornly, sniffing to hold back the tears. 'Why did you stay?'

His blue eyes didn't waver. The look that met her troubled gaze almost made her heart break. 'Because you needed me.'

It was as simple as that. No other explanations needed, clearly. Not once in the time she'd lived with Simon had he even stayed awake when she was unwell, never mind nursed her through it because she needed him. And he was a doctor.

With a sigh, Morgen allowed Conall to help her to the bathroom.

Insisting she leave the door unlocked, so that she could call for his help if she needed it, he leant against the wall in the corridor, wishing that he'd insisted she'd gone home earlier. The least he could do now was make sure everything else was all right for her. He'd tuck her into bed, make sure she had plenty to drink, and give her a couple more tablets to take her temperature down before she went back to sleep again. Then he'd spend the night on one of her silk-draped couches and see how she was in the morning.

She wouldn't like it, but she was in no condition to protest, he thought grimly. Risking Morgen's temper was a risk he was willing to take if he could see to his satisfaction that she was all right.

Switching off the light in the bathroom, Morgen told herself she felt marginally better now that she'd brushed her teeth and eliminated that dead budgerigar taste in her mouth. But it still didn't stop her from swaying slightly as she endeavoured to stay upright and fix Conall's tall broad-shouldered frame with a wobbly little smile.

'All done.'

'Where's your bedroom?'

'I bet you say that to all the girls,' she joked feebly, then wished she hadn't when Conall's handsome brows drew together in what appeared to Morgen a highly disapproving little frown.

'I prefer my women to be in full control of all their faculties before things get that specific, sweetheart,' he drawled, making all the hairs on the back of Morgen's neck stand to attention. What was the matter with her? she thought miserably. Why did she have to be so ultra-aware of this man? What was it about him that made her yearn for the impossible, even when she was ill?

'I wasn't trying to make—make a pass at you or anything.' Turning away, she almost jumped out of her skin when Conall's hand snapped meaningfully round her wrist. Staring up at him, her skin flushed with fever and her legs quaking, she was totally powerless to tear her gaze away from those intense blue eyes as they bored into hers.

'Do you think I would have turned you down if you had? Even in your present unhappy condition, I want you like I have no right to want you. Now, let's get away from the subject before I forget I'm the gentleman I like to think I am.'

In her bedroom, Conall drew the pale lemon voile curtains closed against the night and took a deep steadying breath. He'd left her sitting on the edge of the old-fashioned brass bed, struggling to remove her jacket, while he tried not to stare and imagine her undressing for him.

Already he was in a fever of his own. Being in her

room was unbelievably more erotic than any fantasy he could have conjured up himself, and he could give the average Hollywood director a run for his money in that department. The room was ultra-feminine and made Conall acutely sensitive to his own opposing masculinity. The women he usually dated mostly seemed to prefer a fairly minimalist look in the bedroom, but Morgen's room was a seductive assault on the senses. As well as being filled with the most erotic scents—sandalwood, and something sweetly exotic he couldn't identify—everything around him was a feast for the eyes.

In one corner of the room was a dressing table draped in white muslin, covered with lots of pretty Victorian scent bottles and a silver hairbrush and comb set. The floor was covered in a pale gold-coloured carpet, with an Oriental oval rug by the bed, and in the centre of the ceiling hung an old-fashioned brass chandelier with tear-shaped droplets made of crystal. But it was the bed that drew Conall's attention, and the thought of her in it would haunt his dreams. Covered in virginal white linen, it was an inviting contrast to the midnight darkness of Morgen's hair, and he couldn't help the heat that inflamed him when he imagined making love to her in that bed, that dark silken mass spread out on the pillow behind her.

'Can I get into bed now?'

She'd peeled back the white covers and was starting to crawl beneath them when Conall moved across to stand beside the bed, his casual stance belying the tumult of desire raging inside him.

'You've still got your clothes on,' he reminded her, stern-faced. 'Where are your night things?' He stared, half expecting her to produce a long lacy Victorian nightgown from beneath her pillow.

'I feel too ill to get changed,' she protested. More to the point, she had no intention of putting on her night-clothes with Hunk of the Year standing there watching her.

'You'll regret it in the morning.' Now there was a faint suggestion of a smile ghosting his lips, and Morgen felt her insides teeter as if she was riding a unicycle on a high wire.

'Well, then, you'd better leave me to it.'

As she started to swing her legs onto the floor again, Conall gave her a gentle shove backwards. Ignoring her indignant glare, he let his hands drop to his hips. Morgen's gaze did too, and she gulped when she realised what she was doing.

'Where are your things? I'll get them for you.'

Jerking her head towards the heavy Victorian chest of drawers on the other side of the room, Morgen reluctantly told him, 'Third drawer down. You can't miss them.'

She was right, Conall mused, handling the red silk py-jamas in awe. They were so soft they felt like water trick-ling through his fingers. Desire slammed hard into his groin, and for a few moments he stood perfectly still to ground himself. She wore red silk pyjamas in bed. What was she trying to do? Torture him?

'Put them on,' he instructed, throwing them onto her lap, his voice gruff. 'I'll wait outside.'

CHAPTER SIX

MORGEN was lying in bed staring up at the ceiling when the door swung open and, unannounced, Conall strode in. He was bearing a glass of water on a tray and his hair looked tousled and damp, as if he'd just showered. Around his jaw was the distinct dark shadow of a beard. With his shirt undone to almost the centre of his chest, and minus his tie and jacket, he looked almost too disturbingly attractive for words. Like a living, breathing male calendar cover.

For a moment Morgen couldn't speak, she was so tongue-tied, and if it was possible her temperature soared even higher. Apparently he'd stayed the night—just as he told her he would. She still couldn't quite believe it.

'How are you feeling this morning?'

She didn't mince her words. 'Like death warmed up, if you must know.'

'Here, take two more of these.' Carefully positioning the tray on the small muslin-covered nightstand beside the bed, Conall proffered the tablets, then handed her the glass of water to wash them down with. He waited patiently while she took them, then put the glass back down onto the tray.

'You're still very hot.' Sliding his hand onto her brow, he frowned at the evidence. 'There's no way you can come into work today. Perhaps I should call the doctor out? Have him check you over?'

Morgen wasn't used to this much attention when she was ill, and she still couldn't quite believe that her high-powered boss had stayed the night in her humble little house to watch over her and make sure she didn't get any worse. Protecting his firm's investment, maybe? Or were his reasons even more basic than that? His statement that he wanted her more than he had a right to had played over and over in her head during the night, as if she'd left her finger on the 'rewind' button of a tape recorder. But he could want all he liked, she thought defiantly. It didn't mean that he could have. She had her child's welfare to consider before she went racing down that old road of heartbreak again, and that was where she'd be headed if she became intimately involved with her boss.

There was also the little matter of her ex-husband's behaviour in the past—surely that was enough on its own to prevent her from getting any silly ideas about a relationship with Conall? High-powered men were too into their careers to really dedicate themselves to a proper relationship with a woman—let alone a woman with a child. And hadn't she heard Conall say with her own ears that he would never let a woman get really close? Top of Morgen's list of priorities was raising her daughter, and she wasn't about to indulge in some hot little affair, possibly jeopardising her job and her relationship with Neesha. Even if the idea was getting harder and harder to resist.

'I don't want you to call the doctor. There's nothing he'll suggest other than what I'm doing already anyway. I'll wait until lunchtime and see how I feel, and if I've improved, I'll jump in the car and drive into work.'

'Over my dead body!' Conall's searing blue gaze was like a laser beam boring into Morgen's skull. 'Thank heaven your car's still at work—remember? But even if it was possible, I'd tie you to the bed first to stop you

doing it! Be sensible, Morgen. Stay put for the rest of
the day and make sure you don't venture any further than
this room and the bathroom. Unfortunately I have several
meetings scheduled for this afternoon, and I need to do
some background work to prepare, otherwise I'd stay
with you. Have you got a phone nearby?' he asked.

Morgen reached across to the nightstand at the other
side of the bed for the slim white cordless phone that she
always kept there.

'Right here.'

'Keep it handy. I'm going to be ringing you on and
off throughout the day, just to make sure you're okay. I
might also have to ask you where I can put my hand on
things I need at the office. That all right with you?'

'Of course.'

Their business concluded, Morgen was worryingly be-
reft of words. It didn't help matters when Conall stood
staring at her as if he was having great difficulty in walking away. A little muscle ticked in the side of his jaw. It
seemed to trigger a series of worryingly sensual tremors
in her body that she was helpless to do anything about.
Imagination was a powerful thing, Morgen silently
warned herself. Conall O'Brien could have any woman
he wanted, most probably. Why on earth would he be
interested in a single mother and all the baggage that
automatically entailed? And now he'd seen her at her
worst—oh, no! She hadn't even glanced in a mirror this
morning—never mind brushed her teeth or combed her
hair—she must look like Dracula's mother!

'Thanks for bringing me home, by the way, and for
staying the night. I hope you weren't too uncomfortable
on the couch.'

'I was fine. I used your shower—I hope you don't
mind? I need to go home now, for a quick shave and to

get a change of clothes. I've made up a flask of soup for you in the kitchen—I went through the cupboards and found some tomato and lentil. Make sure you have some if you feel hungry. And ring me if you need anything. That clear?'

He made her feel like a little girl again—that much was clear. Safe and protected—*cherished*, almost—a seductive combination for any woman overdue for a little tender loving care. Morgen smiled her gratitude, even though her head felt as if all the rock drummers in the world were having a jamming session inside it.

'Are you always this thoughtful for your employees?'

Ignoring her question as though it made him uncomfortable, Conall strode back to the door. 'And ring your mother—just to let her know you're not well. I'll see you later.'

And with that he was gone. Morgen dropped her head back against the pillows and gratefully shut her eyes.

His senior associate's PA was pleasant and helpful to a degree, but she wasn't Morgen. And she couldn't make coffee he wanted to drink. Scowling for the umpteenth time that afternoon, Conall glanced up at the slender blonde bearing down on him with yet another cup of the undrinkable brew and forced a smile.

'Thanks, Julie. By the way, did you find that file I asked you for?'

'I'm still looking for it, Mr O'Brien. Could you bear with me for a few more minutes?'

'I need that file if I'm to address this item at the meeting in half an hour. Do your best to find it, will you?'

When she'd closed the door behind her Conall sighed and tunnelled his fingers through his already besieged hair. He needed a haircut, but when he was supposed to fit it into his already impossible schedule he didn't know. Finding himself reaching towards the telephone, he snatched his hand away at the last moment.

He'd already rung Morgen three times. The last time she'd sounded sleepy and husky-voiced, and he'd suffered uncharacteristic guilt because he knew he'd just woken her. If she was going to get back to the office sooner rather than later, he really should let her rest. Trouble was, she'd pricked his conscience with her unstinting concern over Derek, and her accusations to the effect that Conall lacked compassion when it came to his staff's personal problems. Morgen had probably resigned herself to the fact he was a cold, uncaring, arrogant swine.

He winced at the thought. She was a single mum coping on her own. That had to be hard. Even though his own high-octane lifestyle was probably a million miles away from hers, he knew that. But, aside from her provoking his conscience, he missed her. Crazy when he'd only known the woman for just a few short days, but there was no explaining this powerful attraction he seemed to have developed for her.

Every time Conall closed his eyes, even briefly, he saw her in those sexy red silk pyjamas. Last night, when he'd checked on her at around one in the morning and found she'd kicked off the covers and her pyjama top had rolled revealingly up to just beneath her breasts, Conall had sucked in his breath at the sight of her gorgeous sexy midriff.

His friend Mike back at the New York office would no doubt advise him to take her to bed as soon as possible and nip this wild attraction in the bud before it got out of control. Perhaps that was what he should do? Morgen might not exactly like or admire him, but he knew she wasn't entirely immune to him either. It wouldn't be too hard to seduce her, surely? Not a man of his experience…

'Concentrate, O'Brien! What the hell is the matter with you?' Furious with himself, he pulled the drawings spread out on the desk towards him and forced himself to run through them one more time. The door opened as he did so and Julie's blonde head appeared.

'Did you want something, Mr O'Brien? I thought I heard you talking.'

What I want right now, I can't have… Conall's blue eyes stared unseeingly ahead, then he gave himself another mental shake and flashed a broad smile at his temporary PA that had her clenching everything in her body that could possibly be clenched.

'I'm fine. Just thinking out loud,' he said apologetically, then got to his feet to go and stare out of the window as she closed the door behind her again.

'I didn't see your car parked outside.' Lorna McKenzie fussed around her daughter's bedside, rearranging the glass of water on the tray, patting down the soft embroidered counterpane.

With a daughter's radar, Morgen picked up the slight note of suspicion lacing her voice. 'A friend from the office drove me home. My car's still in the car park at work.'

'You should have rung me. I would have come and got you myself. Did this "friend" of yours think to ring the doctor for you?'

It was typical of her mother to assume that nobody else knew how to do anything properly. Briefly shutting her eyes, Morgen silently warned herself not to rise to the bait. When she opened them again her mother was staring down at her, lips slightly compressed and arms folded.

'I didn't want the doctor to come out. It's probably just a viral thing. It'll blow over in a couple of days.'

'And what if you need some proper medication? I suppose you're going to treat yourself with some of those alternative remedies of yours instead?' Lorna sighed and unfolded her arms. 'You are the most stubborn creature on the planet, you really are! Have you managed to eat anything?'

'My friend made me up a flask of soup.' She'd had some earlier, but hadn't felt much like eating.

She wondered what Lorna would say if she knew this 'friend' she kept referring to was actually her boss. The head of the firm, no less. To tell the truth, Morgen was still having trouble getting to grips with the fact that Conall seemed so genuinely concerned about her well-being. Already he'd rung her three times today, and, worse than that, she'd found herself actually looking forward to those calls. Just hearing his voice had given her a resurgence of energy that was better than any medicine—orthodox or otherwise. Dangerous…

'Well, I'm going to make you a nice chicken stew. Neesha's already had tea, but she can have some stew as well later, if she's hungry.'

'What's she doing now?'

'Watching a video. I've told her you need to rest. She's already done her homework, and it's all packed away in her bag for tomorrow. I'll send her in to see you in a while. In the meantime, why don't you try and get some more sleep?'

Morgen made a face, wishing her head didn't feel as if it had a lead weight wedged inside it. 'I don't want to sleep any more. I think I'll just put on my dressing gown and go and sit with Neesha.'

'Well, don't blame me if you start to feel worse later. You just won't be told, will you?'

'For God's sake, Mum! I'm twenty-nine years old, not five! If you stopped treating me like a child and just let me make my own decisions things would be a whole lot happier all round.'

Planting her feet on the floor, Morgen reached for her silk wrapper, pulled it on and headed for the door. Lorna stared after her, her eyebrows arched and her expression wounded, as it usually was when her daughter chose not to take her advice.

'That would be fine if you made a few *right* decisions now and again,' she muttered.

Morgen knew the wise thing to do would be to ignore such a remark. But hurt and anger welled up inside her like a dam about to burst and completely sabotaged such wisdom. Her green eyes furious, she dropped her hands to her hips as she glared at the older woman.

'And what's that supposed to mean? We're not talking about Simon again, are we, by any chance? He left me, remember? He's the one who didn't want the responsibility of fatherhood—so don't act like it was all my fault. Do you think I wanted to be a single mother? You know how hard it's been for Neesha and me, yet you still bang on about bloody Simon like he's the injured party in all this!'

'You could have hung on to him if you'd really wanted to.' Patting down her soft brown hair, Lorna met her daughter's furious look with an aggrieved one of her own.

'Hung onto him?' In disbelief, Morgen's mouth dropped open. 'What exactly is that supposed to mean?'

'You're an attractive woman. It can't be beyond you to work that one out for yourself. You've forgotten how to be feminine since you've been working; that's your trouble. You think you've got to be the tough career woman, act like a man to get what you want, when the reverse is true. Simon was besotted with you. If you'd only used that to your advantage, instead of letting his parents push him around, he'd still be here with you now.'

Swaying slightly, Morgen stuck out her hand and held onto the doorjamb. Because she was so angry her head started to swim even more than usual. And deep down inside she felt betrayed. Betrayed because her mother seriously seemed to believe that she had somehow driven her husband away because she'd refused to use her feminine wiles to keep him interested. Lorna just wouldn't see the truth. Simon's parents had never believed her good enough for their beloved son, and eventually he'd believed that to be the case too—even when she'd become pregnant with his child.

'We weren't good enough for the likes of Simon Vaughan-Smith and his family, Mum. You, me, Neesha…that's the cold, hard truth! We weren't good enough! Why can't you just accept that and move on? What did you expect me to do? Act like I was grateful he'd even noticed me, because he was a doctor and I a mere secretary? Was I supposed to bury my self-respect for the sake of a wedding ring?'

'You're every bit as good as him and you know it!' Sniffing, Lorna pushed past Morgen into the hallway. She turned slowly, digging for the little square of linen tucked into her sweater sleeve. 'I just want you and Neesha not to have to struggle. What harm can it do for a mother to want a good man to look after her daughter?'

Morgen's green eyes glittered as she looked at Lorna, heartsore. 'Simon wasn't a good man, Mum,' she said softly. 'He was a weak man. Neesha and I are better off without him. Things aren't so bad. I earn a reasonable salary, we live in a nice house, I manage to keep our overheads to a minimum most of the time and I've even managed to accumulate some savings. All in all, we don't do badly.'

'No, you don't,' Lorna agreed, dabbing beneath her eyes. 'But you work long hours and don't get to see enough of your child. Who's the one who's been to see her last three school plays? Me. Don't you think Neesha would prefer it to be you, Morgen?'

Already feeling guilty about that, and other similar situations when her mother had had to stand in for her because she was working, Morgen sighed heavily. 'Well, perhaps I can do something about that, at least.' She was remembering what Conall had said about realising that people had a life outside work—about it not being unreasonable to expect to be there for your child's school play.

The charismatic head of O'Brien and Stoughton Associates was a good man—Morgen instinctively sensed that to be true, even if his manner was a little on the brusque side. Perhaps while he was in the UK she could talk to him about cutting down some of her hours here and there, so that she could be more flexible where Neesha's needs were concerned? She'd certainly put in her fair share of overtime since Derek had had his problems. Surely the firm could pay her back by cutting her a little slack?

As soon as she was feeling better she resolved to ask Conall for a meeting. Protocol probably dictated that she go via Human Resources, but why do that when she had a God-given opportunity to talk to the head man direct?

'I'll talk to them at work,' she told her mother now. 'I'll see if I can change my hours round a bit, swap over to flexitime or something. Don't worry, I'll sort something out, I promise.'

'You know it's not because I don't want to look after Neesha, don't you? I love that little girl as much as any grandmother could love her grandchild. I just think that you and her deserve more time together as a family. She's growing up so fast, Morgen. I don't want you to miss all those special times, because they'll never come again. All I want is for you both to be happy.'

Sliding her arm around her mother's thin shoulders, Morgen pressed her close with tears in her eyes. 'I know that, Mum. I know that.'

'Morning!'

Immersed in deep conversation with Richard Akers, one of the senior associates, Conall did a double-take when Morgen's dark head appeared briefly round the door.

'Excuse me, Richard. I'll be back with you in a moment.'

Emerging into the outer office, he stared in amazement at Morgen's busy slender figure as she bustled around her desk, picking up mail, sifting through it, dropping some of it into her in tray and holding onto the rest. She was wearing a red fitted jacket over a white silk top and a knee-length black skirt, her lovely long hair tied back in a sleek ponytail with a slim red ribbon. Had she lost a little weight? Conall's blue eyes narrowed in concern, even though he was secretly fiercely glad to see her.

'And what, may I ask, are you doing back in the office

today? I thought we'd agreed you weren't coming back until after the weekend?'

'I was feeling fine this morning, so I thought I might as well come in. Shall I put some coffee on?'

'Forget the coffee,' Conall growled, acutely conscious of the fact that Richard Akers was waiting in his office, and that the man wasn't known for his patience, yet anxious to reassure himself that Morgen was well enough to be back at work. 'Stand still for a minute, will you?' Pushing his fingers through his hair, he glared at her.

He'd had a haircut, Morgen observed. That edge she'd noticed about him when she'd first met him was definitely back in evidence. As well as looking every inch the successful architect he was, from the top of his expensively cut hair to the tips of his stylish Italian loafers, the air around him seemed to bristle with the power he emanated—as if she were standing on a ley line. Her heart gave a nervous little jump.

'What's wrong?'

Her lower lip had trembled slightly and Conall honed in on it like radar. His whole body seemed to suddenly snap into super alertness. Why was it that work was the furthest thing from his mind when she was around? He'd seriously have to address that little problem if they were going to continue to work together in any sort of harmony.

'Nothing's wrong. I just want to establish that you're actually well enough to be here. What did the doctor say?'

'I didn't go to the doctor. I'm quite capable of judging for myself whether I'm feeling better or not. We give the medical profession far too much credence, in my opinion.'

'Well, you still look a little peaky to me.'

'I'll be fine when I get back into the swing of things.' Her gaze slid guiltily away.

To tell the truth she was still feeling a little under par, but that was surely to be expected after three days in bed and only two after that of being up and about. And she had no appetite to speak of, which was probably why she was looking a little peaky, as Conall had put it. But still, he didn't need to know that. Besides, Neesha was at school during the day, and Morgen had been going a little stir crazy cooped up in the house all by herself. Lorna had dropped by intermittently, of course, but Morgen had persuaded her that she was on the mend and really didn't need fussing over. Work seemed more appealing than it had for a long time. Nothing to do with the fact that Conall O'Brien was there, of course…

'We'll talk when my meeting with Richard Akers is finished.' Striding back to the door of Derek's office, Conall paused to give Morgen a final once-over. Satisfied she would last the day without doing herself some long-term damage, he smiled briefly. 'Don't overdo things, and, yes, I'd like some coffee when you've got a minute.'

'I'll see to it.'

Finding her chair before her legs gave way beneath her, Morgen put her hands to her burning cheeks and sighed. How was it possible for a totally innocent little smile from that man to reduce her to a quivering, shivering wreck? Even Simon, handsome as he undoubtedly was, had never been able to provoke such a violent response in her.

Being glad to be back at work because she needed to get out of the house and back into a routine was one thing—but being glad to be back because of a certain six-foot-two, broad-shouldered, gorgeous blue-eyed male who happened to be her boss was completely another. If she was going to survive the remainder of the time he was acting as stand-in for Derek Morgen was going to have to claw back some professional distance between them.

She was seriously going to have to forget the fact that Conall had rung her every day since she'd been ill at home—and not just to discuss work either. Those phone calls had done her self-esteem a power of good. Not that she'd ever dream of telling him that. All such a confession would accomplish would be to turn their relationship into something more personal than she could handle, and Morgen could not risk such an eventuality. Socially and professionally she and Conall were light years apart— just like she and Simon had been. Never again would she put herself in a position of not feeling good enough. When—and if—she ever contemplated a relationship in the future, she'd be looking for someone who was her equal on every level. Someone she could totally be herself with.

Picking up the morning's post, she tore open the first letter with her small silver knife with unnecessary zeal, then endeavoured to concentrate hard on reading the contents.

CHAPTER SEVEN

MUCH to Conall's growing frustration, he hardly found an opportunity to have a conversation with Morgen all day. There were meetings scheduled in his diary practically back to back, and on top of that he'd spent the afternoon at the Docklands site with Stephen Ritchie and the contract manager, dealing with a particularly sticky problem that had come up. By the time he arrived back at the office it was five forty-five, and Morgen was reaching for her raincoat.

She looked startled when he blew in through the door, and her cheeks went very pink. Conall grinned. He threw down his briefcase onto the nearest chair.

'Still here, Miss McKenzie?' he teased. 'If I didn't know better I'd think you were trying to impress the boss.'

'Seeing as I'm here most days until at least six or six-thirty, that would be an incorrect assumption on your part, *Mr* O'Brien.' Colouring again, Morgen hastily slid her arms into the sleeves of her navy blue raincoat. 'If you're intending on staying a bit I've left the percolator on simmer in your office. Don't forget to switch it off before you go. Well…have a good weekend. I'll see you on Monday.'

'Hey! Not so fast.' Snagging her wrist as she breezed past him, Conall shut the door behind them and manoeuvred her deftly against it.

She felt as if her heart was about to jump straight out of her chest, and her green eyes flew wide in alarm. He was too close—didn't he know that? Breaking all the rules of office protocol, as if he didn't give a damn. If someone should walk in right now he'd be— But how could they walk in when her back was against the door?

Her mind raced wildly as she tried not to notice those enviably long lashes of his, the beautiful sweeping cheek-bones and the bristly shadow of a beard starting to form around his hard jaw. As for his mouth—well, there was no good reason on earth why she should fantasise want-ing to kiss it, was there? Just because his lips looked firm and commanding and seemed to promise a sensuality that only a woman who'd lost the will to live wouldn't crave...that was a poor excuse for feeling her resolve crumble, wasn't it?

'What—what is it?'

'I want to see you tonight. Have dinner with me.'

'I can't.' Panic locked Morgen's throat. It was impos-sible...not to mention dicing with death. She was already experiencing the kind of urges and longings that could get her into big trouble, and if she wanted to make her life any more complicated then she was going about it in the right way.

'Why not?' Quirking a dark eyebrow, Conall loomed closer. Morgen gulped.

'Because—because I always spend Friday night with my daughter. We order in pizza and watch *Top of the Pops* together.'

'Sounds nice. What about tomorrow night?'

'I told you when we first met that I don't get involved with people from work. It's the one rule I don't break.' Tipping up her chin, Morgen challenged him to find something wrong with her reasoning. Surely even he could see the sense in her explanation? One day he might even thank her for it.

'Never been tempted? Even once?' Gravel-voiced, Conall ran his finger down the length of her nose, then drew the pad of his thumb gently round her plump lower lip, as if he were examining something quite exquisite and unique.

Heat assailed Morgen as if she was lying on a beach somewhere with the sun beating down. A slow trickle of perspiration slid inexorably down her back. 'Tempted' was the word. Knowing the soft gasp she heard had emanated from her own lips, she struggled to maintain control, to act sensibly. *Move away*, a small voice of caution in her head advised, and Morgen obediently slid her hand around Conall's wrist to push him away.

That was her first mistake. His flesh was warm and firm beneath her touch, and the fine dark hairs on the back of his hand felt like silk. The contact immobilised her. In desperation she raised her soft green eyes to his.

'I don't—I don't want to be tempted to do something I might regret. I don't want to lose my job when things get complicated—and, believe me, they will. Nothing good ever comes out of office romances, and I have a living to earn and a child to think of.'

'Do you always play safe?' Conall's brow puckered as if the idea really bothered him. 'It doesn't leave a lot of room for spontaneity, does it? Let down a few barriers, Morgen. I won't tell…I promise.'

His mouth was on hers before she could think another thought. Melting warmth throbbed through her body and her whole world suddenly existed only in those marvellously warm and pliant lips of his, expertly coaxing hers into a response that she was helpless to withhold any longer. His kiss was deeply stirring, and filled her with the most sensual longing she could imagine. Hot little tingles of delicious pleasure sizzled up and down her spine.

Welcoming his deeper exploration, Morgen's tongue danced with his, discovering erotic little sensations of velvet and fire with a hint of rich roast coffee, and her heartbeat throbbed like distant drums in her ears as her body found a natural home against the solid male hardness of his.

Breaking the kiss to press his lips against the side of her throat, Conall wound his fingers through her hair, tugging at the silky red ribbon that held her ponytail in place. He groaned when he freed the heavy dark velvet strands and anchored his hand possessively behind her head.

'I think wanting you has become an obsession with me,' he confessed huskily.

His words sent terror of a very particular kind barrelling into Morgen's heart. Simon had always been so disappointed with her sexual responses. Many times he'd accused her of lacking passion. Saying that as well as being his professional inferior, she was also useless in bed—another strike against her suitability as a wife. The memory robbed her of all her pleasure. Especially now, in this too intimate situation with Conall. Already they had gone too far, transgressed boundaries between the professional and personal that they shouldn't have crossed. Was it too late to put the brakes on? Morgen wondered in panic. Could she extricate herself from this wildly impossible attraction to her boss without causing either of them further embarrassment or difficulty?

'I'm sorry, Conall.' Breathing hard, she pushed him away, momentarily thankful for the fact that her hair had tumbled loose around her face because now she could partially hide behind it. 'You're a very attractive man, but I'm not interested in sex with you. I don't doubt that you could have any woman you set your sights on…you're rich and successful with no ties, and I'm a divorced single mother trying to make ends meet. I can't afford to throw away everything I've worked for in the heat of the moment. I have a child, Conall. I need to work to support us both. I need this job. Do you think I'd be so foolish as to jeopardise it for a one-night stand with my boss?'

'Why would you think for a second that your job would be under threat if you slept with me?'

'Because inevitably it would be. It would complicate things. How could it not? We'd see each other every day and it would be—it would be too distracting, for one thing. It would make it impossible for me to work here. I'm not the kind of woman who takes sex lightly, Conall. If you think I am then you've made another wrong assumption about me.'

'And what makes you think that all it would be between us is a one-night stand?' Frustrated and annoyed, Conall stepped back and yanked at his tie-knot.

Leaning against the door for support, Morgen stared. 'What are you saying? That you're looking for a relationship?'

He couldn't answer her truthfully right then, because he didn't know himself. He'd hardly thought beyond taking her to bed and fulfilling the fantasy that had gripped him since he'd first set eyes on her. Consumed by dreams of her that nightly took over his sleep, he wanted a release from such sweet torture. He knew his track record with women wasn't good, and that he had no experience of a long-term relationship. But right up till now it hadn't seriously bothered him. Not when 'short and sweet' had always been his motto. So *did* he want a relationship with this woman? Was he prepared to break one of his own major rules and commit to her long-term? She had a child to take care of. If he wanted Morgen, he would have to start considering her daughter too…

'No.' Answering for him, and smiling to hide her hurt, Morgen straightened and then bent to retrieve the slender red ribbon that lay curled on the floor at her feet. When she stood up again her pretty green eyes had a glaze in them that hadn't been there before. 'I didn't think so. Well, that's fine with me, because I'm not looking for a relationship either. I've already messed up royally once in my life; I'm not in a hurry to do it again. Goodnight, Conall. Enjoy your weekend. I will.'

He let her walk away, silently cursing himself because his wits had apparently deserted him. Why had he taken so long to answer her perfectly reasonable question? He wasn't some insensitive oaf. He should have known from the beginning that she wasn't the type of woman who was into brief sexual flings, even if he had jumped to the totally wrong conclusion when he'd first seen her. He'd quickly learned that she was conscientious and loyal and very clearly put her child first. That much was evident. Just the kind of candidate his mother would label 'marriage material.' He groaned. He didn't want to marry anyone. To Conall, 'long-term' meant more than four or five dates—not a lifetime commitment.

Not wanting to examine his feelings any further right now, he reached for the telephone on Morgen's perfectly tidy desk. As he dialled, he picked up a notepad that was lying there and idly flicked through it. On the first page he opened, he read: 'Saturday, buy Neesha new shoes, then take her to Tumble Drum 2 till 4.' Frowning, Conall tried to decipher what the last part meant as the ring tone purred in his ear.

'Hello?'

'Mother? It's Conall. Are you home tonight?'

'Conall! At last! I was wondering when you were going to get in touch. Of course I'm home. My bridge evening was last night. I'm just in the kitchen, preparing myself a meal. Why don't you come and join me?'

Knowing he'd put off seeing her for long enough, and partly glad of the opportunity to just kick back and relax with someone who knew all his little foibles as well as he knew them himself, Conall dropped the notepad he'd been handling to tap his fingers resignedly on the desktop.

'Okay. I'll see you in about an hour. I'll bring a bottle of wine.'

'Conall?'

'Yes, Mother?'

'Are you all right, dear? Your voice sounds a little strained.'

Sexual frustration, no doubt. Smiling ruefully, Conall sighed into the phone. 'I'm fine. Busy day, that's all.'

'Well, come over and put your feet up. It will be wonderful to have your company.'

As he let the receiver settle firmly back onto its rest Conall realised with surprise that he echoed the sentiment.

'So, you're enjoying being back home?' Victoria Kendall's crystal-blue eyes, so reminiscent of her son's, carefully considered the big man filling the armchair opposite her own.

Hearing the hope in her voice, Conall grimaced. He knew only too well where this conversation was probably leading. But he'd enjoyed a wonderful home-cooked dinner, and two generous glasses of good Chablis, and he was feeling predisposed to be kind. At least that was what he told himself as he replied.

'Yeah, I'm enjoying being back home. There are some things that I've missed for sure.'

'Then why don't you think about buying yourself a place in town? I know Teresa doesn't mind you staying at her flat, but it's not really practical if you're going to be working at the London office for any length of time, is it?'

'The thought had crossed my mind.'

In fact, on the drive over to his mother's Conall had thought of not much else…well, apart from Morgen, that was. But somehow buying a house and his feelings for the woman were inexplicably intertwined. Worrying.

'Seriously?' His mother beamed at him. 'So you really might think about working from the London office permanently?'

'I didn't say that.' Vaguely disgruntled, Conall got to his feet and paced the floor. 'There's a lot of things to consider before I make such a decision.' *Like, how soon can I tell them in New York that I'm transferring back to the UK?*

He wondered how Morgen would feel about that. When Derek returned to the fold she'd no longer be working directly for Conall, but what was to stop him promoting her? After all, he'd need an assistant of his own if he were to work at the London office permanently, wouldn't he? The idea shouldn't hold such ridiculous appeal but, God help him, it did. After that sexy knee-trembling kiss they'd shared earlier he was in no hurry to put an ocean between them any time soon. Even if she did think his motives were less than worthy.

'What's on your mind, son?'

Gently, Victoria came up behind him, the softly stirring classic scent she always wore drifting around him, bringing an unexpected memory of his childhood.

'I know something's bothering you. Call it a mother's intuition.'

'Nothing's bothering me. Least, nothing that a good night's sleep won't cure.'

Victoria put out her hand and touched his arm. 'It's a woman, isn't it?'

A mother's intuition? Next she'd be telling him she had a crystal ball.

'You're like a terrier with a bone, you know that?' But even though he scowled humour flashed in Conall's compelling blue eyes. Delighted, his mother didn't bother to hide her pleasure at the thought her son had finally met someone he was prepared to get serious about.

'Who is she? Where does she live? She must be a local girl if you're thinking of moving back here.'

'Don't jump to any conclusions. I'm not the settling-down type, as you well know.'

'Like father, like son, huh?' Victoria rolled her eyes and shook her head, but not before Conall saw the brief flash of hurt reflected there.

He admired and loved both his parents, but it was true that when it came to relationships he'd taken his lead from his father. Desmond O'Brien hadn't been able to resist playing the field even when he'd married. Eventually, worn down by her husband's philandering ways, Victoria had filed for divorce, but not without deep regret, Conall knew. In her heart she still carried a torch for the man—even now, when he was living on some tropical island thousands of miles away with a woman thirty-five years his junior.

'We're not going to fight, are we?' Guilty and irritated, Conall turned away.

Frustrated, Victoria 'hmmphed' and crossed her arms in front of her soft pink cashmere sweater. 'I know you don't like me drawing comparisons with your father, but just look at the way you conduct your relationships, will you? And I know you've avoided coming to visit me because you hate hearing me say it. I would have given that man everything, Conall…everything. And I did for a while. But he chose to throw it all back in my face with his tawdry little affairs with other women. Don't you want someone special in your life? Someone who'll commit to you and you only? How long do you intend playing the field just because you can? Where is the satisfaction in that? You're thirty-six years old now. About time you started thinking of marrying and having a family. I'm sixty next birthday and I don't want to be too old to enjoy my grandchildren.'

What would his mother think if Conall told her the woman he was crazy about already had a six-year-old daughter of her own? The thought came out of nowhere, and a surge of anger made him push it away again. He didn't want a permanent arrangement with Morgen. All he'd wanted from the very beginning was to get her into bed. That hadn't changed—no matter how different or sweet she was compared to the other women he'd known. She was a single mother and Conall knew nothing about children. Brief as his relationships were, he liked his women to think of him exclusively. He was far too selfish and egotistical to want to share her with her daughter.

'Let's change the subject, shall we?' Affecting a yawn, he dropped back down into the armchair he had recently vacated. 'Let's talk about *your* love-life for a change, Mother. A little bird told me that a certain good-looking widower who's joined your bridge club has been showing more than a passing interest in you lately.'

Blushing like a girl, Victoria fanned her suddenly warm cheeks. 'I'll give that sister of yours a piece of my mind when I see her next! "Good-looking widower" indeed!'

The place was hot, noisy and colourful, and Neesha's excitement at being taken to the Tumble Drum all but poured out of her as she stood jigging around next to her mother. Once they'd paid, and Neesha's name had been logged in the visitors' book, Morgen wound her way past plastic tables and chairs to the front, near where the climbing frames and soft play areas were situated. Then she pulled up a chair, sat down and began helping Neesha take off her shoes.

Two little girls, both in jeans and T-shirts, raced by holding hands and Morgen saw her daughter's pretty face light up. 'There's Chloe and Lily. They're both in my class! Can I go and play now, Mum? Can I?'

She was off like a rocket through the wooden swing gate before Morgen had a chance to steal a kiss and warn her to be careful. She had a mother's natural tendency to spot danger everywhere, but tried not to be too uptight about it and transfer her anxieties to Neesha. Finally, satisfied that Neesha had found her friends and was off climbing a rope ladder in the jungle area, Morgen left her things on the table and went to buy herself a much anticipated cup of tea from the cafeteria.

She'd enjoy having a few minutes to herself while Neesha played with her friends, and if her thoughts happened to stray back to yesterday and that kiss that Conall had floored her with, then it was only natural and who could blame her? Even if he'd made it perfectly clear that he only wanted to get her into bed and nothing more.

* * *

He was completely out of his depth. As he stood scanning the colourful chaos all around him Conall knew if his rich corporate friends could see him now they would swear he had taken leave of his senses. And without a doubt they would be right. To pursue a woman on a visit with her daughter to a children's indoor play arena just because he had the hots for her was not something he would normally ever have contemplated. But Conall had had to throw out his rule book where Morgen McKenzie was concerned, and now, God help him, he was definitely in uncharted territory. He'd even lied to the girl at the check-in desk just now to gain access, telling her that he was Morgen McKenzie's boyfriend, come to meet her and Neesha.

'Whoa! Steady!' His long legs almost buckled as a sturdy young boy suddenly careened into him out of no-where.

'Sorry, mister!' With an apologetic grin the boy was off, chasing after his friend before Conall had got his bearings back.

'They didn't warn me I'd be taking my life into my hands coming in here,' he muttered to himself as his gaze settled on the huge play area full of ropes and ladders, swings and slides.

Where were Morgen and her daughter? Calling at her house on the off-chance, he'd sent up a silent prayer of thanks when he'd found her mother in residence. Once Lorna McKenzie had established Conall was who he said he was, she'd helpfully given him directions to the Tumble Drum and had been only too eager to assure him that Morgen would be there at least until four o'clock.

Spying some empty tables near the front, he made his way towards them, wondering how parents coped with all the noise and the chaos but inwardly experiencing unexpected pleasure at the sight of so many delighted children clearly enjoying themselves. As he was about to sit down on one of the white plastic chairs Conall did a double take.

On a bouncy castle, amid several small girls and boys, was Morgen. Dressed in faded blue denims, belted round her shapely hips with a fringed suede belt, and a tight pink T-shirt that exposed her midriff, she was bouncing up and down with the children as if she was one of them, long dark hair flying and her cheeks flushed with heat. He also couldn't fail to notice that her exceptional breasts were bouncing nicely along with her. Heat slammed urgently into his groin and Conall felt his heart stall in his chest. Was there a sexier or more beautiful woman alive?

Feeling the chair behind his knees, he sank down slowly into it, content to just sit there and watch. What she'd say when she saw him he didn't know, but right now he didn't care. It was enough to just sit and admire the object of his desire at his leisure, and when he heard an appreciative comment from a father sitting behind him with another male friend Conall smiled to himself, knowing he wasn't the only one who was enjoying the impromptu floor show.

Still out of breath from her recent exertions, Morgen froze when she saw the big confident male lounging in one of the white plastic chairs just by the swing gate. In his classic-cut denim jeans, blue chambray shirt, boots and tan suede jacket, he stuck out in the sea of parents and children like a sore thumb—surely he'd be more at home in some trendy up-market wine bar than in a converted industrial unit that had been transformed into a children's play park? What on earth was he doing here? And how had he known where to find her?

Finally able to get her limbs to move once more, Morgen took her time reaching his table, her lips pursed and her green eyes flashing clear disapproval.

'Well, well, well. All this time and I never guessed you were a parent.'

'All this time and I never guessed you like to get so…' Conall's provocative gaze slid deliberately up and down her figure and back again to her face '…physical.'

Heat bloomed in Morgen's already flushed cheeks and throbbed right through her body down to her toes.

'What do you think you're doing here? And how did you know where to find me?' She sat down opposite him in a huff, and Conall had to force himself to peel his gaze away from the luscious shape of her breasts outlined by the tight-fitting T-shirt.

'I wanted to see you this weekend. I dropped by your house and spoke to your mother; she told me where to find you. We need to talk. Specifically, about what happened yesterday.'

'Yes, well, the whole point is that it should never have happened in the first place.' She stuck out her chin, daring him to argue with her. What was wrong with him, for goodness' sake? Couldn't he see that their association was fraught with pitfalls? He owned the firm she worked for! He moved in entirely different circles from her. He'd seen where she lived, so he could be under no illusion as to her personal circumstances. What was his game? Why was he pursuing her like this?

'I'm afraid I can't agree with you.' His deep frown drew his smooth brows together, and Morgen found herself wishing those unsettling blue eyes of his weren't quite so blue…then maybe she would have a chance of staying immune from his charm. Yeah, and the government would declare that everyone should work a three-day week with full pay…

'I'd really like us to see each other outside of work,' he told her.

'And when did you decide this? Yesterday you didn't seem very sure.' Folding her arms across the plastic table, Morgen leant forward a little as she asked the question. For a long moment Conall was simply bewitched by the beauty of her face.

'You know I'm very attracted to you. And if that little kiss we shared was anything to go by I'd stake a bet that you feel the same way about me. So let's knock down a few barriers, Morgen, and come clean. I want you. I want to spend some time with you, and not just in bed. I'd like to get to know you and your daughter better. Are you willing to give me that chance?'

CHAPTER EIGHT

'I DON'T take chances where my child is concerned. I can't afford to get involved with you, Conall, however fleetingly. My first priority is as a mother. I've tried the relationship thing and, apart from having Neesha, came off the worse for trying it.'

Feeling a sudden chill descend on her, Morgen leant back in her chair. Trying to sound as if she meant what she was saying was difficult when the man sitting opposite her was consuming her with his long slow gaze, making her stomach do cartwheels and stirring up feelings she wasn't sure she wanted stirred up.

'So what are you saying? You're never going to have a relationship with a man again?' Despite feeling frustrated with her reasoning, Conall couldn't help a rueful grin. 'That's like showing a kid the biggest box of chocolates in the shop and then telling him he can't have one.'

'For once in my life I'm putting me and Neesha first. Children need stability. Our lifestyle may not be ideal, but it works for us, and that's the way I like it.'

'So what happened between you and Neesha's father? I take it he's the one who made you so anti-men?'

Morgen was discomfited by the fact he made her sound as if she had a personal vendetta against his gender. 'I'm not anti-men. I just don't particularly want one in my life right now. I need all my energy just to do what I have to do. And I'd rather not talk about Simon, if you don't mind.'

To be perfectly truthful, Conall didn't particularly want

to talk about Morgen's ex-husband either. Whoever he was, and whatever he'd done, he'd made a big mistake letting Morgen go, as far as Conall was concerned. Colossal. Conall wasn't the marrying kind, but if he had made such a commitment to Morgen he was damn sure he would have done everything in his power to honour it—despite his mother's insistence on comparing him to his father.

His whole body went on alert every time he was near Morgen—his senses so consumed by her presence that all he could think about was his need to make her his. For the past week, every morning his first thoughts had been of her, and then at night there'd been the dreams... If this went on much longer without resolution he'd be investing a serious amount of cash in therapy.

'Well, let me buy you a cup of coffee at least.'

He started to get up from the table, but Morgen slid her hand across his to stop him. As soon as she touched him she cursed herself for being so stupid. The man was sexual dynamite and her heartbeat was off and running like a greyhound out of its trap. Their gazes met and locked, and helplessly Morgen's fingers curled around Conall's. The connection was so profound it shook her.

'Mummy, I need a drink!'

Guiltily she snatched her hand away as Neesha drew up breathlessly beside the table. Her dark hair clung to her forehead in tendrils and she looked excited and happy. Morgen felt a strong wave of love and pride suffuse her.

'So this must be the lovely Neesha?' Smiling broadly, Conall studied the beautiful child with interest. No need to wonder which parent she got her looks from. Neesha shyly dipped her gaze, then moved closer to her mother.

'Darling, this is Mr O'Brien—the man I'm working

for at the moment. He wanted to speak to me about something so he came to find us.'

'You can call me Conall,' he told her, his expression
somewhere between a frown and a smile, ridiculously
disappointed that Morgen had introduced him to her child
so formally. 'And isn't this a great place? They never
had anything like this when I was growing up.'

'Didn't they?' Her natural curiosity vying with her
shyness, Neesha stared interestedly at the man she'd seen
holding her mother's hand.

'We had parks and museums and stuff like that, of
course, but this must be great—especially when it's raining outside.'

'I can climb right to the top of that platform and swing
on that rope.'

Conall's gaze followed the direction of her finger, his
blue eyes widening in pretended amazement.

'Wow! That's a pretty big achievement for a little girl
like you.' He grinned. 'Seems like us boys have some
stiff competition in the playground these days.'

'Isn't that the truth?' Morgen's lips curved in a knowing little smile and her eyes glinted with amusement.

If he'd been standing next to a volcano about to erupt
Conall couldn't have got any hotter. He had to remind
himself exactly where he was, because his first instinct
at the sight of that heavenly smile was to haul her into
his arms and kiss her until his lips went numb. Not a
good idea, under the circumstances, he mused ruefully.
Not with Morgen's pretty little daughter studying him
intently, as if she was trying to fathom him out.

'Let me buy you a drink. What will it be?' Glad to
have a distraction other than Neesha's beautiful mother,
Conall reached into his jeans pocket for his wallet and
got to his feet.

'You don't have to do that.'

'I want to. Do you mind?'

Morgen gave a little shake of her head. 'No. She'll have some blackcurrant juice, please, and I wouldn't mind a cola. It's thirsty work getting in touch with your inner child, believe me.'

'If you promise to get in touch with your inner child one more time on that bouncy castle, just for me, I'll buy you as much cola as you can drink!' Chuckling out loud at the mortified look on Morgen's face, Conall made his way to the cafeteria.

Thinking of the friends he usually hung around with socially, he reflected that this visit to the Tumble Drum with Morgen and her daughter possibly beat anything he'd done with them hands down. In fact, he couldn't remember the last time he'd enjoyed himself more.

'Can I help you with that?'

Startled, Morgen glanced up from the plate she'd been rinsing and wondered what little devil of mischief had prompted her to invite her boss to dinner. Perhaps it was because she'd been so sure he would refuse? She'd been certain he had far better things to do on a Saturday night than spend it with her and Neesha, but yet again he had surprised her.

Turning up unexpectedly like that at the Tumble Drum was one thing, but agreeing to share pasta and meatballs in front of the TV, watching Neesha's video, was something she hadn't really been prepared for. Now, as Morgen watched his perfectly relaxed figure monopolising her narrow doorway, she wondered how long he would stay before telling her he had to go. It alarmed her intensely to realise she was in no hurry for him to leave.

'I'm just rinsing them to stack in the dishwasher,' she

explained, tucking her hair behind her ear and blushing slightly.

'It was a great meal. Thank you.'

A sexy dimple at the corner of his mouth, Conall smiled, and Morgen immediately wished he wouldn't. It was a weapon that never failed to miss its target, she was sure, and could probably entice her into things that could get her into all sorts of trouble. She was certain she wasn't the first female to fall for it either. How many women had been so expertly seduced by that gorgeous smile? Victoria Kendall, for instance...? And how had that lady felt when Conall hadn't shown up that night for dinner and sent her yellow roses instead? Morgen knew how she personally would feel. Crushed.

'You must be easy to please,' she quipped self-consciously. 'It was nothing special. But pasta and meat-balls are Neesha's favourite, I'm afraid.'

'Then your daughter has good taste. The movie was great too. I don't think I've enjoyed myself so much in a long time.'

'Really?' Drying her hands on a clean teatowel, Morgen leant back against the sink to face him. Every nerve in her body seemed to quiver at the very sight of him.

'Why look so surprised?'

'They're such simple pleasures.' Shrugging, she threw the teatowel down onto the drainer. 'A man like you must—'

'A man like me?'

To her alarm, Conall moved across the kitchen towards her. His glance was very direct and extremely potent. Beneath it, Morgen felt as if her spine had just melted like hot candle wax.

'Just what kind of man do you think I am, Morgen?'

'Not the kind of man who eats pasta and meatballs in the front of the TV with a six-year-old girl and her mother—not usually, anyway. You're probably much more used to five-star hotels and restaurants. You're the head of a premier firm of architects and it's obvious you move in very different circles to me.' Heat surged into her face and her eyelashes fluttered self-consciously downwards.

'And that bothers you?' Conall asked speculatively.

'You start out thinking those differences don't matter...' Her throat tightening, Morgen wished the ghosts of the past would leave her alone. Simon was history. She should have got over how he'd made her feel a long time ago. She shouldn't let feelings of inadequacy ruin her future...or her present. But that was easier said than done. 'But they do.' Her voice cracked. 'They do.'

'Not to me, they don't.' All of a sudden his big muscular body was very close—just a hair's breadth from her own, in fact. Morgen felt her breath hitch as those sensual blue eyes of his gazed hungrily down into her upturned face. 'You're a beautiful, intelligent woman, Morgen. Any man would be proud to know you. No matter where he came from or what he did. Don't you know that?'

Her lip trembled and she sank her teeth into it to quell it. Seeing the gesture, Conall tilted her chin towards him, then dropped a gently experimental kiss on her mouth. Morgen's eyelids automatically closed to absorb the full intensity of his touch. That featherlight kiss reverberated throughout her body like a small but deadly explosion, and set up such a longing inside that she trembled with the force of it. When she opened her eyes again Conall was studying her as if he was really seeing her for the first time. Almost as though her soul had been laid bare to him.

'Whatever it is you've got, Morgen McKenzie, you could bottle it and make a fortune.'

She placed her palm on his chest. Her hand looked very pale and slender, outlined by the sky-blue chambray of his shirt, but it was his heat that undid her. The warmth of his body seemed to burn right through the material.

'Do you say that to all your girlfriends?'

'I can honestly say I've never said that to another woman in my life. And I'm not seeing anyone else at the moment, if that's what you're asking.'

Morgen hesitated before asking the question that had been on her mind throughout the evening.

'What about Victoria Kendall? The woman you got me to send flowers to the other day?'

'What?' A wide smile breaking free, Conall looked heartbreakingly handsome as mirth lit up his eyes. 'Victoria Kendall is my mother.'

'Really?'

'She reverted back to her maiden name after she got divorced from my father.'

'Oh.' Relief flooded Morgen's insides. She wanted this man, but she wouldn't succumb to this tempestuous attraction if he were seeing somebody else. There were certain standards she very definitely wouldn't transgress.

'Happy now?'

'Happiness is such a fleeting thing. It doesn't last.'

'Then live for the moment. Hmm?' His arms sliding seductively round her waist, Conall wished fervently that he could banish every trace of sadness from her beautiful green eyes. He couldn't ever remember feeling that way about any other woman, and he'd dated many.

'So, Miss McKenzie…where do we go from here?'

It was difficult to think straight with the sudden rush of blood to her head. Her expression revealing her anxiety more candidly than she knew, Morgen glanced nervously up at Conall. 'Where do you want to go from here?'

Overwhelming her with another sexy smile, he tightened the strong arms around her waist a little. 'Want me to be frank with you?'

Morgen nodded.

'Your bed would be good.'

She dipped her gaze, her heartbeat going crazy. She knew she should do the sensible thing and say no, but she was suddenly tired of her enforced self-restraint. After six years of celibacy, her body ached for a man's attentions. And not just any man. Only *this* man would do...this dark-haired, blue-eyed giant who had 'heartbreak' written all over him. Right then, Morgen thought her heart was worth the risk.

'All right, then.'

He watched her tug her tight pink T-shirt over her head in the lamplight. Impatience overpowering him, he took it from her and threw it on the bed. The white lace cups of her uplift bra presented her beautiful curves like a sensual banquet, causing heat to flood Conall's body at the sight, making him immediately heavy and aroused. When Morgen reached for the snap on her jeans, his hand waylaid her and jerked her towards him.

His kiss was almost ruthless—all worthy intentions of taking things slowly helplessly abandoned in the heat of passion. Weaving his fingers through her long dark hair to anchor her more firmly to his embrace, Conall let his hand shape and mould her heavenly curves, thoughts of possessing that beautiful body making him a little crazy. He'd staked his claim and—barring acts of God—had no intention of letting her go any time soon. Feeling her tremble, Conall exulted in his manhood, his only desire to pleasure them both in a way that neither would forget in a hurry. He had been aching for her from the moment he'd set eyes on her, and if he'd nurtured any fantasies at all about his perfect woman, Morgen was the living, breathing manifestation of that fantasy.

Sliding his hands down her slim back, he deftly released the catch on her bra, sending up a silent prayer of thanks that he'd accomplished it without difficulty, then removed it completely. It too joined the discarded pink T-shirt on the bed. Her breasts were as lovely as he had known they would be. Voluptuous and womanly, with dusky nipples that just begged for his mouth to pleasure them. Making a little sound of need, Morgen wound her arms around Conall's neck, pressing those same luscious breasts deep against his chest.

'Let me finish undressing you,' he whispered huskily against her neck, and she willingly let him do as he desired, her skin quivering wherever he touched her. When she was naked, he laid her back on the bed and stripped off his own clothing.

Morgen reached out in wonder to caress the flat brown nipples on his magnificent chest, her fingers diverting to push through the springy dark hairs surrounding them. His body was amazing. Wide smooth shoulders, with enough rippling musculature to die for, that incredible chest tapering down to a hard flat stomach, lean hips and long, well muscled legs—now tangling with hers. She sucked in her breath, letting his kiss devour her, the hands that explored his powerful male body as eager to stroke and touch as his own were in pleasuring her.

Conall's movements were instinctive, yet skilled, and he seemed to know exactly where to touch her to elicit the utmost pleasure. He also knew the exact pressure to apply to make her gasp, and Morgen arched her back off the bed, truly believing she would lose her mind if he didn't possess her right now.

Above her in the lamplight, Conall stilled. His blue eyes seemed to burn into her heart with the intensity of his stare. 'I hate to be the voice of reason, but I really need to protect you.'

'Have you—? I mean, did you—?' It was a bit late in the day to be struck dumb with embarrassment, but Morgen was. How could she have been so mindless as not to think of it herself? Was she so eager to bring trouble crashing down on her head?

But Conall was reaching down to the end of the bed for his jeans, withdrawing the requisite protection from his pocket and sheathing himself adeptly. Morgen's heart slowed to beat at a more normal rate. Thank God. Thank God he'd had the foresight to be sensible before things had gone too far.

Moving above her, his big body covered hers, and she slid her long slender arms around his neck then, with a hungry sigh, eagerly received his kiss. As his mouth moved tormentingly over hers, taunting and teasing, nipping and caressing, Conall let one hand slip down her body to part her legs. Morgen had been ready for him practically from the moment he'd suggested they go to bed and, seeing no reason to postpone their mutual pleasure, Conall eased his way inside her, his satin length filling her until Morgen thought she might lose her mind with the intense gratification of it.

'Wrap your legs around me,' he ordered, and she needed no second bidding.

He drove into her hard, his hips grinding into hers as his mouth took possession of first one nipple then the other, nipping and suckling so that Morgen felt the deep primeval connection convulse like lightning from her breast to her womb. Then she was digging her fingernails into that strong muscular back, the tips of her fingers sliding on skin slippery with perspiration, holding on for dear life as he took her over the edge to an intensity of bliss she'd never experienced before. With a fierce groan that seemed to take him by surprise, he quickly joined her. The weight of his body drove her deep into the bed, but there was pleasure in that too, in being held captive in those big strong arms, feeling those slick hard muscles contract beneath her fingers.

Emboldened by his loving, Morgen pushed back his dark silky hair as he raised his head to look down at her, her heart almost stalling in her chest when he smiled.

'You are definitely the nicest thing that's happened to me in a long time, Miss McKenzie.'

'You're not so bad yourself, *Mr* O'Brien.'

'Just one question.'

'What's that?' Morgen gasped as his mouth temporarily captured one of her fingers and sucked on it.

'Why wasn't I informed that the woman of my dreams was working right under my nose, so to speak?'

'Hardly under your nose when you work in New York,' she reminded him, a smile raising one corner of her softly curving mouth.

'My mistake. My *big* mistake.' His voice husky with delight, Conall stole another deeply hungry kiss. When he raised his head again his expression was more serious. 'As soon as I can finalise things with the New York office I'm transferring back to London permanently. Did I tell you?'

Morgen stared. 'No. You didn't tell me. Can you do that?' Her brain racing with all the implications of Conall working permanently in London, she absent-mindedly traced a circle on his bicep.

'Sweetheart, I can do anything I damn well please, seeing as I own the firm.'

Something in Morgen's mind snapped to immediate attention. What was she thinking of—being so delighted that Conall was transferring back to London? They'd just made love, and it was wonderful, blissful, the best thing that had happened to her in ages, but she couldn't allow herself to get swept along with what was happening between herself and this man. He'd just delivered a very timely reminder of who he was, and she was under no illusion that they would enjoy more together than a brief passionate affair.

Men like Conall O'Brien did not commit to women like her—she only had to think of Simon to understand that—and Conall was not a man who had long meaningful relationships with women; that much she did know. Okay, so she'd heard it on the office grapevine, and usually she held no truck with gossip, but this was different, wasn't it? How could she ignore his past track record under the circumstances? This was her livelihood she was possibly playing with—hers and Neesha's. She couldn't afford to lose her job because she'd had sex with her boss. When Conall tired of Morgen—and she was certain he would—and moved on to the next attractive woman, where would she be then? She'd die if she had to see him every day at work, knowing she'd just been a temporary distraction to while the time away now and again.

'Why did you become an architect?' she asked him, hungry for anything—any snippet of information that she could use to point out the insurmountable differences between them—to tell him why a relationship between them just wouldn't work. Because, God help her, he'd stirred up a wild impossible longing inside her that just wouldn't be tamped down, despite her profound reservations on the wisdom of it.

'My father was an architect.' Kissing her fingers one by one, he smiled down into her eyes and made Morgen's heart melt. 'Even as a child I was fascinated by what he did. And when he used to drive me past the buildings he'd designed, and explain to me how he'd go about working on ideas, I was hooked. When he retired I'd already been working for him for about ten years, so I was happy to take over the reins. His partner James Stoughton had retired a year earlier, so I was really the logical choice.'

'And it didn't faze you? The responsibility of taking over your father's firm?'

Seeming amused by her question, Conall grinned. 'No. I knew I could do it. Why should it faze me?'

'You've obviously never been hampered by a lack of confidence. When did you become so sure?' Her hungry gaze roved his face, examining one impossibly handsome feature after another, finding no flaws. Even the tiny lines fanning out from beside his eyes and the deeper grooves bracketing his mouth were fascinatingly compelling to Morgen.

'I've never really thought about it.' Frowning at her, Conall cupped her face between his hands. 'Why so many questions, hmm?'

'We've just made love.' Lifting her shoulders, Morgen tried to ignore the sudden longing that was sweeping relentlessly through her body all over again. 'I hardly know anything about you. That doesn't seem right, somehow.'

'What does seem right is you and me together like this. When I've made love to you again you can ask me all the questions you want…deal?'

As his mouth hovered bare inches from hers, his passionate words intoxicating her and for the moment driving out her fears, Morgen was powerless to do anything else but agree. 'Deal,' she whispered as his lips descended.

CHAPTER NINE

FEELING like a schoolgirl creeping out of the dorm at midnight for a snack, when everyone else was fast asleep, Morgen pushed open the door of the airy modern office, almost dizzy with relief when she saw that she was clearly one of the first to arrive. All was quiet, save for the distant hum of recently switched-on computers down the hall, and in her personal domain—the domain she was sharing with Conall—everything was just as they'd left it on Friday night.

Quickly hanging up her coat, then unpacking her sandwiches and shoving them into a desk drawer, she planted herself on her chair and with her hands pressed up against her temples gave herself a few moments to recoup.

She'd slept with her boss, and it had been a magical never-to-be-forgotten experience, but today she had to work with the man and try to pretend it had never happened. Because when she'd woken on Sunday morning the space in the bed beside her had been ominously empty. No note, no 'see you later' kiss—nothing. He'd left without so much as a by your leave. Taken what he'd wanted and gone. For the sake of her own self-respect, she now had to keep a particularly cool head. Not let him see that his desertion in the early hours of the morning had left her hurt and confused, even though she'd guessed that that was probably the way it was going to be.

It was too late now for recriminations; that much was clear. The deed was done and she had to accept the consequences. At twenty-nine years old, a divorced woman

with a six-year-old child, Morgen was no wide-eyed innocent. She knew how things worked in the world of
office relationships. Basically, you got involved with a
colleague at your peril—because sooner or later your personal relationship would start to infringe on your work.
One of you would end up leaving if things turned sour—
or working life could turn into a nightmare.

Neither was a scenario that Morgen particularly
wanted to contemplate, so she would assure Conall that
she wasn't about to make any claims on him or make
him feel awkward in any way, and no doubt he would
breathe a grateful sigh of relief. All that talk about transferring permanently to London had clearly been just
that—talk. Most men would say what they thought a
woman wanted to hear after they'd made love.

Morgen sighed into her hands. If only he had been a
man of honour, as she'd hoped he'd be. Walking out on
her on Sunday morning had been pretty low. He didn't
deserve to get off scot-free just because sleeping with her
clearly meant nothing to him.

Still, it was pointless getting herself all worked up
about it. She couldn't see how it would serve her at all.
No: if she got even the smallest opportunity today, she'd
force herself to tell Conall that it was okay. He wouldn't
have to walk on eggshells around her, or feel he'd taken
advantage. She was a grown-up and she would act like
one. Whatever the fall-out from Saturday night, Morgen
told herself she'd handle it. Even if her heart ached because she'd believed him when he'd said that he wanted
to see her again, that he was transferring back to the
London office—that she was the nicest thing that had
happened to him in a long time.

Voices in the corridor made her sit up smartly and
reach for the pile of work in her in-tray, but her glance

gravitated automatically to the door as Conall swept into the office, closely followed by his colleague Richard Akers.

'Good morning, Miss McKenzie.'

The formality of his tone hardly surprised her, but it still hurt. Silently acknowledging it was probably for the best, Morgen felt her emotions thrown into further turmoil when she saw him wink conspiratorially, one corner of his mouth kicking up in the suggestion of a smile. Her heart did a cartwheel.

'Morning.' Addressing her response to both men, she wasn't surprised that Richard Akers barely glanced at her. Instead he preceded Conall into his office, his dour face unsmiling. The man had a reputation for being of a bit of a sourpuss, but for once Morgen didn't let it worry her. She was too busy walking on air because Conall had winked at her. Pathetic.

The meeting with Richard dragged on for two interminable hours, during which time Conall had to hand it to the man for surely being the champ at making mountains out of molehills. No wonder Derek Holden had been driven to drink if Richard had been his main point of contact day to day!

He'd started off the day feeling eager and optimistic, but now he felt distinctly ratty and in dire need of at least two large mugs of Morgen's excellent black coffee. Not to mention an even greater need to see the woman herself. That was if she was even speaking to him.

He could have kicked himself for leaving early on Sunday morning, without waking her up to say goodbye. If he'd wanted to give her the impression he was some kind of heartless lothario, playing fast and loose with her feelings, then no doubt he had succeeded. His actions had been almost automatic, he was ashamed to admit, but he'd also felt an absurd sense of panic that his life was suddenly taking a direction he wasn't sure he was ready for. He'd needed to walk and think, and then walk some more. Exercise always helped to get his head together, he found.

He'd spent the whole day trying to straighten out his thoughts. By the time evening had rolled around he'd pretty much made up his mind that he was going to give a relationship with Morgen a proper chance. Having reached that momentous decision, Conall had discovered an urgent need to ring her and let her know that Saturday night had surpassed all his expectations about making love with her. Unfortunately, Morgen hadn't been in when he rang, and even though he'd persisted late into the evening to try and contact her, her phone had just rung on, unanswered. It had irked him that she didn't even have an answer-machine to pick up a message, and he'd resolved to speak to her about that just as soon as he had the chance.

Consequently he'd spent the rest of Sunday wondering where she was all this time—and who with? He knew he was falling for her hard, but right now he had no intention whatsoever of pulling back. Instead he was absolutely resolved to see how things might pan out, for once in his life willing to let a relationship with a woman run its course without anticipating a break-up. *My, my…how the mighty are fallen.*

The sight that met his eyes when Conall stepped into the outer office had his mouth splitting in a grin from ear to ear. Morgen's very cute, very shapely rear end, hugged by her slim black skirt, was wriggling beneath her desk as she apparently searched for something.

'Need any help?'

The sound of Conall's deeply amused rich tones had Morgen bumping her head on the underside of her desk in shock. Feeling her face flame red, she moved out of harm's way and quickly rose to her feet.

Her dark hair was yet again escaping from the confines of its loose knot, drifting across her heated face in feathery wisps of silk. The desire that had seized Conall's body at the sight of her delightful derrière beneath the desk became almost painful.

'I was looking for my fountain pen.' Raising the slim gold pen aloft for him to view, before placing it back on the desk, Morgen struggled to conceal her embarrassment. Of all the undignified moments for him to walk in and find her... 'It was a present from Neesha and I didn't want to lose it.'

'I can understand that.' Moving in closer, Conall reached out to touch her hair.

Jerking back in surprise, Morgen wiped her palms down her skirt, then nervously tucked her blue silk blouse more securely into her waistband to cover her confusion.

'I was just about to come in and make you some coffee. I didn't get a chance earlier, when Richard Akers was with you.'

'Well thank God he's gone now.' Conall winced. 'That man could bore for England.'

Morgen tried to smile, but somehow her facial muscles wouldn't work. He overwhelmed her, that was the trouble—scattered her thoughts with just a glance. But she could hardly afford to have her wits scattered when he'd clearly demonstrated by leaving early on Sunday morning that she had just been a diversion for him...nothing more. Long years without knowing a man's touch had left her vulnerable to the first man she'd really been attracted to since Simon, and now she had to pay the price. If only he wouldn't stand there looking at her, with that sexy little smile of his playing havoc with her senses and driving her heart wild.

'Don't I warrant even the smallest kiss hello?' Unabashed, Conall closed the gap between them to slide his hands up her arms. Trembling with nerves, Morgen stole an anxious glance at the door.

'No. You don't. I got the message loud and clear on Sunday, when I woke up and found you gone, that what we had was just sex…a one-night stand. But don't worry, Conall, I'm not going to make things difficult for you. Some of us know how to act with a little dignity.'

'I know how it looked.' Flushing beneath his tan, he ruefully shook his head. 'But I had a lot of thinking to do about you and me.'

'And what brilliant conclusion did you come to?' She couldn't help it if her voice was scathing. His actions had made her feel cheap…*used* and cheap. Even if the sex had been great.

'I decided I want a chance at a proper relationship with you. That includes getting to know Neesha. I tried to ring you Sunday night and explain but you were out.'

'I had a headache. I unplugged the phone.' There was no thaw in the chilly tone of her voice.

Conall's steady blue gaze didn't waver. 'So? What do you think about what I just said?'

'What do I think?' Morgen pulled away from him, crossing her arms angrily across her chest. 'I think you're spinning me some kind of line, Conall. Do you know how cruel that is? You can sneer all you like at people like Derek, who care too much, but at least I don't think he'd ever consciously use anyone.'

'I didn't use you!'

'No?' She tilted her head to one side and her glance

was bitter. 'Then what do you call having sex with a woman and leaving her the next morning without so much as saying goodbye?'

At the realisation that things weren't going entirely the way he'd planned, Conall raked his fingers frustratedly through his hair. 'I've never had to pursue a woman in my life,' he admitted, gravel-voiced. 'The fact that I've done all the chasing now must surely tell you that it means something more than just sex? What other man would pursue you to a children's play park, for God's sake? I'm serious about us, Morgen. I want us to have a proper relationship. Why won't you believe me?'

'Because I don't trust you.' There. She'd said it. Funny how it didn't make her feel any better.

To give Conall his due, he did look crushed. So he was a good actor…a past master, no doubt, at manipulating women to get his own way. It wouldn't be hard, a man who looked as good as he did.

Suddenly Morgen felt very tired of all these games.

'I've got work to do.' She glanced edgily towards the door again, anxious to bring this awkwardness between them to an end, her heart thumping at the idea that their relationship was a 'no-go' after all. Something told her she wasn't going to get over the crushing disappointment that easily.

'So you're not going to give me a chance to put things right?'

'There's nothing to put right. We're both adults. I knew what I was doing as much as you. Forget about it. I know I will.'

'Liar.'

She found herself suddenly hauled hard up against his chest, and Morgen's senses were all at once consumed by him. Her mouth parted in a little inrush of breath as she saw the blue irises turn almost black, and felt his hands tighten commandingly on her waist. Where he'd all but crushed her against him her nipples ached, and tightened unbearably, already anticipating his caress, helplessly remembering his mouth on them, the heat, the longing, the way he'd made her feel…

'Do really think you can forget about me so easily?'

Lowering his head, Conall dropped a combustible little kiss at the juncture between her neck and her collarbone. The sizzling fall-out burned her all the way down to her toes and back again, and Morgen had to clamp her teeth down hard on her lip to stifle her groan.

'You're a ruthless man, Conall. Right up until now I never knew how ruthless.' Wrenching herself free from his embrace, she bumped into the desk and, flustered, picked up some papers on the pretext of studying them.

'Because I go after what I want?' he demanded, scowling.

Morgen felt the little prickle of perspiration on her brow and sucked in a deep breath. 'Because you don't care who you hurt in the process,' she said softly.

She was wrong, Conall thought bitterly. He was more than aware of the fact that he had hurt her with his apparently casual behaviour on Sunday, and desperately wanted to make amends. If he could turn back the clock and undo his leaving he would do it like a shot. He didn't want to lose this woman. He knew it would be his own fault if he did.

Blue eyes narrowing in concern, he straightened the cuffs on his shirt and blew out a breath. 'I don't want to hurt you, Morgen. If I acted like a jerk on Sunday it was because up until now I've not been entirely easy with the idea of commitment. But I don't want to let this chance with you slip away. What do you say we give things another go? Take it one day at a time, huh?'

He knew by her expression she was wrestling with the idea. Holding onto his breath, he was on tenterhooks as he waited for her answer.

'You weren't just using me?'

His heart thudded almost to a stop. 'I swear.'

'Don't think that I'm unaware of your reputation.'

His dark brows came together at that. 'Oh? And what reputation would that be?'

Uneasy at this new turn in the conversation, Morgen glanced nervously towards the door again. 'Look, Conall, I know you don't go in for long-standing relationships, and I'm not blaming you. I never expected... I mean, don't think that I'm going to make things awkward or difficult for you. What happened, happened. Perhaps it's for the best if we just put it behind us and be adult about this.'

His blue eyes turned wintry. 'I thought you didn't pay attention to gossip? You've obviously heard things that make you doubt my intentions, and you don't believe I can possibly be serious about us.'

'Right now it's hard to know what to believe.'

Again, Conall found he was cursing himself for walking out on her. Now he had his work cut out convincing her he wasn't the amoral bastard she obviously thought him to be.

'You're right. We need to talk properly. Now's not the time or place, but we need to do it soon. Can you get your mother to sit with Neesha tonight?'

Her smooth brow puckering, Morgen thought quickly. 'Probably. Yes...yes, I'm sure she wouldn't mind. But why?'

'I'm going to take you out to dinner so we can talk

like civilised adults, away from the office and away from the gossips. I'll pick you up about seven-thirty. That okay with you?'

Morgen nodded, her head in a whirl. 'Fine.'

'Good. In the meantime I'd be grateful if you could make some coffee…oh, and if you could get those notes transcribed from the board meeting last week and let me have a look at them, that would be good too.'

The door shut behind him with an ominous 'thunk', leaving Morgen staring down at the papers in her hand, wondering why she couldn't make head or tail of a single word.

At seven forty-five that evening, dressed in her one and only 'little black dress,' her make-up applied as perfectly as she could manage it, Morgen sat on her couch sipping anxiously at the small glass of dry white wine she'd poured herself. Okay, so he was late…it didn't mean he wasn't coming, did it?

The last thing he'd said to her before she'd left for the night was that he was going to drop in at the Docklands site for a brief meeting with the contractor before making his way home. He'd booked a table at some fancy restaurant in Chelsea for eight o'clock and had made her promise to be ready on time.

'Well, I'm ready, Mr O'Brien,' she said out loud into the silence. 'Where are you?'

When eight o'clock came and went, with still no sign of Conall, Morgen went resignedly into the kitchen and threw the remains of her half-drunk glass of wine into the sink. There was an awful ache in her heart, and her thoughts were tumbling over one another to be heard. Why hadn't he kept their date? Had he had second thoughts after what she had said this morning? Had he too come to the conclusion that a relationship between them was not such a great idea after all?

The pain of rejection hit her like a fist in her stomach. Hunching over the sink, she stared unseeingly into the enamel basin, fighting to keep the sting of tears at bay, vowing to stay strong even though her heart was breaking. All she could do was thank God things hadn't got too serious—at least Neesha hadn't grown to care for Conall and he wasn't yet a part of her life, as he might have been had things between him and Morgen progressed. *More's the pity...*

Finally, resigning herself to the inevitable, she wiped her eyes with the back of her hand, switched off the light, then got her jacket and car keys and drove to her mother's to fetch her daughter.

Arriving early the next morning, she was relieved to find no sign of Conall. Telling herself she was grateful for the breathing space, Morgen tried to distract her racing thoughts with work. She switched on her computer, logged on to the programme she used for minutes of meetings, then endeavoured to concentrate on the notes she'd transcribed yesterday but hadn't had the chance to type out.

Yesterday had turned into one of those days when things got steadily busier as the day wore on, and she hadn't been able to get the promised notes to Conall as he'd requested. Thinking about that, she fell into anxious speculation about the man himself. Where was he, and why hadn't he turned up for their date last night? He hadn't even had the decency to ring her and cancel. He'd let her down for the second time. She wouldn't give him another chance.

Chewing heavily down on her lip, Morgen read the

typed sentence on the monitor at least three times more without making the least bit of sense of it. Was this a foretaste of things to come? Was she destined to spend her future working days with this man feeling like some lovesick schoolgirl? Thrown into confusion when he was around, her stomach churning like crazy when he wasn't?

'Hi, Morgen.'

She glanced up as Julie hurried into the room, frowning when she saw her fellow PA looking flustered.

'What's up?'

'You haven't heard?'

'Heard what?'

'About what happened to Conall?'

Morgen's stomach lurched wildly. 'What are you talking about?'

'Last night at the Docklands site. He slipped on some scaffolding and fell. He spent the night in hospital with a cracked rib and a bad gash on his shoulder that needed twenty stitches.'

'Where is he now?' Pushing to her feet, Morgen stared anxiously at the blonde girl. Why hadn't someone informed her? But then, why should they? As far as everyone else knew she was only his temporary secretary. And to think she'd spent the whole of last night silently castigating him for not turning up for their date, when all the time he'd been lying injured in the hospital. Her stomach rolled over at the thought. She couldn't bear the idea of that strong, fit man in pain and alone in hospital.

Glancing curiously at Morgen, Julie flipped open the pad she was carrying and tore out a page. 'He's gone back home to his sister's flat in Highgate. He rang me on my mobile this morning and asked me to tell you to go over there. Here's the address. He's got some instructions for you.' She handed Morgen the torn-out page, and her blue eyes widened a little when the other woman all but snatched it out of her hand.

'Thanks, Julie. Can you take my messages? I'll phone you just as soon as I'm on my way back.'

Grabbing her coat and bag, Morgen hurried to the door.

'Give him our love.' Grinning sheepishly, Julie came up beside Morgen. 'Tell him all the girls in the office are wishing him better.'

'Sure.'

Not sure at all that she would tell him any such thing, Morgen hurried down the corridor to the lift.

He opened the door to her dressed in jeans and a light blue shirt opened halfway down, exposing the white bandaging across his chest. There were bruising shadows beneath his compelling blue eyes and his hair looked as if it hadn't seen a comb for days. But to Morgen's starved gaze he was everything she'd ever wanted in a man and more.

Striving to keep her voice natural, she endeavoured to smile. 'So this is what you get up to when I leave you alone? Being an architect these days is obviously a far riskier business than I imagined it was. I'll bet you didn't have the proper footwear on. Is that why you slipped? Last time we were there the place was a quagmire.'

She knew she was babbling, but it was so good to see him up and about when she'd dreaded seeing him in a far worse scenario. Right now she was operating on pure adrenaline alone. He could have been killed, for goodness' sake!

'I'm sorry about missing our date. I didn't have your phone number on me, or I would have got someone at the hospital to ring you.' Unusually subdued, Conall stepped back to let her enter.

His sister's flat clearly had all the comforts of home, with its beautiful parquet flooring, sumptuous furniture and up-to-the-minute entertainment console, but the thought of Conall lying on that big luxurious sofa alone and in pain brought all Morgen's maternal instincts rushing to the fore.

'It doesn't matter. What matters now is that you look after yourself. Are you in pain? Did they give you something to relieve it when you got home?' She was already taking off her coat, throwing it over a chair, then turning to examine Conall more closely, her heart skipping a beat when he glanced back at her and smiled.

When Conall's gaze fell on the woman he'd been thinking about all night, the dull throbbing pain in his ribs that had robbed him of even one hour's decent rest since it happened miraculously faded as if he'd been given a wonder drug. With her long dark hair flowing loosely over her shoulders, and her green eyes wide with concern, he thought she was the most beautiful creature he had ever laid eyes on. He didn't need hospitals or painkilling drugs—all he needed was Morgen. Just being in the same room with her made everything right.

Suddenly all the loose ends in his life seemed to slot into place and find a home. The thought was exhilarating, yet terrifying. When he'd walked out on her on Sunday morning and then faced her in the office yesterday, he really thought he'd blown it. And however ready she was to forgive him now, for not showing up last night to take her to dinner because he'd had an accident, he still had his doubts about her being equally magnanimous about his earlier transgression.

'I'm doing all right, all things considered. Do you

think you could make me some coffee? The kitchen's just through there.'

'Have you eaten? I could make you some breakfast too. Why don't you go back to the sofa and lie down?'

'I don't want to lie down. I want to talk to you. I'll come in the kitchen while you make the coffee.'

Morgen found him a chair, insisting he sit while she busied herself organising coffee and toast. Every now and then she glanced anxiously at the big man cautiously holding his ribs, and her stomach would lurch in fright. Popping some bread into the toaster, she turned and leant against the counter to speak to him directly.

'So how did it happen?'

'Exactly as you said.' Shrugging his massive shoulders like a naughty schoolboy, he grimaced. 'Wrong shoes, muddy surface—then I follow the contractor up some scaffolding and lose my footing. Lucky for me I was only a few feet off the ground. If I'd been up any higher it might have been curtains.'

'That's not funny.'

'No, it isn't.' Wincing, Conall tried to make light of the fact his ribs felt as if they'd been snapped in two and tied back together again with string.

'You should never take chances like that. Where was your mind?' Realising she was scolding him because she was angry he'd been so obviously careless with his own safety, Morgen turned back to the toaster and checked the bread.

From behind, Conall said quietly, 'I was thinking about you, Morgen. I'm beginning to think you've put some kind of spell on me.'

She moved across to the fridge, found the butter she'd been looking for and brought it back to the counter.

Standing on tiptoe to reach up to a high shelf for a mug, she pretended to make light of his statement.

'Don't be silly!'

'Dammit, woman! I'm being serious!'

Her heart pounding, Morgen swung round at the reprimand. She didn't miss the wince of pain that flashed in his electric blue eyes and she was stricken with remorse.

'Please, Conall, don't get yourself all worked up. I can see that you're hurting.'

He swore softly. 'I'm hurting more because you don't seem to be taking me seriously. Just because your husband played around with your feelings doesn't mean I will do the same. I mean what I say, Morgen. I want a relationship with you...a *serious* relationship.'

A wave of shock vibrated through him. Until that moment he hadn't known himself exactly what he wanted. It seemed that walking out on Morgen on Sunday after they had slept together had changed everything. It scared Conall to see how much he might have lost with his thoughtless behaviour...might still lose if he couldn't make her see he was in earnest.

She froze. 'It wouldn't work, Conall. You're who you are, and I'm—I'm—'

'You're...?' he prompted, not bothering to mask his irritation.

'I'm a secretary who works for your firm. I'm a single mother with all the responsibility that that entails, and I can't afford to have a relationship with you. It wouldn't be fair to Neesha.'

'And what about *your* needs, Morgen? What are you saying? That you're going to remain celibate for the next fifteen years, until Neesha is old enough to leave home and have a relationship of her own?'

'Much better to do that than screw her up with lots of different men coming in and out of my life.'

'Lots of different men?' Conall rose slowly up from his seat. A muscle twitched in his jaw. 'Haven't you been listening to anything I've been saying? You seem so sure that all I want from you is a few quick tumbles in bed and that's it. I know my track record with women hasn't been the stuff of romance novels, but then I hadn't met you, had I? I never wanted to commit to anybody before because I too was cynical about relationships lasting.

'It's the old story; I saw my parents' marriage disintegrate before my eyes and was furious when they didn't patch it up and get back together—even though the break-up came about because my father couldn't resist playing around. I thought it was better to play the field a little than get serious about anyone, because I saw how broken-hearted my mother was when my father was persistently unfaithful. I was hoping to save myself from that particular pain. Unfortunately my mother just sees my non-committal attitude towards women as a character trait I've inherited from my dad. Now I see that I was wrong to treat those relationships so lightly. I probably hurt at least a couple of those women I went out with because I wouldn't commit, and I can honestly say that I regret that. They deserved better.'

He walked to the door. 'Think about it, Morgen. Next week I'm flying out to New York for a few days to wind up some business there. When I get back I'd like to know if you and I are going to get together.'

'Get together?' Her expression startled, Morgen glanced at him with troubled green eyes. 'You mean—*live* together?'

'Not straight away, but that's the general idea. I know you're concerned about the effect it will have on Neesha, but I promise you I won't be rushing anything. I'd like us both to get to know each other better first. I'd like to get to know Neesha, and to give her the chance to get to know me. Then, when a little time has passed, I'll buy us a house here in London.'

Morgen smelt burning. She spun round just as the toast popped out of the toaster and saw that it was black. Her hands shaking, she threw the burnt slices into the swing bin in the recess by her feet, then raised her gaze to Conall's again. He was leaning against the doorjamb, looking worryingly pale.

'I'll make some fresh toast. Why don't you go and lie down on the sofa and I'll bring you in a nice cup of coffee? Please, Conall. I don't think you should really be up and about at all.'

'Have you been listening to me?' Grouchy and tired, he scowled.

Morgen's heart went out to him, but even so she was wary of falling for promises that he might not be able to keep. As he admitted, his track record with women wasn't good. Why should she be the exception to the rule?

'Of course I've been listening. And I promise I'll think about what you said. But right now your health and comfort is my primary concern.'

'Shame I didn't nab a spare nurse's uniform from the hospital. Seeing you dressed up in that, with black stockings and suspenders, would do my health and comfort a power of good!' Amused at her wide-eyed reaction, as well as mildly turned on by his own outrageous fantasy, Conall turned obediently back into the living room to stretch out on the sofa.

CHAPTER TEN

BY THE time Morgen returned to the living room, with the promised coffee and toast, Conall had fallen asleep. His long jean-clad legs stuck out past the arm of the sofa, his silky brown hair flopped boyishly across his brow and his features were relaxed at last in the guise of sleep. There was an uncharacteristic vulnerability about him that brought all Morgen's nurturing instincts rushing to the fore.

Leaving the coffee and toast on a side table, she dropped down a little wearily into a nearby armchair and settled her back against two embroidered cushions. Free to pursue her own thoughts at last, she couldn't avoid the truth that was now staring her straight in the face. She was in love with Conall. Head over heels, jump through hoops, crazy about the man.

When Julie had burst into the office this morning and told her what had happened to him last night, Morgen had known then her life would never be the same if she lost him. But whether she was ready to commit to him, as he professed he was ready and willing to commit to her, Morgen still didn't know. There just seemed to be too many obstacles against their relationship working out as far as she was concerned.

Conall was used to just thinking about himself. As far as she was aware, he'd enjoyed a high-octane, fast-living life in New York and, like Simon before him, obviously moved in very different social circles from Morgen. He'd already admitted he'd dated lots of other women—and

141

what if his mother was right? What if he was too much like his father to change? She didn't think she would be able to bear it if he were ever unfaithful to her even once—let alone several times!

And how could she risk her own and her daughter's happiness on a man who knew nothing of taking care of a family, who was unfamiliar with the demands that family made on you as well as all the mundane day-to-day domesticity that inevitably came with it? What if, after a few months, or even weeks, he started to feel trapped? Bored? The feelings he had for her would soon diminish to resentment. These things happened, and Morgen wasn't unaware of the possibility.

But oh, how she longed for him. Just knowing he was in the world made her feel better, while being with him filled her with a kind of restless excitement that wouldn't be subdued. Every cell in her body had become exquisitely sensitive to his presence, as if they were almost sharing the same breath. In bed they'd shared a passion that could light up the whole of London with its force, and Morgen had secretly basked in the power of her femininity, feeling beautiful and desired in his arms.

But what would happen when he introduced her to his friends as his former secretary? Would they look down their noses at her status? Would they think she had somehow tricked him into being with her? And what about his family? How would they react when they knew their handsome successful son had fallen for someone who worked in his office? Remembering how disdainful Simon's parents had been, Morgen shuddered. It would be a cold day in hell before she allowed anyone to make her feel so unworthy again.

Stirring in his sleep, Conall murmured something unintelligible, his sudden movement shaking Morgen out of her painful reverie. She got up, cleared away the coffee and now cold toast, and took them back into the kitchen. Plugging in the kettle, she resolved to make a cup of tea, then ring the office to see if there were any messages. As soon as Conall was awake again she would see what he needed her to do, then get back to the office just as soon as she could. If nothing else, the distance between them would maybe help her think a little straighter.

At four-thirty that afternoon, Conall rang Morgen at the office for the third time.

'Morgen?'

'Conall.' Picking up her pen, she doodled a smiley face on her shorthand pad, trying hard to ignore the fact that the sound of her racing heart was almost deafening her.

'I need you to come over here.'

'Why?' Her back straightening, her first thought was that he was in pain, or maybe needed a doctor.

'I want to see you before you go home.'

'Why?'

She heard him curse, and bit her lip to stop herself grinning.

'You ask too many questions, you know that?'

'It's part of my job. I'm trained to meet my boss's every need.'

'Now we're talking.' His voice turning gravelly, Conall chuckled down the phone. The sound had Morgen clamping her thighs together beneath her straight black skirt.

'Not *that* sort of need. Besides, you're injured. I wouldn't want to risk you hurting yourself any more than you're hurt already.'

'Sweetheart, even talking to you like this is hurting me like you can't imagine.'

Morgen imagined, and felt her body grow respondingly hot. 'If you really need to see me, I'll leave half an hour early and stop by on my way home. I can't be late tonight; I'm taking Neesha swimming.'

'I promise I won't keep you any longer than necessary. Just to see you for even five minutes would be good…and, Morgen?'

'Yes?'

'Make it soon, okay?'

'Okay.' She did another doodle of a face, and this time the smile was even wider.

There was coffee brewing when she arrived, and the delicious aroma filled the flat. Conall waited until Morgen had removed her coat, then insisted she sat down next to him on the sofa. She noticed that he'd shaved and was wearing cologne. It drifted under her nostrils every now and then, tying her senses into a straitjacket.

'Everything okay at the office?' he enquired.

Morgen nodded, trying desperately hard not to notice how long and fine his eyelashes were. 'Everything's fine. Nothing urgent to report.'

He'd obviously turned up the heating in the room, because it was almost too warm. The fact that the warmth might have more to do with Conall's well-muscled jean-clad thigh pressing up close to hers, she didn't dare dwell on. As it was, she was having trouble thinking straight around him.

'Are you still hurting?'

It was only when his blue eyes turned smokily dark that Morgen realised how easily her innocent enquiry could be misconstrued.

'Are you prepared for me to answer that?' His fingers trailed down the lapel of her jacket and slid deftly onto her silk blouse underneath, a mere half-inch from the swell of her breast.

'You've made some coffee. Shall I get us both a cup?' Jumping to her feet, Morgen escaped into the kitchen before he could answer. He followed her there, as she'd guessed he would.

'Don't you want me to touch you?' His handsome face was scowling, and there was frustration in his eyes. Morgen's blood slowed and thickened at the knowledge. Sweeping her gaze down his shirt, to the evidence of the white bandages wrapped around that wide muscular chest of his, she once again felt her heart squeeze at the idea he might really be hurting.

'Seriously, Conall, you need to be concentrating on taking care of your wounds, not worrying about whether I want you to touch me or n-not.' Blushing furiously, she turned away to pour the coffee into two mugs that were on the counter side by side in readiness. But she never got as far as reaching for the coffeepot.

Sure-footed, Conall stole up behind her, his warm breath teasing her hair. As Morgen tensed he deliberately anchored his hands either side of her hips, then nuzzled into the side of her neck with his lips. Morgen sagged against him at the contact—convinced she would surely melt into a puddle at his feet if he kept on touching her so intimately. Her limbs feeling like cooked spaghetti, she released a shaky sigh and let her head fall back against his chest.

'Ow!' His sudden groan told her he wasn't crying out in ecstasy. Mortified, she swung round to see him ruefully shaking his head, his hand lying cautiously against his chest.

'I hurt you! Oh, Conall, I'm sorry. I should have been more careful!'

'Shut up and kiss me.'

'What?'

'You heard me.'

Careful not to pull her close into his chest, Conall captured Morgen's face between his hands, then precisely and expertly lowered his mouth to hers. He'd anticipated her taste and her heat all day, had fantasised about it stretched out on the sofa until he'd had to get up and pace the room to calm himself down. But nothing could prepare him for the blinding sensuality of their kiss. Her response astounded and aroused him, making him lean deeper into the kiss, his tongue swirling around hers, his teeth nipping at her deliciously damp plump lower lip until he was so turned on he knew he had to call a halt before events overtook him. Reluctantly he disengaged contact, ruefully putting at least three feet of chequered vinyl flooring between them.

'They should prescribe you on the National Health. I can't tell you how much better I'm feeling after that.'

Her green eyes bewildered, Morgen stared. 'Why did you stop?'

'Why did I—? Sweetheart, I want you so badly I could take you right now over the kitchen table, but I don't suppose either of us would be satisfied with that, do you?' Gratified to see her blush, and giving a silent cheer that she clearly wanted him as much as he wanted her, Conall smiled. 'Besides, you've got to get back to Neesha. I don't want you to be late for your daughter. As soon as you can next get your mother to babysit, I want you to come over and stay the night with me. Cracked ribs or no cracked ribs—it won't stop me making love to you.'

'Won't it?' Her breathing still a little laboured, and

frustration eating into her bones, Morgen couldn't disguise the longing in her eyes.

'There are always ways and means. I'll while away the lonely hours dreaming some up.'

'Okay.'

She gave him a sweet smile, and her heart swelled with joy. The fact that in the middle of their passionate embrace Conall had stopped to think about Neesha made him rise tenfold in her estimation. Maybe there was hope for a relationship between them after all? She would nurture that hope like a fledgling seed that needed water and sun to bring it to life, and for once she would try not to be cynical about the possibility of success.

'I'll pour us some coffee. What are you doing about food tonight? I don't have time to cook you anything, but I could order you a take-away.'

'I've got it covered. My mother's coming over to cook me one of her specials. What can I tell you? She loves to cook.' And would spoil him rotten if he let her. For once Conall didn't feel irked at the thought.

'She sounds like a nice woman.'

'She is. Perhaps I'll introduce you some time soon?'

Morgen guessed how that would go. She captured the thought before it ran away with her down old roads paved with heartache.

'Hmm.'

Watching him walk away back into the living room, Morgen poured the coffee and tried to convince herself that Conall's mother would be nothing like the Vaughan-Smiths.

'He seems like a very nice young man,' Lorna McKenzie said approvingly as she sat down at the table to join her daughter and granddaughter for dinner. 'I'll be happy for

Neesha to stay over Saturday night, so you can go out on a date. It'll be good for you to have some free time to yourself.'

'Nana said we can make a chocolate cake for tea. Shall I save you some, Mummy?' Glancing up from a forkful of mashed potato, Neesha's pretty face was hopeful.

'You'd better, or else there'll be big trouble! You know it's my favourite.'

'Is it Conall you're going on a date with, Mummy?' the little girl wanted to know.

Feeling both sets of eyes from across the table settle on her with great interest, Morgen glanced from Neesha to her mother and back again. 'Yes. It is Conall I'm going on a date with.'

Dinner, then back to his sister's flat in Highgate to stay the night. Her stomach clenched tight at the thought.

'Good. I'll save him some chocolate cake too.'

Morgen felt her shoulders sag with relief. At least Neesha had not put up a protest about her mother going on a date with a man, and at least she had met Conall and seemed to like him.

Early days, Morgen...one step at a time, remember? The little voice inside that was always with her warned her to proceed with caution. Just because Conall seemed perfectly serious about them seeing each other that didn't mean that they were going to have a storybook ending. In a few days' time he was going to have to make that trip of his back to New York, for closure on his business there, and a few days could be a long time when a man was back on familiar territory, with all the same temptations that had been part of his life there before.

'Eat up, Morgen. Your dinner will get cold.' From across the table Lorna McKenzie's eyes narrowed at the pensive expression on her daughter's face. He seemed like a good man, this Conall O'Brien—even if she had met him only briefly. But then Simon had seemed like a good man too, and look how wrong she had been about him.

Staring at the plans on the drawing board in front of him, Conall made a slight adjustment to an area that had been particularly bothering him. Satisfied his correction was a distinct improvement, he stood back a little to get some perspective on it. A smarting pain in the area of his right shoulder just then made him wince a little, and he rotated his arm a couple of times in a bid to ease it.

His ribs were healing nicely, if still a little sore, but it was the gash on his shoulder that seemed to cause him the most discomfort. Every time it ached he was reminded how foolish he'd been to climb that scaffolding with ordinary shoes on, and in the mud too. It really wasn't like him to be so careless, but then his thoughts had been totally preoccupied with Morgen instead of on the job in hand.

The thought of her now made him realise that he wasn't looking forward to returning to New York at all. If someone else could have gone instead of him he would have arranged it like a shot. But Conall had business there only he could sort out, as well as an apartment he rented that he needed to return the keys on, and friends he obviously needed to say goodbye to. He'd already decided that when Derek Holden was back in the fray—providing, of course, that he'd got a grip on his addiction to drink—he was going to send him out to the New York office and a new life. It was probably just the challenge the man needed. At least it would help take his mind off all the problems he'd had at home.

And as soon as he himself got back from the States he

was going to look seriously into buying a house—a house he hoped that eventually Morgen and Neesha would come to share with him. But first he had to convince the lady that he was in earnest.

'Conall?'

Suddenly she was there, and Conall felt the ache in his shoulder miraculously recede.

'Come in and shut the door.'

'I only wanted to leave these letters with you to sign.' Her expression unsure, she hovered in the doorway, feeling suddenly ridiculously shy around him.

'Come in anyway. I want to talk.'

Finding herself waved into the comfy leather chair opposite Conall's desk, Morgen laid her hands in her lap and waited. To put her at ease, Conall decided to start off with a neutral subject.

'I've spoken to Derek at the clinic. I just wanted to let you know that he's doing fine. He had a few shaky days to start with, but apparently he's now determined to kick the booze and get back on track with his life.'

'That's great news!' Her pretty green eyes alight with pleasure, Morgen leaned happily towards the big man in the chair opposite. 'I knew he could do it!'

'It's early days yet, sweetheart. He's got four more weeks at the clinic, then we'll see—yes?'

'I don't doubt for a minute that he can do it.' More subdued, Morgen leant back in her seat. 'I know you probably saw him at his worst, but he's not the hopeless case you might think he is.'

'I never believed his case was hopeless, but addiction is a disease. Some can beat it; some can't.'

'Anyway, it's the best news. Thanks for telling me.'

Picking up a ballpoint pen from the blotter in front of him, Conall twirled it thoughtfully between his fingers.

'What would you say if I told you he probably wasn't coming back here to work?'

'Why?'

'Because I'm thinking of sending him to the New York office. A change of scene would most likely do him the power of good. New people, new challenges, a new life.'

'I can see how that might work,' Morgen agreed. 'Though I'll miss him, of course.'

'You'll be working for me instead.' His expression brooding, Conall directed his gaze straight at her. He saw the brief flicker of doubt in her eyes and couldn't prevent the sudden knot in his stomach. Did the prospect really bother her that much?

'Because I'm the head of the firm it will be a promotion, of course. More responsibility and more money...how does that sound?'

Under any other circumstances it would have sounded good, Morgen decided. But with her promise to both her mother and Neesha to somehow cut down her working hours so that she could spend more time with her daughter it was really the last thing she needed to hear. Not to mention the fact that she now had a highly personal relationship with Conall that she didn't feel was particularly conducive to their professional one.

It would only be a matter of time before the whole office found out that something was going on between Derek Holden's PA and Conall O'Brien. Potentially it could cause a great deal of resentment and make life even more difficult for her.

'I've been meaning to talk to you about this.'

'What, specifically?'

'Our working together.' Shifting uncomfortably in her seat, Morgen fiddled with a strand of her hair, then, leaving it alone, glanced directly at Conall. 'You must see that it wouldn't work on a permanent basis. Not when we're—we're seeing each other socially. Plus there's the fact that I was going to talk to you about the possibility of cutting down my hours anyway. I need to be there more for Neesha. I've been working full-time since she was a baby. She's growing up so fast, and I'll never have this time back. I've already missed things in her life that I won't get the opportunity of enjoying again. So, thanks for thinking of me, but I really think, all things considered, that you ought to give the job to someone else.'

Glowering, Conall got to his feet. 'Nobody else knows the work as well as you! I had that bubble-headed Julie working for me for those few days you were off sick, and she's an okay PA, but ask the woman to think on her feet and she dissolves into a puddle of girlish incompetence that just brings out the caveman in me!'

To her shock, Morgen burst out laughing. Green eyes brimming with mirth, she clutched her stomach to stop it from hurting. 'And you *don't* act the caveman with me?'

He frowned and sat down again, blue eyes troubled. 'Are you saying I'm difficult to work with?'

'No.' Morgen's voice was firm. 'I'm not saying that at all. I'm saying that if you're serious about us having a personal relationship then I can't work for you as well. You know it makes sense.'

'Trust me to find a woman who's got scruples as well as standards I can't help but admire.' He smiled then, and it was like standing in a pool of sunshine after a grey cloud had passed.

'So you'll look for someone else to fill the post?'

'Not until the next few weeks are up—until I see how Derek's doing. Then I'll give you my verdict. In the meantime I think we should look at how we can shorten your hours. I can see that it's important for you to spend more time with Neesha.'

'Thank you.' Expelling a long sigh of relief, Morgen got up from her chair to leave.

'Where are you going?' Conall demanded.

'I've got work to do.'

He stood up and came round the desk, a glint in his eye that Morgen was beginning to recognise.

'Not until you kiss me first.'

'Conall! Someone might walk in—'

He strode to the door, twisted the catch and locked it. A sexy grin making him look exceedingly wicked, he returned to a gaping-mouthed Morgen and grasped her firmly by the arms. 'Not now, they won't!'

CHAPTER ELEVEN

It was raining when they came out of the restaurant late on Saturday—not heavily, but a slow driving drizzle that made Morgen's dark hair look as if it was shrouded in a filmy net. Slipping his hand beneath her elbow, Conall jogged her to the car, opening the passenger door first to let her get comfortable before sliding in next to her in the driver's seat.

'You okay?' His blue eyes flashed concern as she pulled the collar of her coat up more securely round her ears. It was a particularly chilly evening, and as well as the rain the wind was raw.

'I'm fine. I'll soon warm up.'

All evening he'd gazed his fill of her, but it never seemed to be quite enough. They'd talked, sometimes skirting round more personal subjects to make polite chit-chat, both knowing there was a conversation of a more meaningful kind going on elsewhere in their minds and in their bodies.

In the flat, Conall had adjusted the lighting to low. The softer light welcomed them in from the cold, creating an atmosphere of warmth and intimacy, sending shivers of delicious anticipation scurrying down Morgen's spine. It was scary to want him so much, to need him. It had been a long time since she'd allowed herself to need a man, and Simon hadn't really needed her at all in the way she'd needed him. But Conall was different. They had a *connection*. It was stupid to deny it any longer.

Back at the restaurant Morgen had hardly been able to

do justice to their wonderful meal, because every time their glances had met a small firework display seemed to go off in her stomach, and two glasses of wine had consequently gone straight to her head. Now, as she slipped off her coat and handed it to him, she was alarmed to find that her legs were shaking, as if she'd just got off the Twister at the fairground.

Catching her shiver, Conall hesitated before taking care of her coat. 'Still cold?'

'No. It's lovely and warm in here.'

'Sit down. Make yourself comfortable. I'll get us both a drink.'

'No more alcohol, please.' Her smile was apologetic. 'More than two glasses of wine and I'll flake out for the night.'

'I'm glad you warned me.' His voice deeply sexy in timbre, he smiled in a way that lowered her resistance to zero and made her forget to breathe. On his way to the kitchen he arranged her coat and his jacket on the back of a large comfy armchair and asked her if she'd prefer coffee instead.

'Lovely.' Rubbing her arms in the blue and white silk dress she wore, Morgen dropped down onto the sofa and kicked off her shoes. Curling her stockinged toes into the deeply luxurious carpet, she gazed round at the various prints on the pale-coloured walls, peered closer at the family photographs lining the pine mantel, then allowed her gaze to wander over the eclectic *objets d'art* arranged on shelves and bookcases. Everything was tasteful and beautiful, but obviously said a lot more about Conall's sister than they did about him.

'Why don't you have a place of your own?'

On impulse, her feet took her into the kitchen, where Conall was arranging cups and saucers on a tray, then

pouring sugar from a cellophane packet into a little por-
celain bowl. He appeared quite at home with the ordinary
domestic tasks, and Morgen was equally content just to
watch him. That broad back of his was like an artist's
model's, with the suggestion of muscle rippling gently
beneath his shirt every time he moved, and her eyes
dipped appreciatively to his taut lean behind and those
long, long legs in smart tailored trousers.

'I was renting an apartment in Chelsea up until I left
for New York. To be frank, I never really felt the need
to have somewhere permanent. The last few years I've
been travelling a lot: America, Canada, Australia—what
was the point in having a place that would be empty most
of the time?'

'And now that you've decided to stay in the UK for a
while?'

He stopped what he was doing, turning round to lean
against the counter, his electric blue eyes a stunning contrast to the whiteness of his shirt. 'I'm thinking about
buying a house.'

'Not designing one?' Morgen knew that if she had the
enviable skills Conall possessed she would love to design
a house of her own.

'The thought had crossed my mind.'

Before she had time to think Conall was standing in
front of her, running his hands up her bare arms in her
silk dress, drowning her senses in his potently virile, not-
to-be-ignored maleness. 'But it depends on whether or
not I've got somebody special to share it with me.'

'You'll find someone.' Tearing her gaze away from the
sensual hunger simmering in his, Morgen focused instead
on the little pearlescent buttons on his shirt.

'I thought I already had.'

'You might want to think again.' Her voice low,

Morgen dragged her gaze back up to his, her heartbeat faltering and stumbling at the sheer masculine beauty of his face. 'I've got a daughter, remember? This isn't just about you and me. Have you any idea what it's like to be responsible for a child? You're used to being free and single, coming and going as you please. You can't do that when you have children. Your whole focus is on them, and you never stop worrying about them. That's what you'd be taking on, Conall, and somehow—' She broke away from him to stand in the doorway. 'Somehow I don't think you're ready for that.'

Taken by surprise, Conall was momentarily silenced. *Children...* He'd honestly not dedicated a lot of thought to being a father. Up until now he'd always relegated that possibility to the dim and distant future, convinced that when and if that time ever came he would be mature enough to handle it...unlike his own father.

Having Morgen and Neesha in his life would completely change the way he lived. He'd never even flat-shared before, let alone lived with a woman. There were a lot of new things he would have to get used to, but they weren't exactly things he *dreaded*, he found. It might be sort of nice, having two females about the place. And being able to wake up next to the woman of his dreams each morning was an incentive he couldn't ignore. No. Morgen was wrong about him. He was far more adaptable than she thought. If he wasn't, he wouldn't have decided to transfer back to the UK at the drop of a hat all because he was in love with someone, would he?

In love... The thought swirled over him like a mist, shrouding him in wonder. He felt excited, enthused. His heart stumbling over itself to get a rhythm, he smiled.

In the arsenal of advantages he already possessed, that

smile of his was the most explosive weapon of all, Morgen decided.

'You're wrong about me, Morgen. I want you and Neesha in my life. I want to take care of you both. I may not know much about taking care of kids, but I've always been quick to catch on, and I can learn as I go along, can't I? I won't let you down. If you think this is some kind of temporary whim on my part, then you really don't know me at all. I've never fallen for a woman so hard before.'

Urging Morgen away from the door, he captured her face between his hands. 'What do you say to us getting married?'

If a bomb had ripped through the ceiling just then Morgen couldn't have been more shocked. Dizzy for a moment, she glanced up into Conall's smiling blue eyes and lost the power of speech. *Marriage?* It wasn't something that she had imagined he would ever consider for one second. When he'd talked of buying a house, and sharing it with her and Neesha, Morgen had assumed he meant her to cohabit with him.

Sliding her hands up to cover his, she gently pulled them away. 'We've only known each other such a short time. We shouldn't rush into anything we might regret. I know you're probably thinking of me, but we don't have to get married in order to be together. I'll think about moving in with you eventually, but I really need more time.'

It wasn't the answer Conall wanted to hear. He'd astounded himself with his offer of marriage, and it hadn't been until the words were out of his mouth that he'd realised it was what he desired above all else. As far as he was concerned he'd found the person he wanted to share the rest of his life with, and he wasn't about to let her get away.

'I asked you to marry me because I'm in love with you, Morgen.'

Morgen bit her lip. 'Simon said he loved me too. Words like that come easy at the beginning of an affair, and you've already admitted your track record isn't good.'

Stunned, Conall cursed harshly beneath his breath and stepped away. 'So I'm to get no opportunity to redeem myself? It wasn't as if I hid anything from you about my past. I admitted I've never wanted to commit to anyone before, but I deeply resent being compared to your ex-husband. Can't you see that this is different?'

Morgen wanted to believe him, but she'd lost the ability to trust when Simon had walked out on her. How could she explain to Conall that she'd been absolutely terrified to find herself falling for him? That she couldn't help drawing comparisons with her relationship with Simon because when he'd walked out on her she'd hardly believed she would recover from such rejection. With his parents' disdain of her background, Morgen had lost all sense of self-esteem and worth. What if Conall's family treated her similarly?

'You saw where I live, Conall. You know I don't move in the same social circles as you, with monied, professional people. What are your friends going to think when they find out you've fallen for an ordinary secretary from South London, and a single mother to boot?'

'I can't believe any of this would even bother you! Yes, I've seen where you live, and what I saw was a home—not an empty shell fitted out with designer furniture, but a real home. Something I haven't had since I was a kid. And though it might be true to say that some of my friends inhabit the kind of social circles you hint at, and in the past I've been guilty of using my wealth and connections to my advantage, I personally don't give a damn about any of that stuff any more! I take people as I find them—no matter where they're from or what they do. I either like them or I don't, and the ones I don't like I leave well alone.'

Striding to the counter, he turned on a tap and splashed water into a glass tumbler. Taking a long drink, he turned back to broodingly consider Morgen on the other side of the kitchen.

'And for your information I don't give a damn what people think either way. This is you and me we're talking about. Either you want to be with me or you don't. When you get right down to it, that's the only thing that matters.'

Sucking in a deep breath, Morgen released it slowly. 'I do want to be with you,' she confessed quietly. 'Okay. I'll really think seriously about moving in with you, but I won't marry you.'

Meeting her gaze and recognising the hint of steel in the depths of soft green, Conall felt his chest constrict with deep disappointment and hurt. The first woman he'd ever asked to marry him and she'd turned him down. To say it wasn't a blow to his pride and his manhood would be a huge lie. Returning the glass of water to the counter, he slowly folded his arms across his chest.

'If you won't agree to marry me then I won't ask you to move in with me.'

'That's up to you.' Hot colour shading her cheekbones, and a brief flash of disbelief in her eyes, Morgen turned and walked away.

*   *   *

'I want you to phone that number and book me on a morning flight to New York tomorrow.'

Staring down at the sheet of paper Conall had slapped down on her desk, Morgen swallowed hard. Saturday hadn't turned out at all as they'd planned. After telling him she wasn't going to marry him things had gone steadily downhill. Instead of ending up in bed together, as both had eagerly anticipated, Morgen had found herself asking him to ring her a cab to take her home. Refusing to do any such thing, he'd insisted instead on driving her home himself.

To say the atmosphere between them had deteriorated to a morose silence simply didn't equate with the harsh reality. When he'd bade her goodbye at her door he hadn't even hesitated before striding away down the street back to his car. Morgen had let herself into a cold and lonely house, her mind numb, without even the companionship of her little daughter to help ease her heartache.

'I'll see to it right away.'

'I'll be gone for most of the week. If anything important comes up ring me direct. I've left you my home number as well.'

'Okay.'

Finally she allowed her gaze to lock with his. The anger she saw simmering there, reminding her of hot springs, made her catch her breath. She didn't want it to be like this between them, but how was she going to make things right? Marriage terrified her. Her divorce from Simon had been messy and acrimonious, and she'd vowed to never repeat the experience. She'd had to fight to get any support at all for her child. The thought of marrying Conall only for their union to end in bitter divorce was her worst nightmare. She couldn't do it, and she wouldn't want to make him ever regret knowing her.

'And I've got Richard Akers coming in for a one o'clock meeting. Organise some refreshments, will you?'

She nodded mutely, hating the terse, formal way he was addressing her. Was it going to be like this from now on, until she stopped working for him?

'I'll see to it.'

'I've no doubt you will, Morgen. You're nothing if not professional at your job.'

Before she had even a hope of unravelling his meaning his door had shut, leaving her staring at her computer screen as though she was in a trance.

He was staring out of the window again, his concentration shattered, his fury growing steadily by the minute. Why wouldn't she marry him? The way she'd acted when he'd asked, anyone would think he'd insulted her! She obviously didn't believe he was serious. What the hell had her ex done to her to make her so untrusting? The thought made Conall's gut clench. And what was all that about him moving in different social circles from her? He'd spent the whole of Saturday night and most of Sunday trying to fathom out why she seemed so perturbed about it. The fact was, he should have sat down and talked with her more. Instead he'd let his hurt and rejection—not to mention his anger—get the better of him, behaved like a sulky child who hadn't been able to get his own way. No wonder she'd wanted to go home in preference to sharing his bed!

That thought alone undid him. He'd been walking around as though the ground was covered in tin-tacks since he'd driven her home, sexual frustration almost making him lose his mind. Dammit, he couldn't even look at her without being so turned on it hurt. In contrast, when she turned those damnably soft wary green eyes of hers on him, she made him feel like the man who'd shot Bambi's mother. How to repair the damage before he took off to New York tomorrow? If he didn't at least try he'd spend the better part of a week being impossible to work with. It was a dead certainty his colleagues wouldn't appreciate the fact.

The buzzer sounded on his telephone. Irritably Conall barked into it. 'Yes!'

'I've got Victoria Kendall in Reception, asking to see you. Shall I bring her in?'

What the hell was his mother doing at the office? Drumming his fingers impatiently on the desk, Conall let loose a groan.

'All right. Go and get her.'

In the outer office, Morgen smoothed down her black skirt with nervous hands, straightened her jacket, glanced perfunctorily in the mirror on the wall above the filing cabinet, then walked with what she hoped was a confident air along the corridor and out into the plush reception area.

'Ms Kendall? I'm Morgen McKenzie—Mr O'Brien's assistant. If you'd like to come with me, I'll take you to him.'

Impeccably dressed, with light brown hair and blue eyes as dazzling as her son's, Victoria Kendall shook the younger woman's hand with a smile, then followed her into the corridor.

'I expect he's not best pleased to see me,' she confided chattily to a surprised Morgen. 'He probably thinks I'm going to give him another lecture, when all I want to do is take him to lunch. He hasn't got anything important booked, has he? I know I probably should have rung first but—well, I was in town and sort of acted on impulse.'

Immediately Morgen felt herself warm to this woman. Unexpectedly maternal, despite her glamorous appearance, Victoria Kendall was not what she'd anticipated she'd be. In contrast, Simon's mother had been so cold—supermarket freezers were warmer.

'He does have a one o'clock meeting, but I'm sure he could postpone it until later.'

Now, why had she said that? Conall—not to mention the pompous, self-important Richard Akers—would likely kill her.

'Well, that certainly sounds hopeful! Thank you, my dear.'

To Morgen's shock, Conall was waiting in the outer office, his pacing feet wearing a hole in the carpet as they entered.

'What's the problem, Mother? You know I'm busy.'

'What a greeting! I think I'll turn around and go home again.' Her expression offended, Victoria started to move back towards the door.

Appalled by his rudeness, Morgen jumped swiftly to the older woman's defence. 'Your mother came to invite you to lunch, Conall, and I really think you should go. I can easily postpone your meeting with Richard Akers until later on this afternoon.'

'Why should I do that? And who asked your opinion anyway? You know damn well I'm flying out to New York tomorrow, and I'm up to my ears in work!'

'Conall O'Brien! Since when did you forget the manners I raised you with?' Marching up to her tall, broad-shouldered giant of a son, Victoria stood in front of him and glared. 'Now, I want you to apologise to your secretary immediately! It's perfectly true I came to take you to lunch. She was only speaking up on my behalf.'

'I'm sorry, but the fact of the matter is I'm still too

busy to go to lunch with you, Mother. Why don't you let Morgen make you a cup of tea, and just relax for a few minutes before you set off home again?'

'Was that an apology? Did I miss something?' Victoria frowned at Conall, then at Morgen.

The exceptionally pretty young woman with the glossy dark hair had gone quite pink in the cheeks, she noticed. Also, her hands trembled slightly as she picked up some papers off the desk and shuffled them back into order. Interesting. Was this the woman her son had fallen for? She could easily see why. Her frown was quickly replaced by a dazzling smile that could only be matched by one of her son's.

'Even if you're madly busy there is never any call for rudeness,' she lightly scolded Conall. 'But if you really don't want me to treat you to lunch, perhaps Morgen would like to join me for a cup of tea and a chat instead? You can spare her for a little while, can't you?'

Like a police dog on the scent of a criminal, Conall wrinkled his brow in suspicion. 'Now, why on earth would you want to chat to my secretary?' he demanded irritably.

What could you possibly have in common with her? Morgen finished for him in her head.

That did it for her—that note of insulting disdain that had crept into his voice. It was the straw that broke the camel's back, as far as she was concerned. Throwing the sheaf of papers she had so carefully reassembled furiously down on the desk, so that they scattered everywhere, she turned to Conall with spitting green eyes, her chest heaving with the force of her anger at his insufferable condescension.

'Does making people feel small come naturally to you, or did you take lessons? Well, for your information, *Mr*

O'Brien, I've put up with your bad temper and ill manners all morning, and I'm not going to put up with them for a moment longer! See how well you can manage when I take the afternoon off!'

'Now, wait just a minute, here. I—'

She heard the fury in his voice and, grabbing up her bag, headed out of the door as fast as her legs would carry her. Not really knowing where she intended to go, she pushed open a nearby door as she heard him hurry after her, slipped inside and firmly locked it shut behind her. Inside the small dark room that housed the firm's stationery, Morgen tugged on a slim cord dangling from the ceiling and hefted a relieved sigh when the light came on.

'Morgen!'

Outside the room, Conall rattled the metal door handle back and forth. 'What the hell do you think you're playing at?'

'Stop bullying me! I don't want to talk to you. You can have my notice on your desk in the morning!'

In the silence that followed, the only sound she could hear was the thundering of her heart. A lone tear slid down her cheek, but she impatiently brushed it away. She wouldn't let him treat her like some kind of brainless minion! She just wouldn't! That had been Simon's trick, and Morgen was damned if she was going to let Conall replicate it.

'I'm flying to New York in the morning, remember?' The timbre of his voice was a low growl laced with pure frustration.

'So you are,' Morgen snapped. 'I hope you stay there and never come back!'

'You don't mean that.' He rattled the door handle one more time. 'Let me come in and talk to you.'

'I don't want to talk to you. There's nothing more to be said.'

'There's plenty to be said! Open the door, Morgen, and let me in. Please!'

Hitching her shoulder bag more firmly onto her shoulder, she settled her fingers warily round the key in the lock. 'I'll open the door, but I'm not going to talk to you, Conall, so don't think I am. As a matter of fact, I'm going straight home.'

His height and breadth of chest immediately swamped her as she turned the handle, and to her complete shock Morgen found herself hustled back into the tiny little room, with Conall glaring down at her and the door unceremoniously kicked shut behind him. All of a sudden her senses were completely overpowered by his maleness, and she backed up against some hardwood shelves, her breathing shallow and uneven. She could see the glint of sweat on his brow, and his face looked hard and unyielding in the harsh orange light of the room.

'What—what do you think you're doing?'

'I'm not moving from here until you talk to me.'

'Your mother's waiting in the office. Go back to her. I'll go for a walk and come back in an hour. I won't really hand in my notice. You know I need this job, and I—'

'What are you so frightened of, Morgen?' The sudden gentling in his tone caught her off guard. Biting her lip to stop herself from crying, Morgen exhaled a shuddering sigh.

'I'm not—I just don't want to talk about this. And I—I don't like the way you spoke to me in there…like—like I was somehow beneath you. Please move out of my way so I can go.'

'I'm sorry if that's how I made you feel.' He grimaced.

'I just let my frustration get the better of me. I didn't mean anything by it. Now, please answer my question. What are you so frightened of? I'm staying right where I am until you tell me.'

Everything about him was implacable. Like a hard granite wall that even a wrecking ball would have trouble dismantling. Morgen stole an anxious glance at his intense blue eyes and swallowed to try and ease the ache in her throat.

'I'm frightened of my feelings for you, if you must know! I don't want to want you so much, but I do. It makes me afraid, Conall. You're used to being in charge, giving orders. You're at the peak of your career—wealthy and successful. I was married to a man who had those attributes too, but he thought that made him so much better than me. Because he was a doctor and I was *just* a secretary. He belittled where I came from, where I'd gone to school—what my parents did for a living. He even thought he was better than our baby! His parents turned their backs on Neesha, do you know that? Their own grandchild! By the time our marriage ended I didn't have such a good opinion about myself. I don't ever want to feel like that again. Can you understand?'

At last, Conall could. Seeing tears glistening in her beautiful eyes made his chest hurt. Reaching out, he touched her face, stroked away the moisture on her delicately soft cheek, then dropped a butterfly kiss on her softly parted mouth.

'If I've ever made you feel less than you should, then I'm mortally sorry. I've always thought of you as my equal in every way. You put other women in the shade—you know that? With your beauty, your wit, your intelligence, the way you take care of your child. You're a remarkable person, Morgen. That's why I want you to be my wife.'

CHAPTER TWELVE

A LOUD rapping on the door startled them both.

'Hold that thought.' Smiling wryly, Conall bit back his obvious frustration.

'Conall? Are you in there with Morgen? Why don't you both come back into the office and I'll make you some coffee?'

'Mother.' Ruefully shaking his head, Conall tugged gently at Morgen's hand. 'She won't go away until she gets to the bottom of this, you know. She's not known in the family as "Columbo" for nothing. We'd better go back. I'm sorry if I've been like a bear with a sore head this morning. I had no right to take things out on you.'

Hardly trusting herself to speak, Morgen risked a brief wobbly smile.

'Apology accepted.'

'Do you have a photograph of Neesha I might see?' Sitting beside Morgen's desk, her hands curled around a steaming mug of coffee with a liberal helping of sugar, Victoria Kendall leaned forward with interest as Morgen delved into her bag.

When it came to her little girl—her pride and joy—Morgen had no trouble in producing pictures on request. She had a generous selection in her wallet that she always carried around with her. The fact that Conall's mother professed to be genuinely interested in her child and didn't seem in any hurry to leave made the younger woman warm to her even more.

'Oh, she's beautiful!' Victoria exclaimed, glancing up as Conall came back into the room. Smiling, he went behind his mother's chair and peered over her shoulder at the colour photograph in her hand.

'Just like her mother,' he remarked.

The comment tugged powerfully at Morgen's heart and made her feel as if she was suddenly falling into space. Her gaze touched Conall's and a burst of warmth exploded inside her.

Noticing the longing in that glance in her son's direction, Victoria Kendall smiled inwardly with a feeling of great satisfaction. She'd waited a long time for her handsome son to fall in love, and right now, studying the lovely brunette who sat before her, wearing her heart in her eyes, she prayed he really had found the one. His soul mate.

The only thing that slightly perturbed Victoria was that she sensed Morgen might need some little persuasion in the right direction. Being a single mum, she was obviously concerned for the wellbeing of her child, and wouldn't want to rush into anything unless she was absolutely sure that Conall was one hundred per cent committed to them both. No doubt Conall's reputation with the ladies had preceded him, and it was understandable that Morgen should be a little reticent under the circumstances. But Conall wasn't really a carbon copy of his father. He might have enjoyed the ladies, but he hadn't made any promises he couldn't keep, and Victoria had always felt in her heart that when he eventually found the right woman he would stay completely loyal to her.

When he made up his mind about something he stuck to it, and Victoria didn't doubt that her son would stick by Morgen through thick and thin. Therefore she resolved

to do all that she could to help matters along to a satisfactory conclusion. What mother worth her salt wouldn't?

Handing Neesha's picture back to her, Victoria reached
up and slid her hand across Conall's. 'It's not too late to
take Morgen to lunch, you know, darling.'

Shaking his head with genuine regret, Conall sighed.
'It's a nice idea, Mother, but I really, honestly cannot
spare the time. When I get back from New York, in a
few days' time, I promise the first thing I'll do is take
Morgen out to lunch. Does that make you feel better?'

'I know you'll do the right thing, son.' Confidently,
Victoria smiled.

Morgen worked her socks off to make sure Conall left a
clean slate when he went to New York. At half past six
that same evening she finally switched off her computer,
slipped on her jacket, from where it had hung on the back
of her chair, stood up and stretched her arms wide.
Glancing nervously at the light showing under his door,
she patted her hand against her mouth to capture a yawn,
then stood there wondering what to do next.

She was going to have to go in and tell him she was
going home. It wouldn't be easy, knowing she wasn't
going to see him for at least the next four days, maybe
more. The ache in her heart was deep and irrevocable—
like a physical pain. Why hadn't she given him an answer
when he'd said he wanted her to be his wife earlier? He'd
asked her to 'hold that thought', but would he think because she hadn't brought the subject up again she still
wasn't interested? As far as she was concerned he had
given her the assurance she sought. He didn't care where
she lived or what her background was; he'd told her he
thought of her as his equal.

Oh, God...please don't let him change his mind.

*   *   *

Pinching the bridge of his nose, then rubbing the tiredness away from his eyes, Conall welcomed the distraction the knock on the door brought. Feeling a little frisson of heat zigzag through his body when he saw who his visitor was, he rose from his seat, yanked off his expensive silk tie and threw it carelessly onto the desk.

'I just came to tell you that I'm going home now.'

Her tentative smile slipped away from her lips, as if she was unsure about letting her guard down. The brief tantalising glimpse seduced Conall's already aroused senses like satin sheets against bare skin, and anticipation seeped into his blood and quietly simmered. Dropping his gaze to the vee of her blouse beneath her opened jacket, and the pink cotton that lovingly caressed her comely curves, he felt heat explode inside him, obliterating any last vestiges of fatigue he might be feeling.

'Come in and shut the door,' he told her.

She didn't protest, as he'd thought she might. Having done what he asked, Morgen moved towards him, carefully looping her hair behind her ear, her interested glance on the architectural plans spread out before him on the desk, the blue of his silk tie a vivid splash of colour against the black and white of the drawings.

'Not finished yet?' she asked.

'Sweetheart, I've done all I'm going to do for tonight.' Without further ado Conall rescued his tie, pushed it deep into his trouser pocket, then rolled up the drawings and stashed them by the filing cabinet behind him. His desk clear, he let loose a heartstopping grin that knocked her sideways.

'Anyway, I hope you have a good trip. I'll keep you posted if anything important comes up.'

'Ever the efficient assistant.'

'I try to do my best.'

'I wish you'd said you aim to please.'

'I do.' Puzzled at his meaning, Morgen self-consciously tugged the sides of her jacket across her blouse.

'Then if that's true, please don't do that.'

'What?'

His blue eyes slumberously dark, as if he had just woken from the most languid sleep, Conall rocked her world with the shocking sensuality of his hot direct glance.

'Hide your body from me.'

'I'm…I'm not.' Dropping her hands to her sides, Morgen dragged her gaze away from his before she went up in flames. All of a sudden her limbs felt curiously slow and heavy, as if she was in one of those dreams where she wanted to run but couldn't. Only this time she had no intention of running. Forcing herself to look at Conall again, she unwittingly moistened her lips with her tongue.

For Conall, on the receiving end of that innocently erotic little gesture, desire was swift and merciless in its retribution. All his muscles bunched in an effort to maintain control.

'I need you to take something down for me, Miss McKenzie.' There was a husky catch in his voice that completely undid Morgen.

'I thought you'd finished for the night…Mr O'Brien.'

'There's something I've been wanting to do all day. Do you mind?'

She moved slowly round to where he stood, and her breath stalled in her lungs when he guided her gently back onto the desk, then slipped off her shoes. His touch was warm and sure, and Morgen felt like a cat stretched out on a window ledge, waiting for the sun to come up and caress her with its rays.

Truth to tell, she'd been wanting this all day too. It had been torment to watch him go about his business without being able to touch him. Ever the cool, polished professional, his slightly aloof office persona had tantalised her, playing on her nerves until she'd thought she might scream if she didn't get some relief soon. Now there was no intention whatsoever in her mind to deny herself this sublime intoxication of the senses. She had been craving nothing else since he had stormed into her life, accusing her of not doing her job properly.

Though her natural inclination was to wrap her arms around his waist, he moved his head, indicating that she stay where she was, smiled wickedly, then eased down her pantyhose and underwear with a shockingly erotic artistry that made her head spin. She was immediately damp and flushed. A wave of love consumed her, and carried her along on its crest.

'You're wearing too many clothes,' he scolded softly, but before Morgen's fingers could get to her blouse buttons he captured her hand, the corners of his mouth hitching up in one of the sexiest traffic-stopping smiles known to woman. 'Let me.'

Pushing aside the freed material, his mouth captured a breast beneath the thin silk of her lacy black bra, his heat scalding her nipple, making it surge into a tight peak and shamelessly arch towards him for more. Knowing what she needed, what she craved, he moved to her other breast to lavish the same treatment. The connection deep inside Morgen's womb was electrifying.

Excitement consuming her, she gasped as his hand slid up the inside of her thigh, stroking and kneading the soft smooth flesh he found there, while Morgen drove her fingers through the thick short strands of his hair and hungrily sought his mouth. When their lips met, hotly, desperately, passion ignited like an inferno, leaving them gasping and trembling in its wake.

'Conall, please.'

'What is it, Miss McKenzie?' he teased, his voice a low, hungry rasp against her ear.

'You know.' Twisting her head, she claimed his mouth in another mind-blowing kiss, her tongue sliding in and out of his sensual heat, feeling the rasp of his unshaven jaw abrade the sensitive skin on her chin, her cheek—his male scent invading her everywhere so that her own body felt like a living extension of his.

'Tell me.'

'Love me...please love me.'

He gazed into eyes that reminded him of melting mint-green ice, framed with velvet black lashes. Her lush pink mouth was damp and slightly pouting from the passion of their kisses, and every other woman he'd ever felt desire for melted into oblivion, as though they'd never existed. On fire for her practically since the moment she'd walked into the room, Conall was inside her before he had his next thought. Her heat surrounding him, he felt her muscles flex and contract around him, all his desire, all his simmering frustration and longing for her finally crowning in his deep and voracious possession.

Guiding her hips towards him, then burying her face in the hard strength of his massive chest, Morgen gladly accepted his passionate, urgent thrusts, her heartbeat galloping in her breast, the need in her spiralling swiftly into such profound tension that something had to give soon. It did. The walls of her muscles contracting almost violently around him, she gasped aloud, her nails biting into his back beneath the thin material of his shirt as one final thrust resulted in his own powerful climax and his liquid heat spilling deep into her womb.

Overcome by their profound connection, Morgen lifted her head to gaze, stunned, into his eyes. The love she saw reflected there amazed and astounded her. Reaching up, she pressed a tender lover's kiss on the side of his mouth, then another, then another. Still locked together, her skirt up around her waist and her legs around Conall's hips, Morgen allowed herself to fully experience the sense of delicious wickedness that had invaded her for a little while longer. They'd made love…on Derek's desk, for goodness' sake! She'd never be able to look at that desk again without remembering.

'Have I told you how gorgeous I think you are, Miss McKenzie?' His hand sliding between them onto her milk-smooth white breast, Conall rubbed and squeezed her nipple inside her bra, making Morgen feel that heavy drugging sensation in her limbs all over again.

'As a matter of fact, I don't think you have.'

'Well, you are—and I'm crazy about you. That's why I want to marry you.'

Before she realised what he intended, he'd reached round to her back, tugged her blouse out of her skirt and unhooked her bra. Her breasts spilled freely and unashamedly into his hands as he shoved the material out of the way and lowered his mouth to each one in turn.

'What about living for the—the moment…hmm?'

But her barely gasped words were stolen away by what he was doing to her body. Tipping back her head, Morgen was swept away by the fierce ache that ruthlessly took hold of her, determined to give Conall loving like he'd never known before, so that there wouldn't be one single minute while he was in New York that he wouldn't think of her and long to be home.

* * *

'What's this? You doing a little freelancing on the side, Con?'

Mike Brabourn, fellow architect and friend, directed a trained eye over the plans on Conall's desk, then waited interestedly for his reply.

'You could say that.'

Inexplicably irked by his friend's curiosity, Conall swiftly rolled up the plans and slid them expertly back into their cardboard tube. Picking up a pen, he tapped it on the blotter in front of him.

Mike frowned. 'So what gives? You still haven't told me the real reason you're relocating back to England—and don't try to pull the wool over my eyes either. I know when you're being economical with the truth—I've known you too long, remember?'

Conall remembered. He hadn't shared the news that he'd fallen in love and planned to get married with anyone but Victoria—and even she didn't know about the marriage part yet. He didn't feel it was right, telling her his intentions when he still hadn't had a proper answer from Morgen. They'd had never-to-be-forgotten sex on the desk in his office, but he still hadn't got her to agree to marry him. She'd tantalised him with the promise that as soon as he got back from New York he could have his answer.

So far, Conall had endured three agonisingly sleepless nights, wondering if she was going to turn him down after all. The traffic noise of one of the busiest cities in the world hadn't helped either. He'd found himself lying awake in his plush high-rise apartment, dreaming of a place of his own in the English countryside, with Morgen and Neesha and maybe a puppy for Neesha to play with. The idea had made his imagination catch fire, and finally he'd been motivated enough to get up in the middle of the night and sketch out some plans for a house he suddenly wanted to build...

'Conall?' Mike waved a hand in front of his face, then stopped abruptly. 'The penny's just dropped. It's a woman, isn't it? You've gone and fallen for someone, haven't you?'

Pushing to his feet, Conall dropped his hands to his hips and grinned. 'Is it so obvious?'

'What else would have you staring off into space like you've been drugged? Right, spill the beans. Who is she? What's her name and—more to the point—what does she look like? Is she a babe?'

Conall dug his hands deep into his pockets, then walked slowly across to the huge plate-glass window. Staring out at the teeming city below, with its traffic fumes and furious honking drivers, he sucked in a deep breath. 'She's someone who works in the London office. Her name is Morgen and she looks like a raven-haired angel. Oh, and she's definitely a babe. Satisfied?'

'I would be if I was so lucky to meet such a dream!' Rubbing his hand over his thinning brown hair, Mike shook his head in wonder. 'The women of New York are going to go into mourning when they find out, you realise that?'

'Can't play the field for ever.'

'No,' Mike agreed, 'but a man can have a damn good time trying! You sure she's the one?'

Conall had no hesitation in replying. 'She's the one, all right. From now on, my friend...I'm a one-woman man.'

His flight was delayed. Delayed! Morgen stared up at the blinking green digits on the Arrivals board and bitterly swallowed down her rising frustration.

Six days he'd been gone, and she hadn't had a decent night's sleep since. She'd been prowling the kitchen in the early hours of the morning, making tea, listening to the radio, painting her nails—anything to try and divert her thoughts from thinking about Conall. She'd known she had it bad when she'd put the jelly mould she'd filled with Neesha's favourite raspberry jelly in the oven instead of the fridge, and thrown out her morning's post with the rubbish. And only this afternoon her poor mother had told her to make an appointment with the doctor because she was convinced she was coming down with something viral!

Pushing her fingers through her hair, Morgen sighed dramatically, then reluctantly marched over to a row of chairs and sat down. On one side of her was a youth dressed in a shiny tracksuit and a baseball cap, listening to music on his headphones, and on the other a middle-aged blonde woman in tailored black trousers and a boxy red jacket. Her long red nails fascinated Morgen as, momentarily distracted, she watched them dip in and out of her brown suede handbag for her make-up mirror, then her lipstick.

Catching her glance, the woman smiled. Her make-up was picture-perfect, and her teeth very even and white. It made Morgen remember that she hadn't been able to devote the time she would have liked to making herself beautiful for Conall. She'd had to rush to give Neesha her tea before driving her over to her mother's, then dash back to the house for a quick change out of her working clothes into jeans and a cotton shirt before driving to Heathrow Airport to meet Conall's plane. Truth to tell, she couldn't remember if she'd even stopped to brush her hair.

'Meeting someone?' the woman asked her politely.

'Yes.' Her answer came out in a breathless rush, and Morgen willed herself to stay calm. Not easy when her stomach kept doing cartwheels every time she thought about seeing Conall.

'Anybody special?'

Only the love of my life, Morgen thought silently, her heartbeat going crazy. 'Yes, he's special.'

'I thought so.'

'Why's that?' Curious, Morgen tipped her head.

'I've been watching you walk up and down with that look on your face every time you glance at the Arrivals board for the past half-hour now.'

'Oh?' Discomfited at the thought that her feelings were apparently transparent to a total stranger, Morgen twisted her hands together in her lap. 'What look do you mean, exactly?'

The woman's perfectly arched eyebrows lifted a little to accompany her gently knowing smile. 'The look that a woman gets on her face when she's in love and can't wait to see the man she's in love with.'

'Oh.' Morgen dropped her shoulders, untwisted her hands and looped her hair behind her ear. 'Is it so obvious?'

'Only to a kindred spirit. My husband Graham and I just celebrated our twentieth wedding anniversary, and I'm still as head over heels in love with him as I was the day we met.'

At Morgen's interested glance, the woman introduced herself as Faye Mortimer, then confided that her marriage to Graham was in fact her second marriage—she'd divorced her first husband because he'd been a womaniser and an abuser. The fact was, she continued, she'd never dreamed she would get a second chance at happiness after everything she'd been through. It just went to show that if you didn't allow yourself to become all bitter and twisted about love, love paid back your trust tenfold.

An hour later Morgen had shared her own marriage disaster with Faye, right down to the revelation that Simon had walked out on her when she was pregnant, then blithely washed his hands of both her and their child because he was convinced he had married beneath him.

For quite a while there, Morgen realised, she *had* been bitter and twisted. Right up until the moment she'd known she had fallen for Conall O'Brien, in fact. When that had been exactly she couldn't rightly say, but maybe it was the time he had followed her and Neesha to the Tumble Drum, bought them drinks and sat with her watching Neesha play for the rest of the afternoon—the whole time looking as if there was nowhere he'd rather be on the planet than with them.

Glancing at her watch, hardly believing that so much time had passed, Morgen turned apologetically to Faye. 'I've got to see if there's any more news about his flight,' she explained. 'It's been so nice talking to you, Faye. I'd love to think that in twenty years' time I'll still be with the man I love, celebrating our wedding anniversary.'

Faye smiled. 'If this Conall of yours is anything like the way you've described him, I've no doubt you'll be popping the champagne corks on your twentieth and looking forward to the next twenty years with your grandchildren. Take care, Morgen. It was nice meeting you too.'

Twenty minutes later Morgen was peering over the heads and shoulders of the waiting crowd pressed round the Arrivals barrier, trying to catch a glimpse of the tall, broad-shouldered and devastatingly handsome man she loved. She spotted him straight away, excitement jamming her breath in her throat and making her heart pound. Head and shoulders above nearly everybody else who spilled onto the polished walkway, he was easily the most eye-catching male in the area, and Morgen couldn't suppress the shudder of anticipation that shot through her at the thought of being alone with him later.

Pushing her way through the throng of people at the barrier, she forgot that she usually liked to keep her emotions well under wraps, that in public she always liked to maintain a low profile, that in her book public displays of affection in general were undignified. She raced onto the walkway, calling his name.

Stopping right where he was, the trenchcoat he'd worn in a cold and rainy New York before boarding the plane folded over his arm, and carrying his leather holdall, Conall could hardly believe his eyes when he saw Morgen hurrying towards him. Letting his bag drop to the floor, he simply stood and stared. She was dressed in faded blue jeans, a white cotton shirt and a black suede jacket, with her long dark hair flying out behind her, and she was everything he'd ever dreamed of finding in a woman and more. God how he'd missed her! He'd made the flight from New York to London many times in the past, but it had never seemed to take as long as it had today. Now he was back home, and Morgen was waiting to greet him. Just as he'd hoped and dreamed she would be.

Sprinting the last couple of feet that separated them, without hesitation Morgen threw herself into his arms. Conall almost stumbled with the force of her embrace, the air suddenly leaving his lungs in a powerful 'oomph!' But still he held onto her tight, raining kisses down on her fresh sweet-smelling hair, then desperately seeking her mouth in a hard and hungry kiss that fuelled the longing inside him to fever-pitch and made him nigh on desperate to be alone with her just as soon as he could. The woman was temptation with a capital 'T', and Conall was helpless to resist such potent charms. He was only flesh and blood after all...

'I love you.'

'What?'

Pretending not to hear, Conall stared into her beguiling green eyes, got lost in them for a second or two, then surfaced again with a grin.

'I said I love you—and I want to marry you!' Morgen was sliding her hand up his shirt, holding onto his waist with her free hand, careless that they were receiving highly interested stares from passing disembarking passengers, as well as the public awaiting their arrival. 'I couldn't wait to tell you.'

'So I see.'

'I'm sorry I made you wait for an answer. I wasn't trying to play hard to get.' Planting a brief loving kiss at the side of his jaw, she seemed to think that wasn't enough, and planted another one for good measure at the corner of his mouth. 'I just wanted to have the chance to talk to Neesha about it...about us getting married. Do you mind?'

He wanted it to be right with Morgen's little girl, Conall realised. He didn't want her to think he was going to walk into their lives and claim all her mother's attention for himself. It was important he let her know he cared for her too, and would do anything he could to always keep her feeling safe and loved.

Slipping his arm around Morgen's shoulders, he shook

his head. 'I don't mind at all. I'm glad you did. And was she…was she okay about it?'

Her answering smile was like the kiss of moonlight on a summer garden…sublime. 'She was fine about it. She even helped her nana bake you a cake. I've got it waiting at home, for us to enjoy with a cup of tea.'

'Home?' Conall's blue eyes narrowed.

'My house. You will stay with us until we find something together, won't you? I know it's quite a small place, but it's warm and cosy. Or if you'd prefer to stay at your sister's, I'll understand.'

Conall was surprised at the flash of anxiety in her lovely eyes. 'Your house will be just fine, my angel. As long as we can be together, right?'

It was exactly the answer Morgen wanted to hear.

'And as soon as we get five minutes I want to show you the plans I've been working on.'

'What plans are those?'

'For the house I'm going to build us—you, me and Neesha.'

'Oh, Conall!'

Once again her embrace produced that 'oomph' sound from his chest, but as the last passers-by moved slowly ahead of them Conall found he couldn't wait to kiss his wife-to-be again…and again. By the time they reached the Arrivals barrier nearly everyone else had cleared the area, but the pair of them hardly noticed. They were much too preoccupied with each other to care.

Cosy up to the fireplace with these two classic tales of love beneath the mistletoe...

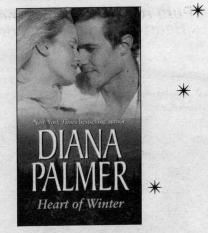

New York Times bestselling author

DIANA PALMER

Heart of Winter

Woman Hater

Having been burned in the past, Winthrop Christopher was wary of women. But when Nicole White had to visit his home, what she found was the most roughly masculine man she'd ever met. Could she ever teach this woman hater to love again?

If Winter Comes

Charismatic mayor Bryan Moreland was on his way to getting Carla Maxwell's vote – until she found out he might be a fraud. As a reporter, Carla had to get to the bottom of it; as a woman, she wanted to lose herself in the sexy mayor's arms. Or was that exactly where he wanted her?

Available 7th December 2007

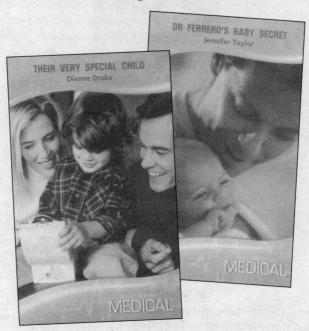

MILLS & BOON

MEDICAL™

Proudly presents

Brides of Penhally Bay

A pulse-raising collection of emotional,
tempting romances and heart-warming stories by
bestselling Mills & Boon Medical™ authors.

January 2008
The Italian's New-Year Marriage Wish
by Sarah Morgan

Enjoy some much-needed winter warmth with
gorgeous Italian doctor Marcus Avanti.

February 2008
The Doctor's Bride By Sunrise
by Josie Metcalfe

Then join Adam and Maggie on a 24-hour rescue mission
where romance begins to blossom as the sun starts to set.

March 2008
The Surgeon's Fatherhood Surprise
by Jennifer Taylor

Single dad Jack Tremayne finds a mother for his
little boy – and a bride for himself.

*Let us whisk you away to an idyllic Cornish town –
a place where hearts are made whole*

COLLECT ALL 12 BOOKS!

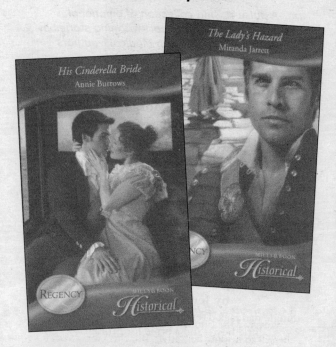

Two Victorian Christmas Treasures

Wicked Pleasures by **Helen Dickson**

Betrothed against her will, innocent young Adeline
Osbourne is resigned to a loveless marriage. Then dark,
dashing Grant Leighton comes along. Can the festive
season lead to pleasures Adeline thought impossible?

A Christmas Wedding Wager by **Michelle Styles**

Lovely Miss Emma Harrison has dedicated
herself to helping her father. But this Christmas,
ruthless and unforgettable Jack Stanton is back!
And Emma can't help but wonder if she made the
wrong choice seven years ago...

Available 16th November 2007

M&B

www.millsandboon.co.uk

MILLS & BOON
100 YEARS
of pure reading pleasure

100 Reasons to Celebrate

2008 is a very special year as we celebrate Mills and Boon's Centenary.

Each month throughout the year there will be something new and exciting to mark the centenary, so watch for your favourite authors, captivating new stories, special limited edition collections…and more!